An essential read for understanding the complexities of narrative medicine.

Mikelionis combines clinical expertise with storytelling, creating a novel that educates as much as it entertains.

—***Amanda Carter,*** Academic Reviewer

An intricate and thought-provoking medical drama

HYBRID is a testament to the power of informed storytelling. Mikelionis's prose is intelligent and evocative, though it risks alienating readers unfamiliar with medical jargon. The plot combines drama and authenticity...

—***Kevin Morse,*** Independent Publisher

An unforgettable exploration of resilience and compassion in medicine.

This is a story that leaves you pondering the thin line between science and humanity. HYBRID delves deep into the intricacies of medicine with a writing style that is rich but occasionally overwhelming in detail.

—***Laura Fields,*** Bookstore Manager

BOOK VIEWPOINT CRITIC

A gripping portrayal of medical triumphs and challenges.

This book resonated deeply with my own experiences in healthcare. Mikelionis captures the chaos, the heartbreak, and the rare moments of triumph with authenticity.

—**Ethan Ward**, *Former ER Nurse and Novice Writer*

An honest and unfiltered glimpse into the human aspect of healthcare.

Mikelionis masterfully bridges the gap between medical and literary worlds. The writing is precise, echoing the clinical setting while retaining emotional depth. The tension in each medical case is palpable... A standout for medical professionals and book buyers seeking authenticity in fiction.

—***Jacob Lenz, Editor,*** *Medical Times Literary Supplement*

A bold narrative rooted in the trials of modern healthcare.

This novel captures the heart of medicine—the triumphs, failures, and ethical grey zones. Mikelionis's experience as a physician permeates every chapter, making it a delight for medical insiders.

—**Richard Kent**, *Physician and Aspiring Novelist*

A compelling fusion of medical ethics and emotional depth.

HYBRID combines medical authenticity with literary skill, drawing readers into the critical decisions faced by a physician. The storyline is both engaging and thought-provoking, striking a balance between intense ethical challenges and moments of reflection... The characters are well-developed, especially Dr. Cameron, whose quiet resolve and complex vulnerabilities propel the story forward... For those in decision-making roles, this book provides a distinctive perspective on the challenges of modern medicine.

> —*Dr. Emily Harper*, Literary Critic and Medical Historian

A profound narrative of compassion and choices in healthcare.

HYBRID is a fascinating look at the intersection of medical science and humanity. The writing is vivid and insightful... Dr. Cameron is a fully realized character whose journey invites deep discussion about ethics in medicine. I would recommend this for book clubs interested in thought-provoking reads.

> —*Dana Lewis*, Librarian and Book Club Facilitator

A riveting depiction of the human spirit in the world of medicine

Mikelionis brings the medical world alive with sharp, realistic dialogue and intricate ethical quandaries... This book's strength lies in its ability to merge clinical precision with emotional resonance, making it ideal for a niche audience.

> —*Sarah Thompson*, Author and Writing Coach

An intelligent, if challenging, read for the discerning audience.

HYBRID is a challenging but rewarding read, offering a rare look at the personal struggles behind medical decisions. The detailed prose might deter casual readers, but it's a goldmine for professionals and enthusiasts.

> —*Megan Foster*, Marketing Consultant for Bookstores

HYBRID

R.J. MIKELIONIS, M.D.

Copyright © 2025 R.J. Mikelionis, M.D.

All rights reserved. No part of this book may be reproduced, stored, or transmitted by any means—whether auditory, graphic, mechanical, or electronic—without written permission of both publisher and author, except in the case of brief excerpts used in critical articles and reviews. Unauthorized reproduction of any part of this work is illegal and is punishable by law.

ISBN: 979-8-89419-464-6 (sc)
ISBN: 979-8-89419-465-3 (hc)
ISBN: 979-8-89419-466-0 (e)
Library of Congress Control Number: 2024904008

Because of the dynamic nature of the Internet, any web addresses or links contained in this book may have changed since publication and may no longer be valid. The views expressed in this work are solely those of the author and do not necessarily reflect the views of the publisher, and the publisher hereby disclaims any responsibility for them.

THE EWINGS PUBLISHING

One Galleria Blvd., Suite 1900, Metairie, LA 70001
(504) 702-6708

CONTENTS

Chapter 1   And Judgment Difficult 1
Chapter 2   Visits and Voices 25
Chapter 3   Two Masters 41
Chapter 4   One Goal 55
Chapter 5   Grandma Millie 73
Chapter 6   Magic 89
Chapter 7   The Hawk 115
Chapter 8   The Run 137
Chapter 9   Autumn Winds 155
Chapter 10 Quo Vadis 173
Chapter 11 A Thin Line 193
Chapter 12 Two Roses 213
Chapter 13 Holding the Line 231
Chapter 14 Fate Gypsies 253
Chapter 15 Soul Search 267
Chapter 16 High Clouds 281
Chapter 17 Gold Standard 303
Chapter 18 Choices 321
Chapter 19 A Christmas Journey 339
Chapter 20 A Frog, A Prince, A Knight 355
Chapter 21 Requiem 369
Chapter 22 The Dragon 385
Chapter 23 Almost A Good Race 401

Epilogue 423
Acknowledgements 425
Dear Reader 427

CHAPTER 1

AND JUDGMENT DIFFICULT

"Life is short
And the art long;
The occasion fleeting,
Experiment dangerous,
And judgment difficult."

—Hippocrates, c. 400 B.C.

"The Faculty of our School of Medicine, and the patients of our medical center, welcome you, our seventy-seventh class of Interns and Residents. Our mission here remains unchanged, from a legacy dating back over two and a half millennia:

"'I shall follow that treatment, which according to my ability and judgment, shall benefit my patient; I will keep him from harm and injury...'

"It is said the olive tree that first bore witness to these words, on the Aegean Island of Kos, still stands. Ironically, that legacy may be cut down in our own time.

"Insurance companies seek to dictate a by-the-numbers, cookbook medicine. Government, through decrees disguised as 'utilization', 'appropriateness', and an alphabet soup of 'DRG's, PCR's, and MAAC's' rations medicine, then places the blame on physicians. Lawyers, with the benefit of one-hundred percent hindsight, define medical perfection. All these forces seek to turn physicians from being doctors for their patients, into 'providers of health care' for the industrialization of medicine.

"Despite this, while we, your teachers, still have a voice, your work and learning here will continue to be based on traditional values. You will polish your years of medical training from theory into practice. In the process, you will eat, drink and sleep medicine. Your goals and ours will remain one and the same: 'To cure sometimes; to relieve often; to comfort always.'

"We cannot make you into true physicians for your patients, any more than we can guarantee you won't become forced 'providers of health care' for an industry of insurance and governmental medicine. But when you are finished here, you will at least know the difference.

"Guard that knowledge well. You may be one of the last to have that privilege. What you do with that knowledge, in your future journeys, is up to you."

After speaking without a microphone to the combined crowd of nearly two hundred Interns and Residents, Mark "Track" Sullivan, Assistant Professor of Medicine, loped off the podium with the stride of a cheetah leaving its lookout post. Dr. John Cameron smiled: Before med school, "Track" had been his running coach; he still moved as if the quest of his own journeys resided over the next horizon.

Dr. Cameron tried to spot the two Interns that had been assigned to him, but in the mass dispersal from auditorium to cafeteria, the attempt was useless. Besides, there was still time before rounds to visit his canine charges.

. . . . .

M.R. VI cocked its ears: With a mixture of distant Alsatian past, more recent golden lab fuzziness, and a German Shepherd's instinct to keep its ears at martial attention, M.R. VI followed the approaching footsteps before the door had opened.

Dr. John Cameron closed the door softly behind him, as if to avoid disturbing the rows of silent cages. Atop high basement walls, light from the sun's world melted through barred windows, then crashed in multi-colored shards across the cages. M.R. VI wedged his muzzle between the colors and the steel.

John Cameron stopped and fingered his pockets: Nothing, not even a few crumbs; he'd forgotten today. M.R. VI lifted its wet muzzle in anticipation, and struggled onto its forepaws. The back arched, then straightened; for a while it looked as if the hind legs would follow. But M.R. VI slowly settled again. Head swaying side to side, ears now at half-mast, M.R. looked like a dejected circus clown without an audience.

"There, big fella," Cameron stroked under M.R.'s neck, "it's going to be all right."

"Mutation Rover VI": That was the name "Track" Sullivan had given him. "Rover" for all of Dr. Sullivan's canine lab charges; numbered for the times Dr. Cameron had tried his experiment; "Mutation" had been added when Cameron hadn't explained what he'd been doing, but muttered something about an experimentally induced mutation.

Now M.R. VI was still alive. Nine days after the implant, and still alive. Under Cameron's hand, M.R. VI turned onto his back, smooth-shaven belly waiting to be scratched. In dawn's light streaming in through barred windows, Cameron could see the sallow jaundiced hue fading from an underbelly dotted with closing metal staples. The staples would be ready to come out tomorrow. And M.R. VI was still alive.

Cameron filled M.R.'s water bowl, fetched the food mix, and added a few biscuits. M.R. VI made a throaty noise; his tail slapped out the rest of the message.

Before turning to go, Cameron glanced back at M.R. VI. "Damn," he muttered. That familiar knot rose from his stomach. Across a parking lot and five flights up, in the lab room of Medical Ward B, Cameron still felt the knot.

Dr. Max McDaniel, Intern, glanced at his watch: Seven twenty-five. Five minutes early. "Looking a bit pale. Want some coffee?" Max asked his Resident.

"Oh," Cameron looked around absently, "sure."

Max looked for a cup between the Gram-stains, microscopes, and slides. "If a lowly Intern may remind you, Dr. Resident Cameron, you're leading the charge today on morning rounds, before our thirty-six-hour call duty."

"I'll be all right. The Attending can't make it?"

"Dr. Atwood called in. Grand-Rounds case on another ward."

Max' face showed that Dr. Atwood wouldn't be missed. "What about you? Late nights on that secret project of yours?"

"Who told you that?"

"Now don't get sore," Max bobbed on his toes like a guard who'd just made the first of his free-throws. "Track told me about it. In case you were really wiped-out tired sometime, so we could give you a break. He figured since we're buddies..." Max flashed his high school yell-king toothpaste-commercial grin, "we are, aren't we?"

"Sure. Go on."

"So he told me. I don't think he's told anyone else. And I sure haven't."

"Joel knows?"

"Nope...Speak of the..."

Dr. Joel Saxton, white Intern's smock neatly buttoned up his neck like a military dentist, glanced up from his patient cards: "Got nine here. How 'bout you, Max?"

"I don't count 'em."

"You should. We'll each probably get another twelve during call. We've been averaging thirteen. Besides," Joel's jawline squared below ears well clear of his sculpted haircut, "if we keep that high a census, and our Medicare patients in too long, the DRG's just might smother our hospital out of business. Right, Dr. Cameron?"

John Cameron couldn't have cared less about DRG's. And he'd already told Joel he didn't need to address him as "Doctor" away from patients. Cameron shrugged. "Ready? Rounds, gentlemen. Let's go."

On summer mornings the long, bright white corridors stretched never- endingly and cool under their feet. Max wore sandals and white socks. Doors opened regularly on either side of the ward corridors, punctuated at corners and intervals with the flickering glass partitions of nurses' stations.

Joel flipped a patient card to the top of his deck: Mrs. Ellen Samuels, 501A. They went into the room; Joel stopped at the foot of the bed. He recited the vital signs, then paged through the chart. "How are you, Mrs. Samuels?"

"Oh, pretty good, I guess..." The metal hospital bed, railings up at the sides, dwarfed Mrs. Samuels, reclining at a thirty-degree angle in a sea of white sheets.

Dr. Saxton unslung from around his neck a triple-headed stethoscope resembling a miniature tank turret. "Good," he listened to her chest. "Sounds clear today."

Mrs. Samuels sank back into her bed with a few panting breaths. Her mouth moved uncomfortably like a fish out of water.

Dr. Saxton reviewed the history: "Mrs. Samuels came in being tired and short of breath for two weeks. She's been on digoxin, propranolol, and disopyramide. Her physical exam showed a grade 1 out of 6 systolic heart murmur, clear lungs, no neck vein distension, no peripheral edema. Vital signs were normal." He ran his hand through short, wiry hair. "So initially we thought maybe emphysema/COPD, or early congestive heart failure. But arterial blood gases didn't show enough oxygen drop or carbon dioxide elevation to account for her shortness of breath; pulmonary function tests likewise. Chest X-ray was clear, and so was her EKG; cardiac enzymes were normal." Saxton stroked his meticulously trimmed mustache. "So, she's been here four days, and still no firm diagnosis, Dr. Cameron."

Cameron turned to Max: "Dr. McDaniel?"

Max glanced from the chart to Mrs. Samuels. "Well, there has been no cough, no temperature, no increase in respiratory rate with her shortness of breath. Also, no chest pain. Still, because her EKG did show a new incomplete Right Bundle Branch Block, I would wonder about a pulmonary embolus..."

"Done. Lung scan was negative for blood clots," Joel Saxton smiled.

Cameron pulled a chair next to Mrs. Samuels' bed. Her hair, not completely gray, was strewn like autumn after winter's first snowfall. "What we're saying, Mrs. Samuels, is we're not sure what's causing your trouble. Dr. Saxton has done a good job at checking the possibilities, and now we can tell you some things you don't have. For example, you don't have heart failure, because that would overload fluid into your lungs, which we'd hear, and also see on a chest X-ray; the extra fluid would also show up in your weight, in fuller neck veins, and leg swelling. In the same way, your EKG's and blood tests show no evidence of heart damage or heart attack. And without cough and temperature, and with a normal chest X-ray, there's no pneumonia. Now emphysema, which we call COPD for 'Chronic Obstructive Pulmonary Disease,' could give you symptoms like you describe, but the arterial blood gases Dr. Saxton ordered..."

"The ones they take from the wrist?"

"Yes."

"They had to do it twice, and it hurt more than from the arm ..."

"I know," Dr. Cameron patted her hand, "but we had to find whether the shortness of breath was from lack of oxygen, and we can do that best from an artery. In your case, the oxygen was seventy-nine, near normal."

"So my oxygen was okay?"

"Yes."

"Then why am I short of breath?"

"That's a good question, Mrs. Samuels. And we haven't found the answer, yet."

"Oh my, I'm sorry... " The brow wrinkled, deepening her eyes into shadows of contrition. "I don't mean to be so difficult. I'm sure you're trying very hard."

"That's quite all right," Joel fingered his deck of eight more patient cards. "So, what do you think, Dr. Cameron? We've worked up the problem, coming up negative. Should we send her home with clinic follow up?"

"What would the discharge diagnoses be, Dr. Saxton?"

"Basically, either CHF DRG # 127 or COPD DRG # 088 add up to the same number of hospital days. While we can't make congestive heart failure stick, we probably could COPD—since her lab tests were not totally normal, about seventy-nine to eighty-five percent—I think we could go with that."

"Do you think that's what she has?"

Dr. Saxton fidgeted. "That, and eighty-one years, and perhaps depression to account for the rest." He replaced her card into the rest of his stack.

Cameron remained seated, and looked at Mrs. Samuels. The corners of her mouth turned down like sad commas. "Are you still tired and short of breath?"

"Yes..." Her hand fluttered briefly arranging her sheets, like a small bird lost in her polka-dotted hospital gown.

"You know, Mrs. Samuels, when we find the cause of a problem, we can usually correct it, or make it better. But sometimes we can't solve a problem right away, and we need more time. How about giving us a little more of that?"

She smiled and tugged at his hand. "Sure."

"You know, there are some sayings in medicine that help us when we're stuck. You want to hear one, Mrs. Samuels?"

Her small hand fluttered again. "Sure!"

"One goes like this: 'When you hear hoof-beats, don't look for Zebras.' In other words, when faced with a set of symptoms and findings, don't go looking for the rarer diseases, like Zebras, but for the more commonplace horses."

Mrs. Samuels thought a bit, then smile-wrinkles came to her still brilliant blue eyes. "Does that mean in my case we're through looking for horses, and now we've got to go on to Zebras?"

"Not yet, Mrs. Samuels, not quite yet. But I think we better keep you a few more days."

Joel tapped his nine patient cards. "No discharge, then?"

"Not unless we have something more than emphysema, age eighty-one, and depression. Any questions?" Cameron paused. "No? Then-let's take a walk, gentlemen."

Max and Joel glanced at each other. They knew what that meant. Overtime rounds. If they didn't have any questions, he was sure to have plenty.

Cameron stepped into the hallway, which at times became their conference room. "Dr. Saxton, how many eighty-plus people do you know?"

"You mean patients?"

"I meant just what I said."

"Well, people...Ah, I guess I know a few...my grandparents, some others..."

"Are they always tired and short of breath?"

"No, not really."

"May we conclude then, that for most of them tiredness and shortness of breath are not a usual part of life?"

"It would seem so, Dr. Cameron." Joel's fingers let the cards slip into his pocket, then curled around the stethoscope.

"Dr. McDaniel, what about the possibility of depression accounting for the symptoms?"

"She does appear a bit depressed at times. But when you interviewed her, she smiled more often than you'd expect from someone depressed. If depression is a problem, it's not likely to be a primary one, but secondary to whatever else is bothering her. But I'm not sure what that diagnosis might be either."

"So, gentlemen: Do we go with Zebras now, start all over, or ask a consultant to bail us out?"

"Hell, if we didn't have call and new patients coming in," Joel reminded everyone, "I'd like to check on some more unusual possibilities." Joel looked down: His eyes were on his shoelaces, his heart on the day after call, and his mind on whether he'd have enough energy left over for Jody, even if she didn't require preliminaries and came directly to his room. Jody, with harvest-moon curves...

Cameron's voice sliced through Joel's thoughts. "And you, Dr. McDaniel?"

"Something bothers me here. Her symptoms are so simple, so common, so..." he finished searching for another word, "basic. It's as if this is what medicine's all about: Finding and mending what lies behind symptoms like hers. I'd like to work through this, if we can."

"Medicine is many things, Dr. McDaniel." Cameron's eyes, a high mountain lake's blue-green, seemed to drift far away. "Not only finding diagnoses for symptoms, but finding the human being inside each patient, each with fears, hopes, needs, and dreams. Sometimes, that's all we can do."

"Point taken," Max inclined his head. "Cameron's corollary number one, twentieth century."

"No. Hippocrates, fifth B.C., and Sir William Osler, nineteenth. By evenings rounds, gentlemen, I want another report on our patient's status."

. . . . .

At 502B, Jessie Lucas cleared her throat several times, then peered at them through oversized glasses. Her tall, thin frame rested like a pelican atop her bed and pillow. "Good morning, Max," she gave him a grin wide as a rainbow.

"And how are you Mrs. Lucas?"

"Pretty good today. That medicine must have worked. I'm not short of breath like I was last night. But it kept me up all night peeing, too."

Jessie was eighty-nine, and as grandmotherly as Mrs. Samuels. It was difficult to imagine either of them saying "pee." That was Jessie, though.

Max finished presenting the vital signs, a summary of the history, exam, and the recent lab. Dr. Cameron listened. Then he asked questions, and tracked the details of Mrs. Lucas' course like footprints on a forest floor: What had brought her to the hospital? What other conditions were involved in her present status? What could be done to improve them?

Rounds continued down the white hall, along rooms 503 to 525. Each contained its own world; they had between ten and twenty minutes for each world's story. Between rooms 506 and 507, Joel whispered to Max: "I don't think Cameron was satisfied with my presentation of Mrs. Samuels. Give me a hand in the case?"

"Sure. We'll hit the library between admits."

"Thanks." Joel relaxed and was able to think of Jody again.

Between 509 and 510, Barbara Davis, R.N., placed a chart in Joel's hand: "First admit, Mary Wilson's back. Same thing—asthma. Any initial orders?"

As Joel glanced at Barbara, he realized he was more tired than he'd thought. He hadn't noticed her walk from the nurses' station. Ordinarily there would be no missing curves like hers from a hundred yards away. Everything was in exact and full proportion, an hourglass only the Swiss could make, and the Italians design. The hourglass waist drew in tightly like a gymnast's, above hips rounding smoothly as a rose petal. She was like Jody, only more—and more aloof. Joel glanced away from Barbara, trying to gear his brain down towards the chart.

"Well, would you like me to start an IV?" Barbara didn't like it when she was stared at like that. It had been all right at first. But now too much of the same had become old. Even if they had the smooth cover-boy looks of Joel Saxton—who could do an aftershave commercial walking on a beach with a surfboard, or sitting on a Harley—she was fed up with their line 'em and wine 'em routines, in which 'no' existed only as an alien vocabulary.

"Hi, Barbara," Max glanced over her shoulder at the chart. "Joel's up for the next admit?"

"Anna Wilson's back."

"You want me to take care of her, Joel?" Max asked. "I took care of her the last time."

"If you'd like."

"No problem. Can you fill me in, Barbara?"

"She's worse than last time: Not taking *any* of her medicines for two weeks. She denied it at first, but I checked her pill bottles, and they'd hardly been touched. She said she'd felt so good, she didn't think she needed them."

Though auburn hair to the shoulders usually framed Barbara's face with curls, Max noticed she wore it up today. On Barbara, it looked like a princess' tiara. "What was done in the ER.?"

"They gave her IPPB with zero-point-three cc's terbutaline in three cc's of saline, chest X-ray, and CBC. They also ordered a D5/W and four-hundred mg aminophylline drip over twelve hours; but I guess they got busy, because they didn't start it."

"Let's start her IV here – D5/W, Dextrose and water, and increase the aminophylline to five hundred mg every twelve, since she hasn't taken her usual medicines. Continue the same IPPB every four hours. I'll see her within the hour, unless you think she needs it sooner."

"She's also coughing."

"Let's get a gram stain for white cells and bacteria. Hold the culture and sensitivity unless she gets a temp."

"Usual diet and activity?"

"Regular diet, no caffeine, and up ad lib."

Barbara finished writing the orders. Max reminded her of a lifeguard on a far-flung Australian beach, with wildly-curled sun-bronzed hair, and the shoulders of a rower. He didn't have Joel's smooth cover-boy looks, but seemed the friendliest of the trio. Yet under his cheerful disposition there was something else—an area of limited access, a cave walled off deep inside, boarded up like an abandoned mineshaft. "Anything else?" Barbara asked.

Max turned to Cameron, who replied without a pause: "Two liters oxygen flow, and a stat EKG if her pulse is irregular. Keep us posted if her vitals change. Sometimes", Cameron added, "just when we think we have patient and problem figured out, they will surprise us with something different."

"She wanted to know how you were, Dr. Cameron."

"Mrs. Wilson? That's sweet. Give her a hug for me; tell her we'll see her soon," Cameron smiled.

Barbara noticed Cameron didn't smile that often. When he did it was a shy, tentative smile. Though handsome, with bluish eyes that seemed even lighter when contrasted with his dark hair, it was in a less displayed manner, matching his personality. He wore shirts baggy at the waist, and an occasional flowery tie, especially after admissions of cases that were sad. His smile become even less noticeable then; and the ties got wilder as he smiled less. Cameron was as precise as Joel wanted to be, and perhaps more mysterious than Max appeared. Though Cameron's friendliness was also less displayed, its manner betrayed no hidden bounds, no limits to his commitment. His was the quiet tenacity and loyalty of a bulldog. It would be an interesting year, Barbara thought. Even for this large and bustling Medical Center, the two Interns and their Resident made for an unusual trio.

Cameron turned to Barbara before resuming rounds: "Let us know if Mrs. Wilson begins to go sour." Barbara's eyes were clear blue like an emerald sea; like the sea they had the power to draw voyagers sometimes dangerously close to the abyss. At others, they were flat and cool, like a sea becalmed between icebergs. Hers was an unnerving beauty. When combined with the capacity to measure others without emotional effort, it became a beauty of ice. But it was also a beauty that could easily attract, and burn—fire. Fire and ice walked back to the nurses' station, leaving a wake of daydreams.

Joel shook his head and grinned: "Well, what do you know? I wonder what it'd take to be the lucky guy?"

"Maybe nothing," Max said. "Or everything."

"Then, gentlemen," Cameron smiled, "we have all the bases covered here. Let's finish rounds."

. . . . .

They were two patients short of finishing when the Red Blanket came. Chest heaving, eyes rolling wildly, he shouted, gagged, coughed, and wheezed. He was about nineteen. The red tag identified him as a John Doe. His wrists writhed bloody against the restraints.

Joel was next up for the admit. If someone had told him that John Doe was foaming and fulminating with rabies, Joel would've believed it. He tried to check the vital signs – pulse and respiration were both high. Blood pressure and temperature were impossible to take. Joel tried to talk to him. Gurney bars bent as John Doe flailed in spasms not unlike grand-mal epilepsy, except he was awake. Obscenities wheezed out in torrents, then smothered in drowning gasps. Joel tried to listen to his lungs and heart, but the flailing worsened. A look of terror gathered in John Doe's eyes. Then one hand ripped through the bloody restraints.

"Cameron! Max!" Joel put all his weight in one hand. "What's going on?"

Cameron turned down the lights and whispered: "Talk softly. Any stimulus will set him off. Easy now, easy…" Later he was able to listen to the chest, and left the stethoscope on for Joel.

"Crackles all over…" Joel whispered over the heaving chest. "Sounds like pulmonary edema, heart failure. How'd he get that way?"

They secured the restraints.

"Max, bring oxygen. Don't put it on yet. Just point it his way. Make your moves slow. Talk soft."

"P.C.P.?" Max asked.

Cameron nodded. "Acts like it. That's not all, though."

Patty Aldrige, R.N., rolled in an IV cart. "How are we going to get the IV in?"

"We'll need a soft cath, Patty. And lots of padding."

"Toxicology's back: He's also got heroin on board."

"How much?"

"Moderate, not the worst we've had."

In the dimly lit room, Cameron threaded the IV in by feel. The gasping for breath and writhing continued. "Something doesn't add up here. What do you think, Joel?" Cameron asked softly.

"Can you get the pulmonary edema from large doses of heroin?"

Cameron nodded. "What were his blood gases from the ER.?"

"pO2 of forty-four, pCO2 fifty. Those are terrible—acute respiratory failure!"

"Unusual," Cameron shook his head: "Blood gases don't match the heroin tox levels. Wait a minute. What about…what about street or folk antidotes for heroin?"

"Many, I suppose," Joel bandaged the wrists. Max helped pad the IV.

"…And one fits," Cameron clenched a fist: "Milk! There's a folk belief that intravenous milk cures heroin overdoses. That would give him clots of milky fat globules in his lungs—pulmonary fat emboli—and respiratory failure." He paused. "Patty, have social services run down his I.D.—family, friends. Find out if that's what happened. Joel, get two one-cc ampules of Naloxone. A stat portable chest film for edema, and a lung scan for emboli. Follow his blood gases every hour."

"Diurese some water out of him?"

"Not too much. Probably won't help if he's got fat emboli."

"Lasix eighty IV.?"

"Forty. And get his lytes before and after – with that low oxygen and acidosis, he doesn't need a low potassium from Lasix to make his heart more irritable."

Whether from medication or exhaustion, John Doe finally became calmer, and Joel finished his workup.

Max and Cameron went for lunch. The cafeteria was in its usual turmoil of Interns, Residents, and nurses trying to squeeze a few minutes of leisure between gulps of their noon meal. The tables were white and of the same size, and the chairs ate holes in the tiled floor. Max filled his tray with coffee, hamburgers and fries, and some extras in case Joel didn't make it down. "You know, it's nice to have you as my buddy, and my Resident. The two ever get mixed up in your head?"

"Nope. I keep the two apart. You too, I hope."

"Sure. I respect you as a teacher – Socratic method and all that. That's why I'm curious about that project you never talk about."

Cameron shook his head.

"Why not?"

"Nothing to teach," Cameron shrugged. "Just a wild idea that's got zilch chance of working."

"By idea you mean theory?"

"I guess."

"And in practice?"

Cameron shrugged again.

"I know you, John. Something's brewing. And if it's your theory, it can't be too far-fetched. Even if it is, you're probably doing something about it."

"I told you: Nothing to teach."

"So forget that. As a buddy, then: You've been driving yourself too hard. Why?"

Cameron laughed. "How'd we become such buddies, anyway?"

"Quit changing the subject. You looked at Barbara like she was a hundred miles away. That's not how you usually look at her. And you haven't checked out a single nurse the entire time we've been here. May I remind you that's how we became buddies: The Intern/Resident party found my jaw scraping after that blonde pony-tailed beauty. She was so beautiful, and ignored me even more beautifully. You sat me down, pushed my drink away, and told me she wasn't as beautiful inside as she was outside."

"I noticed her too."

Max let out a whistle between his teeth. "And?"

"And...nothing. Gorgeous, of course. Depends on how far ahead you were looking: A day, a night, a week...or whatever. Whatever would be bad with her, though."

"Maybe I was only looking for a day and a night."

"That's the problem," Cameron shook his head. "You weren't. You were remembering someone else."

"You're right," Max shrugged. "Who did she finally leave with, anyway?"

"Roger Taylor."

"Taylor, the Surgery Resident? That figures. He's as smooth and cool as they come."

"You know what he told me?" Cameron laughed, "he was looking tired one day, and just sat down and said, 'they just want sex... doesn't anyone want to talk anymore'?"

"Maybe he's wearing down."

"I doubt it. Never underestimate the power of recuperation."

"Is that a medical or a personal pearl?"

"Both. Especially in Roger Taylor's case, should your taste buds run across the same female again."

"Point taken. What about you?"

"Taste buds resting."

"We're not on call Saturday. Let's go to the Continental."

"Maybe."

"No maybes. You need a break."

"Sure," replied Cameron, then, "maybe..."

Max finished his tray and stood up, bouncing on his toes like a guard on a free-throw: "Hell, we're going," he grinned.

. . . . .

They had six more admits before evening rounds. Joel finished his latest workup. "You know, about that John Doe heroin and P.C.P. overdose? Cameron was right down the line: Chest film confirmed pulmonary edema and shock lung; lung scan was consistent with multiple small emboli, like fat particles from massively fragmented bones."

"Only our boy didn't have broken bones."

"Exactly. Social Services tracked down his sister, and then some buddies who admitted to the I.V. milk 'antidote.' And you know what? When told that causes milk clots of fat in blood vessels, one of them muttered about using low-fat next time."

"If there is a next time," Max shook his head. "Well, no one said it would be easy."

"Not this hard, either," Joel added.

Before the hospital clinics closed at 7 pm, Dr. Roger Taylor called from Surgery Clinic for transfer and admission to Medicine of a patient with a rapid pulse rate. Such transfers were facilitated Resident-to-Resident, since Interns were by nature more suspicious of any "lateral" transfers that increased their workload, especially from other wards or services—viewing them as potential "dumps"—difficult cases that had gathered downhill momentum, and were seeking a place to hit bottom.

Joel glanced at his just completed chart, and waited for the arrival from Surgery Clinic. He looked at Cameron: "Why are you such a soft touch for difficult cases?"

"This one shouldn't be difficult. We're just taking her because we're on call."

"Just recently when we weren't on call, there was Adams, with multiple myeloma, also from Surgery. She couldn't talk, eat, or do anything else. She had one foot in the next world, and her other on a banana peel. It took twenty minutes just to draw her blood, because it was so thick from myeloma."

"We got her eating, and home in a wheelchair, didn't we?" Cameron asked.

"Sure. Now you've got a rep for taking all the bad cases."

"That's why we're here."

Joel looked at Cameron. At times he seemed so incredibly old fashioned. Of course, there was the challenge of doing everything just right, and then maybe, just maybe, turning a hopeless case around. More often, after a lot of work and several unavoidable complications, they checked out of Hotel Earth. Now government computers had begun to tally up the complications and deaths under each doctor's name. After a few years, the computer could make one look good, or could make one look bad. All with little foundation in reality, since computers didn't differentiate whether the complications had taken place in cakewalks, or in mortal combat with severe and chronic disease of every organ system.

That message hadn't been lost on Joel. His solution was simplicity itself: The less complex and difficult the cases, the better the computer results. So there was no reason for taking the difficult ones. Joel had no intention of becoming a scapegoat for any system. But perhaps Cameron didn't yet know about the great computer in the sky.

"John, you do know all the deaths and complications are being tracked by Medicare computers."

"I suppose they are."

"So the more difficult cases you take, the greater the red ink and liability in your computer collection."

Cameron nodded.

"Ours too," Joel pointed to Max. "Why would you want to do that to us?"

"You need the practice," Cameron smiled. "Now get some dinner, and I'll see our new patient."

Joel shook his head: "Was he serious or joking?"

"Probably both," answered Max.

Joel looked at his watch. "It's past dinner. Will you still give me a hand with Mrs. Samuels?"

"Sure. But I know someone in the kitchen. Let's grab a tray and take it to the library."

"You sure they'll feed us?" The cafeteria crew picked up trays promptly at 7:30 pm. With nearly two thousand patients and staff to feed, there was little room for deviations from schedule.

"Don't worry. She's a sweetie."

Down five flights and through double doors, a dietetic Intern was going over next day's menu. Tight reddish curls hovered like sunset over the pale cloud of her complexion. She took them inside the kitchen and loaded up a tray.

"Thanks, Jennie, you're a lifesaver."

"Go on you guys, you're on call, aren't you? You want anything else?"

"No. Got to move on to the library."

"See you."

Joel balanced the tray past the double doors. "Max, what's difficult about the Samuels case is I've already looked at it from hundreds of angles—cardiac causes, pulmonary causes, same for hematologic, metabolic, and endocrine causes—nothing comes up. Sure she's got a few abnormalities here and there, but none of them add up to what she's telling us. I know Cameron's not happy with my presentation of the case."

"Have you thought of presenting a person, instead of a case?"

"What do you mean?"

"What you've got on those cards, Joel, are details. Very important ones, but still just details. You can't squeeze a person onto those cards, or onto programmed formulas."

"I know." Joel was silent awhile. "Maybe it's because I don't want to carry people inside me. You know, when something happens, maybe it's better to carry cards than people with you..." He paused. "How many have you lost so far, Max?"

...Blood welled up the trachea...an artery pumped, eaten through by cancer...drowning the lungs...blips across an EKG screen, finally a flat line—a machine signaled the end of a human being. "Two," Max said.

"Same here," Joel wiped his forehead. "It's easier to file away a card, after someone's gone..."

. . . . .

Across campus, the Medical School's library stood brilliant as a stage, cavernously huge. But here the hospital's library was an old converted dining room. A stand-up lamp in a corner sent shadows over worn tomes lining all four walls. Sections of faded carpet had been worn into dull paths across the room, from lumpy couch and wooden chairs to bookshelves, and back again. Generations of Interns and Residents had paced within the confines of this room, their attention undiverted by plush carpets or contoured seats, and the dim light was probably kinder to their tired eyes than the bright banks of lights of the library across campus. Late at night, when those brilliant lights went out, and the large and beautiful library was as empty as a forgotten museum, the dim light of the hospital library still outlined someone shuffling from bookshelves to a couch with fractured springs. Tradition did not always side with fancy and flash. Tradition sometimes couldn't be bought.

"Where do you want to start, Joel?"

"There's something strange I didn't notice before, Max. Mrs. Samuels' kidney function is down a bit. I don't know why I didn't see it before—a urine creatinine clearance of thirty-nine—but her serum creatinine was normal at one-point-five. Wait a minute, I didn't order a creatinine clearance..."

"The lab slips's got Cameron's name on it."

"I knew it! He's probably got the case figured out!"

"Well, then so can we. Interesting, though, that the normal serum creatinine didn't give us any hint of her renal insufficiency."

"That amount of kidney impairment wouldn't be enough to give her symptoms, though."

"You're right. But what if it's not a disease at all?"

"What do you mean, Max?"

"Look, we've checked out most disease possibilities. What if it's something else?"

"Like what?"

"What medicines is she on, Joel?"

Joel plucked out his cards: "Digitalis, propranolol, disopyramide, terbutaline inhaler..."

"What if it's a side effect of one of the meds she's taking?"

Joel whistled: "Especially if that medicine is cleared by the kidneys! If her kidney function is down, it could accumulate to higher levels, with side effects!" By now, Joel had appropriated the idea as his own. "You check on the first two, and I'll take the rest."

Between ransacking the pages of THE PHARMACOLOGIC BASIS OF THERAPEUTICS, the P.D.R., and the COMPENDIUM ON DRUG THERAPY, they wolfed down their dinner.

Max shook his head: "Digitalis gets a clean bill. Her dig levels were normal, and side effects of it wouldn't account for her symptoms anyway. Now propranolol could do it, since it can make you tired, or precipitate shortness of breath or asthma. Still, that should clinically show up on her pulmonary function tests, and it hasn't. Besides, her propranolol dosage has been very low, and it's not cleared by the kidneys, but metabolized by the liver, so changes in kidney function would not affect it."

"Wait," Max paused. "She also has gall bladder stones. Wouldn't that alter her liver function?"

Joel paged through the chart. "Her liver functions have been normal. We found stones incidentally on ultrasound after a clinic visit, looking for an aneurysm. Found no aneurysm, and she refused all thoughts of surgery for GB stones, since she's felt no problems with it. She told Surgery Clinic the same thing, and they didn't pursue it." Joel dove into the books again. "I think I've got it! The disopyramide she's using for her arrhythmia is cleared by the kidneys. For her creatinine clearance, the dosage should be twenty percent lower than what she's getting now. And it can produce unexplained tiredness and shortness of breath."

"Let's see," Max double checked.

"Think that's it?"

"Sure looks like it."

"Just in time for evening rounds," Joel grinned. "Let's not keep Dr. Cameron waiting."

They found him in the lab room, writing an admission.

"Can I talk to you about Mrs. Samuels before rounds, Dr. Cameron?"

"Go on."

"I think I've found the problem."

When Joel said "I" instead of "we", Cameron cast a glance toward Max, but said nothing.

"Too high a level of disopyramide," Joel continued, "in the face of an unexpected lower kidney function, could produce the side effects that Mrs. Samuels feels."

"Good possibility. Good work, Joel."

"There is one thing, though: How do I..."

"How do you what?"

"Well, that is, I'll lower the dose, or stop it..."

"Your choice, Dr. Saxton."

"But..."

"But what?"

"How do I tell Mrs. Samuels she's sick from the medications we gave her? I'm the one that prescribed it at clinic four months ago."

"Just tell her."

"She'll think I'm stupid or something." Joel paused, his face brightened: "Will it hurt her if we don't tell her? I mean, we could just change it."

Cameron thought about it. "No, I guess not. It probably wouldn't hurt her." He began to walk away.

Max gave Joel a subtle elbow in the ribs. Then, "wait," Joel added, "I wouldn't feel right about that either."

Cameron turned around. "Why?"

"I don't know. Somehow it doesn't feel right."

Cameron looked at him.

"It's a gray zone, I guess." Joel placed his hands in his pockets. "I mean, it wouldn't make much difference one way or the other, but…"

"There will be many more gray zones waiting ahead, Dr. Saxton. We all start in a simple and safe white zone. Though we wish it would always remain that way, the world around us—whether in medicine, or anything else—casts nets of gray and dark about us. The nets can be made of many things—power, greed, force, fear—but whatever they're made of, things are never the same again. Compromise begins: A little gray here, some more there; from one gray compromise stone to another, until at path's end there's only surrounding darkness. Remember then, that first compromise, that first choice of gray. They add up only too easily." Cameron's voice trailed off. "So you're right, it wouldn't make much difference for Mrs. Samuels whether she knows or not. The difference would be inside us."

Joel stared at the ground.

"Evening rounds, gentlemen. Let's go."

· · · · ·

At 501A, Mrs. Samuels looked out from her sea of white sheets. A smile briefly touched her lips, a butterfly fluttering its wings once on a petal, then gone. "Hi," she said.

Dr. Saxton opened her chart, and cleared his throat. "Mrs. Samuels, I think we can help your problem by readjusting the medicine dosages."

"Sure," she smiled at them. "So do I have horses, or Zebras?"

"Well, we probably just have to correct your medicine dosage a bit, to allow for a mild decrease in your kidney function that we didn't expect. You should feel better in a few days…" Joel wanted to say more, but couldn't. He looked towards Cameron.

Dr. Cameron pulled up a chair next to Mrs. Samuels. "Dr. Saxton is right. You had a small drop in kidney function, usually not enough to worry about. But sometimes, when certain medicines we prescribe are eliminated by the kidneys, and those kidneys aren't functioning at full capacity, the medicines accumulate in your body at higher levels than we intended. Now medicines are neither good nor bad in themselves. They all have potential benefits and potential dangers. We try to use a drug only when the chances of potential benefits, in our judgment, outweigh the chances for undesirable side effects. Sometimes that's a hard call to make. In your case, the drug disopyramide was of a higher dosage than needed in comparison to your kidney function, quite likely producing the side effects of tiredness and shortness of breath. We'll correct this now, and I think you'll feel better. Do you have any questions?"

"No. It's nice of you to tell me about it. When can I go home?"

"As soon as you feel better. It may take a few days to eliminate it from your system. We'll talk about it again tomorrow."

Before they finished rounds with Mrs. Samuels, another Red Blanket arrived.

CHAPTER 2

VISITS AND VOICES

Visits last
    the mandatory
    time for a written report

…Oft the story's told
    in less than a heartbeat
    but lasts a lifetime.

Voices tell
    tales of lives
    to be understood

Before their heart
    beats
    can be mended.

7 p.m. After eighteen patients, Medicine clinic was closed. "Mrs. Darrow didn't show," Dr. Cameron said.

The nurse shrugged. "What are you going to do? Make a house call?"

· · · · ·

Lost Creek Way lived up to its name. As house numbers began to predictably line up, the road forked: to the left, empty dirt ruts; to the right, a path blocked by a gate. The path wound into desolate foothills, flanked by an occasional house.

John Cameron got out. The gate creaked, then settled onto the gravel road. Cameron found the numbers above an empty garage a half-mile down. Across a dry elbow of the creek that doubled back on itself, overgrown weeds parted by car-ruts led to an entrance. An empty flowerpot gathered paint flaking from the doorsill.

Cameron knocked. After a third time, there was a faint "door's open."

Mrs. Darrow, ninety-two years old in July, sat on a recliner, feet up. "How are you, sonny?"

"I was wondering why you weren't at the clinic today."

"My daughter couldn't move me. Knees hurt, and my back so I could scream."

"Did you fall?"

"Two weeks ago."

A cream-colored plastic bucket was near her. It had rained that night.

"Roof leaks?" he asked.

"No. That's to pee in."

Dr. Cameron examined her: First the heart and lungs; then hips, back, extremities, and neurologic. Her knees were swollen like cabbages under the robe. He felt something doughy along her lower back. He checked for a decubitus ulcer. It was feces instead.

"Who takes care of you?" he asked.

"My daughter. But she can't always, you know. It's too hard for her."

"You can't stay here like this, Mrs. Darrow. You need more help."

"Where can I go?"

"We have to get you to a hospital."

Mrs. Darrow didn't answer.

Around them, family portraits faded with age showed a woman in a print dress, cradling a child; another with three children in front, and a wide-shouldered, somber-mustached man standing behind. Then the children grown: Girls in prom dresses, an Army picture of the boy. Similarities ran like rivers into the sea.

"You should come to the hospital," Cameron repeated.

"I'm afraid."

Surrounded by a past that was gone, hanging on to a present crumbling around her, the future held fear and the unknown.

"You'll be on Med Ward One. I'll be taking care of you, Mrs. Darrow."

· · · · ·

Cameron hadn't forgotten this time. He kept breakfast's bacon strips wrapped in a plastic bag in his pocket. Whether M.R. VI would be capable of enjoying them was another matter. Indeed, that M.R. VI was still alive at all was another matter.

M.R. VI had no such doubts: As the still warm bacon strips approached in Cameron's hand, M.R. VI barked a lively greeting punctuated by affirmative tail wags. M.A. VI sat up on wobbly haunches, stiffened his back, then with a rabbit-like push of hindquarters, went upright on all fours. Like a friar who'd surfaced from a deep cellar after a prolonged fast, M.R. dispatched the strips crisply, followed by a silent prayer for more.

Cameron gave M.R. VI the last piece of bacon, and smiled. It was, of course, an unscientific departure from an otherwise tightly controlled experiment. There may be those who might wonder whether it had been the bacon strips, or Cameron's genetic engineering, that had regenerated a new liver in place of a dead one.

Cameron opened his Journal:

August 2, 6:30 am:

"M.R. VI's skin jaundice and eye icterus resolved. Stood on all fours. Frisky. Ate extra ration of bacon strips. Implant wound closed without erythema, discharge, or swelling. All metal staples removed. Vital signs normal."

Cameron closed the journal. Next time, he resolved to save some of the bacon for himself.

· · · · ·

Leaving the cafeteria before morning rounds, Max bumped into a pensive "Track" Sullivan.

"Sorry, Dr. Sullivan, I didn't see you coming around the corner." Besides being one of the best attending professors at the medical center, Dr. Mark "Track" Sullivan also ran the cellular physiology research lab, where Cameron dabbled in his secretive project. Initially, Dr. Sullivan had gained his reputation as an outstanding sports and exercise physiologist (rumor had it he'd been tapped as a chemical wizard for the Olympic team). But then he'd abruptly changed the course of his research to basic cellular physiology. That move had undoubtedly cost him among circles devoted to not rocking the research boat, and set back his standing at the medical school. But he'd continued to run his lab at the same furious and uncompromising pace that had earned him the nickname "Track" during his running days in the quarter and the half mile. It was said he could still run competitively if he wanted to (and in the same breath that it had to do with some of his biochemical wizardry). If so, Cameron—who'd been one of Track's foremost runners when he'd coached—had never mentioned it. Tall, almost gaunt, with legs and arms lanky as a windmill, and short-cropped hair that stood as if bristling in the wind, Track resembled a cheetah at loping speed even when he stood still.

"Have you seen Cameron?" Track asked.

"No. I think he missed breakfast this morning. We had a busy last night, though. Maybe he just grabbed some shuteye."

"Has he said anything about the lab lately?" Track's long fingers wandered around his belt, and he swayed from side to side, as if he were uncomfortable standing still.

"Not really."

Track's forehead creased. The look from his deep-set eyes within high cheekbones brought to mind a cheetah's visage, veldt grasses parting before its stalking step. "Max, there've been strange things going on at the lab. I told you that before. But now even more than strange:

Phenomenal. You see," he continued, "I've been dealing on the cellular level, trying to observe how chemical, toxic, or infectious catastrophes change cellular systems beyond repair. If we can see how, when, and where these changes take place, maybe we can find a way of blocking or repairing those changes. No other way to help humans, so we had to use animal models for research: Mostly dogs self-poisoned by Amanita P. 'Deathcaps' and beyond vet's help.

"In these cases of toxic hepatitis, with rapid necrotizing changes, obliteration of the acini, portal triads, biliary inspissation..."

"You mean, basically a dead liver," Max put in.

"...Exactly. The animals die of liver failure. As with all liver failure, pain is minimized since they lapse into a coma from the liver's inability to metabolize." Track paused. "Cameron worked on animals that would die anyway. But after Cameron had given them some sort of genetically re-engineered tissue implant, several have lived longer than expected. Seems while I've been working at the cellular level, he's been dealing with subcellulars and genetics. Now his last dog is quite alive and well, apparently regenerating a totally new liver out of nowhere—three weeks after it should have been dead!"

"Why hasn't Cameron told you about it?" Max asked.

Track shrugged, like the nervous twitch of someone over-eager at the starting blocks. "We've run together, you know. He's complicated as a runner. And complicated as a person. Usually terrible at the starting blocks—just about last one out; sometimes awful in the middle, too; sometimes even awful at the finish. At times, he'd feel someone coming up on him, and totally break his stride." Track Sullivan shook his head: "How does he tick? How does he work? Officially, Cameron's not even at the lab—no name, no grant, not a part of any official research team. He's done most of it himself, using leftover and borrowed equipment. Evenings and nights, since mid-medical school. No questions asked. No answers given. Just work. He's like that." Track glanced down the long, narrow corridor leading from the cafeteria to the elevators, as if measuring in terms of a quarter mile. "There were times, you know, times when he'd forget everything else...his body, his soul were one. He'd hit just right, nothing would shake him—knees high, head back like a colt running a race on storm's tide. A race just to see whether life's blood or shore-breaking waves would win, without really caring which prevailed." Track's eyes gleamed: "He was the fastest then; for a few moments, the fastest I have ever seen."

Max smiled: "Not faster than you."

"There are things you don't know about people—sometimes never come to know. You can't be told of them, or learn of them. You have to feel them, close to you, like on the run..." Track shook his head. "I wouldn't want to run against him, on a day like that. You might have to kill him, or yourself, doing it."

So his calm Resident had a wild side as well, Max pondered.

Track's hands dropped to his sides, ready to move on. "Listen, I've kept you late for rounds. I know you're Cameron's friend. He may be onto something big. The kind of thing that can break one's stride. Keep an eye on him. We'll talk later."

. . . . .

Max climbed the five flights of stairs slower after last night's call. Cameron and Joel were finishing their coffee.

"Hi."

"You all right, Max?"

Max nodded. "Sorry I'm late."

"Coffee?"

"Had some in the cafeteria."

"Then rounds, gentlemen. Let's go."

At 501A, Mrs. Samuels arranged and patted the sheets around her waist. "Hello, doctors." The corners of her eyes sparkled with a tiny wink.

"Hello, Mrs. Samuels. How are you feeling today?" Joel asked.

"Fair. A bit better."

Joel brought out his patient cards. "Less short of breath and tired?"

"Well, I haven't walked yet, but I don't feel tired. Maybe a little short of breath still."

Dr. Saxton's tank-turret stethoscope connected his ears to Mrs. Samuels' chest. "Lungs are clear, Dr. Cameron. Heart unchanged." Joel checked his card: "That makes four days of hospitalization, with a primary diagnosis of 'Respiratory Signs and Symptoms,' DRG number one-hundred, and secondaries of COPD, mild, and renal insufficiency, also mild. Can we discharge her home?"

Cameron's glance went from Joel's cards to Mrs. Samuels. "We can have her walk today, and see how she feels. If there's resolution of her symptoms, our diagnosis is confirmed, and we can reasonably send her home tomorrow. That is, Dr. Saxton, unless you'd like to present her case to Dr. Atwood—attending nearby at Med Ward II—I'm sure we could borrow him and get his opinion on Mrs. Samuels."

"I believe we can keep Mrs. Samuels another day, Dr. Cameron. I wouldn't want to cut into Dr. Atwood's busy schedule." Atwood's presence wasn't particularly sought, nor his absence missed.

"Fine," Cameron smiled.

At 504A, Mrs. Anna Wilson greeted them with wheezes between words: "Good morning...doctors. I feel better...already..." wheeze… "Just perfect!"

"Good morning, Mrs. Wilson." Max went over her vital signs: "Respiratory rate's better but still elevated in the thirties; pulse tachycardic with some P.V.C.'s. Theophylline level in the therapeutic range at thirteen, giving us some leeway before we get into the toxic twenties. Chest X-ray showed emphysema with no changes and no pneumonia; likewise sputum showed minimal white cells and therefore no infection. Arterial blood gases improved slightly from an initial pO_2 of forty-nine," (Cameron raised his eyebrows—a usual normal pO_2 was around ninety), "to fifty-three on room air, while her pCO_2 went from fifty-one to forty-seven. Initial E.K.G. showed rapid tachycardia with three to four premature ventricular contractions—which have now increased to about seven per minute, but are unifocal."

"I don't know..." wheeze… "about you...but I feel...just dandy!" Mrs. Anna Wilson stammered.

"You're feeling better?" McDaniel asked.

"Sure! I don't even..." wheeze… "know why I'm...here."

Dr. McDaniel listened to her lungs and heart. Wheezes moved in and out like a vacuum cleaner scouring one spot. From the foot of the bed, Cameron could hear them without a stethoscope.

"I'm glad you're feeling better, Mrs. Wilson," Max said. "But last time you wanted to leave, you had lost half your blood, and your first unit transfusion was still dangling unfinished in your arm."

"That's not true..." wheeze… "Tell him...Dr. Cameron...how good I'm...doing." She looked at Cameron with a smile that spanned the length of her glasses. Cameron pulled up a chair, trying to remain stern. By now he realized Anna had a way of getting others to agree with her despite the possible consequences.

"Mrs. Wilson, can I talk with you for a minute?"

"Sure, dear."

"And will you listen?"

"I do listen to you, dear..."

"Dr. McDaniel is trying to say we may be fighting a losing battle. You and I both know you have emphysema, complicated by asthma. If you take your medicine regularly, most of the time you can stay out of trouble. But when you stop, your lungs get tight and shut down. You get status asthmaticus—asthma that's irreversible for a prolonged period of time. It doesn't respond to the usual oral and inhaled bronchodilating medication. So, we need to use intravenous medication, and even standard amounts of that don't usually reopen your lungs.

"Now these medicines can speed your heart, which is already beating wilder from your lack of oxygen. And as we push the medicines to their limits to reopen your lungs, we also push the heart faster than we'd like. If these don't work, then we have to use large doses of steroids that work negatively on your immune system. For you, since you've had ulcers before, these can be particularly dangerous, because these steroids can weaken the stomach's ability to heal itself. And as Dr. McDaniel mentioned, you nearly bled out once from ulcers."

Cameron paused and looked at Mrs. Wilson. "So you see, when you skip your usual medications, we are forced to use even stronger ones, which are a double-edged sword: We need them to keep you alive, since your oxygen drops to levels incompatible with life. Yet these stronger medicines could also kill you. Mrs. Wilson, you don't know how much we worry, every time we have to increase a dose, or add another medicine."

"Oh there..." wheeze "...you know I'll be... all right." Mrs. Wilson took Cameron's hand: "You're not...mad at me..." wheeze, "...are you?"

"No, I'm not, Mrs. Wilson. I know it's important to keep a positive attitude. But when it gets in the way of taking the medicines you need, then it's not positive anymore, and just hurts you. So, promise me you'll take them from now on."

"I'll try, dear... Don't get mad...at me... You'll see how...I get better."

Cameron stood up. "Your plans, Dr. McDaniel?"

"I'd like to transfer Mrs. Wilson to the telemetry unit, so we can monitor her heart rate as we push the theophylline level up. Also increase oxygen to three liters, then follow-up with blood gases and clinically. If there's no improvement, we may need to start high dose steroids like prednisone, and continue her anti-ulcer regimen."

"Dr. Saxton, anything to add?"

"I'd consider an upper G.I. series, if one hasn't been done recently, to make certain there's no active ulcer disease."

"Last upper G.I. was three months ago, showing scarring only," Max added. "Recent stool occult bloods negative times three—so not likely active ulcer disease."

Cameron turned to Mrs. Wilson. "We'll be seeing you this evening at telemetry. You get better now, you hear?"

"I will...Thanks, dears."

In 508, the only darkened room, their previous John Doe—now Lester Brown—breathed in halting rasps.

"He's been more calm the last two hours," Barbara Davis spoke in a whisper. "Hasn't slept though, and goes wild whenever lights go on. Pulse up to one twenty-eight, respirations in the thirties, temp ninety-nine point eight, and blood pressure down to one zero six over sixty. Won't eat or drink, and resists any nebulizer or oxygen mask."

Joel glanced towards the charts, which Barbara held cradled under her breasts. They spanned almost the entire chart. "Thanks, Barbara!" Joel's words startled Lester into a teeth-grinding grimace. Joel took a step back, then continued: "Condition unchanged, or worse. Repeat chest film showed more fluid of pulmonary edema, and arterial blood gases show an even larger reversal of pO_2 and pCO_2—the O_2 was forty-six, and the CO_2 sixty-three. Repeat doses of naloxone gave no improvement. Sputum gram-stain showed no white cells or clusters of organisms indicative of infection. Blood cultures also negative so far."

Joel stopped, and Cameron waited.

"What do you think, Dr. Cameron?"

Cameron didn't answer. Instead of reminding Joel that plans were not made—regardless of amount of lab work done—without first examining the patient, Cameron did it himself. Previous examination attempts had provoked extreme combativeness, controlled by four-limb and torso restraints. This time only a weightlifter's grimace showed—Lester was getting tired. Cameron loosened the torso restraints, and listened to the heart and lungs. All sounds were represented: wheezes, rhonchi, and rales; the heart kept its drum-beat distantly behind.

Cameron finished the exam. "You were saying, Dr. Saxton?" Joel decided to listen to the lungs before he spoke. The triple-turret stethoscope went to work, and afterwards Dr. Saxton solemnly announced: "He seems to have developed shock lung. We've been unable to remove edema fluid from his lungs via diuretics. I'm not sure how else we can help him. I'd suggest a Pulmonary consult."

Cameron thought about it. "Dr. McDaniel?"

"I agree he has shock-lung syndrome. He hasn't responded to our therapy, which is not unusual, since this problem carries a high mortality rate. Whatever caused it—multiple fat emboli from the milk IV, heroin, and maybe PCP, or combinations—we've run out of therapies. Pulmonary will probably snow him with tranquilizers and intubate him for positive-pressure breathing."

"Why have we run out of therapies?" Cameron asked. "Dr. Saxton?"

"Well, if it was cardiogenic shock, we could dry him out with diuretics, unload the heart with vasodilators, improve heart muscle function with inotropes. But..."

"But what?"

"Well, we've already tried diuretics—they're not working. I mean, they're working, but not on the lungs, where we want them. The same would happen with the rest."

"Ah," Cameron paused. "Why?"

McDaniel wondered what Cameron was leading up to. "I suppose they're not working because this isn't cardiogenic shock," Max put in, "but lung edema mostly due to fat emboli. Now if these emboli were due to lung blood clots, we could treat them with anti-coagulants."

"But they're not," Cameron affirmed the obvious, then waited.

Joel and Max were puzzled.

"I suppose there's nothing else we could do then," Cameron offered, "to dissolve the fat clots."

Max was beginning to see some light: "Fat can be dissolved. There are solvents, but..."

"But what?"

The light disappeared again. "Nothing we could use in the body. I mean, what solvent could we use?"

"Indeed," Cameron stroked his chin. "Seems to me there's one rather commonly used, though not exactly for that purpose."

"Alcohol!" Max suddenly exclaimed. "But could we get enough of it in to make a difference?"

"He won't eat or drink," Joel pointed out.

"We could use one hundred percent absolute ethanol, two-hundred proof stuff," Max pondered. "It should be sterile enough for an IV drip, and we could monitor his blood alcohol levels."

Cameron turned to Joel. "What do you think, Dr. Saxton?"

Joel wavered between his chance to bounce someone to the Pulmonary Ward, and the tantalizing possibility of trying something new that might decrease the number of needed hospitalization days. "Far shot, but it could work."

"Then, gentlemen, I shall call the Pulmonary consult; and since prognosis is grave regardless of what Pulmonary recommends or does, you shall research the literature for any data on fat-emboli dissolution by alcohol in man, and their results. In the meantime, we'll add steroids in an attempt to stabilize the patient's lung membranes, and we'll monitor his status. Then depending on how Mr. Brown does, how well Pulmonary fares, and what we'll find, we'll make further decisions."

· · · · ·

Rounds between 508 and 525 saw life continuing in a multiplicity of forms and life supports: Some were silent, some screamed; some had vacant stares, and of those some were held in restraints; some were pensive, others jovial despite the number of tubes attached. IV's were standard fare, like the branches of a tree, carrying over six different medicines along four different lines. Then came bladder catheters, nasal cannulas for oxygen, and nasogastric tubes to put the stomach to rest. Tubes dangled like awkward rainbows with more hope than promise that tomorrow would be better than today.

Rounds were almost over when Med Ward II became overloaded with O.D.'s on their call day, and Dr. Cameron accepted the overflow. The elevator door opened with their new patient from the ER.

She was in her late teens. Wild hair the color of burnt caramel fell mane-like over her large green eyes. A few youthful pimples swam in the pallor of her face. The eyes moved constantly as she kept up an incessant stream of chatter. Joel glanced at the I.D. bracelet over her ankle: Christina Rourke. Under the bandages on her wrists, lacerations crisscrossed superficial to the tendons. But the veins had bled enough to saturate the dressings, even after suturing in the ER.

Joel checked the chart, then called Cameron.

"Toxicology is negative," Joel explained. "The ER. apparently sent her thinking she was an overdose, needing med ward care. But she isn't an O.D.—looks like a clean cut-n-paste job. We could lateral her to Psych ward, and the lacerations could be followed as an outpatient. What do you say?"

Until now, Chris' face remained without expression. The high cheekbones were uncreased below eyes that moved swiftly, but blinked infrequently. Her long neck matched the sinuous lines of her slim waist and shapely breasts. If not beautiful, she was at least pretty. Incongruously, no emotions shadowed her face until Joel's words to Cameron. Then, as if some painful memory had surfaced first through her eyes, their deep green became sea-drenched emeralds, with tides rushing between cheekbones and her finely curved nose. Her lips became moist and bright red.

Joel became uneasily silent. He offered the chart to Cameron.

Cameron didn't open it. He sat down next to Chris. "Chris," he said quietly, "how can we help you?"

She seemed startled by the words, awakened from her sea-dream. "I don't know. Do you think I'm fat? Do you think I'm ugly?"

Cameron brushed a lock of hair from her forehead. "I don't think so. Why do you ask?"

"I hear voices, you know. Voices all the time. They say many things. Usually that I'm fat, that I'm ugly. I look in the mirror, and that's what the voices say. Sometimes, they talk to me so much that I...I..." She held up the bandaged wrists to Cameron, then dropped them limply at her sides, like childhood's too soon abandoned rag dolls.

"How long have you heard the voices?"

"Maybe two...no, three years..."

"Are those voices a part of you, your own voices, or someone outside you?"

"They sound like outside me, telling me...bad things, about me."

"Do you know why the voices began three years ago?"

The eyes closed, bringing darkness, perhaps forgetfulness, to her green eyes. No, not forgetfulness: Tide-washed despair returned to her face; tears rolled down lips devoid of smiles; smiles that had been forgotten long ago, along with those abandoned rag dolls.

"I did stuff... a lot of it. Everything and anything... pot... LSD... coke... speed..."

Rag dolls, perfumed lace—all had been replaced by thrills unknown, journeys into spaces where childhood fantasies abruptly ended. Twisted webs had veiled and trapped reality into a thick winter sea-fog. And when the foghorns sounded, only nightmare forms appeared: Alien forms, creations of chemical phantasms in brain-space. Phantasms that had frozen the person she could have been into an eternity of fake experiences, gathering dust like plastic flowers in restaurant corners, without anyone ever noticing.

Cameron didn't ask more, or ask why. He knew that permanent chemical brain changes could have occurred. If she was lucky, and only LSD flashbacks were involved without permanent psychosis, perhaps after another three years the voices would improve. There was no way of knowing now, and she needed time to find out. Time that perhaps she wouldn't give herself.

Chris didn't say more either. Her face froze into its past expressionless cast. Perhaps it kept her from crying.

Cameron touched the back of her hand: "Just remember, Chris, if the voices come back, saying anything bad about you, they're wrong." He searched for more words, but there weren't any. He felt like giving her a hug, but couldn't. It would be difficult to explain to the Intern he was teaching. But that was only an excuse: Cameron didn't do it because he was afraid. Afraid of many things, outside and inside. Somewhere between the 2 am med school crammings, three-day marathons of hundred-page tests, and forty-hour call days, less had remained of love than of disciplined learning. Yet even that was an excuse: He was simply afraid, like everyone else. Afraid to open himself, afraid to love, afraid to lose. Afraid of memories that might hurt; afraid of running a race when the difference between winning and losing was so small. Afraid to engage not only the mind, but the heart, in the battles for lives—because sometimes those battles were lost, and the heart paid a greater price than the mind. So like everyone else, he'd built islands and walls. Perhaps better. Because he'd had more practice.

"Let's see what we can do for her here, Joel," Cameron said quietly. "She'll probably wind up in Psych soon enough as it is."

"Shall we start her on an antidepressant or something?" Joel asked.

"We may have to, I suppose, but for now, just talk to her."

"You mean do a history and a physical?" Cameron looked back.

"That too."

He thought about seasons. Even deepest winters broke like butterflies from a cocoon: Ice floes cracked, with seals wandering at their edges; thick tundra thawed into spring grass, for hopping white rabbits. But for Chris, the sea-fog of frozen winter might never lift for a warm gale on her face, nor a spring-burst of sun dance before her green eyes.

It was late into the night before Cameron finished. Work came automatically by now. Only dealing with emotions didn't. Instead of going to the Resident quarters to sleep, Cameron walked to the sixteenth floor. A boarded-up door barred passage to the rooftop. He wedged a board out, and walked outside. Dim glows of dawn shimmered like the smooth skin of a laughing girl's breasts above a low-cut dress.

Cameron undid his shirt and tie, and sat back against a ledge. In sleep's twilight, he recalled what Chris had said, about the voices. He remembered when he'd first thought about medicine: He didn't yet know then the many different worlds that existed, or how they lived and how they died. He remembered...a basketball game: The end of their second year, after finishing their first clinical hospital rotation. They began playing after midnight. The four of them. Two-on-two. At 3 am it was 142 to 146. At 4 am 168 to 170's... A different kind of game: Something had happened to them. It had happened differently for each, yet the same. The four of them knew it, without having to say anything. They played like they had never played before. They played with their sheer desperation—one last attempt to escape. They knew how it was no longer a game. They too, had finally heard their own voices: Their old world had died, and their new one would be totally different—not even always their own.

"Yes, Chris," Cameron whispered over the rooftops, "we all hear voices, sometimes."

The voices of those they couldn't help enough.

CHAPTER 3

TWO MASTERS

"To fulfill the physician duties, I solemnly swear in the presence of my teachers, confreres and our entire people:

To work honestly and conscientiously to promote the protection of public health and the development of the human personality in all directions;

To pursue with all my powers the study of medicine so that I contribute towards its flourishing and to seek when necessary the advice and help of my teachers and colleagues;

To love the sick, to be attentive and concerned about them;

Not to apply the medical knowledge to the detriment of human health;

Not to impart to others any information that was entrusted to me by patients when it does not endanger society;

I shall always be mindful of any medical duty, of my high responsibility to the people, to the Communist Party and to the socialist state. By selfless work I will make the effort to earn the love and the respect of the entire people.

I swear to behave in an exemplary manner in my work and in my daily life and to be an active fighter for the upbuilding of communist society as well as for the information of the communist consciousness in our people. This oath I promise to keep all my life."

—*Solemn Oath of the Physicians of the Soviet Union, 1963.*

Cameron returned the call from Dr. Gregory Neuhaus, Director of Medical Education.

"Got a minute, Dr. Cameron?"

Whether he really did or not was irrelevant. "Yes, sir," Cameron replied.

"Then come and see me."

"When, Dr. Neuhaus?"

"Now will be fine."

Cameron was ushered into an office that was spartan, as far as director's offices go: Table, four armchairs, one picture on the desk, and a disarray of papers. A small bookcase lacked the volume and shine of a lawyer's even smallest library; the tomes weren't leather-bound, but were cracked and worn to the texture of rough sand.

"Do sit down, Dr. Cameron."

Cameron was beginning to worry. He'd never seen this office, for any reason, even at the time of his appointment as Medical Resident. Dr. Neuhaus had been a name, a reputation, and the boss. Cameron had always figured it was better never to have to see the boss.

"Glass of water, Dr. Cameron?"

"No, thank you."

Dr. Neuhaus poured himself a glass of seltzer water. "We're having a bit of a problem," he began. "I trust you can keep this in the strictest confidence."

"Yes, sir."

Neuhaus took another sip of water. "A senior Oncology Resident—perhaps you knew Dr. Arhends—shot himself last week. Family's been notified. No one else knows."

Cameron remembered him. Arhends had been a bulk of a man, big as a defensive lineman, and still jovial despite being in a specialty—Oncology, the treatment of cancer—that saw more people die than it could cure. But not without giving them several more months to years before it happened. Enough time to get to know the patients. Enough time to feel it when they died.

"He was found in Resident's quarters, pillow between gun and temple. I suppose we'll have to come up with some explanation..." Neuhaus' eyes drifted off, perhaps towards an imaginary window the office didn't have "...besides working with cancer patients, day in and day out." His voice got very quiet. "I suppose few could understand that."

Cameron understood. But didn't say anything.

"I'm sorry, Dr. Cameron," Neuhaus returned from his drifting. "Here's the bottom line. We're already short two Medical Residents, and now this...ah, happened. Means we've got Interns without Residents to guide them. I need at least two reliable Residents to rotate extra rounds with selected Interns. You're here because you're capable. And for one more reason. Know what that is?"

"I'm not sure, sir."

"I didn't think you'd turn me down in a time of need. Am I right?"

"Yes, sir."

Dr. Neuhaus stood up. "Good. I hope this will be temporary, and we can secure more help in mid-rotation."

"Yes, sir."

"In the meantime, we'll need to reassign some Interns. The ones on the new schedule have to be capable of handling more responsibility, such as evening rounds on their own. One of them will be Dr. Max McDaniel. Will you tell him for me?"

"Yes, sir."

"In his place, your new Intern will be Dr. Lucy Carlton. Of course, you'll be rounding with Dr. McDaniel on the extra morning rounds, according to the new rotating schedule. That should work out well, producing two good teams out of one."

"Yes, sir."

"Are you always this formal, Dr. Cameron?"

"No, sir. I mean, yes, when the situation calls for it."

Neuhaus smiled a bit. "Are you happy here, Dr. Cameron?"

"Yes, sir."

"Good. I've heard good things about you."

"Thank you, Dr. Neuhaus."

"My secretary will give you the new schedule. I trust it will be satisfactory. Rounds on rotation will begin at six a.m. this week. You'll also be available for any questions or help those Interns may need during the day. Good luck, Dr. Cameron."

"Yes, sir." Cameron turned to go.

"Oh, Cameron..."

"Yes, sir."

"Usually, I know more about my Residents and Interns than anyone thinks." Neuhaus' hands fidgeted, "I guess sometimes...it still is not enough. Arhends never came to me with any problems. I just didn't know."

"I'm sure of that, Dr. Neuhaus. None of us knew." Or felt it, Cameron thought.

Dr. Neuhaus looked at him across the room. "I guess I needed someone to know that."

· · · · ·

Rounds went first to Mrs. Anna Wilson in the Telemetry Unit. Wires connected the surface of Mrs. Wilson's chest to a portable scanner the size of a pocketbook, fastened to her waist. Her heartbeats were continuously transmitted to an EKG telemetry console at the nurses' station. Alarms were preset for dangerously low or high rates, as well as other unusual heart beats. Though her rate remained rapid, telemetry alarms and lights for her rhythm had been calm lately. Mrs. Wilson adjusted her nasal oxygen cannulas.

"How are you, Mrs. Wilson?" Max had an idea, but asked anyway.

"Not so...good," she wheezed out. Her chest heaved like an open tent caught in a cross-draft.

Max recited the vitals quickly, dispensed with more questions, and moved his stethoscope over her chest. Sibilant wheezes moved in and out like grinding brakes.

"We may have to step up our schedule a bit. Despite pushing the aminophylline drip to fifty per hour, oxygen, and aerosolized bronchodilators, Mrs. Wilson..." Max searched for a way to put it "...is not doing any better. Theophylline level isn't back yet, but I doubt we can push that much more. I'd like your permission to begin steroids, Dr. Cameron."

"Looks like we have little choice but to proceed that way." Cameron took Mrs. Wilson's hand: "Be sure to tell us if your stomach starts to hurt, even a little. I know you hate to complain, but this is very important. The steroids will decrease your ability to feel inflammation and pain, so that any damage to your stomach can be far along before you feel much pain. So please tell us right away of any problems there."

Mrs. Wilson took a deep breath. "I sure...will," she tried to smile.

Once in the hallway, Cameron stopped. "Dosage of steroid, Dr. McDaniel?"

"Methylprednisolone IV, sixty to one hundred milligrams, every six to eight hours."

Cameron stroked his chin. "There's an old saying about severe asthma, and the use of steroids: 'Too late, too little, and too long.' We usually start them later than we should, at too small a dose, and then continue them for too long—getting less benefits, and more side effects. How about two hundred milligrams? We'll begin to taper in twenty-four to forty-eight hours."

Max wrote the order: 1. Methylprednisolone, 200 mg IV q 8 h.

"Now what about her stomach, Dr. Saxton? What could we do to protect it ahead of time?" Cameron asked.

"What medication is she on now?"

"Antacids and famotidine, usual dosages," Max replied.

"I suppose we could add a cytoprotective agent like sucralfate. But I'm not aware of any studies that show a greater benefit from using such a combination of drugs over what she already has now," Dr. Saxton concluded.

"Dr. McDaniel?" Cameron asked.

Max thought a while. "Since each medication works on a different level—the antacid by neutralizing acid, the H2 antagonist by decreasing acid production, and the sucralfate by coating—then theoretically they bring different mechanisms of healing, which may be additive. My feeling would be to go with all three, especially since sucralfate is not absorbed by the body, and wouldn't add significant side effect risks."

Max and Joel looked to Cameron to resolve the impasse.

"The choice isn't easy. Both points are valid, so there is no absolute right or wrong way to proceed. Let's spend some time on this," Cameron paused, "since situations like this won't be rare.

"In medicine," Cameron continued, "we lack the benefit of hindsight for every patient's situation. Absolute answers in medicine exist only for analysts or reviewers—after the outcome is already known. In this, medicine has something in common with chess: The demand for skill and judgment is greatest when one acts in the present, to predict and produce a future result. To analyze past outcomes, more hindsight and arrogance are needed than skill.

"In our present situation, Dr. Saxton's point is well taken: The idea that 'if a little medicine is good, more is then better' is usually not true, and often dangerous. On the other hand, we have a life-threatening condition: If the patient's breathing doesn't improve, she will likely die. But if we give her steroids to improve her breathing, she may reactivate an ulcer and bleed to death. So maximum therapy to suppress ulcers is also reasonable, with the theoretical advantages mentioned by Dr. McDaniel. On balance, in this case, we may have more to gain than to lose by using all the medications combined."

Max added the orders for antacids, famotidine, and sucralfate.

Barbara Davis joined them at Mrs. Jessie Lucas' bedside. In theory, nurses were to round on their patients with doctors. In practice, the last few years had seen such a steady escalation of regulations and paperwork that it had come to usurp most of the nurses' time and priority. There were nursing admission forms to be filled, nursing assessment forms, pain evaluation forms, psychologic profile forms, family profile forms, social profile forms, day sheet and progress note forms, daily flow sheets, discharge planning forms, and still to-be-developed forms by supervisors whose task was devoted not to the care of patients, but to the formulation of new forms. And of course, all forms came in multiple layers and copies.

Whether the forms had been initiated by hospital, supervisory nursing, insurance, or governmental bureaucracy, the end result was cumulative and the same: The breeding of fine, pedigreed paperwork, which in turn demanded yet more bureaucrats and supervisors to oversee its proper completion. There was as yet little realization that when paperwork or electronic records are treated first, patient treatment necessarily came in second, or even last.

By now, paperwork's destiny had become so bloated that only five minutes were allotted for nurses to make rounds on each patient with their doctor. Rather than compress patient care into this time, nurse-physician patient rounds had become more a relic than a standard. Nurses like Barbara Davis were the few exceptions who somehow squeezed extra time from their stack of papers, and still rounded with doctors on their patients. Such patient-care zeal, however, was rarely rewarded by nursing supervisors as favorably as paperwork perfection.

"Good morning, Barbara. Thanks for rounding with us."

"Good morning to the dynamic trio." Barbara noticed Cameron's shirt collar wrinkled over his tie, Max's socks the same as yesterday's, and Joel's usually neat smock crumpled as if it had seen several hours of R.E.M. sleep compressed into one. "You had twenty-one new admissions last night. Everyone okay?"

"Couple of close ones, but they're all hanging in."

"How about you guys? There's cookies and tea in the nurses' station, if you'd like."

Cameron noticed Barbara wasn't wearing any makeup. Her eyes looked even bluer, softer—not a fire this time, but dawn's glow. "Thanks," he replied. Cameron remembered a time from long ago: Eyes of blue like that, looking out over a harbor, ferries leaving their soundless foam-tracks under a pearl-clouded sky with dusk's ruby edges. It seemed long ago, and it was better that way. Better, to forget.

Joel stared at Barbara's white jumpsuit. He imagined its full contents soft like a great bowl of jello. He fingered his patient cards like a new deck that needed shuffling.

Barbara disengaged herself from Joel's glance. It was one of the reasons she hadn't worn make-up: Perhaps the stares would cease; perhaps eyes would stop their rush to strip layers of clothes from her breasts and thighs. She was tired of being the Barbara that lay naked in mind's eye. There were times it felt different: When Cameron looked at her, she felt someone had touched her hands, her face, before her body. But Cameron's glance was brief, Joel's prolonged and clinging. It was difficult to react accordingly, to separate her own feelings, and be able to judge those of others as they fleetingly brushed by. Mostly she put them all in the same place. And away.

Joel shrugged when Barbara looked away. Like Roger Taylor, the Surgery Resident, Joel wasn't used to his glances being deflected. Besides, there would be Jody tonight: If not overflowing, at least exquisitely filled out, peaks and curves tightly gliding like a cat on the prowl.

Max tried to avoid looking at Barbara, but the rising curves of her hips meeting the small of her back drew his sleepless eyes like a dream he'd left too soon. By now he knew that beauty sometimes came with love, often without—and at times with such power that in gaining that beauty he'd lose himself.

Barbara reviewed the vitals, medications, and nursing care for Mrs. Jessie Lucas. "B.P. one-sixty over ninety-five; pulse eighty-three; respiratory rate twenty-seven; afebrile; weight one eleven."

From the foot of 502B, Max could see Mrs. Jessie Lucas' condition had deteriorated: She lay limp against the inclined pillows; her wide pelican-grin was gone; lower eyelids drooped like little pools collecting rain beneath a window. Max studied the chart, pondering the sudden change. "What's bothering you, Mrs. Lucas?"

"Oh, Max," she cleared her throat. "I'm not feeling so good."

"What can I do for you?"

"I don't know, dear. I'm a bit short of breath again."

"Can you sit forward a bit, so I can listen to your lungs?" She had to take his arm to pull herself a few inches from the pillow.

"Enough?"

"It'll do fine." As she breathed in, Max could hear her usual gravel-grinding rhonchi of many years standing. There were no fine rales—sounds a bit like brushing silk—of congestive heart failure to be heard under the rhonchi. And no asthmatic wheezes.

The large hospital gown covered Mrs. Lucas' thin, bird-like frame like a tent. Dr. McDaniel didn't need to move the gown off her shoulder to listen to her heart—his arm and stethoscope fit under the tent. Heart rate, rhythm, and murmur remained unchanged. Mrs. Lucas lay back against her pillow, tired from the effort of bending forward. Dilated neck veins pulsated up to her jaws. Max pressed lightly above a neck vein, then with another finger milked the vein down. It filled up two-thirds of the way to the jaw. That was about four centimeters above normal.

"Have you had any chest pains, Jessie?"

"No, dear."

"Cough?"

She shook her head.

Max loosened the tightly tucked covers around Jessie's feet, and pressed his fingers around her ankles, observing for any remaining indentation of edema fluid. There was none. Her ankles remained as smooth and bony as ever.

"Well, how am I, dear?" Jessie used the term in a familiar yet polite manner, as if sipping high tea at Queen Victoria's salon.

Max ran the data through his mind: There had been no weight gain since yesterday's one eleven. Fluid balance was also even—little less than a quart in, a little over one out. His eyebrows rose: "I know you're not feeling well, Jessie. But there haven't been any significant changes since yesterday..." Except for the veins, Max thought.

"You know, dear, I'm feeling so weak and short of breath..."

"I know. Mind if we ask Dr. Cameron about this?"

"Sure, go ahead, dear."

"Dr. Cameron, Mrs. Lucas was admitted six days ago with shortness of breath due to pulmonary edema and cardiogenic asthma. While her wheezing is gone after digitalization and diuresis, her symptomatology has returned. She's short of breath again, but seemingly without her previous accumulation of fluid. In fact, she's now nine pounds less than at admission. So congestive heart failure symptoms are unlikely. She's also had no chest pain, no significant tachycardia, tachypnea, or fever to indicate a pulmonary embolus or clot. And lack of a temp also makes pneumonia unlikely." Max paused. "She's always had rhonchi, so her lungs are difficult to evaluate for subtle changes. Only the neck veins are overdistended by four centimeters. This would be compatible with C.H.F., but again, no other signs of congestive failure are present. Cardiac constricting tamponade could also do this, but no other signs are present for it, either."

Cameron had been watching Jessie. "Does it feel like the wheezing you had before?"

"Not exactly."

"And you're not coughing, and didn't have any chest pain?" Cameron repeated the question, since it no longer surprised him when patients changed their answers even ten minutes later. "No, dear."

Cameron checked her lungs, heart, and neck veins. "I agree, Dr. McDaniel. We have conflicting data, and therefore no simple answer.

What would you like to do to resolve this?" Before Max could begin, Cameron turned to Joel, immersed in his patient cards. "I'd like your opinion, Dr. Saxton."

Joel made an effort to recover: "Well, I'd run a few tests..."

"What tests would you like?"

It was one of Cameron's rules that teaching rounds were just that—for all of them to listen and learn from all patients. And another was to avoid making uninformed mistakes. After weighing the two, Joel decided to pass rather than bluff: "I'm not sure at this point, Dr. Cameron."

"Knowing you're not sure is also important." Cameron left it at that, and turned to Max. "Dr. McDaniel, what would you like to do now?"

"We could get a chest X-ray this morning, give her two liters flow of oxygen, and reexamine this afternoon."

"Reasonable. Maybe also get arterial blood gas measurement before we give the oxygen."

Max pressed Jessie's long, thin fingers. "We'll see you this afternoon, Jessie."

"Thanks, Max."

At the end of the hall, Barbara left them. The nurses caring for patients on the other half of the ward were too busy—"managing" the "health care team" of nurses' aides, clerks, supervisors, nursing coordinators, social workers, insurance coordinators, home-care coordinators, quality-control reviewers, and utilization reviewers—to make rounds on their patients with doctors. In the past, even without such a formidable "health care team," patients had somehow gotten better. Unfortunately for the future, they would have to get better in spite of the several more tiers of "health care team" paper workers to be added, few of which could be counted on to respond to the real and basic needs of bedpan, sponge and towel, and T.L.C. In fact, such response would steadily diminish, since power and importance lay with those "managing" others who actually did the work. And when one rewarded a "health care team" most for handling computers and "managing" papers, and least for bedside patient care—surprise—that's what one got.

They went on to the next room—the darkened one. Plastic tubes caught the light from the hall like a pale string of Christmas lights: One tube carried oxygen to Lester Brown's nostrils; the other dripped clear fluid into his veins. He lay quiet, the covers ruffled over his chest.

Dr. Saxton spoke in whispers near the doorway: "Pulse unchanged in the one twenties; respiratory rate in mid-thirties; blood pressures in the one hundreds over sixties; a low-grade temp of one hundred point two. Since he's been calmer, we've been able to supply him oxygen, and his pO_2 now is fifty-two, but the CO_2 sixty-four." Joel approached the bed. "Good news is he's more quiet. Bad news, he may be in a coma." Joel drew the covers back slowly and placed his stethoscope under the restraining vest.

In less than a blink, the vest grew taunt, and the restraints snapped against their metal bedposts. Joel heard a roar as the stethoscope ripped from his ears.

Joel drew back, then retrieved his stethoscope. "Dr. Cameron," he announced, "the patient is not in a coma."

While Saxton's ears still rang, his patient's storm abated. The arched back sank down onto the bed; the tortuous breathing resumed.

"What do you have on the alcohol idea?" Cameron asked.

"No textbook sources, but three articles on ethanol use for fat emboli: Two were single case reports, somewhat favorable; the other was a series of nine patients with presumed fatty embolization from the marrow of multiple fractures, sustained during massive trauma. Sufficient conclusions about treatment efficacy couldn't be made, due to small sampling, different age groups, and possible direct lung injuries."

"Dr. Saxton, what do you think?"

"This is an unusual case, and there's little written to go on." Joel touched his ear, and glanced at the patient card in his hand. It was a card he could do without. "I'd say he's a candidate for the I.C.U., or the Pulmonary Service."

"We've got a problem," Cameron checked the IV tubing and oxygen lines, "the I.C.U. is full, and with a waiting list. As for Pulmonary, I've checked with them, and they don't want him. Technically, he's still an overdose, and therefore a medical rather than chest case."

"Do they know how critical he is?"

Cameron nodded. "Sure."

"Meaning they don't want a death added against the Pulmonary Service."

Cameron knew Joel was right. As with any regulations imposed by those with only superficial knowledge of what they tried to regulate, the Feds new reporting system produced more effects than intended—like multiple ripples on a pond from a single cast stone. "They'll come to intubate him, though," Cameron added, "and give us a consult."

"Mighty nice of them," commented Joel. "They'll tell us what to do, and we take the rap when it fails."

Cameron thought it over. "Dr. McDaniel, any serious side effects, besides the obvious, from the ethanol treatment in that series?"

"None apparent."

"Any other comments, Dr. Saxton?"

Joel warmed to the alcohol treatment idea. "Well, he's got no visible means of support. If this works, the hospital and society won't have to foot as much of his Medicaid tab."

Cameron counted silently to ten. "Gentlemen, shall we go outside to finish rounds?" Cameron maintained his usual impartiality in teaching, allowing others to think and evaluate without interference. There had only been a few years difference between Cameron's and Joel's medical training. Yet John Cameron had learned disease diagnoses by name not code, and faced a named enemy—on behalf of his patient—with whatever arsenal he had at his disposal. Joel Saxton's medical education began when the government assigned I.C.D.M. code numbers rather than names to diseases, and DRG numbers for treatment. Patients had a Medicare number, doctors a "provider" or "vendor" number. The whole process, from birth to death, could be accomplished for a number, by a number, and according to numbers.

With diseases numbered but nameless, the enemy became less menacing; with treatment aimed at satisfying government numbers and edicts, the arsenal dwindled to whatever the numbers would allow. The personal wars of medicine against disease—with patient's lives at stake—had become institutionalized skirmishes, managed by numbers, with budget and bureaucracy at stake as much as lives. History didn't hold any examples of wars being won without becoming important on a personal level, or without exceeding the national budget for entertainment.

In his darkened room, Lester Brown waged his own losing battle. Gentlemen, let's examine our options," Cameron continued. "On the one hand, we have intubation: When all's said and done, it can be a life-saving procedure, but it's also invasive. Adding any tube to any body orifice adds discomfort and increase chances of infection. Both present a problem in this case, since he doesn't need a pneumonia on top of his shock lung, and the discomfort of an endotracheal tube can be considerable. On the other hand, while it may be theoretically possible to aid dissolution of fat emboli with alcohol, we know little about it, and so can consider it experimental. Evaluating its use involves its potential hazards, which we could control by monitoring blood levels; and, on the other hand, a very poor prognosis with any other therapy, including intubation."

Joel couldn't leave well enough alone: "And intubation and a respirator, whether it did or didn't work, would be prolonged and cost a mint."

Cameron kept his tone just as detached and impartial as before: 'What physician's oath did you take, Dr. Saxton?"

"The usual one—Hippocratic. We also had the choice of taking the Declaration of Geneva, by the World Medical Association. I took them both. Any reason?"

"Just wondering." Near the darkness of Lester Brown's room, Cameron's voice and face remained distant and inscrutable as the shadows. "You see, both the Hippocratic and Geneva Oaths affirm a physician's primary concern for the benefit of his patient. The only one I know that calls for equal responsibility to society and state, as well as to the patient, is that of the Soviet of the U.S.S.R, in 1963."

In the silence that followed, if there was any change in the color of Saxton's face, the room's darkness was to his advantage.

Cameron broke the silence. "Our patient is getting worse, and we have some decisions to make. Each patient deserves the best we can give. The best of our ideas, old and new. And he deserves all the caution we can provide. Leave me your list of the ethanol articles and I'll go over them. In the meantime, I'll ask Pulmonary to place him on a respirator. We'll reevaluate Mr. Brown in the afternoon."

CHAPTER 4

ONE GOAL

"Medicine arose out of the primal sympathy of man with man, out of the desire to help those in sorrow, need and sickness...and whatever is done with this end must be called medicine."

—Sir William Osler,
The Evolution of Modern Medicine, 1913.

B efore lunch, Cameron went downstairs to Radiology. "Dave, got a minute?"

"Sure, John. What's up?"

David Guttman, senior Radiology Resident, sported a beard, medium paunch, silvering sidelines along his temples, and a measured walk that belonged on the high seas, giving him a crusty mariner's look. Cameron liked him because he was straightforward: He called his X-rays carefully, but without the many "ifs, buts, and possibles," that often rendered radiograph reports devoid of meaning for those who'd ordered them.

"Jessie Lucas—she's worsening, but clinically hard to tell if it's lungs, heart, or both. Her lungs sound terrible, but they always do, and she's got more heart murmurs than a purring cat. Neck veins are up, but no weight increase or edema."

"Sounds like a problem. Let's see," Guttman dimmed the room lights, letting the white, gray, and black shadows dance in front of the porcelain-white viewbox. He scanned the entire thorax first—a bird's eye view—then from the outside in, like an eagle's circling glide towards the earth. The bones came first: Ribs, back, shoulders, neck, looking for mineral loss, tumors, blood vessel indentations, arthritic changes. Lung air spaces were next, with tissue edges of the pleura, then the reticular blood vessel network. Towards the center, he measured the mediastinum—the central space containing the great vessels, lymphatics, esophagus—and finally, the heart itself. He did this methodically, eyes rhythmically widening, then narrowing, like a player eyeing a basketball hoop from various angles—the hook, the arch, the lay-up. Finally, he ran past it and went for the basket—the information Cameron needed. The moves had been there all along, before the ball dropped in. "Your best bet is early congestive heart failure: Lungs are hard to evaluate, with that old scarring, and heart size hasn't changed much from before; but there are engorged upper lobe vessels, left atrial enlargement, some fluid in the right horizontal fissure, and there," he pointed to a variation in the sea of gray markings that had escaped Cameron's gaze, "I'd call that interstitial edema. Of course," he paused, "that's for your info only. I'll have to dictate it out as scarring, maybe a suggestion of left atrial enlargement, and minimal interval changes in vessel and interstitial markings, not diagnostic of increased venous pressures, and clinical correlation is necessary."

"Right, Dave," Cameron smiled. "I'm glad you gave me the scoop first."

"No, I'm serious. That's the way we'll have to dictate our reports from now on. Policy change right from the top."

"Why? That's not your style. You've never sent reports like that before."

"Now we'll have to. Apparently, in a recent lawsuit our wording was used against us. If we'd been more ambiguous, and less specific, the outcome could have been different."

"So you're reinventing a new game for radiologists: hedge-pursuit."

"Neither invented it, nor played it before, John. You know I've always given you specific reports to work with. But orders are orders. And we can't have mega-million-dollar lawsuits hurting us, either. If that means rephrasing a few reports, so be it. I'm not happy about it, but medicine's got to survive."

"What will medicine be like, if it survives like that?"

Guttman balanced on his mariner's legs. "Probably same as our courts and lawyers are now, I guess."

Cameron said nothing.

"I'm sorry, John. You can always come down and we'll go over the films like we have in the past—off the record."

. . . . .

The cafeteria was a moving conglomerate of white, splashed in places with colors like a carousel. Noise level lagged behind a rock concert; it was just as well it was a floor away from patient care. Getting one of the over three hundred seats was a ticket to halftime entertainment at Med Center's finest. Max had saved Cameron some lunch.

"So now you're going over to your lab during lunch hour?" Max asked.

Cameron shook his head. "Just went to Radiology."

"Still won't tell me about your project?"

"You make it sound so mysterious. It's just an idea."

"An idea that's working, according to Dr. Sullivan."

"I wouldn't want to disappoint him again," Cameron said.

"Explain."

"He was my track coach. I messed up at an important meet." Cameron paused. "Anyway, about the 'project', as you call it. I'm not sure where to begin. It's a crazy idea."

"Just tell it, crazy and all."

"Has to do with genetics and cancer. Let's start with the cancer part first: What does it do? Why is it so feared?"

Max didn't have to think or try to remember. That first time came back to him: His second year, on Pediatric rotation... It was the first time he saw crimson clouds in the back of a child's eyes, blood flowing from tiny vessels flooded with leukemia cells, bursting and unable to clot—eyes of a heavenly observatory, but with hell let loose inside. The child didn't understand yet, smiled at him and tried to play with toys that were hard to see; she felt the toys with her hands ...and felt a medical student's face, lined with its first attempt to hold something back... But tears would have done neither of them good. "I always touch faces," said the child, as her small hands searched Max' face.

"It kills," Max said slowly. "It kills children, old people, and anyone in between."

Cameron nodded. "But why does it kill?"

Max tried to focus, to put emotion aside. He shook his head: "It grows... into organs, riddles everything, spares nothing...just grows."

"You're saying it takes up space – grows and takes up space –right?"

Max nodded.

"But the liver takes up space and grows; so does the spleen, muscle, heart. What makes cancers so different?"

"It doesn't stop growing."

"That's one thing," Cameron paused. "There's one more: In return for occupying space, all the organs do some work. Cancer doesn't—it takes up space without doing useful work. That's the reason it kills."

"Never looked at it that way before."

"Next observation: The more a cancer tissue is differentiated, that is, specialized for a certain function, the more its cells resemble a normal organ. At the extremes, types of tumors such as adenomas—that actually produce hormones and hence specialized work—are benign and no longer cancerous. At the other extreme—the most undifferentiated cancers, least resembling any normal tissues—are the most malignant."

"True." Max agreed.

"Another observation: Some cancer lines are virtually immortal: They could be grown in nutrient cultures for generations past what any specialized, working organ tissues could sustain."

Max nodded agreement, without any idea where this would lead. "Now for the genetics portion," Cameron continued: "Embryonal or fetal cells in their early stages are also undifferentiated, not yet specialized for any particular organ or work. You can't tell which cells will become bone, liver, heart, so forth. At this stage they still have an unlimited potential for growth and cell division, much like cancers. Yet as soon as cells commit to differentiate, to specialize and become a certain organ, and do that organ's work, the number of their cell replications becomes finite, and their lifespan limited."

"Something like the theory of a three billion beat limit per human heart?"

"Something like that." Cameron paused. "That was the sane and simple part of the idea. Now comes the crazy part: Maybe somehow the qualities of enhanced tumor growth and longevity could be harnessed and controlled, at the same time making genetic alterations to produce a more specialized cell type, one that does the useful work of a desired organ."

Max followed: "Like the fetal qualities of fast growth, longevity, and later specialization into particular organs. That no longer sounds so crazy."

"The really crazy part is that something like that actually seems to be working. I started out just toying in the lab with DNA and messenger-RNA from liver tumors—hepatomas induced by Rous sarcoma virus. Then about two years ago, probably more by accident than design, a genetic alteration occurred that 'mellowed' the Rous induced tumors. Instead of turning normal liver cells into malignant ones, it began transforming them into hybrid cell lines with the combined characteristics of normal and tumor cells. Under the microscope, where previous cancerous cells simply 'stacked' indiscriminately, the hybrid cells followed a more orderly growth pattern, with side-to-side inhibition. But the hybrids grew faster, and outlived their non-transformed clones.

"At first, I thought it was due to some lab aberration or error. But when it happened consistently, I retraced steps, and confirmed how the transformation happened."

Cameron paused. "The next steps were slower and full of dead ends, but after some tinkering and modification, the transformed hybrids resembled fetal tissue of any particular organ cloned. I continued to work with transformed hybrid liver clones. After enzymatic analysis, I found they not only grew and proliferated, but did an honest day's work as well—detoxified, conjugated, metabolized—just like any normal liver cell."

"This is a bombshell! You've been working on this alone?"

"Who else'd believe it? Mentioned it to one of my Profs once—he looked at me as if I'd had a close encounter with strange mushrooms."

"And Track? He believes in you."

"That's just it. I don't want to disappoint him. I'm just happy to borrow his lab for odds and ends. How it turns out..." Cameron shrugged.

"Published any of it?"

"Are you kidding? I've had enough with keeping cell lines and clones alive, borrowing equipment, and getting a bit of work done. Scientific papers with chi-square statistical probabilities are not exactly my style."

"So how far have you got?"

"Not very. Did some implants of hybrid clones into livers of dogs that were in hepatic coma. Seems to be working."

"What do you mean 'seems'? Is it, or isn't it?"

Cameron stopped, as if afraid that talking about it could somehow wipe out what he'd been working on. "So far, yes."

"Do you know what you're saying? Do you realize what this could mean, Cameron?"

"Maybe I do," Cameron looked down. "Maybe that's why I don't want to risk placing so many hopes on it."

"I'll be..." Max muttered.

"Anyway, it needs more work," Cameron continued, "time to gel, to confirm."

"I'll be..." Max repeated. "What if you published some of it, got a grant, moved faster—have you thought of that?"

"Maybe I wouldn't even get a grant. Maybe I've done all this because there have been no schedules to meet, no grants to file, no 'crats to please. No," Cameron looked away, "besides, there's my Residency to finish now, and no time for grants. And tonight's clinic, and tomorrow's call day."

Lunchtime was over. On afternoon rounds, Mrs. Samuels' face lit up with her usual tentative smile, then she looked down, as if afraid to give or receive any bad news.

"How are you doing, Mrs. Samuels?" Dr. Saxton asked.

"Oh, better. I walked a bit today. Felt stronger today."

"Good." Dr. Saxton went over the vitals, then listened to the heart, lungs, and checked the abdomen. "Stable," he pronounced with satisfaction, "and within normal limits."

"Could I go home then?" Mrs. Samuels eyebrows, usually dropping like a basset-hound's ears, suddenly arched up at the prospect of improvement and home.

Saxton glanced at Cameron's nod. "Don't see why not. We'll write prescriptions for your medication. Bring them with you when you come to clinic next week. Make sure you keep your appointments, because we still need to check your blood pressure, and lung and kidney functions. Don't do more than you feel up to, and since you have gallstones, follow a low fat, low cholesterol diet. Any questions, Mrs. Samuels?"

"No, I don't think so. Thank you for helping an old woman with a lot of complaints."

"You're welcome. And you had reasons for your complaints, Mrs. Samuels. If you still don't feel good, don't hesitate to tell us. Also let us know if you decide to reconsider surgery for your gallbladder. It still wouldn't be a bad idea."

Mrs. Samuels shook her head. "It hasn't bothered me," she looked down as if not wanting to be reminded of more problems. "Why should I take it out if it hasn't bothered anything?" As if resolving it for herself, she patted the sheets around her, and tilted her head with that evanescent smile. "I'd rather not, you know. I'm an old lady. You'll still let me go home, won't you?"

"Of course. We just wanted you to think about it."

She smiled more broadly now, including a flash of pearly whites. She took Joel's extended hand. "I know you all worked very hard for this old lady. I feel you're my friends." She patted his hand, "I thank you all for that."

For once Joel slipped the patient cards into his pockets without thinking about DRG's. Max looked straight ahead. Cameron remembered her smile long after he'd left the room. Inside, emotions ran submerged like quiet veins of volcanoes. Outside, Medicine's methodical, scientific process went on: There were twenty more patients to go. "Gentlemen, let's continue rounds."

In the next room, Jessie Lucas no longer sat up in bed. She lay on several pillows, arms holding sheets up to her chin, like fragile wings drying in the sun.

Dr. McDaniel went over the vitals, then looked at Jessie. "You're still short of breath, Mrs. Lucas?"

"Yes, dear."

"Did the oxygen help a little?" Like a pair of broken glasses, her nasal cannulas hung askew, one portion in the right nostril, the other whistling oxygen above the bridge of her nose.

She nodded.

"No chest pains, no leg pains, no cough?" She shook her head.

Max examined her: Lungs sounded as gravelly and enigmatic as ever, with any and all possibilities represented; the rest of the exam was unchanged.

Max turned to Cameron. "We're in the same situation as this morning. Arterial blood gases were low normal. Radiology report of her chest film was non-committal—'possibly increased venous pressure, but not diagnostic of congestive heart failure' was how they put it."

Cameron had noticed Jessie's veins now filled thickly to the jaw, doing an irregular pulsating dance. "What do you think, Dr. Saxton?"

"Ambiguities in this case seem to call for a differential diagnosis of congestive heart failure, emphysema or occult asthma, pulmonary embolus, valvular heart disease, or even a primary heart muscle dysfunction like cardiomyopathy. Since it doesn't appear the problem can be resolved clinically," Joel continued, "further decisions should probably be guided by lab tests. An EKG and MUGA scan can evaluate cardiac muscle function; echocardiogram to evaluate valve function; lung ventilation and perfusion scan to rule out pulmonary embolus; and pulmonary function studies to evaluate emphysema and asthma. A CBC, sed rate, and chem panel would also assess the possibility of infection," Saxton summed up, "and other organ involvements." A brief grin at the end confirmed he'd studied the problem, diligently trying to recoup from his morning-rounds lapse.

"Comments, Dr. McDaniel?"

Max stroked his stubbly chin. "Dr. Saxton's suggestions are thorough and reasonable. Mrs. Lucas has had many of those tests in the past. Yet somehow, I feel they may be as ambiguous now as they were before. Undoubtedly some should be done, but which, and in what order, I'm not sure. I do agree with a sed rate and perhaps an A.N.A.—since Mrs. Lucas has dermatologic lupus, she may also have it systemically, which could account for the symptoms."

Cameron helped Jessie sit up, then pumped the neck veins down, and watched them fill again, thick and high. "Well, what do you make of all our talk?" Cameron asked, pressing her hand.

"I believe you're trying to help me, dears."

"So we are. Right now, we're working to find the best way. I know it can be trying for you, being checked so often in a teaching hospital."

"Everyone's been so kind," she cleared her throat, "and you've paid so much attention to me." Her eyes looked like she was about to cry.

Cameron tucked the bedsheets back under her chin, like they'd been before. "It'll be all right, Jessie."

They went into the hall. "Gentlemen, your coverage of choices is thorough. One part remains—easier or more difficult, depending on how you look at it—to make a decision from the choices presented. Dr. Saxton, how about you?"

"I'd begin with the lab tests, and hold treatment pending their results, since we aren't exactly certain what we'd be treating at present."

"Dr. McDaniel?"

"I'm not sure a battery of tests will make her situation less complex. The tests will take about two days, and we'll still have to make a decision. I feel a bit confused and paralyzed by the situation."

"You've both covered the choices well—and perhaps to the extremes," Cameron began. "But there's nothing wrong with extremes, so long as all are covered, and balanced. Why the paralysis, Dr. McDaniel?"

"Like Dr. Saxton, I'm uncertain about the diagnosis, and so I am reluctant to treat."

"You want to nail down a diagnosis, absolutely, before treatment?" Cameron asked.

"Well, not absolutely. But with more certainty."

"Do you have any preferences, based on what you know, about the diagnosis?"

"The neck veins are unusual for her. I'd say most likely congestive heart failure."

"Dr. Saxton?"

"Given the choices, I'd also likely pick C.H.F., either secondary to valvular disease, hypertension, and/or cardiomyopathy."

"Good," Cameron encouraged. "Now which lab tests would you choose first? Or would you still go with the entire list?"

"Put it that way, I'd stay with an EKG, echocardiogram, and blood tests as discussed."

"Any reason to withhold treatment, Dr. McDaniel, while we're doing these?"

"A diuretic trial, if we monitored her potassium and watched for dehydration, might help if she has C.H.F. And it wouldn't hurt if she has something else."

Cameron glanced at both. The same impartiality that allowed others their opinions also made his own thoughts inscrutable. "Gentlemen, you've taken a complex and enigmatic situation…"

Joel and Max looked at each other, thinking: *And screwed it up even more.*

"…You recognized it as such," Cameron continued, "and came up with reasonable differential diagnoses. You have a plan for diagnostic action, and a reasonable interim treatment trial. At the same time, you've pointed out and avoided the pitfalls of overtreatment in the face of uncertain diagnoses, and of undue reliance on 'shot-gunning' for all possible lab tests before you can do anything. I don't believe anything more can be asked." Cameron smiled, "We've all learned something. Thank you, doctors."

· · · · ·

Before the end of rounds, and the start of evening Medicine Clinic, Cameron remembered they hadn't seen Christine Rourke.

"She's stable," Joel said. "She's had a Psych consult, and I was planning to send her home in the morning."

"All the more reason to visit now." Cameron replied.

Dr. Saxton briskly recited the vital signs and laboratory results. "How are you doing?" he asked rather stiffly. He felt less at ease with illnesses that weren't quantifiable by numerical data or lab tests.

"Not so bad, I guess," she answered.

"Psych consult thinks Miss Rourke will respond well to antidepressants. She's medically stable. I'd like to discharge her home in the morning, with Psych Clinic follow-up, if that's all right with you, Dr. Cameron."

Saxton was probably right, Cameron thought. Not much more could be done here. She'd return on some rainy day, or some holiday, when more voices inside told her how alone and different she was. Others, too, sometimes felt such rainy days around life's edges: Greeting holidays alone, or waking on Sunday mornings with nothing ahead but empty walls. They too, felt a sadness akin to hers, only from silence, not voices. Most would then take a walk in the park, go fishing, or run in the rain to a movie. A few, like Chris, were neither well enough to do that, nor crazy enough to forget the sadness. She'd stare at the mirror—seeing yet not seeing, hearing yet not hearing—the sad voices that paralyzed her. Eventually those voices would become real enough to open her wrists, or open her mouth to a bottle of pills. Still, it was probably time to let her go. Hospitals usually didn't diminish that sadness. Sometimes medicines bought time. Perhaps that, like brief springs over polar ice, was all there was.

"Dr. Cameron?" Joel asked again.

Cameron nodded. "Follow-up with Psych Clinic, and with you in Med Clinic."

"Why would she need Med Clinic, or me?" Joel puzzled.

Cameron stared at him. "In a way, maybe you and Med Clinic need her more than she needs you."

Dr. Saxton's mouth first opened, then shut, as he thought about that.

Christine Rourke gave Cameron a brief smile—a touch of sun on half-open petals. "Do you think it would help if I returned to school? Maybe if I'm busy there'd be less voices?"

Cameron returned the smile, then looked at Joel.

Dr. Saxton hesitated at first. "Yes, that's a good idea, Chris. You can tell me about it at clinic." He placed the chart under his arm.

They walked back into a corridor that seemed shorter now that rounds were over. Multiple doorways faded into distance like fenceposts at dusk in a rear-view mirror.

"That wasn't so hard, was it?"

"No," Joel replied. "Thanks."

After evening Medicine Clinic, Max returned to the lab room to get his rucksack.

"Doing anything tonight?" Joel asked.

"Nope." Max changed into his jogging sweats and sneakers. "I'm meeting Jody for dinner. Want me to call and see if we can make it a foursome with one of her girlfriends?"

"Thanks, but I'll just read and fade into bed. How do you keep it up, Joel?"

"I go to bed at an early hour," he grinned.

. . . . .

The streets were quiet by now. Some of the day's remaining heat hovered over the sidewalks as Max jogged home. Like the others, Max had the choice of staying at the Intern/Resident quarters, or live off the medical campus. But he'd had enough of high-rises around him. The run back at times seemed strangely unreal, especially after call-nights—like a childhood's recurrent slow-motion dream chase. It was as if he could choose two pathways in time: One, to remain on the adrenalin edge of the last thirty-six hours; the other, to suddenly disengage gears like a racecar going into neutral uphill.

Max coasted to his small two-room apartment, got his mail, threw most of it onto last week's pile in the corner, and lobbed copies of Time and Postgraduate Medicine onto the bed. He decided on a shower. Despite the stubbly face in the mirror, the shave would hold 'til tomorrow.

He propped a pillow and got into bed. He remembered he hadn't had dinner, but the refrigerator was empty. After getting through a few articles in Postgraduate, Max began Time, an anniversary issue of Hiroshima, August 6, 1945, decades before he was born. It was strange, he thought: Though he'd been a marginal case himself, hardly a paragon of learning, and in fact came as close as anyone to vanishing into the sidelines of human driftwood, somehow he'd managed to escape that fate, finish five years of college, then another four of med school. During that time, he became somewhat acquainted with sciences, history, and literature. Yet it didn't take a fraction of that to realize the chronicles of history were merely cyclic repetitions without, in fact, much deviation from the same pattern. Attila, World War I, World War II, Pol Pot in Cambodia—all were repetitious—only the names and places were changed. The repetitions, of course, came on a swifter and grander scale as the technology of the times would allow.

Though such technological evolution had exploded by leaps and bounds, human behavioral evolution had lagged far behind. The same "civilized" world that regarded the decapitation by sword of men, women, and children as a "barbaric" relic belonging to an illiterate past, accomplished the same on a greater scale by bombs that slaughtered hundreds of thousands. That it did so at the push of a button was "advanced, technological, and civilized." What the button did, from the standpoint of combatant and non-combatant victims, surpassed the "barbarism" of ages past enough to make Attila himself envious.

Max had thought that at least in med school he'd find a place where the pattern of increased destruction following increased technology would be reversed, where civilization meant human life came first, and all other creeds, philosophies, and ideologies could not change or corrupt that goal. His belief had not been misplaced. Though he'd encountered human foibles and failures, in medicine life's progress was slowed but not reversed. But even here the scales were not favorable: He'd learned to cure some diseases, alleviate many more, and before his career was over, he'd save some perhaps five thousand lives. Yet one bomb, in less than one second, could snuff out over two hundred lifetimes of such work. But those were the only odds he had to work with.

Outside the windows, light had faded and gone. Shadows on the ceiling melted into darkness. Max' eyes closed. His hand loosened its grip on <u>Time</u>, open on page forty-nine, and an atom bomb with the heat of the sun, fell onto to the floor...

· · · · ·

Behind the door to room 723, Intern/Resident quarters, as Jody undressed, Joel watched the beads of perspiration between her breasts.

Her jeans lay like a second skin at her feet; legs rose to a pelvis tilted just enough to give her a swayback stance. She stopped, curving her shoulders forward, and looked at him. Her light eyes were framed by wisps of dark curly hair, gathered in back. He placed his hands above the smooth roundness of her hips, then slowly, in one caressing motion, moved upwards and unfastened her bra. Rather than dipping down, her breasts bounced upward as they were freed. Tan lines ringed her rosy nipples like caramel around a strawberry ice cream scoop topping a sugar cone. Joel dried the moisture between her breasts with his lips, then carried her to bed. The softness of her hair brushed against his arm.

"Joel, promise me something..."

"What, Jody?"

"I've got to leave early. Anatomy test tomorrow."

"So we'll study together."

"I'm serious. I'm pulling between a C and a D right now."

"I could help, I mean, really."

"You'll help if you're just satisfied with the main course," she laughed, "no seconds, no dessert."

When he fell asleep, Jody didn't wake him as she slipped from bed and out the door to the nursing students' dorms.

· · · · ·

After briefing and signing out to Dr. Erskine's on-call Med 3 team, Cameron went for a quick dinner at the hospital cafeteria. He checked through his lab notebook as he ate: M.R.'s I to V had all died within six to fourteen days. Samples of their livers had shown massive cell death, especially in M.R. I and M.R. II. M.R. II, Cameron remembered, had been a Great Dane/Lab mix. He remembered all the M.R.'s, but he'd had a harlequin Dane pup, when he was still a pup himself. Its name had been Dana—Dana the Dane. One evening, Dana was hit by a car. The pup didn't move afterwards. Cameron lifted the Dane pup carefully, cradling the head and neck. The eyes were still open. When the head turned slightly, Dana's whole body shuddered once, then the eyes closed forever. Its neck had been broken. Cameron carried Dana in the dark, and returned him home next to his doghouse.

Now Cameron worked on them, and had to watch them die. He tucked a few leftovers away between napkins for M.R. VI. At the end of the day, walking from the hospital to the lab building, he still felt like that day he'd carried Dana home in the dark.

Perhaps it would be different now, he thought. M.R. III and M.R. IV had a few islands of cell regeneration, then M.R. V even more—a good portion of a liver's lobe had regenerated. The progression of improvement in the M.R.'s most likely meant his modified surgical techniques, and changes in the number and size of his cellular implants had made a difference. On M.R. VI, he'd added still another technique. If it worked, it would be the first time an organ had been regenerated from a recipient clone hybridized with cancerous tissue.

Cameron didn't think of it as his own achievement, but as an example of nature repeating a pattern of balance. As in physics every force had an equal and opposite reaction, so in biology an equilibrium existed: The same sickle cell that in its severe disease form brought suffering and death, in its milder sickle cell trait protected against malaria; plant and sea poisons also doubled as antineoplastic remedies against cancer; snake venoms dissolved blood clots; dread viral diseases like smallpox had led to the concept of vaccines protecting against infectious agents; other viral illness (including AIDS) demonstrated how the genetic code could be altered, in turn helping produce missing enzymes, or correct hormonal deficiencies. Similarly, the obviously negative effects of aberrant cancer genetics contained a hidden positive potential. Cameron had simply followed his belief in a principle of cosmic balance: Where negative forces existed, so did positive ones; where the potential for "evil" existed, so did the potential for "good"—neither allowing a lopsided victory over the other. Extending it further, would the universe continue to expand? Or eventually contract and annihilate itself? Would life continue? Or become extinct?

Cameron was no expert in these areas, but from his own experiences in medicine, he suspected the outcome would be close—and perhaps not even absolute and predetermined, but changeable. The question was not whether God played dice with the universe, but whether the dice were loaded: Perhaps by God; or perhaps by man, under God's gaze?

Cameron heard M.R. VI's greeting before he'd reached the door. M.R. VI stood, muzzle wedged between cage bars, with an expression akin to nose-on-window pane. Cameron unfolded the napkins, and the leftovers disappeared between M.R. VI's jaws. Clearly, M.R. IV was on his way to recovery. It would be different for both of them now: For M.R. more blood analyses and biopsies; for Cameron more procedures and work. But tonight, they still had time for rest.

Cameron opened the cage door, and watched M.R. VI glide out under his own power. The once ghostly and jaundiced canine now stretched its body in a way that if motion were language, his would be a comfortable Southern drawl. Cameron sat on the floor next to the cage, finishing entries in his notebook.

M.R. VI casually sniffed the corners of the room, examined a few cages, then returned to face Cameron. His notebook lay on the floor, next to the hand that had dropped it. Cameron's chin rested on his shoulder at a neck-twisting angle. M.R. sniffed in front of Cameron's face and mouth. Satisfied that the breathing was normal, M.R. lowered his head onto Cameron's lap. M.R. yawned once, as if settling next to a fireplace. Moon shadows drifted through the narrow skylights, settling like blankets of woven dreams upon a man and a dog, on the floor, asleep.

CHAPTER 5

GRANDMA MILLIE

*DEPARTMENT OF HEALTH AND HUMAN SERVICES (HHS)
HEALTH CARE FINANCING ADMINISTRATION (HCFA)
42 CFR (CODE OF FEDERAL REGULATIONS) PART 405:*

"Under Section 1886(d) of the Social Security Act, enacted by the Social Security Amendments of 1983…a prospective payment system for Medicare payment of inpatient hospital services was established… Under this system, Medicare payment for inpatient hospital services is made at a pre-determined, specific rate for each discharge. All discharges are classified according to a list of diagnosis-related groups (DRG's). This list contains 470 specific categories."

412.60(C-2) "Each discharge will be assigned to only one of DRG… regardless of the number conditions treated or services furnished during the patient's stay.

412.42 (a) "A hospital may not charge a beneficiary or Medicare…even if the hospital's costs of furnishing services to that beneficiary are greater than the amount the hospital is paid under the prospective payment system."

Cameron poured himself a cup of coffee, and watched the others wake up. Max was clean shaven; his recently washed shirt still pretended to be stay-pressed, and fresh white socks showed under hospital-issue cotton white pants that had shrunk. Joel had fared better with the leg lengths, but the doubly starched hospital smock crackled as he poured another cup.

"I trust everyone had a good night's sleep," Cameron looked at them.

Max glanced up from a piece of paper, but remained silent. "Don't everyone talk at once." Cameron waited, then stood to start rounds.

Max dropped the piece of paper: "Says here I'm transferred from your service. Why am I being transferred?"

"I'm sorry, I was supposed to tell you first. Not my idea, came from the top."

"Director's office?"

Cameron nodded. "It's not a black mark; the opposite, in fact. Only several Interns were chosen to work more independently for a while. It was necessary. We'll still be on scheduled rounds together."

"What about you? What about those extra rounds, and..." Max paused—he'd been about to say "lab work"—but finished with "...your extra work?"

"It will get done."

"Yes, I suppose so."

"Who's taking Max' place?" Joel asked.

"Lucy Carlton."

Joel had seen her a few times. Perhaps he wouldn't miss Max that much after all.

"Well, gentlemen, rounds."

At 502B, Jessie Lucas clasped her long-fingered hands. "Good morning, dears." A throat-clearing hack sent her Adam's apple bobbing like a pelican's gullet. "I'm feeling much better today."

"Then it is a good morning, Jessie." Max went over the vitals. Pulse 98, respiratory rate 26, blood pressure 164/94, temperature 98.4, weight 109 pounds. He noted she'd lost one and a half pounds. Her neck veins were half as distended. But as the stethoscope skimmed across her chest, Max picked up more rales and rhonchi than a metal detector over Normandy's WWII invasion at Omaha Beach. Her heart still heaved its anterior left ventricle against the chest wall, pounding her ribs like a boxer's sixteen-ounce gloves. The heart muscle was enlarged, somehow tricked into squeezing out abnormal pressures as high as the ceiling, past valves hardened and stretched, along highways of stiffened blood vessels. But her heart stubbornly beat on, like a primordial ooze building and seeking life. It was a tortured Timex, a gorilla-stomped Samsonite, a mountain-driven three-hundred-thousand-mile station wagon—all rolled into one. Some three billion diligent heartbeats, without a vacation. Now needing a little help from her friends.

Max studied her chart: Electrocardiogram had shown left ventricular chamber hypertrophy; echocardiogram confirmed cardiac enlargement of all cardiac chambers, thickening of the muscle of the left ventricular wall, and calcified and thickened mitral and aortic valves. The sed rate was normal, and the anti-nuclear antibody (A.N.A.) not back yet.

"What do you think, Dr. McDaniel?" Cameron asked.

"Mrs. Lucas is doing better. We'll still need to get her blood pressure down, but we can switch from IV to oral diuretics. While decreasing the diuretic, we'll also decrease her potassium supplement. We'll check potassium levels, and confirm her improvement with a follow-up chest X-ray."

"Dr. Saxton, anything to add?"

"No. That ought to do it."

"Thank you, dears."

In the hall, Cameron renewed the conference. "It's Scylla and Charybdis time," he announced, likening their decisional navigation to the ancient mariner's dreaded steering between the straits mythologically guarded by Charybdis' whirlpool, and Scylla's rocks.

Max and Joel looked at each other, trying to guess what lay behind Cameron's dramatic overture.

"We'll have to steer between the whirlpool of extra fluid pushing her heart into congestive failure, and the dry rocks battering her kidneys if we don't leave enough fluid to keep them primed and trickling. There won't be much room to steer between those narrow straits: We need to keep her on the dehydrated side so her heart pump's work is easier, but at the same time, her kidneys are sclerotic, and won't accept much dehydration before failing."

· · · · ·

A rattling cough greeted them before they entered the telemetry room. "Hello, dears..."

"Hello, Mrs. Wilson. You're still coughing a lot. Are you short of breath?" Max asked.

"Not...very..." Mrs. Wilson adjusted the oxygen cannulas around her nose.

Dr. McDaniel went over her vitals: Pulse 114, respiratory rate 34, blood pressure 145/90, afebrile. He listened to her chest. Mrs. Wilson's status asthmaticus wheezes vibrated the chest wall enough for a deaf man to feel, as her intercostal muscles struggled to push air past bronchial tubes plugged with secretion and constrictions of asthma.

"How do...I... sound?"

"Maybe a little better, Mrs. Wilson. Your respiratory rate is a little slower, and your arterial blood gases showed some improvement to an oxygen of fifty-five, although the carbon dioxide was fifty-four." But Max wasn't totally convinced. "Be sure to tell us if you start getting tired and breathing gets harder. It may take the medicine a little longer to do the job, and you may need a respirator until then."

"It's getting...easier... Don't want...a respirator." Spasmodic coughs jolted Mrs. Wilson's speech like marbles over a roulette wheel.

Cameron watched the intervals of breathing between her words. He wasn't convinced either. He listened to her lungs.

"Mrs. Wilson, having to constantly fight your breath could be dangerous. At least think about a respirator if you start feeling worse."

She shook her head. "No... respirator."

Cameron palpated her abdomen. "How's your tummy? Any pains at all?"

"It's... fine. Just... perfect."

In the hall, Cameron turned to his Interns: "What do you think, Dr. McDaniel?"

"She hasn't improved as much as I'd like, but I think we can wait a little longer before really pushing intubation and a respirator. Besides, she was pretty emphatic about not wanting it."

"Dr. Saxton?"

"She's balanced on a fine line, and she could go either way. So I don't have a preference—we could recommend more strongly a respirator now, or we could wait."

Cameron wasn't sure if Joel had said what he believed, or was hedging. Now was the time to make decisions, with plenty of help still available. It wouldn't get easier later. "Her pulse was a bit high," Cameron remarked casually.

"Could be from the hypoxia and stress of her asthma," Dr. McDaniel paused, remembering something, "or also from the theophylline. But her theo level was eighteen point five—normal, though getting up there."

Cameron had a hunch it might be higher now. "Check the orders, Dr. McDaniel. See if the on call-team increased the dose."

"I'll be...they upped the IV drip to sixty per hour! How did you know?"

"They probably didn't have her level back yet, and didn't believe me when I told them not to push it. So when she worsened last night, they did the usual—increased the dose."

"So we'll repeat a level to confirm, and DC their order?"

"Right. And we'll check on her in the evening."

· · · · ·

In room 509, life was suspended from a transparent respirator tube reaching Mr. Lester Brown as he lay face up, to a squat box like a table with dials and gauges—the MA1 respirator. Respirator: "An appliance fitting over the mouth and nose, for the purpose of altering the air before it enters the air passages; air is supplied under pressure to the lungs, inspiration and expiration are automatically regulated by means of valves operated by electromagnetics... " Where dials and gauges ended, the MA1's umbilical cord stretched to an electric outlet on the wall.

An endotracheal tube, a foot-long transparent tube the size of a little finger, was inserted into the windpipe via nostrils or mouth; a soft balloon-cuff between tube and windpipe ensured a seal without air leakage from respirator to Mr. Lester Brown's lungs. The endotracheal tube within the windpipe produced a universal avoidance response—conscious patients struggled to pull or pry it out whenever they could—so sedation was a common necessity. But Mr. Brown's hands remained still at his sides.

Dr. Saxton went over the vitals: Pulse 108, temperature 100.3 rectal, blood pressure 102/64; respirations set at 18, with 90% oxygen, tidal volume 900 cc's, and sigh at 6 per hour. "He hasn't been conscious since last night, even without sedation for the respirator. On ninety percent oxygen, his last pO2 was forty-nine, pCO2 fifty-two, and pH seven point three-o. I just listened to his lungs before rounds," Dr. Saxton continued, "and they sounded terrible. Gurgles and wheezes of fluid and edema. Pulmonary consult increased steroids for shock lung, but it doesn't seem to have helped."

Lester Brown's skin was moist and waxy. The lungs sounded as Joel had described. Cameron pocketed his stethoscope. "What do you think, Dr. Saxton?"

"I'm not sure what else we can do. Even the Pulmonary consult had no other suggestions."

"Dr. McDaniel?"

"Unless we can pull some rabbit out of a hat, I think he's going to die."

"Got any rabbits?" Cameron asked them.

"Only the alcohol-solvent idea. What did Pulmonary think of it?"

"They're satisfied he won't die on their Pulmonary service," Cameron answered. "As far as they're concerned, it doesn't matter much what we do, so long as it's by the book. They don't think the alcohol will work, but don't see how it could harm, either."

"So they approved it, then?" Saxton asked.

"I didn't say that. They won't commit on paper. It's a probable death, and they want as little part as possible."

"What do you think, Dr. Cameron?"

"I read the alcohol solvent articles;" he said it without inflection, as someone reading the Bible alone. "It's a chance. What about you, Dr. Saxton? He's your patient."

Saxton shuffled the patient cards in his fingers, then replaced them in his pocket. "I think he'll die if nothing else is done. He'll probably die even with the alcohol treatment. But it's worth a try."

Cameron nodded. "If it was me, I'd want it done. Let's go with it, then. Order the absolute alcohol from pharmacy, and start the IV."

The two-hundred proof, absolute alcohol arrived from pharmacy, and they began piggy-backing it slowly into the main IV line, giving it in short bursts every four hours, with alcohol levels checked often, and Mr. Brown's status reassessed periodically.

Afternoon rounds went by quickly, followed by progress notes and paperwork. They sent two more patients home, leaving sixteen remaining before next day's call.

"Let's all go to dinner," Max proposed, "while we're still on the same call team."

"We'll always be on the same team, Max," said Cameron.

"Save me a tray," Joel asked, "I'll check on Mr. Brown first."

Max was pensive. "So, who do I call for complex cases like Mr. Brown, or Mrs. Samuels?"

"I'll be on rotation with you once or twice a week. The other days you'll have another Resident or an attending available."

"Isn't this schedule going to add quite an extra load on you?"

"Sure."

"What will you do about the research lab?"

"Same as now. Keep on going."

Before leaving for dinner, Cameron received a call from Dr. Trent, Med Team 2. "We've got a Jane Doe O.D. here, from the ER. Her I.D.'s returned as Tammy Clarendon. Your team, Dr. Max McDaniel I believe, took care of her before."

Cameron knew what this was leading to. "And?"

"Traditionally, we'd bounce her to you, since you took care of her earlier."

"Only after you take care of her admission, Dr. Trent."

"She'll probably just stay for the day, after we get her washed out and stable."

"You aren't thinking of delaying her gastric lavage to transfer her here, are you, Dr. Trent?"

"Look, I'll meet you half-way: We'll do the washout, then transfer her to you."

"Make sure she's stable when you send her."

The Intern on Med Ward 2 had already finished the physical exam. The patient was in her early twenties, tall and shapely even under the red blanket that had been thrown over her for the trip from ER to Med Ward. Admission papers were on a metal chart, next to a plastic bag pinned to the red blanket. The bag held a bottle of pills, phenobarbital 1 grain, # 80—six pills were left from a prescription dated one week ago. Her freshly washed hair hadn't yet dried; it lay in auburn curls about her shoulders, like Sleeping Beauty in a bad dream. The Intern wondered what story she'd used to obtain the pills, and why she'd washed her hair prior to attempting suicide. He shook his head, then squeezed the web of her neck. There was only a slight twitch of her lids, enough to reveal the brilliant sea-green of her eyes. Though her tan lines could have graced the cover of <u>Cosmo</u>, and the in-between the centerfold of <u>Playboy</u>, the Intern worked within an eyeblink of death. Time was too short, her connection with life too tenuous, for a centerfold view of the world.

A large, clear plastic bag filled with five liters of saline and magnesium sulfate as a cathartic hung from the IV pole. Three feet of thick clear plastic tubing dangled downward to the bed, ending in a Y connecting two additional clear tubes.

"Suction ready?"

The nurse nodded. She pushed a shiny steel bucket towards the bottom of the gurney. One end of the Y-tube was in the Intern's hand, the other end dropped into the steel bucket.

"You think she'll fight?" asked the nurse.

The Intern shook his head: "She's too far down. We'll have to watch for aspiration." It was a double-edged sword: When the patient was too awake, he or she usually grappled, scratched, and bit down on the nasogastric tube or anything else nearby. But when the patient was in a deeper coma, with little reaction to the tube's passage, the outcome could even be worse—without a gag reflex to protect the airways and lungs from regurgitated gastric contents, a chemical (food and stomach acid) pneumonitis was often fatal.

There was little reaction as the Intern slipped the gastric tube past the teeth, oropharynx, and into the esophagus, then stomach. Stomach contents welled up the tube: A gray frothy slush of unidentifiable food particles, rice and carrots. He taped the tube along the cheek, then allowed the gastric contents to drain from tube to bucket. It was thick and slow, and when the flow stopped, he clamped the arm of the Y-tube emptying into the bucket, and opened the one dangling from the fluid bag above. "Let's wash," he said. A third of a quart of solution cascaded from the graduated plastic bag into the stomach. He listened for its sounds in the stomach, to make certain none was leaking back into the lungs. After another third of a quart, he reclamped the upper line, then reopened the one draining from stomach to bucket. Rancid food and solution swirled out into the bucket: The stomach wasn't really "pumped" in O.D. cases, but repeatedly flushed out with a solution of water or saline.

"I see something—yellow tablets?" The nurse removed and saved one from the bucket.

"Good. Let's keep going."

"More saline?"

"Hold it, she's a bit distended. Flow's stopped." The Intern adjusted the clamps. "Add about fifty cc's." A trickle began out the tube, but it also came out of her mouth.

"Suction! Get more suction!" They lowered her head, sucking out a paste of refried beans. Some of it dribbled onto her neck and surrounding towels. She hiccoughed.

"Aspirated?"

The Intern shook his head. "I think we got it in time."

They continued lavage until no tablet or food particles returned, and the color was clear. By that time the bucket was full, and a second overhead bag had been emptied. The Intern pulled off his gloves. "Let's stop."

The Resident, Dr. Trent came by. "Done? I've got her set for transfer to Cameron/McDaniel's team."

Med Team 2, from the sixth floor, transferred Tammy Clarendon to Med Team 1, fifth floor. Max examined her to make certain she was stable and out of immediate danger.

"How's she doing?" Cameron asked.

"They found her just in the nick. She should make it, this time."

"The last time, did she tell you why?"

"No, wouldn't talk," Max said, "wouldn't say anything at all."

"When they don't tell you why," Cameron thought out loud, "they'll usually keep doing it. Until one time...we can't save them anymore."

· · · · ·

Downstairs, they saved a dinner tray for Joel. The cafeteria was nearly empty at this time of the evening. "You know, I'll miss Joel—patient cards, DRG talk, and all. Anyway, Cameron, what do you think about all these DRG's and stuff mandated by the Feds?"

Cameron glanced at his tuna-casserole dinner, then leaned his chair back. "Well, 'Diagnostic Related Groups' are a gimmick by the Feds to control the cost of medicine for the Medicare population. When the Medicare program first began in nineteen sixty-five, there were nine and a half million senior citizens over sixty-five, with a life expectancy to seventy years. By nineteen eighty-three, there were twice as many, over eighteen million of them, with life expectancy to seventy-four and a half years. That's over twice as many senior citizens, with their life expectancy doubled from age sixty-five.

"At the same time, costs went from six billion to seventy billion. That means in nearly two decades, unadjusted medical costs for Medicare rose ten-fold—five-fold if adjusted for inflation—to give twice as many senior citizens almost five more years of life. Put it another way, that figures to about fifty million extra person-years of life expectancy, for about ten thousand dollars per person per year. Not a bad deal.

"By comparison, in the same period, the defense budget went from forty-seven billion to two hundred thirty-five billion—an exact five-fold jump."

Max smiled and shook his head. "How do you remember all that?"

"Hey, insignificant compared to what we had to learn in med school. Besides, since everyone's attacking medical costs, I figured I'd look up the facts. Not sensational headlines, but a bit more sane perspective."

"So go on."

"Now we have thirty million senior citizens, with a life expectancy to seventy-seven years. And the same federal government that promised unlimited Medicare in nineteen sixty-five, decided it was too expensive by now to deliver on that promise. Rather than admit this, and declare that they would be rationing rather than paying, one of the things they did was set up the DRG scheme: Hospitals would be paid a certain amount for a certain diagnosis, no matter what the real cost of diagnosis and treatment would be. Something like a contract with Boeing or Lockheed for a specific fighter plane for a specific price. But people are not machines or fighter planes. Some with a diagnosis of pneumonia may be critically ill; others may have a mild viral pneumonitis. Some may have other organ diseases, and complications that must be carefully treated besides pneumonia. Others will have chronic debilitating illnesses besides their acute problem. No category will fit each individual patient.

So, enter the government's concept of an 'average' patient. While this may well apply to planes, tanks, or guns coming off an assembly line, no two people came off the assembly line of life the same. I don't know about you, Max, but I've yet to see an 'average patient' outside a textbook."

Max nodded.

"Besides the dubious concept of 'averaging,' DRG's also change medicine into a business. There's a business side to every private enterprise, and that's not bad. But when the business aspect is controlled by parties other than those delivering the service—in this case doctors, and those receiving them, patients—you lose the <u>private</u> from private enterprise. And that one little word is what built this country vastly different from many others.

"Now, Medicare patients no longer have any say how DRG funds are spent related to their individual care. And that physicians have a say is a temporary illusion: Independent decisions can only be preserved by economic independence. For example, more than fifty percent of all health care costs come from the last year of life, and half of that is spent for the last <u>two months</u> of life. Still, with the old system, that last year has been slowly and consistently pushed later and later. Yet now, when eighty-two-year-old Grandma Millie has a stroke, then a gastrointestinal bleed, and maybe pneumonia on top of it, why not save a few hundred or a few thousand bucks in her care, before she dies? Before DRG's, a few Grandma Millies would make it through with maximal care, and with the extra thousands spent. Now, with DRG's, there's more profit to be made with less hospital care rather than more. In fact, with DRG's—an early death is the ultimate in savings! Of course, no one will be that blatant: The catchwords will be 'cost-efficiency ratio,' 'sensible cost containment,' and 'quality assurance,' which in reality are just the opposite."

"Don't you think the public will intervene when this comes out?"

"They haven't yet. Besides, who's going to tell them? Most laws today purposely hide their real meaning from the public. The entire Constitution of the United States is a clear, concise twelve-page document. But the legislation on DRG's alone spans fifty obfuscating pages. Politicians create this complexity and crapexity to make it appear they are giving the taxpayer a great deal for virtually nothing; lawyers thrive on interpreting it; and bureaucrats make their livelihood implementing it into something even more complex. No...no one will want to admit what's going to happen to Grandma Millie."

"Don't you think doctors will do something about it?"

"For one thing, Max, they can't. Policies are set in Washington, even medical policies. For another, once economic incentives begin to drive institutions in a certain direction, economics will also roll over individual doctors like tanks over eggshells: 'Sorry, doctor, your style of medicine is just too expensive for us; go find another hospital to work in.' When enough hospitals and medical business chains say that, doctors will listen—they have families to feed like everyone else. And instead of remaining patient advocates who work for their patients, doctors will do the bidding of their new paymasters—Mega-Medi business chains, hospital chains, and Washington, D.C. Whoever pays, calls the tune."

"Joel seems to be in the band already," Max remarked.

"He was taught DRG's before the physician's oath. Sad, but not entirely his fault. In a way, he's the end product of society's wishes."

"Speak of...sit down, Joel."

"Talking about me?"

"Sure."

"It'll have to wait until the status report on Lester Brown.!"

"And?"

"He's responding! After the second alcohol drip he's getting better!"

"You're kidding!"

"No, really! He's awake and looking around!"

Cameron put his fork down, Max left a napkin on his dinner. They trotted upstairs and into Mr. Brown's room.

Mr. Brown sat halfway up, one hand still in restraints, the other waving the endotracheal tube he'd just pried loose from his windpipe. The respirator alarm was going bonkers.

Mr. Brown appeared in no immediate danger, and Joel regained his composure. "Mr. Brown, these are doctors Cameron and McDaniel. Drs. Cameron and McDaniel, meet Mr. Brown. His last medication dose was three hours ago." Joel looked like a Santa on Christmas Eve.

"What the hell's going on?" asked a perspiring and puzzled Mr. Brown. His voice was hoarse and rasping.

"You've had a bit of an illness. You're getting better now, Mr. Brown."

Lester stared at the white bed, metal railings, IV tubing dripping crystalline fluids into his arm. His head bobbed, inebriated. "Wow...I don't remember. Where am I?"

"You're at Medical Center. Been here three days."

"Wow..." He shook his head like a dazed surfer after tumbling in a wave. He glanced at the IV again, eyes focusing with recognition: "That bad, eh?"

"We'll talk more in the morning. For now, get some rest." Joel listened to the chest, then turned off the lights.

A voice called after them: "Will I be...okay?"

"Sure. You'll be okay."

As they started for the cafeteria, nurse Patty Aldridge intercepted them: "Glad you're still here. I know you're off duty, but Mrs. Wilson's gotten worse. Could one of you see her, please? I don't think the on-call team knows her as well."

Cameron shrugged. "I'll be there."

"I might as well recheck our O.D. in the meantime," Max decided. Mrs. Wilson seemed to have turned the corner with her breathing rate down to thirty, and her wheezes sounding less tight—bagpipes instead of whistles. But her pulse had remained high, pushing into the one hundred and twenties, with increasing premature beats. Cameron puzzled over it, then found the aminophylline IV drip still set at sixty per hour instead of their ordered forty. He shut it off, and wrote an order to discontinue it until the aminophylline level returned from the lab.

The dinners awaiting them were cold. They didn't seem to mind. "A rose," Joel grinned. "Would you believe Mr. Brown would get better?"

"They're all roses when they get better."

"Lester Brown Rose," Joel repeated. "Anyway, what were you guys saying about me before?"

"We were talking about DRG's, and well, how earnest you were about them."

"Why not? If things don't go well with DRG's, some hospitals will close their doors. Who'll care for patients then?"

"Maybe the bureau-craps at Washington, D.C.," Max grinned.

"That's low, Max."

Cameron intervened. "Look, we can't disregard DRG's, and we should do our honest best with them. On the other hand, if hospitals are squeezed closed by DRG's, then that's society's problem, not ours. We didn't go to school to ration care, but to provide the best medical care possible. If society doesn't want to spend more than eleven percent of its GNP on medical care for its citizens, while at the same time it spends sixteen percent on entertainment, then let society shoulder the responsibility for rationing. If politicians, businesses, and bureaucrats wish to ration medical care, let them do so. Doctors should neither be used as instruments nor be the scapegoats for rationing. I'm not going to tell Grandma Millie, or her family, that she has to die, because there isn't enough money to care for her."

"Who's Grandma Millie?" Joel asked.

"Grandma Millie is Lester Brown, Jessie Lucas, Anna Wilson, and all those who are almost, but not quite, at the end—for whom we still need to do our best."

"Hey, isn't this our last day of work together?"

"Anyone have a toast?"

They lifted three water glasses. "How about to Lester Brown Rose, and Grandma Millie?" Joel offered.

CHAPTER 6

MAGIC

"There are more things in heaven and earth,
Horatio, than are dreamt of in our philosophy."

—William Shakespeare, Hamlet, c. 1600.

MR VI huddled against the side of his cage, pretending not to notice the wads of dog chow strewn across a corner of the room. MR's cage door was open, and one food bag bore unmistakable signs of toothed entry. The identity of the fanged perpetrator was less of a mystery than how he'd gotten out of the cage.

The morning crew hadn't arrived yet, so Cameron set about cleaning. Though not ecstatic about MR's toothsome adventure, at least it meant MR was hungry and healthy. MR inspected the cleaning process from afar at first, then closer, motioning approval with his tail. When Cameron bent down to scoop, MR waved his forepaws in the air, and placed them on Cameron's shoulders.

After cleaning, Cameron examined MR VI. The underbelly was clean and well healed, without jaundice; flanks were without ascites fluid, lungs and heart sounds normal. As if to prove the point, MR danced a few steps on his hindquarters; his tongue flopped to one side, resembling the grin of a distant lupine cousin playing a role in Little Red Riding Hood.

Cameron entered in his log:
"Aug. 10, 6:45 a.m.:
"MR VI afebrile; pulse, respirations, blood pressure normal. Gained ¾ lb. Normal abdominal exam, no tenderness or ascites. Normal canine behavior."

Cameron added the normal liver function tests, normal urinalysis, normal immune globulins, and minimal anemia.

MR lay next to Cameron's feet, tail pounding out a regular beat. Cameron closed his notebook, then scratched behind MR's fuzzy golden ears. "Hey, did you know we have the same initials?"

MR cocked his ear-tips.

"MR VI, meet Medical Resident 3. MR 3, meet MR VI." Cameron extended his hand, then took a deep breath: "Let's dispense with the initials," Cameron put his notebook on MR VI's fuzzy head, "I shall dub thee Wildwolf."

He' refused to name them so far, because losing named ones was even worse.

With more puzzlement than solemnity, Wildwolf peered from under the notebook; golden eyes rimmed by a faint dark mask lent a bit of credence to his newly adopted lupine name. Then, with an inclination of his muzzle, Wildwolf lifted his paw in greeting.

. . . . .

Lucy Carlton, balancing sixteen charts between arms and chin, closed the lab door behind her with a stroke of her foot. She hoped to find a few peaceful minutes for chart reviews prior to Dr. Atwood's rounds.

Cameron was already there, eyes hovering above the microscope.

"Good morning, Dr. Cameron."

Cameron made additional notes, then returned from the microscopic dimension. "Hi, Lucy. You really don't have to call me 'Doctor Cameron,' except for more formal occasions, like patient rounds."

"Especially Dr. Atwood's rounds," Lucy twittered in her unusually high voice, resonating like crystal, and probably polished in a girls' finishing school that taught how to smile even with braces on.

Cameron glanced at her pile of charts. "You can look over Robinson's chart, with possible cardiomyopathy, and Jessie Lucas and Lester Brown's charts for rounds."

"I thought the last two were going home today, Dr. Cameron."

"They probably are. And there you go again, Dr. Carlton."

"Again what, Dr. Cameron?"

"Called me 'Doctor Cameron', Dr. Carlton."

"Oh," her smile gleamed wide like a beaver contemplating a dam across a stream. "I'm not sure I can get used to dropping the 'Doctor' part." Prior to beginning a sentence, she had a peculiar way of looking down, thinking a bit, then brushing her hair back as her neck arched up. "Do you always tell your Interns ahead of time which cases will be presented on attending rounds? Did you tell Saxton, or McDaniel?" Her wide smile had drawn thin.

Cameron sensed he'd touched a raw nerve. Normally, Residents did choose patients at random to present for attending rounds. "As a matter of fact, yes" Cameron replied gently, "for the first two weeks. You're not getting special treatment."

"I want to be respected," she looked down, then threw her hair back. "It's just that...I know behind my back it's said I use men—to get that kind of treatment. Ever since I was a little girl, I suppose I began learning how to do that. Most girls do," she looked straight ahead. "You know, it's not entirely our fault: Getting special treatment or breaks because of looks doesn't just happen, it needs encouragement from others along the way. And there was plenty of that," she added in a wry, half-moon smile, "plenty. Maybe at times part of me still falls back on that. But now all of me wants to stand on my own two feet, on my merits alone, with respect for me and my abilities," she paused, "and not my ass."

Cameron said nothing. She was right. When she'd arrived a week ago to take Max's place, they'd probably, though perhaps subconsciously, assessed her measurements before her I.Q. In all fairness, the lowermost of these was not simply a measurement, but a work of art. It attracted eyes like a magnet, much as the earth drew Newton's apple. Even if that tendency was understandable, what wasn't understandable, nor excusable, was the importance it was accorded and how it stopped further consideration for the being inside.

"Good morning!" Saxton bounced the door open, patient cards in hand. "No mercy on Atwood's rounds!"

Lucy busied herself with the charts. Saxton glanced at her powder-blue blouse, conservatively open only one button. He judged for tightness and how far it brimmed within her Intern's white coat. He hoped she'd stand up, to see the rest. It wasn't that bad, after all, not having McDaniel around.

Attending Professor Dr. Archibald Atwood stepped off the elevator, and confirmed 7:30 a.m. on his Rolex. He'd been doing this for nearly a decade, and was hoping to retire soon, at least from this portion of his work. Known to be a fastidious stickler for details, his application of same didn't always extend to what needed to be done for the patient. For all his knowledge and intelligence, connections between his textbook references and patient care were at times tenuous.

For Dr. Atwood, Cameron usually chose to present patients that were already worked-up and recovering, rather than real problem ones. Dr. Atwood didn't seem to mind – in fact, he looked upon rounds on Dr. Cameron's ward as a welcome interlude.

Attending rounds with professors and assistant professors generally went on for two hours, and were designed to stimulate learning, throw light on difficult patient cases, and serve as quality checks in teaching hospitals. Joel led off by presenting Mr. Lester Brown, who was sitting up in bed, breathing without additional oxygen, and as usual since his improvement, looking puzzled about all the attention lavished upon him. Joel's enthusiastic presentation was followed by a disappointing lack of understanding on Mr. Brown's part that they had saved his life, and an equally expressionless Dr. Atwood.

Cameron tried to take the edge off: "The patient was admitted <u>in extremis</u>, with an extremely poor prognosis. Both conservative and innovative treatments were tried. While it's likely our ethanol-solvent treatment helped dissolve the milk-fat emboli, it's also possible some other mechanism aided the cure. What we have here is only a series of one, that merits further study, not proof of treatment efficacy."

Without comment, Dr. Atwood solemnly walked out to the hall. The others followed. He pursed his lips between his fingers, as if reluctant to continue with what he had to say. The reluctance lasted but a polite moment, since Dr. Atwood was at his best whenever the opportunity presented itself to point out flaws after the fact. "Dr. Cameron, you are correct the only thing you have is a series of one. And I'm glad you realize it doesn't prove anything. However, I'm concerned that this experimental procedure was undertaken at all. The consequences of such action could have quite a negative effect on your career."

The long way of getting to the point was also a characteristic of Dr. Atwood. As medical director and partner of a large clinic specializing in P.P.O./ H.M.O. insurance contracts—just as the language in these contracts—Dr. Atwood could use the long way of saying very little, nothing at all, or even the opposite of what he appeared to say.

Cameron didn't reply, but Lucy Carlton instinctively sprung to his defense: "Dr. Atwood, the patient was dying a few days ago. And now he's about ready to go home..."

"Young lady, is this your patient?"

"No, but..."

"Consider yourself lucky you weren't involved in the case, and prudently keep it that way. Now, if I may, I'd like a word in private with Dr. Cameron."

Cameron tried to concentrate on the discharge instructions for Mr. Brown, as he followed Dr. Atwood.

"Dr. Cameron, first let me apologize for perhaps being unduly harsh about this past particular method of treatment. I know your reputation is excellent and exceeded only by your dedication. I simply wished to impress upon our greener Intern charges the need to proceed with more conservative forms of treatment first, and to consider alternatives only with utmost caution and expertise."

"I couldn't agree with you more, Dr. Atwood."

"Good. No hard feelings then, eh, Cameron? Besides, it was a bit of a smoke screen to speak to you in private about another matter. In fact, several doctors at our clinic, myself included, have been impressed by your potential. We'd like to make you an early offer, if you will, about your future career. As you know, Moderna Campus Multi-Care Clinic is aggressively pursuing a greater share of the able-bodied patient market. Among other things, Clinic hours have been extended to ten p.m., and we need capable staffing in the evening hours. In your case, we'd be willing to double the usual salary, <u>and</u> (he emphasized), count your part-time as full-time towards future partnership in the Moderna Campus Multi-Care Clinic. What do you say?"

"Dr. Atwood, this comes as a surprise. I'm thankful, but my duties here..."

"Dr. Cameron, you are an intelligent and capable young physician, with a promising future. Look around you: Inner city hospitals are dying, inundated by the likes of the John and Jane Does, Mr. Browns, and Medicaid and Medicare payments, or rather non-payments. You're now caring for the most difficult cases, for the least gratitude, and least financial reward. Any future here is locked into a pattern of failure. You're intelligent enough to see the handwriting on the wall, and what awaits institutions like this.

"On the other hand, M.C.M.C. will be the vanguard of a whole new concept: Aggressive pursuit of profitable contracts, carefully chosen from companies with good medical track records, and further improved by our methods of computerized medical care management." Dr. Atwood failed to mention all profits would be removed at the top, for Board of Director's salaries, share dividends, and "expenses." If what was left wasn't enough to cover medical contingencies that arose, well, then bankruptcy laws would force contracted doctors to care for patients for free, while the Clinic and Board of Directors "reorganized"—and the same, of course, kept their previous profits.

"The Clinic will also be affiliated with a strong private hospital chain, integrating all services under multi-clinic and hospital-chain umbrellas. Computers will pre-screen and contract with only the healthier of patient and company populations. With a board of directors of lawyers, businessmen, and accountants, business will run more efficiently, creating profit and non-profit divisions to shuffle funds as needed. I hope you can see the advantages of my proposal, and are willing to come aboard, Dr. Cameron. It would be a wise career move for many reasons."

"Dr. Atwood, your offer is most generous. Unfortunately, rotation schedule adjustments have left little time for other activity."

Dr. Archibald Atwood eyed the situation with the look of a gambler, considering what odds and offers to make next. "Think about it, Dr. Cameron. We could make additional salary adjustments and partnership arrangements. Contact me when you're ready, before you make any other decisions." Dr. Atwood pressed his M.C.M.C. card into Cameron's hand.

After Attending rounds were over, Cameron and his Interns took a break in the lab room.

"Hope he wasn't too hard on you," Joel remarked.

"Nothing happened, really."

"The facts are behind you, and we're behind you," Lucy added.

"Seems like he could be dangerous," Joel ventured.

Perhaps more dangerous than you can imagine, Cameron thought: The business part of medicine disguised and controlled by insurance companies and boards of directors. "There is one more thing we haven't mentioned on today's rounds, and I wish Dr. McDaniel were also here to hear it. Because it wasn't just 'a series of one' we had: Our patient is alive. Whether by coincidence, by conservative treatment, or really due to our special treatment, Mr. Brown is going home today. Without any treatment, he would now be dead. You've worked one-hundred plus hour weeks, admitted more patients per call night than any other place I know, and through it all evaluated the patient well, followed with prescribed treatment, and when no other recourse was left, you were able to come up with a novel yet reasonable approach that may have saved the patient's life. The system still works. You doctors made it work. Now let's get back to it."

· · · · ·

Three weeks later and on another floor, Dr. Sullivan held attending rounds with Med Team 5's Dr. McDaniel and his Intern Partner Carlos Schmidt. Carlos Schmidt, as his name implied, was an interesting blend of Teutonic tenacity and Hispanic temperament, ranging from calm to intense.

Dr. Track Sullivan arrived early, as usual, but more pensive. His moves were abrupt, even for him, like a cheetah pacing its cage and staring at the bars, as if at any moment they might melt away. Rounds began in the same brisk manner, as they followed in the wake of Dr. Sullivan's lab coat along the corridor.

Max and Carlos each presented four patients. Carlos' last one had lung cancer, which seemed to increase Dr. Sullivan's pacing even more. The presentation was posthumous, since the patient had died the day after learning she had cancer. The cancerous nodule was still small, with no apparent spread to other organs. All indications were she'd died of lack of hope, and fear.

"So, Dr. Schmidt, what is it about the word 'cancer' that evokes such fear?" Dr. Sullivan began.

"The problem is based on statistical reality," Dr. Schmidt began stiffly. While part of him exuded Mediterranean *joie de vivre*, the other, especially at work, mentally goose-stepped. "Cancer cure rates have improved significantly, with up to fifty percent 'cures' at five years after discovery. Still, this also means a fifty percent death rate within that time. A rate shared by few other diseases."

"What are the mechanisms of cancer that produce such dismal results?" Dr. Sullivan asked.

"Probably because in many ways cancer is unique, a fortress unto itself. It hides from host defenses by various means: By being unspecialized and undifferentiated, by producing blocking antibodies, or by simply overwhelming host defenses after reaching a certain size." Carlos was reaching his own full mental stride; you could almost hear his heels click. "Tumors even lay down their own supply lines from the host, for example by stimulating hormones that bring additional blood vessels into its zone of growth."

"It seems, Dr. Schmidt, that tumor tissues have an astounding capacity to be bad."

"Or an astounding capability to do good for themselves only, at the expense of their host."

"Do you foresee, Dr. Schmidt, any circumstances where those capabilities might be of some good to the host? After all, we've put viruses and bacteria to use as agents cloning insulin and vaccines; and fungal poisons that kill bacteria are used as antibiotics."

"I believe this to be different, Dr. Sullivan, both quantitatively and qualitatively. Tumor cells can reproduce at rates that double even every few days. That's not a quality that's likely to be tamed."

"Dr. McDaniel, your opinion?"

"Well, there may be some features of tumors that aren't entirely bad. Rapid growth, little differentialization in early stages of growth, and therefore low antigenicity evoking little immune response are also characteristics of fetal tissue."

"How might that be helpful, Dr. McDaniel?"

"I'm not sure..." Max realized Dr. Sullivan was fishing in Cameron's research waters. "Perhaps under certain circumstances these might aid in tissue regeneration."

Carlos had been pondering the matter, and his foot tapped out a marching beat. "Dr. Schmidt, you have something to add?" Dr. Sullivan asked.

"I believe similarities between fetal tissue and cancer cells are only superficial. Fetal cells undergo a rapid growth stage, which gradually slows, then stops altogether. Cancer cells, on the contrary, could grow on forever. And while fetal cells differentiate into useful organs, cancer cells never do, continuing a parasitic existence. The control of growth and differentiation in fetal cells would be impossible to achieve with tumor cells."

"Hmmm," there was a twinkle in Track Sullivan's eyes. "Well, thank you, Dr. Schmidt." Rounds were over, but Dr. Sullivan made no motion to leave.

Carlos Schmidt looked at his watch. "If you'll excuse me, I still have a few labs to draw this morning."

Max stayed while Track settled into his chair. The long legs splayed out in front, toes occasionally flexing as if still in spiked track shoes. "I see you've been talking to Cameron," Track said.

"Not recently, actually."

Sullivan went right to the point: "What do you know about Cameron's doings in the lab lately?"

"Not much more than last time. Haven't talked to him much, and besides he doesn't go into details. Even if he did, I'm not sure I'd understand, Dr. Sullivan."

"Skip the 'Dr. Sullivan' stuff." Track eyed him sideways, as if watching the starter for a clue about his trigger finger: "So you don't want to tell me, for whatever reasons, and I suppose I could name a few. I don't blame you. This is far too big to be trifled with. It's Semmelweis discovering the source of puerperal fever; Jenner inoculating himself against smallpox; Pasteur... You're rubbing elbows with history, Max.

"You're smiling, but I know you believe some of this. Believe this also: At one time history thought them to be fools, or crazy." Track rubbed his chin. "Unfortunately, this may be no different. So, if I know you, you won't breathe a word of it until the time is right." He paused for a gulp of air, as if taking a walk-lap after a race. "What I know is this: That M.R. VI is still alive, over one month after its own liver died. It's living with a brand-new liver. Regeneration went through an explosive state—fetal, tumorous, whatever you want to call it. Now that growth is controlled, normal." Track observed Max' face for any reaction, then continued. "I know all this from the biopsy slides Cameron left near the microscope."

"He just happened to leave them?"

"No," Track smiled. "You have to understand—if Cameron seldom has time to tell me anything, neither does he hide any of it." Track mused, "perhaps it's time he should. He's so methodical, you know. Everything is labelled, from initial dying liver cells, to his implants, to serial biopsies afterwards." Sullivan paused. "He implanted some sort of unusual fusion or hybrid of tumor and normal cells, that grew in place of the old liver. It grew and it functioned, in a controlled fashion. I can't tell the difference now from the previous liver." Dr. Sullivan shook his head: "As Carlos said, it's impossible... And Cameron just did it." Track fell back into his chair, finally relaxed, and closed his eyes.

Max thought he'd fallen asleep—it wasn't that uncommon for Residents, or even Professors to be awake one moment, reading or eating—and asleep the next.

Track's eyes opened again. "And it wasn't a fluke, Max. He's begun another one, sent in by the vet, dying post amanita poisoning... Three weeks ago, Pooch was dying, now it's following same healing pattern. If this keeps up, I won't have room or food for all the live dogs he'll have in my lab!"

"Why are you telling me this?" asked Max.

"Several reasons. For one, I wanted to tell someone. Can you understand that? It's so big... it's like trying to sleep the night before an Olympic race. Just knowing someone else is in the same boat makes it easier. For another, it's also too big to leave unfunded like this. Cameron hates paperwork—it would take him years to apply for a grant, if ever. But sooner or later, he'll need more funds and equipment than he can just scavenge. He'll need to expand the animal experiments, then finally turn to human applications. You know how many people die of liver failure each year? How many lives this could save? And if he can perfect this technique for the liver, why not other organs? Can you imagine? But it's going to cost money, lots of it. And the sooner we can fund this, the sooner it's going to save lives."

"Why not ask Cameron directly about grants and funding? He could give you all the information you need to apply for them."

Dr. Sullivan looked pensive. "Then again, he may not. He's one for details, and might feel he isn't ready to make the claims he needs to make in order to get the really big grants, the kind of grants this project requires. Or he might think it'll interfere with his Residency program. He might even decide not to let me apply for him." Sullivan paused. "At least, if he doesn't know, he can't tell me not to apply."

"Maybe it <u>would</u> interfere with his Residency."

"Not really, it doesn't have to. I can arrange it so all he'll need do is direct the project. Others can work for him."

"Maybe that's not his style."

"You're right. It isn't. But eventually it'll have to be. This project's too big to drag along anonymously, on leftovers from labs like mine. I already know what he's done eclipses anything I might achieve. What I've done in my lab pales by comparison."

Max studied Track, trying to sense what lay beyond the outstretched figure with running reflexes still intact. Ambition? Laurels at the end of another kind of race? Or a simple wish to lend a hand, run one relay of it? Max observed the face before him: Lined with creases, some of which were made where jaws had clenched to suppress pain; a face that did not seek nor flee danger, nor seek the easy way out; a face capable of danger itself. Ah... but not the face of one who'd ride on the efforts of others.

Track sat up. "I know what you're thinking: 'Why is he doing all this? What's in it for him?' Look, I know a big project when I see one, I'll be happy aplenty to lend a hand in producing it. If history remembers me for nothing else, that'll be enough. I'm not after taking credit, or taking over, even if I thought I could. I'm just a doctor, who still wants lives saved. To speed that progress will be enough."

"I still don't understand why you're talking to me about it."

"Perhaps you don't understand the world of grantsmanship, Max. No, I guess you don't. Let's just say I'm trading my name for something I'm not certain of, something wild. I don't have to sacrifice my career needlessly, if I'm not even in the ballpark. I thought you could tell me if I was, if what I've figured matches what Cameron's told you."

"What you're asking places a lot of responsibility on me, Dr. Sullivan."

"It's a big responsibility for all of us."

Max thought about it, then replied with a glint in his eyes: "I have to say you're on the right track."

Dr. Sullivan uncoiled his frame from the chair and stood up. "Good," he smiled. "I've already sent the grant application."

· · · · ·

It had been a while since Cameron had made bar rounds with Max at the Continental: Dim lights, tables lined with brew, and on the dance floor tapestries woven of flesh, sounds, and movement under splashes of color like coral reefs teeming with tropical fish.

Max waited at a table. "I thought I might have to come and drag you out of the lab, Cameron. What'll it be?"

"Moosehead."

"Good. I already got you one. So, how's the lab going?"

"Wildwolf's doing fine. All lab tests normal."

"Who's Wildwolf?"

"Decided to name the pooches. Wildwolf was M.R. VI."

"Means they must be going to live, if you're naming them."

"Yes," Cameron agreed with a trace of surprise in his voice, as if he himself hadn't expected it.

"Did you have to use immuno-repressive therapy to prevent rejection?"

Cameron shook his head. "No rejection. Theoretically, the implants are derived from the host's own previously cultured and hybridized liver cells. There aren't significant surface antigen differences to evoke an immune response."

Max whistled. "Unlike organ transplants, you don't have to type and crossmatch for host and donor compatibility, or worry about rejection by the immune system!"

"If it continues to work as planned," Cameron nodded.

"So what's next?"

"More lab tests, biopsies, tissue cultures, and typing of hybrid cell lines."

"You suppose you'll be applying for a grant for all this?"

Cameron shrugged. "You're starting to sound like Track Sullivan. No, I don't think I'm ready for that yet."

Max finished his draft, and changed the subject.

"How's Mrs. Wilson?"

"Got better and went home."

"What about the premature beats she was having?"

"Her theophylline level was high," Cameron nodded. "When her dose was dropped like we ordered, they went away."

"I know," Max said. "I checked on that. Two of our orders to decrease the dose were ignored."

"You're right. The first order was just plain missed. They caught the second, but a nurse found the drip shut off, so she just restarted it at the previous dose. It wasn't corrected for another nine hours."

"Shouldn't there be an incident report on this?" Max asked.

Cameron glanced at him. "Probably would be the right thing to do."

"Who's going to do it, you or me?" Max asked.

"What do you think?"

"She was my patient at the time. I'll be glad to file one."

"You might think about it," Cameron paused. "Right thing to do—but maybe wrong time. You're still an Intern. Sticking your finger into the bureaucratic machine can get you swallowed whole."

"Sounds like you've had some experience with it."

Cameron nodded. "You see, we're alike, though in different ways. We're both rebels. For me, despite the outward conservatism of a rock, deep down there's an inborn wild streak, far below in a cave, lying like a dozing dragon under a mountain of tradition and self-control. For you, I'd guess on a past caught up in wilder surroundings, over which self-control and a basic conservative down-home streak triumphed as well."

Cameron looked away. "But being rebels for whatever cause, we often bleed against the walls we're planning to storm and liberate, believing righteousness will conquer all. Truth is, the costs are usually high, and despite paying them, there's often still failure."

"Something like that happened to you in the past?"

"A few times. As in Mrs. Wilson's case, medication orders not followed, lab tests not done, but usually more mundane and basic things not done—like weights not taken, fluid input and outputs, and vital signs. Yet the incident reports I filed were soon followed by two or three against me. For example, after quoting a nurse as stating patient appeared to have 'greenish pus' in his wound, I was asked to explain in a letter why I had used the shorter version, while she maintained she had stated 'material like greenish purulence.'"

"Did you write the letter?"

"Typed it, Webster's dictionary and all, explaining the essential equivalency of the two statements. At the time, as an Intern, I had about as much time to type letters as a bull has to take a crap in a bullring. Generally, I found reports were written, papers passed hither thither, each with a higher level of C.Y.A: A quiet concert of paper lullabies, leaving the bureaucratic boat calm. None of it changed anything for the better. Waters that were quiet and inactive wanted to stay that way. So, I just stopped."

"Are you saying we shouldn't even try, Cameron?"

"Not at all. You do what you believe you must. I'm just pointing out large bureaucracies, even medical ones, aren't ideal for learning and correcting mistakes. Now that you know what lies ahead, your decisions won't be blind."

"Just drop it, then? So, what about Mrs. Wilson? She turned out well, but what about the next one?"

"There are other ways, sometimes," Cameron paused. "You could list it as a 'complication' in the discharge summary. That way, if Q.A. picks it up, it's up to them to do something about it."

"And if Quality Assurance doesn't?"

Cameron looked at him: "I don't have all the answers, Max. I can't tell you what to do. Only to pick your time and ground when you can, and to do battle when you must. Besides," he smiled and downed his mug, "rebels like us will never run out of battles, windmills, or damsels in distress."

"Speaking of damsels," Max winked, "don't you have a lady, or shall we say, 'significant other'?"

"Not lately."

"Not going out much either. That can put you in some distress."

"Sure does, at times."

"So how come?"

"I could ask you the same question, Max."

"Remember that Intern/Resident party, when you said I was seeing someone else in that girl? Well, you were right. Met her skiing at Taos, long blonde hair nearly touching the snow when she bent to adjust her bindings. When she stood, her body was long and taut, and her eyes met mine like glows from a fireplace. Mentally I contemplated a bearskin rug and champagne and music..."

"So, what happened?"

"The cabins were right next to the lifts, fireplaces with little chimneys curling smoke, and even a sleepy St. Bernard at the doorstep of the inn—cozy as a chalet with Swiss chocolate. All so damn romantic... but you know how it is: I had to leave in two days for exams."

"Did you keep in touch?"

"Her boyfriend arrived the day after I left. And I don't think my letters afterwards came as often as he did."

"And at the time, you probably respected her, and all that..."

"It felt like we had all the time in the world, Cameron..."

"I understand. It happens like that sometimes."

Max set his mug down. "Now, what about you?"

"You want the romantic, or the regular version?"

"Whatever's comfortable."

"Neither, then."

"That's not exactly fair."

"It seems far away and long ago," Cameron began. "I can't tell if it was yesterday or years ago—I guess our minds anesthetize us like that. Her eyes were deep blue..."

"The romantic version, I take it?"

"...Eyes like that, and freckles around her smile, and dark hair that made her eyes seem even bluer. She was an aerobics instructor, with a perfect S-shape. I went to the gym to work out at times, as a break between Path and Physiology classes."

"Go on."

"The first time I saw her, it broke my concentration, and I wrenched my shoulder lifting—couldn't lift well for three months. We saw each other on and off, on a medical student's schedule. One day a varsity oarsman came in, tanned to perfection, crew-paddle logos on his T-shirt, and a body long enough to reach the chin-up bar without a jump. Her blue eyes fluttered, she purred like a kitten, and I didn't stick around to see the rest."

"Maybe you should have."

Cameron shrugged. "I didn't think the real thing should be that difficult." He paused, drifting to time long ago, without mentioning the real, but most difficult of all.

Max twirled an empty mug in his hand: "Another?" Cameron nodded.

"You know, sometimes it seems unfair that we just talk about the gorgeous girls, and how the attention goes to 'beautiful people' over others."

Cameron smiled: "I can usually find something attractive in everyone, know what I mean? Everyone's got something of his or her own. Sure, there are girls who have everything—from tip of sunshine curls, to sensuous ankles. But no one comes into this world with nothing."

"Maybe."

Cameron scanned the room. "Alright. Consider the girl with the dark blouse, there. Bit on the heavy side, let's say generous. But then, she's big all over and proportioned, with a waist that still cuddles in. And I like the way she moves on the dance floor."

"Comfortable," Max nodded.

"Now directly opposite, in the blue—definitely heavy. If the other's generous, this one's overflowing. Still, she's got a smile wide as a half-moon, and happy as Bugs Bunny."

"I see what you mean. But that's still not exactly fair—they're both stacked like post offices with Christmas cards. A man could get lost in those bosoms, and still come out smiling."

"You're missing the point, Max. That's not all that counts. But that's what they have, and it's not wrong to appreciate it. Now there, with the short hair and 'New York' T-shirt—not much up front behind those letters, is there?"

"Right. But there's something about her."

"What?"

"They're small, all right. But firm, no need for a bra."

"And she doesn't have one. But see, in her own way, she's as delectable as the others. Depends on your taste."

Max warmed to the subject: "There's something else about her... Her hips, thin, but their curves flaring right from her waist."

"See? Now think about it, Max. What do you look for first? What catches your eye?"

"You mean like personality, intelligence, humor?" Max smiled. "Okay, the truth: In fact, it's the hips. Hips, shaped back just so," his hands moved as if his dream had just materialized. "What about you, Cameron?"

"Look, it doesn't matter. It's complicated, yet simple; detailed, yet plain."

"Why do I get the feeling, Cameron, while I got down to the bottom-line, so to speak, you're elevating to a more scientific level?"

"Elevating..." Cameron smiled, "but not necessarily scientific. Seriously, Max, there may be a hidden truth, a hidden reality, to what you said. Hidden—or even expressed—by that 'bottom line.' Think about it: We begin as the fusion of two cells, then grow and divide into four, eight, sixteen cells, and so on. Initially, all these cells look alike, undifferentiated. We don't know which will become heart, brain, muscle, skin. But eventually, genetic material directs itself to form all these, and whatever's necessary to sustain life."

"Sure, all wondrously complex, and all that."

"Complex, Max? In a sense, life is beyond understanding. It shouldn't really exist."

"Either you lost me, or we've been drinking too much."

"Third Law of Thermodynamics, entropy: Roughly states all matter/life in the universe is continuously falling to a lower level of energy or complexity."

Max glanced at his empty mug. "We started with firm breasts, S-shapes, then went on to life and Thermodynamics? Where are we going next?"

"With any luck," Cameron smiled, "where we began. You see, if life, and the evolution of life, is a progressive combination of matter and energy to produce yet more complex forms of matter and energy, then entropy and life are opposing forces."

"I think I understand: Entropy vs. Life; life vs. entropy. The one a building process, the other a destructive one..."

"Exactly. Life is nature's way of battling entropy!"

"That's a trip, looking at it that way."

"A trip, and a battle. In that sense, we're just ammo in that war."

"Another beer?"

"Sure. Chilled mug."

"And I'm a waiter at the Hilton?"

"Don't flatter yourself, Intern. You don't make that much money!"

"Go on, oh mighty Resident!"

"Now it would seem that for more complex combinations of life to take place at all, they should have some advantage over the less complex forms—in order to defy entropy and continue to exist."

"Seems reasonable," Max nodded. "What are we doing? Rediscovering Darwin?"

"Bear with me. We agree then, that entropy dictates the eventual breakdown of any matter/energy or life system that doesn't have an advantage in combating entropy. Example: A rock, not having many advantages in remaining as it is, breaks up into boulders, boulders into dust, and its dust eventually vaporizes into atoms. In the same way, human beings die and degrade into entropy's atomic and subatomic infinity."

"But..."

"But what, Max?"

"Things we define as 'living' do have an advantage, and live on, in a way."

"How's that? Muscle, protein, bone—all that eventually loses to entropy—'dust to dust.' Where's the advantage in that?" Cameron quaffed his beer.

"Playing the devil's advocate with me? All right," Max leaned back in his chair, "I'll play. For one thing, living organisms reproduce, so even after one individual dies, more follow. Also, in the case of man, we further defy entropy by building more complex structures from simpler ones."

"The pyramids of Egypt are wearing, Max; the gardens of Babylon are no more, and so it will be with man's other monuments. But you're right, life does go on, new forms springing from the old," Cameron pondered awhile. "So, if life's a process of combating entropy, then maybe evolution is life's will or weapon in the battle for survival?"

"Sounds reasonable," Max nodded."

Cameron leaned forward: "Life, and evolution, have designed mammals on four feet with prominent forebrains and prominent olfactory bulbs able to detect one particle per billions of others; designed biped animals with hands left free for toolmaking, and a brain with convolutions of cells that a roomful of transistorized computers couldn't duplicate; and designed insects that build castles and form societies to divide their labor."

A waitress brought their drinks, pouring them close to the sides of the inclined mugs to avoid oversudsing. She was tall, with black coat-and-tails cut high above her hips, over leotarded legs that belonged to a girls' basketball center.

They watched her, then Cameron continued without missing a beat: "Blood pressure, pulse, respirations rise, all under subconscious chemical, hormonal, and electric micro-impulses, and their controlling feedback loops. These in turn, are governed and fine-tuned by our genetic makeup."

"Right." Max observed the lofty legs and hips fading into the distance.

"She evoked a variety of responses, didn't she? My own was moderate, but then, I'm not a 'leg man.' Your response, Max, was greater and lingering."

"I'm not a leg man either. There was something else about her... her hips." Max whistled softly.

"Confirms your predilection for hips. Now where do you think that comes from?"

"Come to think of it, I don't know. I always supposed it was something taught or acquired. But on second thought, probably not—in high school, whenever my buddies and I talked about it, we never had the same tastes. In fact, the different forms, angles, and flares of hips were quiet beyond their appreciation."

"What color were her eyes?"

"Don't recall."

"What color do you like, Max?"

"Preference for dark green."

"That's why you didn't recall. They were blue. Why do you suppose you like green?"

"Don't know," Max shrugged, "guess I just like what I like."

"Do you like the color green generally, as in clothes, or cars?"

"No, just eyes."

"Ah," Cameron paused. "So her hips got your motor running, but her eyes didn't. She's already communicated with you without saying anything. Why do you think that is?"

"Pretty basic. Some call it 'chemistry'."

"Basic, yes, and chemistry, yes. But what's behind that 'chemistry'?"

Max shrugged, and let the beer linger, "Who knows?"

"Suppose I told you that for some appearances, features, and colors, there's also a functional and physiologic correlate. Example: Neurologic and motor-coordination testing has shown that people with dark-colored eyes have a greater accuracy in accomplishing tasks during movement than people with light-hued eyes. Conversely, those light-hued or blue-eyed people have a greater accuracy while standing still. So, if you've got a clutch-play to make in basketball, for an on-the-move-shot, maybe your odds would be better with a dark-eyed player, but for a free-throw with a blue-eyed one."

"Let me get this straight," Max set his mug aside, "You're saying some appearances may also be telling us about function?"

"Why should it come as a shock? We diagnose Down's from hand and eye creases, Marfan's from length of fingers, and scalp hair whorls usually sit over the dominant hemisphere, indicating right or left handedness, to name a few examples. So there may be more to our predilections and tastes than meets the conscious eye."

"Then my preference for green eyes, and a certain hip structure with dimples atop sacroiliac joints may be more than an accidentally acquired trait?"

"Neither accidental, nor acquired, Max. Consider what we already talked about: Growth, differentiation, specialization, from the initial fusion of sperm and ovum to a complete and complex organism. All orchestrated under RNA/DNA control. RNA and DNA that dates back millions, even billions, of years, slowly changing, defying entropy, continuing to organize into higher complexities of insect, fish, and animal life. Life's simply the ability to replace new forms for those that fell apart, for those that 'died.' Yet in that sense, nothing ever 'dies.' Parts may cease to exist, break down into atomic dust, but not before leaving reproducible DNA behind—to be changed, in time, by life's weapon or will to survive—evolution."

"I should have known you'd get genetics in there somewhere."

Their waitress returned, refilling their mugs with the same suds-free ritual. "You guys seem lost in some deep debate," her eyebrows curved in a smile, "politics, philosophy, religion?"

"Worse. The basis for all three—genetics."

"Is it serious?" She flashed a brief but full-lipped smile.

"Just a little beyond Darwin and the Japanese," Cameron replied.

"Name's Elaine Mathiesen," she said. "Well, what about the Japanese?"

"Long story. Basically, some of their computerized geneticists believe in directed evolution."

"Interesting," her eyebrows rose. "Might depend on how you define your terms."

"Max McDaniel," Max introduced himself, "and this is John Cameron."

"Glad to meet you. I wouldn't mind staying and talking awhile. But for now, I'm just a waitress. Instead of hustling my brain, I've got to hustle my..." She bent forward at the waist, turning and lifting one hip back in a trajectory that would have drawn envy from a line of chorus girls. "Let me know if I can get you some Japanese beer," she smiled as she left.

Max stared, then shook his head. "Where were we?"

"Just about right here," Cameron smiled: "Now, did those hips communicate, or what?"

"I'm being serious."

"So am I, Max. look at it this way: We've got RNA and DNA that orchestrate all functions from blood pressure to color of eyes to shape of toes. Why wouldn't it also exert some choice over how it propagated itself? There are trillions of possible combinations, and a multitude of relative strengths and weaknesses in any organism. For those relative weaknesses, it would be reasonable to seek a mate with complementary strengths, and in return, provide a complementary strength to a mate's weakness. Such abilities would grant life-forms one small advantage over entropy."

"If what you say is possible—that DNA strands could somehow search for strengths and weaknesses of potential mates—how could they read or communicate them?"

"Ah, there it is!" Cameron exclaimed: "The tone of songs and brightness of feathers in species of birds indicate their ability to withstand parasitic infections; their song contents may reflect their learning abilities, since their brains cells multiply during their season of song. And who knows what her hips were trying to tell you?"

Max looked away between tables where Elaine bent over as she brought drinks. Part of her cleavage showed, and the longer she bent forward, the more her bosom threatened to fall out, creamy white mounds slowly sliding against her fitted V-cut vest. "If that's some sort of genetic language," Max whispered, "not one word's being wasted."

Cameron waited patiently until Elaine had gone, and Max's gaze returned. Max shook his head: "Now what were you saying about some Japanese geneticists?"

"They jumped on their computers, and looked at nature's and their own experiments. Unlike Darwin's prediction of random evolution by haphazard mutation, they found beneficial mutations and changes occurred at a rate significantly exceeding what would be expected from random chance alone. As in the old argument about evolution: Of what benefit would a half-sized wing be, if flight can be accomplished only with full-sized wings? Random changes would indeed be expected to yield incomplete results, like half-finished wings, that confer no benefit. Yet reality yields different results."

Max remained silent, pondering. "That would mean some other mechanism directs the tendency for genetic changes to be more beneficial than expected from random chance alone."

"Right! Now it's estimated that after all genetic material that's needed for functions of daily living is accounted for—from sleeping, to walking, to producing hormones to fight infection—much less than fifty percent of it alone would be sufficient to do the job! That also means over half of our genetic material is either totally superfluous, or has some other function."

"Hmm," Max jumped the gun, "let me guess. Your theory is some of that 'superfluous' genetic stuff isn't superfluous after all. Instead, it may be in charge of reading and communicating—through outward signs—some of the inner genetic workings of an organism."

Cameron put out his hands and smiled.

"Pretty wild theory," Max mused.

"Pretty wild communication," Cameron nodded, noticing Elaine return for more table rounds. A girl in a white dress with a red sash over her shapely waist smiled from a nearby table. Her smile was friendly and rabbit-toothed; from the side, the white dress clung below her waist to her bottom like a comma. Her girlfriend, in powder blue jeans, looked their way, and brushed back the curls from her forehead.

"What do you think?" Max asked Cameron, glancing towards them.

"I think we ended where we began, about what we liked," Cameron smiled. "But it's late, and we've both got call tomorrow. I don't think we have enough time to put theory into practice."

"Not even on a subconscious genetic level?" Max glanced at the girls.

"We've already done that. That's the easy part. And that's why I'm dragging you back home. Tomorrow I'm scheduled to make early rounds with you and Carlos."

"Right," Max sighed. The reality of work drowned out the pulsing rhythm of the Stones' "Let's spend...let's spend the night together..." Max polished off his beer. "How's Jessie Lucas doing?"

"Did well; went home. She said to thank you."

"Those were quite the patients—Jessie, Anna Wilson, Lester Brown. But they all made it."

Cameron nodded. He remembered the day Jessie went home: She shook hands with each of them, and added, "thank Max for me, too." Afterwards, she leaned over and confided to Cameron: "You do look good in blue, dear. Wear that shirt more often." After she'd gone, there was that quiet feeling of emptiness—like a school corridor after graduation—all lit up, but with no one there.

"Sort of grow on you, don't they?" Max remarked.

Many patients did. Of those, some returned, some died; others remained in memories, fading slowly like color photographs. Memories' photographs continued to grow, each day adding to yesterday's images, new faces of illness, recovery, death, until all entwined—entwined in one long story of struggle and courage. Courage sometimes so great it gave more than it received, even while dying.

Everyone that worked on the wards bore those memories—different, yet the same. Of faces lined with pain; or relaxed in the arms of Morpheus; or anxious over fate's uncertainty; or finally resigned with the knowledge of a story's end. Some smiled through it all, others stemmed back tears. A few, from the little ones at life's first steps of the rainbow, to those nearing horizon's end, never really knew or understood what was happening to them. They stared back with wistful looks: Half-smile, half-question in their eyes. But they were all united in hope. Each, in his or her own way, carried the light of hope. And whatever that way was, it brightened the days of those who worked there. Even when that hope sometimes ended, and the light finally went away from their eyes, hope's memory remained—a part of the photographs that would never fade.

Max and Cameron were silent awhile. They had studied the science that made it possible; continued to learn the art that brought it to fruit. But it still felt like magic when it all worked well—and someone that had been sick went home healed.

"Yes," Cameron said. "They do grow on you."

CHAPTER 7

THE HAWK

Every day, for the past few weeks, the hawk perched, like a mysterious sentinel, atop a high pole over a highway exit. Looking neither up nor down, but staring straight ahead, he remained motionless waiting.

Waiting for what? The city's highways, byways, and exits were not a particularly hospitable place for man, beast, or bird of the clouds. What drew it from its dominion of the sky, to endless slabs of concrete roamed by metal beasts on wheels?

Yet no matter the weather, the hawk continued at his chosen post. The last three days it had rained. The hawk still stood, feathers ruffled like gray wool against the rain and wind. It brooded in lonely vigil on whatever secret he'd brought down from the sky.

In a gray suit and tie, hair neatly trimmed about the ears in executive-assistant style, a young man in his twenties moved briskly along the shining corridors, then made a quick tight turn near a water cooler and a maze of doors. He knocked impatiently on the glazed regulation window bearing several titles, none of which made any immediate sense.

"Come in."

"Mr. Werner, I think you should take a look at this grant application."

"So?"

"I thought it might be one of those you want to keep a special eye on."

"Thank you. Leave it on my desk." In the newcomer, Jacob Werner saw himself in his long-sleeved white shirt and tie, and wondered what he was still doing here. Hopefully it was only a temporary stint. At any rate, it was quite undemanding, and made good cover for the rest of his specialized abilities. Still, deep down, Jacob Werner was a man of action, unused to sedentary paper chases behind a desk. A frown formed above his crisp mustache as he thought about it. He glanced at a small stack of papers in a shiny black tray marked "In," and the few memos to his left. There were no "Out" trays on his desk. Jacob Werner smiled again. The easy smile was also a routine ingredient of his work.

As the gray-suited young man received no further comment, he prepared to leave.

"Doing well, Bob. Keep up the good work." Jake's benign smile curled under his mustache: Good work indeed, he thought. Hardly anything reached his desk that didn't need to.

The words, "keep up the good work" cascaded like warm bureaucratic back-pats over Robert Cook. Recently sent by a branch of the H.H.S.—Health and Human Services, before its name changed from Health, Education, and Welfare—to play watchdog and oversee fiscal dealings with the National Institute of Health, Bob was eager to prove his executive mettle. His job was to calculate not only the N.I.H. research costs of a particular grant, but to project, in dollars and cents, the potential future costs for the H.H.S. of applying discoveries of that research to the general public.

As Jake had explained, it wasn't that the government was uninterested in implementing costly discoveries, but that the timing had to be right, from the point of view of their entire Medicare and Medicaid Budget.

Facts and figures had to be checked, timing had to be planned, and any delays in research, if necessary, could be compensated later by expediting needed programs at a more "proper" time.

Bob occasionally wondered about Jacob Werner's own job descriptions and position at the N.I.H. It seemed to be a liaison post between the Department of Health and Human Services, and the National Institute of Health. Checks arrived from either the N.I.H., or the H.H.S. But whatever Jacob Werner's exact role was, his activity wasn't plagued by the same ambivalence: Though less versed in the scientific and research aspects at hand, Jake was neither indecisive nor introspective, and had little trouble deciding how to deal with the grant applications he reviewed.

"Oh, Bob...who else knows about this?" Jake glanced at the grant application and Bob's analysis.

"Only Thompson, but it won't concern him any if we lighten his desk load of another grant app. Besides, he only checks for margins, double-spacing, and that it generally belongs here rather than between the covers of Vogue."

"Good." Jacob Werner straightened his tie and stood up. "I'll take care of it from here. You're done with it, and never saw it before. Right?"

Bob nodded, glancing back at the research application, on the desk near the "In" tray. The name on the application was that of John Cameron, M.D.

. . . . .

After midnight, Max took a breath and waited for his eleventh admission. At this rate, he'd go over fourteen, more than some Interns admitted in an entire week at other hospitals. Still, he felt more stiff than tired—like after a long car ride in a small back seat. Max smiled as he thought of New York state's flap over hospital staff working hours: A reduction to not over 80 hours per week, with at least 8 hours off between shifts of 24. It had to be difficult to concede, for one of the most "doctor-bashing" states in the union, that perhaps doctors were overworked and underpaid—since even working them at the newly reduced rate of still twice the normal average would cost the state nearly three hundred million dollars more yearly. Meaning the state had been getting this, and more, for free all these years.

For his own part, Max felt less of a need to be protected by the state than from the state. The same politicians and legislators who called for continuing recertification of the medical profession would be appalled by the notion of proficiency testing of their own ability to initiate only necessary, fair, understandable, and constitutional laws. And when was the last time legislators spent an entire day in a nursing home, or with a small business, or in the shoes of an assembly-line worker? Insulated by dozens of "staffers" from their constituency, most legislators touched down to real earth about as often as Marie Antoinette. And any government that spent forty- two million dollars of the taxpayers' money to prosecute Ollie North could probably use a refresher course in governing. Max smiled and wondered if the world wouldn't be better off by paying politicians to simply go home, and do nothing, write no new laws, no new regulations. The savings in paper alone would be tremendous.

Max's musings about the shortcomings of others was, as is often the case, brought to a close by a reminder of his own. The nurse caring for Mrs. Ellen Samuels called to report increasing post-operative pain. Max walked to her room, noting under the night-light the new pallor of her face and the perspiration on her forehead. Her teeth weren't clenched, but she appeared too weak for that.

"How are you doing, Mrs. Samuels?"

"Hurts a bit."

Mrs. Samuels had returned several days ago with increasing right upper abdominal pains. X-rays and ultrasound had disclosed a hugely dilated gallbladder, along with the stones they'd already known about.

Technically, she should have been Joel Saxton's patient this time around, and from there to surgery. But since it appeared like a short stay on a medical ward before gallbladder surgery, and Max had cared for her as well in the past, he'd called Joel and Cameron, and kept Mrs. Samuels, before her transfer to Surgery.

Gallbladder removal—cholecystectomy—had been done two days ago. They found not only the gallstones, but a gallbladder infiltrated with adenocarcinoma, producing the fluid that had dilated it to the size of a melon, and spreading the cancer to the nearby liver.

"We'll give you more medication, Mrs. Samuels. Let me know if it doesn't take care of the pain."

She nodded.

Max wrote an order to double the Morphine sulfate I.V. Attending rounds with Dr. Sullivan would be in the morning, for questions and further treatment. But it was doubtful chemotherapy or anything else could cure Mrs. Samuels. Besides, it would be difficult to explain the reasons for enduring the medications' side effects, since Mrs. Samuels didn't really want to know what she had.

"We'll see you at rounds in the morning." Max touched her arm, blue from where the I.V. had infiltrated once. She seemed to be losing more weight every day.

"Thank you, dear." She closed her eyes.

How long had the cancer been there? How could they have diagnosed it if it didn't show up on X-rays? Would it have made a difference had they been able to diagnose it earlier?

Questions without answers were interrupted by a new admission. New, yet not quite: The face was familiar from the days on Cameron's team. Max checked the name tag attached to the limp wrist, half expecting the customary Jane Doe. Apparently, the ER. was familiar with her also, since the name tag already carried the positive I.D. of Tammy Clarendon.

It was her third O.D. in as many months. Whatever her reasons were, she was persistent in her efforts, and someone just as persistently found her, to be brought here and treated in time. Sooner or later one of the links would fail, or a complication would develop, and the name tag wouldn't be the hospital's, but that of the morgue.

Max did a swift exam, where minutes and perhaps seconds counted. He glanced at the ER vital signs: Heart rate, blood pressure, and temperature were all down, and her respirations would hardly have fogged the clearest of mirrors. There were no visible head or neck injuries; pupils were equal but barely reactive to light. Heart sounds were faint, and lung sounds minimal; abdomen bore no signs of trauma. Under the "Red Blanket" and hospital gown, the skin was smooth and unbroken, save for a bruise over her left hip. Dr. McDaniel tested reflexes, searching for whatever tenuous connections remained between her brain and the outside world.

Perhaps at another time, another place, the beauty that rested in her features—even at this extreme moment—could be better appreciated.

For now, in the cold analytical light of diagnosis and treatment, there was no room for emotion. The beacon that would guide them through the storm didn't alter with the weather.

Present diagnosis: Overdose, intentional, probably due to a combination of tranquilizers and a muscle relaxant. Treatment: 1) Immediate gastric lavage; 2) supportive therapy of IV's, respirator if needed; 3) confirmatory toxicology in progress; 4) post-recovery mandatory psych consult.

"Large bore lavage tube," Max asked the duty nurse. "Scissors." Max enlarged a few of the holes that peppered one end of the lavage tube. He moved swiftly, automatically—almost ritualistically, as in a ceremony to exorcise death. "Ice, please." He immersed the tube in a bucket of ice water. It would stiffen the tube and ease its passage. Towels had already been placed around the patient's head, and the pillow removed to straighten the angle of the neck. Max checked the teeth for bridges and caps. "Ready?"

The nurse, Mary Clemens, held the suction cannula, and nodded.

Dr. McDaniel opened the patient's mouth with his left hand, and guided the tube with his right, past the teeth, into the pharynx. He waited between breaths, when the trachea would be closed, then tried to curve the tube into the esophagus. She gagged and bit firmly down onto tube and one of Max's slower fingers. Though initial exam revealed consciousness to be minimal, Max was learning consciousness could be quite variable. But now that he stopped, she was Sleeping Beauty again, lavage tube dangling from her mouth.

"Lidocaine jelly," Max asked. He applied the clear, viscous anesthetic jelly over the tube. "Let's try the nose."

The tube curved into the left nostril, moved two inches, then refused to budge. Max withdrew the tube and wiped it again with anesthetic jelly. After straightening her neck, he curved the tube into the right nostril. Max pushed gently. A trickle of blood oozed from the nostril onto the lips. Tammy grimaced and arched her neck. Max withdrew the tube and wiped it again with anesthetic jelly. After straightening her neck, he curved the tube into the nostril. It stopped again at about two inches. Max nudged the tube while rotating it slightly. A hardness gave way, and the NG tube advanced. Her neck bucked as if in mid-sneeze.

"Hold her straight." Max waited and slipped the tube into the esophagus between breaths. She gasped a few times. Max held the tube immobile against the nostril with one hand, and listened to the gasps with his stethoscope in the other. Breath sounds were equal on both sides, meaning the tube wasn't obstructing one of the bronchi. Stomach contents welled up the tube. Max taped the tube securely against nose and forehead, and let the stomach contents drain before commencing lavage. The procedure had taken two minutes and fifty seconds. It would take nearly a half-hour to carefully lavage everything out.

Afterwards, Max wiped his forehead. He glanced at Tammy Clarendon: This time, all had gone well. Sleeping Beauty would live for another day. How long was another matter. Though beauty hadn't eluded her, apparently the meaning of life had.

. . . . .

Morning rounds began an hour and a half later. After last night's admissions, there was no lack of difficult medical problems to present. Dr. Sullivan arrived early—"start early, finish early," he'd say. One could almost see his body coiling at the starting blocks. Carlos was tempted to ask if he still ran—but that would be like asking Arnie Schwarzenegger if he still lifted weights.

Carlos led off with the first patient presentation, then alternated with Max. Their last one was Mrs. Samuels.

"We've got a problem," Max said. "She's got cancer, but doesn't know it. In fact, she doesn't wish to know."

Dr. Sullivan stopped. "We can make an exception to rounds by the bedside. Go on."

"Mrs. Samuels was admitted over two months ago, while on Dr. Cameron's service. She'd complained of tiredness and shortness of breath. Our work up then was entirely negative, until we realized her kidney function was a bit down, and a drug had probably slowly built up to give her those symptoms. She improved after we stopped it, and appeared better until a few days ago, when she developed persistent pain in the right upper quadrant, nausea, and vomiting—all the symptoms of cholecystitis and lithiasis. Exam signs matched her symptoms: Increased temperature, tenderness near the gallbladder area, and a positive Murphy's sign. Lab showed a mild increase in bilirubin, alkaline phosphatase, and SGOT and LDH liver enzymes. Interestingly, it was known two years ago that she had gallstones, confirmed by ultrasound. But without further symptoms, Mrs. Samuels decided she didn't wish surgery.

"Problem is, at surgery now, along with one of the largest dilated gallbladders seen and four stones inside, she also had cancer there and studded along the liver." Max shook his head. "She was always so worried about something bad happening to her. And now it did. Maybe she had a premonition. Before surgery, she simply said she wasn't interested in knowing what she had."

"What was the tumor type?" Dr. Sullivan asked softly.

"The pathologist hedged a bit, but thought it resembled a primary hepatoma. There was no apparent spread to other organs."

"Any tumor in the gallbladder?"

"A small infiltrate in the distal wall. It was probably that and not the stones that dilated her gallbladder. And come to think of it, it probably wasn't just the kidney dysfunction that had increased disopyramide drug levels in her past admission: It's also metabolized by the liver, and her liver impairment may have contributed to the higher drug levels. It fits." Once again Max wondered if the outcome could have been any different had they found out earlier.

Dr. Sullivan leaned forward and looked at him. "Let's examine this more. Cancer was inadvertently found in the liver and gallbladder during surgery for stones. How long the cancer's been there is difficult to estimate. At any rate, hepatomas are rarely found in time to cure them. So, the surgeons send her back to Medicine because there's nothing more they can do."

"And because they don't want the complications and death on their service," Carlos added. Carlos Schmidt wasn't noted for being particularly shy about his opinions.

Track smiled, but said nothing.

"They really can't do much more for her, can they? But neither can we, and that's what makes it so frustrating," Max added.

"What are your thoughts now, Dr. Schmidt?"

"Well, radiation's not particularly good for that area, but chemotherapy's not that much better. Prognosis is poor."

"Dr. McDaniel?"

"There are some alternative therapies—hyperthermia and monoclonal antibodies, I think. But they're only offered at a few research centers, and are still mainly theoretical and experimental. I agree with Dr. Schmidt—the prognosis is dismal." Max remembered that barely a parking lot away Cameron was working on a problem just like this. For Mrs. Samuels, that might as well be light years away.

Dr. Sullivan seemed to continue his thoughts: "You're right," he said looking at Max, "some research won't be on time for Mrs. Samuels."

The Interns were silent.

"So, what are your plans for Mrs. Samuels?" Dr. Sullivan asked.

"I don't know how or what to tell her. I'm not particularly good at this," Max held the chart, and looked down.

"None of us are, Dr. McDaniel, but it happens to be part of our work. That's why we have rounds, to learn from and with each other."

"I know we're taught to tell patients the whole truth, straight and like it is. But damn it, I'm not sure she wants to know. In fact, I know she doesn't. I've even asked in the roundabout, if she had any questions about the operation and what was found, leaving it to her to inquire if she wanted."

"And?"

"I believe she could sense the bad news behind my questions. I asked two mornings in a row. She simply said she had no questions. No questions! Now, how do I tell her?"

"Any ideas, Dr. Schmidt?"

"There are at least two schools of thought on this, and perhaps many in between," Carlos began. The more he intellectualized, the more likely he was covering his emotions. "In one, a patient must always be told the whole truth, at all times. No matter how painful, truth is served first. From an ethical point, one can hardly fault this. Proponents of this view feel any other approach assumes a larger-than-life role for the doctor, who then makes decisions not only about diagnosis and treatment, but also as to what knowledge might be best for the patient. In their view, this is at best paternalistic, and at worst what they term 'playing God.'

"On the other hand, there are some who believe not all patients wish to know the worst. Especially when no good treatment is available for a disease anyway, little may be served by delivering or confirming news of gloom and doom, which could even further shorten the remaining lifespan through depression. Besides, the reason given for imparting such news—that people have a right to know how much time they have left—may well be invalid, since prognostications about remaining life can be notoriously inaccurate by several multiples. Therefore, supporters of this view argue that knowing when, what, and how to say something can also be part of the treatment. While they do not advocate a blatant lie, they feel information should be tailored to a patient's wishes. Nearest relatives, of course, would be fully informed."

"Your dissertation about the schools of thought was quite thorough, Dr. Schmidt. Now, what do you think?"

"You mean personally?"

Dr. Sullivan nodded.

"I don't have the certainty others may have in these matters..." Carlos cast off his Prussian cloak, then continued: "But perhaps certainty is for books, and doesn't always apply to all people in all situations. I believe each doctor has to do what he believes is best for his patient. That can't always be found in books, nor learned through pre-formulated theories."

Dr. Sullivan squinted, as if watching some far-off finish line. "How would you approach this patient's situation?"

"First, I would check the alternatives," Dr. Schmidt's Teutonic precision returned. "Is there a possibility that treatment may significantly enhance or prolong her life? If so, she should be told, because informed consent must be obtained prior to treatment. The surgeons have already turned her over to us, so there's little hope for any further surgical treatment. As for medical treatments and chemotherapy, I'm not familiar enough to say."

"Suppose I provided that information, Dr. Schmidt: For her disease, response to chemotherapy, with some individual variability, has been poor."

Carlos took a deep breath. "In that case, there would be no overwhelming medical reason to inform this patient of her probably incurable cancer. How and what she's told would probably best be left to the physician who knows her most, and in accordance with her own and her family's wishes."

"Who would that be for her?" Dr. Sullivan asked Max.

"Well, Joel Saxton and I took care of her, but she always did like Dr. Cameron. I'm not attempting to avoid decisions or giving news, but she really did relate to Dr. Cameron best."

"Will he come and talk to Mrs. Samuels with you?"

"Of course."

"Right, then. For next week's rounds, we'll discuss chemotherapy of abdominal cancers." Rounds were over. Dr. Sullivan was gone with a few steps of his lanky stride.

. . . . .

There were as many lab tests usually to be drawn as there were patients. About half were routine draws, with easily visualized veins. The other half ranged from the merely difficult, to the impossible. Difficult were young women with alabaster skin and veins like feathers; older patients with muscles wasted away from the sides of veins, leaving them unanchored and rolling like worms avoiding a fishing hook; and emaciated patients with parchment skin and gossamer veins that burst like webs upon contact with a needle. Impossible were the extremely obese, with veins snugly buried within rolls of fat, and drug addicts with only the ghostly remnants of scars in place of veins, from fingertips to toes.

Dr. McDaniel reached 409B, Tammy Clarendon's room. A white rectangle of sheets was neatly folded and tucked under her chin. A thin IV line disappeared like a kite's string under a cloud of sheets, to the arms folded across her chest. In the curtained twilight of the room, her peaceful rest could have been sleep, coma, or death. Her breathing barely lifted the cloud of sheets. Max set his phlebotomy tray down, and sat next to the bed. For a moment, he placed his hands over his face, and closed his eyes. It was strange how quiet and thin were the threads of life: A transparent line of colorless, tasteless oxygen, bringing fuel to feed the body's combustion engine; clear tubing ferrying sea water's primordial contribution of dissolved salts and ions—the fireflies of the bloodstream—providing tiny bursts of electricity linking the vastness of the nervous system, and igniting each heart's beat.

Max opened his eyes. Perspiration gathered on Tammy's forehead like beads on a pale lily. Somehow, somewhere, her heart had decided life wasn't worth living. And that was more difficult to cure than any disease. A few beads rolled down onto her curly auburn hair.

Nightmares? Did the daytime phantoms driving her to suicide not even retreat during sleep?

When Max unclasped the hands from his face, she was awake, looking at him. "Where am I?"

"You're in the hospital. You'll be all right."

"I recognize you. You're Dr. Max ... something. You and Dr. Saxton helped me the last time." She paused. "Why?"

"That's my job."

"You know I'm going to do it again."

"I figured you might."

"So why do it? Why try to save me?"

"Because maybe you won't do it again."

"Why wouldn't I?" She laughed with a thin, desperate sound. The perspiration from her face rolled onto her neck and hospital gown, gathered loosely everywhere except over her breasts.

"To determine that, we'd have to know why you're doing this in the first place." Max held up her small wrist with linear scars across it.

"What do you care?" Her light green eyes flashed defensively. "All you have to do is wash me out, stitch me up, stick IV's; and when it's done, let me go."

"That's all I <u>have</u> to do," Max nodded. "Both you and I know that's not enough."

"You mean you care what happens to me afterwards?"

"Is that so hard to believe?"

She nodded, and her face came to rest in her hands, sobbing. "Look...I don't want...anyone...involved..." She stopped herself, wiping tears and mingling them with some left-over mascara across her cheeks.

"Here," Max held out his handkerchief.

She hesitated, then took it. "Thanks."

"Are we going to talk about the why?"

She blew her nose into the handkerchief, and shook her head.

"Why not?"

"It won't help."

"We won't know that until you tell me."

She fidgeted with the handkerchief. "I suppose I could try..."

"Good. Is that a promise, then?"

Eyes downcast, unsure whether to be bashful, or frightened, she nodded.

"Listen, I've got to finish drawing lab samples—yours too. Then I'll be back, and we'll talk." Her veins were like spider webs on translucent crystal. He had to pack warm towels over her arm, to make them stand out, and finally thread a vein for a sample. "Now remember—you promised, Tammy." He placed a band-aid over the venipuncture site, on a now warm hand.

She reclined her head on the pillow. "You'll come back, then?"

"Yes. That's my promise."

. . . . .

As they talked, someone in surgical blue scrubs entered 406, Mrs. Samuels' room. He had the steady, self-assured gait of one who regularly held others' lives in his hands.

"Hello, I'm Dr. Roger Taylor, of the surgical team that operated on you." He glanced through her chart. "How are you doing?"

"Well...all right. I think I'm getting stronger now," Mrs. Samuels replied.

"Seems like everything is in order," he paged through the chart, nodding. Then he examined the incision—an ochre ridge riding above a glistening belly—a line held closed by the living glue of fibrin, platelets, and collagen. The ridge crested over the taut, pale skin of the domed abdomen, laced with spidery blue veins, while ascites fluid continued to slowly pour from the tumors inside her. "Good," Dr. Taylor said. "This will be your last surgical follow-up visit." He closed her chart. "Of course, you can't expect too much with this type of cancer. Any questions?"

Like a fish out of water, Mrs. Samuel's mouth opened, without a sound. Her eyes closed, as if a falling curtain could protect her from reality a while longer.

"Oh, hasn't anyone told you yet? At surgery, the gallbladder was large and full of stones, as expected." A plastic bag on her bedside table held several olive-like stones. "I see you already have them," he paused. "We also found nodules of liver tumors. There were too many of them, and we couldn't get them out." He shook his head. "I'm sorry."

His voice had been like his hands, trained to be even and steady, to scientifically carve and dissect disease away. He was gone. Voice and steps echoed behind, measured on rhythms of one who held lives in his hands while others slept.

· · · · ·

Max almost bumped into the surgical Resident in blue scrubs, talking to Barbara at the nurses' station. "Hi. A bit far afield today, aren't you?"

"We do like to finish follow-up on our surgical patients," Taylor commented.

Max nodded, with a strange premonition about something. He had no more labs to draw in Mrs. Samuels room, but quickened his pace towards her. She was on her side, away from him.

"Mrs. Samuels?" He touched her arm. She didn't move. "Mrs. Samuels," he repeated walking to the other side of the bed. She wasn't crying. Her eyes, resting within cheeks and lids puffy like donuts, stared far away.

"Is it true what he said?" Her eyes didn't move, and she didn't use any specific words, banishing as much as she could of her fears.

"I've called Dr. Cameron. He wants to talk to you." Max patted her hand. It lay limp, like a rag doll on a worn safety blanky.

"I'm so afraid..."

"We'll be here talking care of you."

"You promise?" she asked him.

"Yes." For the second time today, he'd made a promise. This time he wasn't entirely sure what he was promising. Perhaps at this point that didn't matter so much as simply confirming he'd do his best. "Dr. Cameron and I will return soon," he put her hand down gently. "Now, if you'll excuse me, there is something I have to do."

Max left Mrs. Samuels' room, rounded the corner, and almost slammed into the nurses' station. "Barbara, page Dr. Cameron stat!" The surgical Resident was walking away. "Taylor!"

Roger Taylor had certainly heard his name before. But when the tone stopped him in his tracks, there was no mistaking how it was used. Taylor at first felt bewilderment, then annoyance, then anger, in rapid succession. He wheeled around, to face Max's approach.

"You saw Mrs. Samuels, didn't you?" Max said.

"You've got a problem with that?"

"Depends on what you told her."

"I told her what she should have already known—that she has liver cancer."

"Just like that?"

"What do you want me to do? Embellish it? It's still cancer, no matter how you say it."

"For her, it's basically incurable. What you say, and how you say it is the only thing that matters to her."

"I suppose you medical types get off on that. When there's nothing you can do for a patient, you've got twenty different ways to talk about it."

"If there's nothing more to do, why don't you at least not make it worse. In your case, that's easy: Just stay away."

"Look, don't blame me that she didn't know! There are decisions to be made—perhaps chemo, radiation, or whatever else. And if nothing else, then to get her affairs in order. She has a right to know."

"Don't you think we've thought of that? And not just in the blink of an eye that it takes to tell her she has cancer? Maybe she even has the right not to know. Did that ever cross your mind? Or do you just specialize in telling patients with all the tact of a bulldozer, that since you can't cut it out, they're going to die?"

"Maybe we could have cut it out, if you'd diagnosed it earlier!"

"So take time off from surgery, engage your brain, and diagnose it yourself, if you're such a hot shot!"

Barbara walked to them. "Do you mind? It's getting a bit loud. Could you continue this elsewhere?"

"Nothing more to continue," Taylor shrugged. "This clown's been all over me like a sweat suit in a sauna. He needs to chill out."

"I'll cool it as soon as you bozos leave my patients alone," Max replied.

Barbara Davis was glad when Cameron arrived. He saw Max and Taylor locked into trouble, and walked straight towards them.

"Is this your Intern, Cameron?" Taylor asked.

"Yes, he is." Technically, that was no longer the case.

"Better reel him in, before I file a formal complaint."

"Let's not get stressed out. Our jobs provide enough of that as it is, Dr. Taylor. Dr. McDaniel, I believe we have some work to do. Let's go."

Cameron took Max out of earshot. "What was that all about?"

"Taylor told Mrs. Samuels she had cancer. She doesn't look good. Her will is gone."

"Shall we go see about that?"

"Let's."

"Listen, I'm sorry about this. I hope it won't cause any trouble for you. I don't know what happened—something just snapped inside me."

Cameron looked at him. "Dr. Taylor was probably wrong in telling her like he did. But you were wrong also, Dr. McDaniel, chewing him out. You get wound up sometimes—and then you uncoil. That's you. But we can't afford 'just snapping' in medicine. We've all got things to work on. That's yours."

They reached room 406. Max sat down, and Cameron pulled up another chair. "Hello, Mrs. Samuels. Shall we talk a bit?"

"What's to talk about? I'm going to die."

"Wait a minute. Who said you were going to die?"

"That other doctor. At least, I think he did. Not in so many words, but..."

"Well, what exactly did he say?"

"Exactly?" I don't know. But he said I have...cancer. They found it all over the liver. Isn't that the same thing?"

Cameron shook his head. "It doesn't have to be. Cancer is not the same as dying. It's true many people die of cancer. But not all of them. And people die of car accidents, heart attacks, and all sorts of things. Nothing is certain in this life—not even what a certain disease will do to you. So no one can really tell you where, or from what, you will die. Does that make sense?"

Mrs. Samuels barely nodded.

"Besides, there's all types of cancers, or tumors. They all have distinct genetic mutations and genetic code differences. Few are ever alike. Therefore, since tumors are all uniquely different, and so are people, there's no textbook way to predict what will happen. Yes, some people die, but we do save up to fifty percent. And in some others, the tumors can go completely away, even without treatment, and for no known reason. So you see, Mrs. Samuels, it's a bit premature to talk about dying. Right?"

She nodded, a bit more vigorously. "So it doesn't mean I'm going to die in a week or two?"

"No. It certainly doesn't."

"What about pain? I'm so afraid to die in pain. You always hear how someone suffered so much...I had an aunt... No, I don't want to remember that."

"It doesn't have to be that way, Mrs. Samuels. You haven't had much pain up to now, right?"

"Well, not a lot..."

"There's no reason to suspect that will change much. And even if it worsens, we do have strong medicines if we need them. There's no reason for you to be uncomfortable."

"You mean that?"

"Yes."

"Sometimes you hear the treatment is terrible, makes you feel worse than you did before. I don't want that. What's it called—chemopharmacy?"

"Chemotherapy. And you don't have to take it if you don't want."

The donut-like swellings around her eyes were the same, but there was more sparkle within. "Thank you," she said. "You'll still be taking care of me all along?"

"Of course, Mrs. Samuels."

"Thank you both." She took Cameron's hand like a child, as if expecting his large hand to surround hers, and keep it from harm. Cameron held it in his, with that way he had, making it seem he could lift a K.O.'d boxer as gently as he could a premature baby.

"You're welcome." Outside, Cameron made a note on her chart and returned it to Max.

"What did you write?"

"Some of what we talked about."

" How do you get all that on there?"

"You don't. Some of what we do, perhaps the best of it, can't be put into words. If you ever get to the point you can, then you'll know you have forgotten what medicine is all about, or never really learned it in the first place. Take care of her, Dr. McDaniel. Keep her comfortable."

Max looked back at her room. "You did say it before, didn't you Cameron?"

"What?"

"You said that medicine was many things, and diagnosis is just one of them. Sometimes, getting to know the human being inside was the best we could do."

"Yes." Cameron looked away.

"Still..."

"What?"

"I wish ... we could have done more."

Cameron nodded. His stare remained far away. "I think that's the way we're supposed to feel."

"Doesn't it ever get you down, Cameron?"

It wasn't how Max had meant it. But Cameron thought of the years of tinkering, changing hybrid cell lines, experimenting. For the first time, what he'd been doing with borrowed time, in borrowed labs, connected with what it really could mean to someone in need. A vague sort of guilt settled upon him. What if he'd worked harder? Perhaps had pushed for a grant? Would he'd been able to offer to reconstruct Mrs. Samuels liver, instead of dispensing words of hope? Cameron left, without answering the question.

Carlos met Max in the lounge. "Heard you and the Surgical Resident had some words, with little in common. Everything all right?"

"Sure."

"How come you didn't present the O.D. case to Dr. Sullivan—you know, Clarendon?"

Max shrugged. "The medical part's not the most difficult part."

"Know what you mean: Toxicologies, wash-outs, routine psych consults ... then they're just back again. You think we ever accomplish anything?"

"I don't know." Max left for Tammy's room.

Eyebrows rose in 412 as Max walked in. "I thought I heard your voice in the hall," Tammy greeted him. "You got into it with someone?"

"Everyone's heard by now?"

"I didn't hear anything. Just recognized your voice. What was it about?"

"Difference of opinions," he shrugged. "I'm sorry if it disturbed you."

"I'm sure there was a reason for it. Did you win the argument?"

"Wasn't a question of winning or losing, but doing the right thing."

"And did you?"

"I think so. But there was no need to do it loudly."

"At least you know what the right thing is," she commented. "I don't think I even remember that anymore."

"Why do you say that?"

"Because it's true. I've screwed up my life. And I don't have any way of fixing it..." her eyes stared blankly ahead.

"So ending it is better?"

She didn't reply. A look of despair came over her face: It was like watching flowers iced under an early frost, or a fawn pursued by wolves and cut off by a raging river.

Max touched her hand.

"You don't understand," she finally said. "I've done things...that can't be changed. The past is always going to be with me... No escape." She shook her head. Cut off by the river, the fawn prepared to die.

"Tammy, the past doesn't have to be fixed, changed, or anything at all. It *is* past. Over. You don't even need to escape it—only leave it where it is. Gone."

She was silent awhile, then looked at him. "You could be right. Maybe the past doesn't need changing. But the past also changes you, what you are now..."

"In some ways, the past changes us all, Tammy. But it doesn't have to dictate what your future's going to be, forever and ever."

Her jaw jutted defiantly, as if daring him to put into practice what he'd said. "I've done drugs. All kinds. What do you think about that? I'm a drug addict."

"I already know that, from your chart. Luckily, you didn't take them IV, and you're also lucky they didn't hurt you more."

"That's strange, because I was trying to hurt myself."

"Well, I'm glad you didn't."

"Glad? Why?"

"Does there always have to be a reason?" Max looked at her: The face was round, softly proportioned, delicately accented by full cheekbones. A pert, small nose kept harmony with the rest of her features, and only a button of chin—with its own flavor of stubbornness—escaped the otherwise perfect facial symmetry. She didn't smile at all, Max noticed. Yet when the lips, softly rounded like everything else, parted for words, her teeth flashed in a beaver's grin, with a hint of dimples. Max resolved he'd see her full smile eventually.

Her emerald eyes looked at him, then down. "I guess it doesn't really matter."

Max felt anger at first—anger at himself. Perhaps also anger at her beauty. Did he really want to help her? Was his intent only medical? Or did he want to help, but for the wrong reasons? Where did one end, and the other begin? Max finally stopped thinking about it, and lifted her chin. "It doesn't matter. You matter."

"No..." she had difficulty going on, "not when you find out about me."

"That's not important now."

"No? Listen to me! How do you think I got the money for drugs?" She pushed his hand aside. "I don't even remember what began first, the whoring, or the drugs ..." She shook all over, but began again: "So you see, I'm a prostitute. That's what I do for a living. Cheap hotels, expensive hotels...it's all the same—johns, prostitutes, pimps ..." She let out a sardonic laugh: "You, how could you understand, or care?"

Max said nothing. He touched her hand.

At first, she didn't cry. Then her shoulders shuddered, and she fell against him, no longer holding it in. After a while, she moved from the wet part on his shoulder and touched it, trying to brush off the tears. "Sorry..." she said.

"I'm not."

There was silence.

"Aren't you..." she began, "I mean, don't you have to send me out, now that the O.D.'s worn off, and I've had my shrink consult? Isn't that how it's done?"

"I suppose so. Do you want to leave?"

Her eyes were unsettling as she glanced firmly past him, far away. "Yes."

"I don't want to send you out yet. But I can't force you to stay. You can leave A.M.A.—that's 'against medical advice'—by signing a piece of paper."

"Why would you want to keep me?" Her eyes settled on him, as if searching for something. The rest of her face betrayed no emotion as to what that might be.

"It could do you good."

"You still care, after all I've told you?"

"I still care."

"For a drug addict, prostitute, whore?"

"I understood it the first time." He paused, looking at her: "You seem to confuse what you've done, with what you are inside, and what you could be."

She pondered, and her eyes flickered a brief glow, like candles at home on Christmas Day. "Are you sure about this?"

He nodded. "Yes."

"Then I won't sign out." For the first time, the hint of a smile played around the puddles of her dimples. Just as soon, the candles went out, and the puddles looked like they'd fill with tears. "There's more..." she said quietly.

"I'm sure there is," he said gently, "but not today."

"Are you ready for it?"

"I think so." He placed her hand gently on the covers.

"I'm sorry. I don't even know your last name."

"McDaniel. Max McDaniel."

"Thank you, Max McDaniel."

· · · · ·

On the evening way home, Max saw the hawk again, at his post. Maybe, like the rest of God's creatures at times, he was just alone in the rain.

CHAPTER 8

THE RUN

The 440. Four turns and then a full-blown sprint all the way. Last race of the season: State finals, senior year.

His start was bad—as usual, and his own fault. Starts were his weakness. He knew it, and the coach knew it. He'd been taken off the 100 and 220, races too short to play catch-up.

Perhaps Cameron wanted it that way. He felt better running from behind. Perhaps it was the challenge, or the ability to set his own stride, or maybe simply fear of the unknown behind him. The few times he'd had a good start, he didn't feel deserving of the race: A quirk of the starting gun? A rush of reflexes and adrenalin just tenths ahead of someone else?.. Time shaved without grueling elbow-to-elbow dues.

So this final start didn't really matter that much. By the end of the second turn he was third, a favorite running position: Two ahead, and not enough time left to think of the pack behind. Time accelerated and something inside kicked in. Sun above in the crystal-dry summer air... nothing was impossible...

Flying feet paid no attention to the cinder track they so swiftly left... That was the race: The flying... By the third turn he'd matched elbow-to-elbow up front. Then began to pull away. Alone.

The air rushed by, the sun; the field behind didn't matter. He flew his own race... Into the last turn, straightaway unfolding... He'd go past the finish line and into the stands...

Just before turn's end, on flying feet that didn't worry about the ground, he heard and felt it at the same time. An ankle turned in on touching down. On a straightaway perhaps he could have pulled back into balance. On a turn it buckled. His soaring crumpled to the ground.

He returned to his feet, lame comparison to his previous run... limped across an already broken finish line. Lying still on the grass beyond, he looked up at the unchanged clear blue sky.

The race was in the flying, he knew. Simply running it wasn't enough.

"Track" Sullivan's face surfaced above him. "You ran your own race, Cameron. Your own, all the way."

Cameron tried to smile. "I flew part of it..."

"You flew all of it."

Cameron continued to look at the sky.

"The race doesn't matter, Cameron. You won the run."

Jacob Werner gazed at the view from the ninth story office. He rolled the cigar between his fingers, but didn't light it. He'd decided he liked the view, the thick carpet smothering his footsteps, the smell of leather armchairs as he sat down. Under his crisp mustache, Jacob Werner stood and smiled: In time, with his cards played right, anything was possible. His smile continued to hold the proper mix of congeniality and deference required for the occasion. Jacob Werner didn't speak first.

"You boys are doing a good job, Jake." Terrance Liverpool usually began his requests for something he needed with a pat on the back. He replaced the box of cigars on a desk that was even more remarkably free of activity than Jake's own had been: Besides the box of cigars, there was an engraved brass fountain pen set, and nothing visible to use it upon.

"I'm glad you think so," Jake replied.

"That last grant request was particularly interesting. Had our experts brooding; turned a few heads at the top." Terrance Liverpool leaned against his desk; though quite tall, he still preferred to begin from a standing position. Younger than Jacob Werner by a few years, Terrance had the correct credentials for his job by birth. The impeccable tailored double-breasted suit always remained buttoned; this time the dark blue was jauntily set off with a crimson school tie. It was as if Terrance himself had been part of the interior decorator's office design. Terrance Liverpool could have comfortably belonged to an evening television series related to banking or oil.

"What did you think?" Jake inquired blandly.

"We won't fund it, of course. But that's not all."

"Oh?" Jake said vaguely. Glancing at the desk again, Jake realized why he liked it so much. Besides the lack of clutter, there was no lighter to go with the cigars. Sometimes even the lack of something displayed power—in this case, the power of favors granted or withheld. Jake nodded at Terrance's new touch. For an instant, Jake relished the idea of lighting his own, but decided against it. All would come in due time.

"Not funding this one isn't enough, Jake. It's got to be stopped cold."

Jake sighed and placed the cigar inside his coat pocket. Perhaps he'd been hoping for a mistake, a slip on Terrance's part. He knew that wasn't likely soon. "If it's not funded, won't that be enough to stop it?" Jake asked disingenuously.

"Look, Jake, this project never has been funded! He's accomplished this on his own. He's done enough already that sooner or later it will get out – in scientific journals, medical meetings..." Terrance went behind his desk and sat down. "We can't let that happen."

"I can see that." Jake paused. "How are we going to do that?"

"It's not a question of stopping it forever, of course. Just a matter of time, Jake. Five, maybe eight years, when the Department of Health and Human Services feels funds are more available, the idea more ripe, and plans for actual implementation are laid out more carefully. You understand? Until then, we ice the idea, perfect it, plan cost-effectiveness, availability, and eventual delivery to eligible segments of our population. We could even develop it in the meantime as a useful backup in certain cases, say, if some V.I.P.'s absolutely needed it. It could be done discreetly, by a selected medical team on a classified basis."

"Sounds reasonable," Jake smiled. He didn't ask whether the list of V.I.P's would include Terrance and himself. He already knew the answer, and planned to do something about it.

"The point is, Jake, we can't just open this up tomorrow for everyone. Even if this guy, Camden something, can do it tomorrow, we can't do it tomorrow. We can't fund another organ transplant, or organ regeneration program, proceeding willy-nilly into the green-dollared health sky. Total health costs are rising by fifteen percent per year, a bite of eleven-point-two percent out of the G.N.P. Kidney transplants alone, for which Medicare began picking up the tab in nineteen seventy-two, were two point three billion dollars back in nineteen eighty-five. Adding any other organ transplant program could add tens of billions per year. And what about this doc's proposal? This organ regeneration thing could chew up funds as fast as anything we have now. Not only that, but with the potential for considerable prolongation of life, think of all the extra folks and extra years Medicare would have to pay for. They'd live into a riper old age, developing more chronic and debilitating conditions that would have to be cared and paid for. Just that would be enough to wipe out all the savings we've achieved by freezing the docs' and hospitals' payments.

"So, you see, the more successful such grant proposals would be, the more they'd be handing us financial disaster. They wouldn't be happy about that on the Hill. That's why we're here. To protect what we already have. To protect the system from bankruptcy."

Jake noted with interest Terrance's ability to mold and manipulate words and figures to depict the opposite of the truth. If Terrance was doing it for Jake's sake, he needn't have bothered—Jake's <u>modus operandi</u> wasn't built on excuses, but expediency; he scorned those who pretended otherwise. And while Terrance was at his best reciting figures and deriving facts from them as he wished, Jake preferred facts derived from actual observations. But if not overly impressed with figures, Jake also realized any climb to the top involved a facility to wield figures—with more emphasis on frequency than accuracy, and more relish than relevance. In this he'd found a great teacher in Terrance Liverpool.

"We can't let that happen," Terrance paused for emphasis. "The impact of future progress must be weighed with careful foresight. Right now, large segments of society can get any medical service, and try to get Medicaid and Medicare to pay for it. But in Britain, for instance, there are no kidney transplants for those over fifty-five. How do you think they keep their total medical expenses under seven percent of their G.N.P.?" Terrance whistled admiringly. "Guidelines and eligibility, Jake, that's how! To control expenditures, we set guideline requirements and eligibility limits—we place each dollar where it will do the most good! Sure, the idea of triage and rationing is a hard one to sell. It's not popular when it comes from the government, and doesn't exactly bring in the votes. But the concept can be introduced in more subtle ways. For example, simple name changes: Triage becomes 'eligibility'; rationing becomes 'utilization review' or 'guidelines'. And suddenly, you've got a package that flies!

"Take D.R.G.'s, passed in nineteen eighty-four, as part of Medicare amendments to Section 1886 of the Social Security Act," Terrance settled comfortably into his role of economic evangelist. "D.R.G.'s set pre-planned limits for hospital days and dollars paid for any particular diagnosis, regardless of how many actual days or dollars were spent. We introduced the concept of the hypothetical 'average' patient and the hypothetical 'average' illness, and declared we've allocated enough funds to do the job. Now, it's up to the docs to get it done. And that's the beauty of it: We control the purse strings, but don't get the blame for the actual rationing, er, utilization itself. If the poor bastards can't do the job right with the funds we've set, it's their problem, not ours. We've got them doing our jobs!"

Terrance Liverpool swiveled his chair to face the view from his ninth story office: "Guidelines, Jake; guidelines and eligibility. They are the keys. It's not easy to plan for the good of our society as a whole. It's not a matter that can be left in the hands of researchers, entrepreneurs, or self-interest groups, like docs or the A.M.A. It must be thought out, planned objectively and centrally—by people with all the economic facts, and none of the biases. We must be those people, Jake." Terrance swiveled back to his desk.

It had been an admirable performance. Jake refrained from applauding, but understood why Terrance Liverpool held his job. "What can I do to help?" Jake inquired blandly.

Terrance eyed him: "It shouldn't be a particularly difficult one for you, Jake. This Camden whatever is an unknown lone-wolf researcher, without impressive credentials, just a doc." Jake observed how Terrance simply dismissed someone who'd studied twice as long, and probably trained four times as hard, as Terrance himself. Underestimating an antagonist was a flaw that could prove costly, Jake noted. "So, he either runs with us, or we break him," Terrance continued. "But we must approach him carefully, without spooking him. First, we have to be quite certain he's reasonable and open to offers. If not, we'd rather he didn't know anything until we take action. If he doesn't know what hit him, he won't be able to cause problems."

Terrance caught Jake's glance: "No, nothing that drastic. Nothing physical, Jake. If he's reasonable, there will be no problem. If not, we'll simply make him more unknown that he already is, totally discredit him, snuff him out personally and professionally. You can do your usual work, with your usual help available, and whatever else you reasonably need. We do expect you to use good judgment. We can't stand by you if you don't. Understand? Of course, there will be the usual bonus for the job done right. Any questions?"

"A couple, if I may. First, do you want this doc to immediately cease working on the project we discussed?"

"Not necessarily cease. We do want a lid on it. But there are options. If he wishes to work for us, it may simply involve a 'delay'—we might call it a 'time expansion', if you will—to perfect the idea, and plan the logistics."

"If he agrees to a delay, excuse me—a 'time expansion'—but asks for how long, what should I tell him?"

"We'd have to be completely certain of the man and his motives, Jake. He'd have to be absolutely reliable. One way of assuring that would be his unconditional agreement to a time frame that's totally our decision. In essence, he'd be selling his idea to us; he could continue to work on development, but management would be totally ours. Of course, our inducements would also be guaranteed. You've seen figures on our buyouts before."

Jake nodded, warming to the smell of action. "Understood. What if he agrees at the start, but later has second thoughts?"

"There would be the standard contracts, and enough other guarantees for smooth operation."

"Hmm...What if he doesn't seem approachable to possible offers or compromise?"

"Ah, that's what you're going to determine, Jake. We want a complete profile on him, in every direction. That's <u>before</u> you take any other action. Findings will be profiled and analyzed by our computers, then independently double-checked by our experts. Results will be finalized in a joint meeting, at which you'll be present. You will receive further instructions thereafter."

"Isn't this a bit unusual? Most of the time, you leave it up to me..."

"Jake, you're good. I know that. But this could be a very sensitive issue if not handled right. It has many people worried. We want the utmost finesse."

"Sounds like I should be honored to be even participating," Jake smiled.

"Correct. I was the one who insisted on you. Don't let me down."

Jake was thrown momentarily off-guard: Was Terrance actually being sincere, or carefully managing and reinforcing loyalties? "So, as I understand it, you don't want me to take any action yet?"

"Not yet, Jake."

"Just gather information?"

"Correct."

"Why didn't you say so before?"

"I wanted to see if we were on the same wavelength first, Jake, the same ballpark. As usual, we are."

"As usual," Jake smiled.

"We need this within a week, Jake. Complete. Can you do it?"

To avoid making it seem overly easy, Jake paused. Then, "sure."

"Good. Then appointment here, same time, in seven days," Terrance smiled and extended his hand.

"Right." Jake shook it, glancing one last time at the large, shiny, empty desk.

· · · · ·

Dr. Max McDaniel stood by the bed and read the entry on the chart once more:

> "...Final impression of multiple drug abuse, depression, paranoidal ideation, inadequate personality...culminating in several suicidal gestures and attempts. Prognosis: poor. Inpatient treatment not covered by Medicaid, nor likely to benefit in the long term. Referral to half-way house, with antidepressant PROZAC 20 mg, and incremental doses of 10 mg per week until adequate response or 50 mg reached. Psychiatric Clinic follow-up in one week."
>
> James J. Turner.
> Psych Resident II.

Max couldn't recognize Tammy Clarendon from the chart and finally closed it. "So," he asked awkwardly, "are you going to the half-way house?"

She shook her head. "I can't."

"Why not?"

"It won't do any good."

"You mean you won't try."

She sat upright on the bed, hair combed, but not wearing makeup, waiting for her clothes and discharge papers. She tried to look away. "It's not that simple, Dr. McDaniel. I wish it was."

"What's so complicated about it? You'll have a place to stay, a fresh start."

"You still don't see, do you?" She continued to look away. "People know me, they'll come looking for me. Do I have to spell it out for you? I'm worth too much money for them to leave me alone."

Max said nothing.

"I thought you'd figured that out. But I guess we're not even in the same ballpark, are we?" She faced him now, eyes set in shadows, trying to convince him of a terrible truth, and at the same time banish any dangerous illusions and hopes of her own. "Girls like me, we're the pimps' bread and butter. We're bought, rented, traded, sold—we're for 'johns', pictures, magazines, movies."

"Why are you telling me all this?" Max slurred his words, head down, as if hit by an unseen jab.

"Because I want you to leave me alone. I want you to realize nothing can be done."

Max gathered himself slowly, as if getting up from the canvas against the count. Looking at her now, the smile that had flourished briefly on her face seemed like a dream, summer butterflies scattered by a gust of autumn wind. "I don't believe that," he said finally. "Maybe I don't understand, or maybe I'm a fool, Tammy...but I don't believe nothing can be done."

"You're not a fool, Max. You just see things in mirrors of kindness," she said softly. The summer butterflies returned to her face.

They both sat quietly, wondering perhaps where new worlds might lead, or end. Seasons, reasons, and questions without answers flew by.

Max looked up first. "I suppose there's no place of your own you could go they wouldn't know about?"

"Don't have a place of my own."

"Have you tried any of the half-way homes before?"

She shook her head, meeting his gaze.

"I know you're afraid, Tammy. But what can really happen to you there? You can't be the first girl this has happened to, and they've got people there to help you."

"Maybe not there," Tammy began to shake, "maybe nothing will happen while I'm there. But afterwards..." her shaking continued like a chill near fever's end "...no one gets away. Some girls tried. Two died. The others would have been better off that way." A look of terror swept her face: "After they got done with one, they sent what was left of her south of the border... Another, after they did things to her, they forwarded her someplace... No one returns after they're forwarded, Max. They're worth little where they go, and nothing back here." Her shaking intensified and her pupils dilated: "I don't care about dying, Max. But I don't want that to happen to me... No more."

He held her to keep her from shaking. "Neither do I."

By the time she'd calmed down, Max had thought about it. "Look, there has to be a way out of this, a place to start. A half-way home is as good as any. No one's going to come in and grab you out of there. I'll come and see you, I mean, if you want. We'll take one day at a time.

"By the time you're ready to be out, we'll have another plan. I won't let anything happen to you."

"Max, you don't know who these people are," she pushed herself away. "I don't want to do that to you." Her voice was firm, and a woman's eyes flashed over the face of a child.

"So, letting them hurt you instead is going to solve things? Look at me, Tammy. Please give yourself a chance."

"I don't want them to hurt you, too. You don't deserve it."

"They couldn't hurt me as much as not knowing what's happened to you—that you might still be hurting yourself, or that they might be hurting you."

"Why?"

"Maybe a hundred different reasons, Tammy. Maybe only one. It doesn't really matter. All I know is, your future doesn't have to be like your past." Max stood as the nurse brought Tammy's clothes and discharge papers. "I'll be back in a few minutes."

When Max returned, Tammy sat with her arms clasped around her knees, head down and hair to one side, exposing the delicate length of her neck. She didn't hear him enter. A worn blue dress with a crewneck drew in at the waist, then pleated down to above the ankles. Waves of auburn hair lay like evening sky over the deep blue sea of her dress.

"Tammy?"

"Oh, Max" she looked up. Her face went blank for a moment, then refocused. "I'm ready to go."

"Where?"

"No particular place."

"I called a cab. For the half-way house. Here's the address."

"Don't have a reason to go there."

Max looked at her. "Yes, you do."

Her eyes went far away again, glowing yet sad, as if watching the sun melt into earth's horizon at dusk. She inclined her head. "Will you come visit me?"

"Absolutely."

"Then maybe I do have a reason."

Max extended his hand. "Got everything?"

She smiled a little. "Don't have much." She took his hand and stood up.

A taxi waited at the hospital entrance. "It came so soon..." she said. Max pressed her hand and said nothing. Tammy realized she was still holding his hand. She raised it up to her cheek. "You're sweet."

"Promise me, Tammy..."

"What?"

"Promise you'll be there when I come visit."

Her eyes were soft, without their previous fear. "I will." She got into the taxi, and Max closed the door.

As the taxi pulled away, Max could have believed all that had happened was only a dream. Then he saw that look of fear return to her eyes, as she looked back and waved goodbye.

· · · · ·

Five stories up, after evening rounds in the lab room of Med Team I, Cameron looked up from the microscope: "What was it you wanted to talk about, Lucy?"

"Dr. Cameron, did you know Dr. Arhends?"

"What about him?"

"Look, I know they're keeping what happened with him under wraps. He happened to be my Resident on the Hematology/Oncology

Service—he was a very dedicated doctor, and a nice man. He understood patients from their point of view, had the ability to walk a mile in their shoes. That's probably what happened to him: One day he went out a mile too far, and just couldn't make the trip back."

"Dealing with cancer is not the easiest part of medicine," Cameron acknowledged, waiting to see what else Lucy had to say.

"Dealing with <u>patients</u> who have cancer," she corrected him, "is probably at medicine's sharpest emotional cutting edge."

Cameron nodded. Suddenly he felt inadequate about his own slow research efforts. It had been a hobby, a pastime rather than an obsession, removed in a way from the daily lives of people who might need it.

"He was a perfectionist, like you, Dr. Cameron, though I suppose you're a bit more mellow about it."

"Dr. Carlton, you can leave out the 'doctor' from my name—remember, I'm 'more mellow' about it."

"Yes, but this is a medical matter, Dr. Cameron. Perhaps I'm more comfortable this way. At any rate, Dr. Arhends was working on several projects before he...died. One of the things that concerned him most was the lack of clues, or epidemiologic tracers, for cancer and some other diseases. I mean, coronary disease has its smoking, sedentary, diet, and cholesterol factors to mark it; emphysema has pollution and cigarette smokers; valvular heat disease has rheumatic fever, and so on. But for most cancers, we have no good tracers.

"Now suppose certain viruses cause an increase in cancers, say, twenty to forty years later. I mean, that's not unthinkable, since 'slow viruses' have been found to cause late neurologic disease, and the ravages of tertiary syphilis visit the brain decades after initial infection. Or suppose even a few of the hundreds of viruses people get over a lifetime later cause something else—how could we translate this into medical knowledge connecting the two? There was even a patient in clinic with measles <u>and</u> chicken pox at the same time, which is not supposed to happen, but it did. What could the results of that be in ten to thirty years? Maybe nothing—probably nothing—then again, maybe something. Maybe there are significant connections between some of the infectious diseases that we take for granted, and more serious disease later in life, ranging from autoimmune thyroid disorders to rheumatoid arthritis. The point is we won't be able to make the connections unless we look.

"But now, if a patient has a mild disease, such as flu or bronchitis, it's just buried someplace in a chart of one hundred pages—hell, some charts are thousands of pages!" To hear Lucy say "hell" was like witnessing an Ivy League coed walk into a prom with a sweatshirt on. Cameron's mouth gaped. "Sure," she continued, "we can figure out a certain viral gastroenteritis causes polio, if it happens right after that infection. But what if a disease takes years, or even decades to develop? How can we connect the two in a chart of one hundred to a thousand pages? Minute details of multiple illnesses lie buried there, without a common thread, and without any simple way we can identify and retrieve any particular illness, or the sum total summary of all illnesses. We're taught in medical school how to diagnose and treat diseases, but only rudimentarily are we guided on how to record and organize that into a meaningful whole over a patient's entire lifetime. It's as if we're using electron microscopy to peer into life's secrets, but are still transcribing them onto stone tablets."

Cameron flashed on his own pages full of contributions to medical records, with little overall sense of where the patient's health history had been, or where it was going. He couldn't help feeling she was right. "So where do we go from here?"

"That's what Arhends was working on. He showed me what he was doing, and it made sense. I don't know, maybe I just liked it because I get lost in charts more easily than others. I mean, I can talk to a clinic patient about the stomach pains he has this week, but I'm not sure if the symptoms are like those he's had in the past—from esophagitis, hiatus hernia, or peptic ulcer—or whether they're unconnected, and a totally new problem. And did the patient already have an upper G.I. to check for ulcers? Or an ultrasound of the gallbladder for stones? Or a nuclear gallbladder scan? Or any one of twenty more tests? Which ones were done? When? With what results? That's not easy to find in hundreds of chart or electronic pages with little organization. Meanwhile, eleven more patients are waiting, and the one in front of me expects an answer."

"Maybe if we worked like lawyers," Cameron smiled, "we could go over each patient and chart for hours, days, even months.... Of course, by then, the patient could be dead."

But Lucy was on a roll, ignoring Cameron's remarks: "So I can either review a cumbersome chart, or start the work-up from scratch, beginning with all kinds of tests anew. Since it takes less time to order lab tests than review a case history and think about it, that's what most of us do, though it may not be the best or most economical way."

"You're right, Lucy. We have a lot of ground to cover—from past symptoms, diagnosis, and treatment, to a patient's present condition—and with only a short time to do it. It must be done right, and it's not just you who gets bogged down. But we either ignore the lack of cohesion, repeat lab tests already done, or fall asleep with eyes red over charts, electronic or paper, thick as pillows. So, what do you have up your sleeve?"

Lucy pressed on without answering: "Not only do we wind up repeating lab tests, but perhaps not even the right ones. Or perhaps when a new piece of the puzzle falls into place and we're near making an elusive diagnosis, we don't notice all the previous pieces already in place, so we miss it again. And all because patient charts resemble tomes of information warring against organization, rather than road maps."

"Granted. Now what?"

"Dr. Arhends had been working on a new system, like the <u>Weed</u> system years back, only more comprehensive. It's basically a summary of all significant diagnoses over a patient's lifetime, arranged yearly and by organ systems—such as respiratory, cardiovascular, and so on. In abbreviated form, there could be three years per page, including medicines taken, and special consultations. He also developed a matching laboratory summary. Since the summaries are arranged in rows and columns, information can be gathered at quick glance. New information is added at the end of each visit, as needed, and can easily be adapted to electronic charting." Lucy set down a chart with multicolored pages.

Cameron glanced at them: "Blue, pink?"

"Sure. The summaries are easier to pick out. Colors were my choice; the rest was basically his. Want to look at them?"

Cameron didn't figure he had a choice. He went over the papers. Organization was deceivingly simple: The diagnostic summary followed along organ systems, much in the order a physical exam was done; the laboratory summary included rows of tests arranged in common order. What was unusual was the precision of columns and rows, that distilled a patient's history, instead of having to dissect it out of the innards of a patient chart. Even more unusual was that someone hadn't thought of this a long time ago. "A bit like the wheel," Cameron whistled, "simple, but essential."

"A mode of transportation," Lucy nodded, "for thoughts."

"It's got potential, Dr. Carlton."

"You can call me Lucy," she grinned. "Now I need your permission to add these to my patients' charts."

"Sounds like a lot of work. But I don't see why not."

"I'm hoping once I get it started, other Interns and Residents will see the summaries and continue adding to them."

"And if they don't?"

"Well, as you said, they can hardly miss the colors. And if they follow-up on it, after a few years the charts can be analyzed for any positive impact the summaries may have had." She swung her shoulder length hair. "If they don't, well, I'm willing to take that chance. I believe Dr. Arhends was onto something. I won't let it just drop."

"He left it in good hands," Cameron said.

"Does this mean I can start using it?"

"Yes, Dr. Carlton. Of course, all the rest of your work must be as before. This will only be an addition."

"Thanks, Dr. Cameron."

And thank you, Dr. Arhends, he thought. Something of him had remained in their midst. Lucy Carlton carried it forward with a zeal that took Cameron years back to a race that had been his best, and his worst. It had also been his last. After that summer came his first year of med school, and a part-time job in a research lab, learning the nuts and bolts of extracting DNA and isolating messenger RNA. Working with the riddles of genetics and the building blocks of life had been one of Cameron's lifelong dreams, much as other kids on the block dreamt of rebuilding roadsters and Corvettes. Ahead of him now waited a new adventure, a new track, with a long run ahead. Finish line unknown.

Cameron finished up and went to the cafeteria for dinner. He saved some leftovers for the canines, which made it a tossup whether the chorus of barks greeting his entrance at the research lab were for him, or for the treats. Wildwolf showed off by standing and balancing front paws upon the bars, head cocked after each bark, waiting to see if he'd been understood. Apparently he had, since Cameron released him and the other M.R.'s to feed them.

Afterwards, M.R.'s 7 and 8 followed Cameron, M.R. 9 rested, and Wildwolf investigated the bunny and guinea pig cages with obvious interest and unclear intentions. But exam time cut Wildwolf's visitations short. He hopped onto the exam table without hesitation, and turned onto his back, pawing the air, with a silly grin from jowls that flapped upside-down. The other M.R.'s were also easily coaxed onto the exam table, with the enticement of post-exam bone treats. M.R. 9, with the most recent belly scar, would have been just as content to bypass the exam, and go directly to the treats.

Cameron recorded the entries in his log, then turned off the lab's main lights, leaving only the spot brights over the microscopes and desk. He liked those soft patches of light, diffusing into a calm and undistracting darkness. Shadows from his pen and moving hands played across the light, as he checked tissue cultures and slides. The mind focused on some answers, then wandered onto even more questions.

Two and a half hours later, Cameron closed his files and log, replaced biopsy and tissue slides in their drawers, and returned all cultures to their incubators. Rose-colored temperature indicators blinked, and orange dials glowed like instrument panels on a nocturnal transcontinental journey. In reality, the journey was even more remote.

The M.R.'s were already asleep. Like children asleep past their bedtimes, Cameron lifted them and carried them to their cages. Wildwolf followed Cameron with his eyes, wide awake as his master. Perhaps it had been similar a long time ago, near the edges of the glacial ice: Somewhere, a wolf had approached a cave for shelter, and found the warmth of man's fire. Perhaps the wolf had remained there, at the fringes of the warmth; perhaps man, seeing the fire reflect strange colors from its eyes and fur, allowed it to stay. Or maybe its gray old muzzle was covered with ice, as it lingered, tired and cold. Perhaps it had simply been a child, then as now, ever bringing something fuzzy and lost home—a motherless wolf-pup—that the youngster just refused to let go, as children oft do.

However it had happened, this much was clear: Somewhere, sometime, man and animal understood each other. Wolf came to share man's shelter and warmth, and in return wolf-dog became man's hunting companion and nocturnal guardian. Cameron knelt and stroked Wildwolf's muzzle.

After tightening his shoelaces, Cameron opened a drawer and took out a brand-new leash with a silvery clasp. Sensing the occasion, Wildwolf sat still, chest full and ears as erect and dignified as possible. Cameron clasped the leash to Wildwolf's collar.

Out in the night, with fog curling in darkness around their feet, and senses keyed more on legs and stride than their eyes—they ran.

CHAPTER 9

AUTUMN WINDS

"Items such as masks, cannulas, and tubing are not covered for oxygen systems purchased on or after June 1, 1989."

—Medicare Bulletin, No. 89-6, 9/89.

"(oxygen) Coverage is not provided for:
- patients with angina pectoris in the absence of hypoxemia;
- patients who experience breathlessness without cor pulmonale or evidence of hypoxemia;
- patients with severe peripheral vascular disease resulting in clinically evident desaturation in one or more extremities;"

—Medicare Bulletin, No. 89-5, 8/89.

"When a percutaneous transluminal coronary angioplasty (PICA) is performed, a surgical 'stand-by' team is usually available to provide surgical intervention should such become necessary. Unless such surgical services are rendered, members of this team <u>do not</u> provide identifiable patient care and, therefore, <u>such stand-by services are not covered</u> by Medicare."

—Medicare Bulletin, No. 89-5, 8/89.

"If PRO preprocedure authorization has not been provided, Medicare will not cover these services:
- Cholecystectomy
- Major Joint Replacement
- Bunionectomy
- Inguinal Hernia Repair
- Transurethral Resection of the Prostate
- Coronary Artery Bypass Graft
- Carotid Endarterectomy
- Hysterectomy
- Complete Peripheral Vascular Bypass
- Cataract Surgery

—Medicare Bulletin, No. 89-5, 8/89.

"Charges for injections, e.g., vitamins, given simply for the gen-eral good and welfare of the patient and not as accepted therapy for a particular illness will be denied."

—Medicare Bulletin, No. 89-5, 8/89.

"Routine physical examinations and screening procedures are not covered by Medicare."

—Medicare Bulletin page 12, No. 86-1, 1986.

"Medicare does not cover routine pap smears."

—Roche Biomedical Laboratories, 9/1/89.

"In the absence of injury or direct exposure, preventive immu-nizations (vaccination or inoculation) against such diseases as polio, diphtheria, tetanus, etc., is not covered."

—Medicare Bulletin, No. 89-5, 8/89.

"Code 99058 (office services provided on an emergency basis) is not covered by Medicare."

—Medicare Bulletin, No. 89-5, 8/89.

"... autologous bone marrow transplantation for these conditions will be denied as not medically reasonable and necessary: Acute leuke-mia in relapse..."

—Medicare Bulletin, No. 89-5, 8/89.

"And your suggestion that cost savings would be the government's overriding consideration is obscene."

—Pete Stark (Dem. – Calif.)
House of Representatives of the U.S.,
Health Subcommittee Chairman,
During testimony on Bill H.R. 1692, 1989.

"Please come in." A male secretary looked over Jacob Werner's I.D. card. "Mr. Werner, we've been expecting you." He announced Jake's presence over the intercom, and a door buzzed open. It led to a small waiting room, empty but for several chairs. Another door unlocked, and Jake stopped into a large suit with oval mahogany desks, flanked by computer banks, two giant TVs, and a projection screen.

Terrance Liverpool sat at the head of one table, with three panel members seated a respectful distance away. Terrance motioned Jake to join them. With only five people, the large suite appeared mechanical, devoid of personality. Then again, the carefully appointed suite, guarded by double ingress and no windows, had been designed for such faceless tasks: Among them, it analyzed personalities, in order to change them, buy them, erase them, or destroy them.

"Jacob, meet our panel of psychological experts, Ron and Johnny. And this is Drew, our economist and statistician. Drew, tell us about this grant proposal. Exhibit 'C', and what it would mean."

Urbane in a light gray suit only a cut below Terrance's (perhaps purposely so), Drew wielded a pointer caressingly over one of the screens dotted with figures. "The following are projected data for our 'C' file. First, for a basis of comparison, we have cost figures for the application of previous medical technologic advances. Take for example, transplants: 1985 saw nine thousand two hundred and six total transplants." Drew's pointer punctuated the screen: "719 heart transplants, 632 liver, 130 pancreas, 30 total heart/lung. And the numbers grow yearly. To date, over 90,000 kidney transplants have been supplied, and at present there's still a waiting demand for 10,000 more. Specific initial costs for kidney transplants ran over fifty thousand dollars, while those for liver transplants range to five times as much. Heart transplants were over hundred thousand, but if all restrictive criteria were removed for recipients, total cost for heart transplant programs could reach well ten billion."

Drew skipped over a few slides. "So far, we've been able to slow transplants considerably by simply dragging our feet on federal organ-finding networks. There's also an added clause that 'advancing years, or those beyond 53 to 57' would not be considered suitable candidates for heart transplants—by definition excluding Medicare patients over 65.

"On the other hand, younger patients have to wait 29 months to obtain Medicare coverage, by which time they're no longer alive to need the transplant."

At intervals, or after making a point, an efficiently packaged smile flashed across Drew's face, in rhythm with the pointer's flicker atop the screen. "Now, cost for the transplant procedures themselves, or for similar technology, pales by comparison to the added maintenance costs for extended longevity achieved. And once technologic advances are applied, further technology—and funds—are consumed to maintain them." The smile flashed on again. "The greatest additional expense occurs," the screen changed data, "with the increased longevity. You'll note these patients continue to require care for a variety of unrelated conditions, over a longer lifetime—demanding an ever-increasing slice of the Medicare budget." The smile flashed on again. "In fact, for every dollar spent on a life-saving transplant, another two will be required for further medical care over the added lifespan. To put it more bluntly, gentlemen, it's that added longevity in a tax-negative population—one that consumes more tax benefits than it pays out—that's the massive underbelly of our Medicare budget iceberg."

Drew paused for effect, with his same smile. "As for project 'C', based on our previous data, even at a fifty percent success rate, here's what we'll have." The pointer followed numbers across the screen. "Actual procedural costs for some sort of genetic implants or transplants might be somewhat less than for full-fledged transplants. Initial estimates are two hundred million for the first year, climbing to over two billion within three to five years." Drew let that sink in.

"Also, please note the two-for-one added costs for longevity, as we discussed previously, escalating the total costs within a few years to nearly five billion dollars."

Terrance whistled.

"Of course," Drew continued, "that's assuming Mr. Jacob's data is correct," he nodded towards Jake. "And we must keep in mind there may be some revolutionary new genetic concepts involved. We don't have much experience in this field, so the numbers could go even higher."

"What makes you say they'd go higher?" Jake inquired.

"Well," Drew smiled, "they seldom go lower than predicted."

"Other questions?" Terrance asked. "Then let's get on with Ron's report and analysis on the 'C' information you've provided, Jake. Afterwards, we'll discuss disposition and implementation. Please go on, Ron."

"Of course," Ron smiled, "we're going on the assumption that the data Mr. ah...Jacob provided is correct." (Last names were studiously omitted to avoid overfamiliarity in clandestine operations.) "You know the saying: Garbage in, garbage out; versus what we hope to be doing, precious stones in, diamonds out. He, he..."

Jake's countenance remained as unclouded as expressions around a high-stake poker game. Terrance waited for the rest, impassively Olympian.

Noting the lack of acknowledgment, Ron cleared his throat. "Ahem. The subject in question, a John Cameron, graduated from the University of Washington, School of Medicine five and a half years ago." Ron's monotone was punctuated by silent changes on the monitor screen, displaying a curriculum vitae dating back to grade school. "Such aspects of the subject's past are no doubt already well known to Mr. Jacob," Ron remarked, intending to make amends for his previous comment. Jake nodded.

"Here are med school grades by subject, and National Boards Parts I, II, and III. There are some interesting, but unpredictable patterns—average or high average on most subjects, exceptional in a few others." Ron paused. "An interesting sideline here: He ran track, high school and college, mostly sprint events. Not bad, but again, unpredictable performances. He was trained the last few years by—and here's a coincidence—Dr. Mark Sullivan, who's the chap who actually applied for the grant for ah...J. Cameron." The monotone continued, accompanied by image changes on the screen. "Here's a stint as an oarsman—four and eight-man crews, could row either port or starboard. Again, unpredictable performances, and too short for a heavyweight crew."

Jake smiled to himself—"unpredictable performances"—that meant sometimes just running on guts. Cameron could prove to be an interesting adversary, Jake mused. He liked the prospect of landing a tough fighting fish. That was the difference between himself and the others—while he desired position and power, he disliked the inactivity that went with it. Activity for Jake meant direct challenges, the field of the outside world, not data banks and boardrooms. Away from what he was used to, boredom would set in, like a lonely beer in an empty bar on a Saturday night. Eventually, of course, retirement would creep up, and then a change of pace together with power and position, would be enough. Enough to forget the past, the jungles, and wars they weren't allowed to win. Until then, his present tasks would keep Jake entertained, and he had plenty of time to observe the powers that be, and to plan his inclusion among them.

The slide show was over. Projection had stopped on data about the grant application, and cost numbers for the research project itself.

"Thank you, Ron," Terrance looked across the table. "And what have you got for us, Johnny?"

Bearded and thick set, Johnny looked the part of an analytic psychologist, more so than Ron, who was the meticulous statistician of the two. Even down to the shoelaces, Ron had his tied to exact even length, while Johnny was lucky to have them on at all, let alone tied in any fashion.

Johnny stroked his beard. "Well, both general statistical and coned-down analysis of 'C's profile show no large or obvious areas we can wedge into. A brief romantic interlude in college, which ended rather suddenly; grades correspondingly dip a bit there; athletic performance parallels same. Other life changes leave no visible impact. That is, despite setbacks, overall performances continue unchanged or follow his own uniquely erratic pattern: Mostly solid and reliable, occasionally dipping below; and sometimes, for no apparent reason, even inspired. In short, for our purposes, basically unpredictable."

"What's the bottom line?" Terrance inquired in an unhurried cadence, savoring the words.

It was then Jake realized how much Terrance relished playing the game, and his role in it. That was the key to his cunning efficiency. Perhaps the key to his downfall as well, Jake noted. He himself was also in the business of "managing" people—a euphemism at times for destroying them. But Jake's motivation was conflict, a battle of wills. Terrance's, he now knew, was to obtain a lock on power so absolute as to shape events at will, and voyeuristically watch it happen.

"The bottom line," Johnny pondered: "I'd have to say we've seen no major openings to work with so far."

Terrance's eyes narrowed. "No chinks in the armor, then?"

"Oh, there are always chinks," Ron added quickly. "We just haven't found them yet. Given more time..."

"Unfortunately, gentlemen, we don't have more time. Besides, could you guarantee any you might find would be sufficient for our purposes?"

"It's an unknown," Johnny shook his head. "Even if we do find an opening, we'd be dealing with a highly individualistic background, in which neither power nor money were that important. Add to that his ability and dedication to pursue an unlikely goal over years, without much backing, and you've got a difficult situation. I sense if we'd try to alter his path in conventional ways, it may prove unsuccessful, and perhaps ultimately dangerous."

"What's your opinion on this, Jake?"

"I'm no scientist or expert in the theory of psychology," Jake inclined his head politely. "I do see a man with no booze, broads, gambling, or drug problems. I'd have to agree with the learned gentlemen: Long hours, little pay or recognition, so there's got to be another motor driving him. That's for him to know, and us to find. But I'd bet it's under individual control, and someone else isn't going to run away with it. The rest doesn't matter, as far as I'm concerned."

"Thank you so much, gentlemen," Terrance closed the meeting abruptly, with the finality of a slam-dunk, or the closing of a book. His manicured hands remained calmly clasped in front. "We're all professionals here. I need hardly remind you that matters discussed were of a highly sensitive nature to the well-being of our society. Your knowledge of it ceases beyond these four walls. You have all been helpful, gentlemen. A service well rendered is not forgotten. Jake, will you please wait in the anteroom?"

"Certainly, sir."

Jake thumbed through old copies of Life and Discover as he waited. An ad caught his eye. On a full page, fine mist hovered over a lake at dawn. Ripples extended like smoke rings from a verdant shore. A moose waded knee-deep, its antlers silhouetted like gnarled tree roots against the crystal waters. It was an ad for some "mist" or other liquor. Jake wondered what connection alcohol had with the moose, the mist, or the lake. Not that Jake didn't enjoy his drinks. But neither moose nor mist were to be found in them, and the lake was best found as when going fishing. Jake well understood the realities that promoted packaging with beautiful girls drinking, eating, standing, or sitting on whatever was being promoted. In that context, the moose was even an artful departure. But Jake disliked that kind of misrepresentation. There was enough deceit in the work around him, and his own, that he had to constantly remind himself where the deceit should end, and reality had to begin.

Terrance buzzed the door open again. "You were insolent to those experts, Jake, right under their noses."

"What do you mean?" Jake inquired blandly.

"Never mind. I don't think they noticed it, from their towers. Besides, as you said, theory is not action."

"I said that?"

"You thought it," Terrance seemed to look right through him.

"You should have let me handle it in the first place," Jake replied calmly. He thought it better to show bluster than ambition.

"I already told you," Terrance smiled, "some of it was out of my hands."

"And now?"

"Back in my hands."

"What do you want done?"

"He must be effectively silenced. By that I mean thoroughly compromised and discredited. No hard methods: Just quiet and selective undermining at the right places. You know what I mean—an outcast to his peers, no longer a danger to society." Terrance paused. "In the process, it should also be fairly simple to acquire the basis of his ideas: Copies of papers, notebooks, lab experiments. Then we can get our boys working on it, so in case we need it for unusual circumstances, such as illness or accident in friendly heads of state, the technology will be there."

"What's the budget, Terrance? I'll need to influence a few people."

"Usual system. Anything within reasonable bounds, in light of what we're trying to accomplish."

"Thank you, sir. Time frame?"

"Process in motion immediately; effectively underway within the month; complete in three to four. Gradual enough to avoid arousing suspicion. Understood?"

"Correct, sir." Jake waited.

"One more thing, Jake."

"Sir?"

"I can't let you do this without asking you one more question." Terrance fixed him with an impassive stare. "Are you convinced what you are about to do will be for the eventual good of the society of the United States?"

Jake replied without a moment's hesitation. "Of course, sir. Aren't you?"

· · · · ·

Day after call night, 5:45 p.m. Max was finally off. He had to think about what he needed to do now. It seemed odd not to have to do anything. He remembered he wanted to see Tammy. He showered, changed, and skipped dinner. Package under arm, he rang the doorbell and waited.

After giving his name, Max was ushered into a waiting room resembling an uneasy blend of a dentist's office and a Victorian tea parlour. The slender young man showing him in fit neither, his sideburns and long hair more reminiscent of the soul-exposed sixties.

He waited silently as Max sat down, with no further introductions asked or given, until Tammy arrived.

She smiled. "Want to follow me?" They went past the kitchen and an L-shaped corridor. "It's tiny," she apologized, opening the door. "Can I get you anything from the kitchen?"

"No, I'm fine."

She looked at him. "Let me guess—just off call, and haven't eaten?"

"Yes, but..."

"I'll be right back." Before Max could say anything, he was staring at three walls and a door ajar. The room had only a chair, a bed, and a bedside drawer, reminiscent of standard hospital furnishings. Max felt at home. A hairbrush, toothbrush, and two pocketbooks shared the room beside a small gooseneck lamp. Tammy was back with a platter of cold cuts, an apple, and a glass of milk.

"Thanks, Tammy."

She sat on the bed. "Will it be enough?"

"That's just fine."

"You surprised me by coming today, Dr. McDaniel."

"If you insist on calling me Dr. McDaniel, I'll have to address you as Miss Clarendon." Max stopped in mid-bite. Tammy's face and smile were drawn to one side, her left cheek and eye puffy and darkened. "What's that?"

"Nothing...I ran into a door."

Max could see under the makeup blush two violaceous bumps about knuckle-width apart, under the eye. Max now recalled how suspiciously the slender young man had regarded him in the waiting room. "Tammy, tell me what happened. This time leave out leaping doors."

She looked down. "I didn't want to be... any trouble here, you know."

"Tammy, you didn't cause this problem," he lifted her chin. "Now tell me."

"They were waiting for me, I guess. I went to take out the trash yesterday morning...they grabbed me from their car, tried to pull me in. I was lucky, managed to bite a wrist."

Max sat next to her, and touched her cheek. "Now move your eyes up and down, there. Now side to side." He tapped gently over her sinuses. "Good, I don't think anything's broken. Any problems with your eye or vision?"

"I can see you look really nice, so I guess I don't have any problem," she smiled her askew smile. "You know, it's strange how I used to be afraid. I'm not anymore. Even after this. I think it's because you're here. I mean, I know you're not here all the time, but I still feel that way."

Max pondered something. "You shouldn't have to be afraid, Tammy." But now he realized what she'd said in the beginning was true: They'd probably be back. While Tammy became less afraid, he was sensing more danger ahead. "I need to know their names; in case something happens. And where they hang out, where they live. I need to know all you know about them. Who pulls the strings?"

"Max, I thought you said nothing would happen. Why all this worry?"

In the face of danger, or when patients faced disease, often there came denial. At times it was helpful. At others, it stood in the way of prevention. "Probably nothing will happen, Tammy. But if it does, I want to be ready."

"What are you going to do, Max? Without sleep after a night on call you're going to go look for them?"

"I'm here, aren't I?"

She touched his hand, then looked down. "I know. That's why I'm not afraid. You came, Max. I don't understand why, but you came. I feel different around you. I feel...things I shouldn't have a right to feel."

"Why do you say that?"

"You still don't know much about me, what I've done..."

"I understand you're not happy about your past. I'm here for who you are now, and who you're trying to be."

"I wish sometimes I could believe in me, the way you believe in me." She shook her head. "But what I know of my past prevents me from feeling...no, prevents me from following what I feel."

"Why?"

"Doesn't seem like that be fair to you."

"What wouldn't?"

"Nothing..." She turned her head away.

"Right. That explains everything." He found her emerald eyes and felt a shudder shake his being. "Anyway, you still need to tell me about those guys."

"From yesterday? The one's just a driver. Bill—we call him Gopher—he's got a space between his front teeth and is just a big lug who doesn't mean much harm. I don't think he can do anything but drive around and look scary. I suppose if someone really graphically explained to him what was going on, he might even find it revolting. As it is, he just sees smiles on pretty ladies, dressed the way he likes to see them, and men with money changing hands, some of which trickles down to him."

"But he'd follow their orders? He's loyal to them?"

"Sure. Never had a real family. I guess he's found a place to belong, whatever that place might be. That's what makes him loyal."

"That makes him ultimately dangerous."

"I always felt there was a little kid inside that gorilla," she said. "But I suppose little kids can be mean, too."

"What about the other one?"

"That one's not a fun guy. He's one of the outfit's enforcers, and dangerous. Jerry—don't know his last name 'cause mostly we don't hear their last names—he's really a different sort from Gopher. One of the girls, who reads a lot, nicknamed him Gar, short for gharial crocodile, for his funny teeth, close together and zipped tight. Most of the girls couldn't relate to Gar, though, so Gator stuck instead."

"Gopher and Gator. That's really going to help when I look for these guys. What else did you girls come up with?"

"Not much. You see, the one that liked to read a lot—I guess it was her escape from things—one day decided to really escape. She was a real beauty, and they figured they couldn't afford to let her go. They made an example of her, for the rest of us. They found her, made a few movies of her, you know, the kind they really didn't care what they did to her. Afterwards she disappeared. They showed the movies, as a preventive measure, to some of the girls thought 'unstable' or at risk of getting away. I never saw them," Tammy choked off a hollow laugh, "I guess they figured me, if anything, for an escape with drugs down under. Anyway, Gator was rumored to be in one of those movies, hooded, but the girls could tell from other things..."

"What I need is names, Tammy; hangouts, clubs, car license numbers, that sort of thing."

"Why? I don't want you to find them! These guys aren't in your business of saving lives! Being a doctor won't impress them, or increase your chances of surviving. A few girls had boyfriends that tried to help. I don't know what happened to them—only rumors. I do know the girls stayed."

"I don't plan on meeting them as a doctor. And probably not alone."

"The police won't help."

"Probably not."

"Well, I don't know how you're figuring, then. But I don't figure on getting you killed."

"Neither do I. And the more I know about them, the safer you and I will be."

"I'll give you what I know," she finally said, "only if you promise me you'll be careful and get help when you need it."

Max nodded. "Deal."

After he finished writing it down, she looked at him: "Is this part of your routine patient care?"

"You're not a routine patient."

"I'm a bad news lady for you. I've screwed up my life enough. Why risk yours?"

"Sometimes risks aren't that important, Tammy. Sometimes you can't run away from them. At others, you don't want to."

"That's a stubborn answer."

"You've got to be stubborn to win."

"Win what?"

"You out of their hands."

She looked at him without blinking, and he felt that shudder move through him again.

"I guess if you're willing to risk that much, I can at least risk rejection." She placed her hand behind his neck, and drew closer. "I must look a sight with this goose-egg over my eye."

"A beautiful sight."

"No rejection?"

The gaze of her eyes was like a whirlpool, and Max didn't try to say anything. Her other arm came around his back. When their lips met, breathing was no longer that important. Afterwards, he cradled his arms around her waist and held her.

"You know," she broke the silence, "I don't usually kiss..."

"Shh," he drew her tighter. "It's all right."

She rested her head between his shoulders and neck. "With you here, it's almost easy to believe that."

"Good." He touched her hair.

She smiled and pushed him away. "Not so good! You haven't touched your dinner. Here!"

"And you haven't opened your package," Max pointed to the hastily wrapped box.

"For me? What's the occasion?"

"You're the occasion."

Tammy undid the wrapping and ribbon carefully, as if planning to save it. Out came a pair of knee-high wool socks, dark green sweatpants, and a light green sweatshirt top. She drew it across her chest. "Just the right size! I'll put it on for you."

Max looked around. "You don't have to do it now. Next time'll be fine."

"You got it for me. So, I want to put it on now. You know how women are—we've got to try everything on right away. So out you go while I change. Won't be a minute."

When the door opened, her long hair lay combed over her shoulders, and her emerald eyes matched the green of her clothes. She turned around: "What do you think?"

"The clothes look good. You look even better."

"My favorite colors! Here, sit and finish your meal." Tammy stood and paced: "I feel so good right now, you know what I mean? Even this goose egg and yesterday morning—that doesn't mean anything compared to this!"

"It means you have to be very careful, Tammy."

"Sure," she nodded, "I will be. You want another sandwich or glass of milk?"

"Listen, I'd like to stay longer. But I'm starting to fade. I better get back for some shuteye."

She hugged him. "I'll miss you!"

"When do you want me back?"

"Tomorrow," she grinned.

"Tomorrow's clinic. But I could get here after clinic."

"No, I'm kidding. I know you can't come every day."

"Not every day, but tomorrow's fine. Besides, the day after is call again."

"I'll have one of these every day," she touched her shiner, "if this is the care I'll be getting." She held him tight. Then, as if reflecting and deciding something…she slowly let go. "You better go, Max."

In the waiting room, the same slender young man read a magazine. "That's Tom Barnes," Tammy said. "He's done with the program here, wants to stay on as a counselor."

"Trustworthy?"

"You bet; quiet, but a very nice guy."

"Could he be bought?" Max asked.

Tammy paused, then shrugged, and slowly shook her head.

Max understood her pause. "I'm sorry. I didn't mean it that way. I wanted to know whether your past acquaintances could enlist him, for a price, to trap you. I shouldn't have said it that way."

"Why not? You were asking for the truth. And the only truth I've always known was anyone could be bought, in one way or another: Drugs, sex, money, power. Maybe here I'll learn different."

"Tammy, I know you've sold parts of you in the past. That doesn't mean you sold your loyalties, your beliefs, your soul."

"Maybe not. I tried to kill those instead."

"I'm glad you didn't. Wait here a second." Max and Tom exchanged a few words and parted with a handshake.

"What was that about?"

"Asked him to keep an eye on strange cars hanging around and their license plates."

"Thanks, Max. I'll walk you to the car."

"We just talked about you being careful. If you walk me out, I'll just have to walk you back again. See?"

Tammy accompanied him to the door. It was dark and a cold wind blew. She shivered.

"If you need anything, Tammy, or anything starts happening, call me. You know the hospital number, where I am most of the time. Here's mine," he pressed it into her hand.

She held it without placing it in her pocket. "Max, how can I? What do I tell them at the hospital? They'll ask who I am when I call for you. I don't want them to relate me...to you."

"Tammy, how others relate and evaluate people is their problem, not ours. Those who've got time to ponder about someone else's life in detail either lack one of their own, or have nothing better to do. Just ask for me, give them your name, and tell them you're a friend."

"That simple, eh?"

"That simple," he nodded.

Tammy stared at the branches of sidewalk trees, thin and bare in early winter, their silent shadows rocking in the wind, weaving spiderwebs out of the lights of passing cars. "You think everything will be that easy?"

"No. Perhaps not that easy. But it will eventually all work out."

She looked past his shoulders, at the trees. "Have you ever wondered, Max, if trees feel?" She inclined her head. "I mean, they blossom in spring's sunlight, produce fruit in summer's warmth, then let the winds of autumn brush their leaves away, to greet winter cold, bare and asleep."

"I don't know. Maybe they do feel, to do those things."

"I'm not sure whether I should be happy that they feel life around them, or be sad since they might also feel the pain..."

"Maybe a bit like you, Tammy?"

She shook her head. "No, Max. Now that I've known happiness, even if for a brief time, it's worth any pain I might have had."

Max pressed his hands around hers. The wind blew in gusts, heavy with the smell of coming rain.

CHAPTER 10

QUO VADIS

A place we all come from
  ...a place we all go
The time in between
  ...we choose on our own.

Attending Professor Dr. Paul Morrison arrived for rounds at precisely 07:15:30. He was punctilious by nature, and meticulously groomed—like a movie star clobbered by three villains at once, and emerging victorious with not a hair out of place. Like his demeanor, his questions cut precisely, and at times unexpectedly. No amount of smoke screening oratory could cover up ignorance or inattention in his presence. Though he was a scourge to those unwilling to work hard, he gave as much of himself as he expected of others. At those rare times when even he didn't seem to know the answer, he'd pause, hands clasped under his chin as if in prayer, breathing slowly and evenly like a tai-chi instructor, until noiseless gears combined senses, hunches, knowledge, and experience into a lineup of possible solutions.

"Good morning, doctors."

"Good morning, Dr. Morrison." Their unison reply was reminiscent of marine recruits saluting their Drill Instructor. They fanned out across the ward's halls like a platoon securing a bridge. Before achieving their objective, without breaking stride, Dr. Morrison noted the Orders of the Day had been broken. "Dr. Cameron, I presume you're acquainted with requirements for clean (he meant sparkling, like his own oxfords) shoes? Your choice of suede, which can't be shined, was clever. However, a Resident should be an example to his team. By showing respect for yourself, you show respect for the patients you treat."

One of the Interns suppressed a snicker.

Dr. Morrison turned around. "Dr. Saxton, would you be so kind as to tell us how we can deduce Dr. Cameron's been spending his early morning hours in the canine lab, which perhaps made him feel exempt from our more mundane attire requirements?"

"Ah, well..." Saxton gave it up, not even attempting a diversionary tactic.

"Dr. Cameron's shoes carry dry kibble particles," Dr. Morrison began. "Since we can assume those were not from his own breakfast, and since the university's experimental labs have a limited range of animal species, from the type of food particle we can conclude Dr. Cameron's been working in a canine lab." He paused. "You see, Dr. Saxton, powers of observation can be honed even from the humblest of places. And unearned humor, during patient care hours, can be best left where it belongs, on the TV set." Dr. Morrison had said it plainly, but without rancor. And he expected to say it only once. His quarrel wasn't so much with lack of facts or knowledge--but against inattention, laziness, and lack of commitment to continue learning—he waged war.

Rounds continued smoothly thereafter, and Dr. Carlton had concluded a patient presentation. "Technically good," Dr. Morrison noted. "Clinically good" was even better, but any accolade from Dr. Morrison was an achievement.

"You whore!" Came a yell from about room 509. "You're bleeding me to death!" A phlebotomist—lab technician who drew blood samples—scurried out of the room, shaking her head.

"We were about to present Mrs. Gates next," Cameron calmly remarked. "Dr. Saxton?"

Dr. Saxton didn't need to consult his patient cards. "Mrs. Gates, sixty-four years old, was brought by her husband five days ago, with multiple complaints. Chief among them were bedsores, left arm pains, and headaches." Joel flashed back to the evening Mrs. Gates arrived. He'd drawn her chart from the gurney: "Hello, Mrs. Gates, I'm Dr. Saxton. I'll be taking care of you while you're here."

"What's this place? I don't want to be here!"

There was no emergency Red Blanket on her gurney, but Joel knew there were cases more difficult than emergencies. At least emergencies achieved a certain clarity near death, a quick vision that if something wasn't done for a particular organ system, there wouldn't be additional time to improve anything else. Treatment had to be swift, to the point. Then it either worked. Or it didn't.

But others swirled like castaways at the brink of some nameless ocean's giant whirlpool, slowly but inexorably drawing closer, without ever achieving that final clarity. They never looked quite right, and felt even worse. Despite the use of all present medical knowledge, they refused to fit any known patterns, resisted exact diagnoses, and remained enigmas to the end, awaiting future medical knowledge that for them would come too late.

"What can I do for you, Mrs. Gates?"

"Nothing! You can't do nothin'!" Dry lips pouted with thin spittle drawn between.

Perhaps she was right. But it was his job to try. A sense of futility settled over him. He tried again: "Anything bothering you?"

"Everything's bothering! Everything!" She shook her head violently from side to side. The rest of her body lay bloated, immobile, wheezing dysrhythmically like a whale beached out of water. Below a sparse mantle of graying hair, coarse dark hairs grew over beard and mustache areas.

Joel remembered trying again: "So what's bothering you the most? Can we start with that?"

"This," she moaned, lifting a padded left arm with her right hand. Joel had examined it. It was softly padded, to keep her paralyzed left hand from stiffening like a claw.

"Take it off! It hurts!"

Joel had been puzzled, but took the splint off as she requested. Then he concentrated on her more obvious problem of wheezing. "Are you short of breath?"

"A little." Each breath's end rattled like a chainsaw caught in a log.

"Are you coughing?"

She looked at the ceiling. "I don't want to be here."

"Do you have any chest pains?"

"Fuck off!"

"Dr. Carlton," Dr. Morrison interrupted Joel's thoughts, "what do you notice about Mrs. Gates expletives?"

"Ah...they're quite frank...I mean, very explicit."

"We realize that. What else?"

"I'm not sure what you mean: Her speech isn't slurred; it doesn't always make sense, but sometimes it does..."

"What else?"

"Some of the expletives are repetitive..."

Dr. Morrison nodded. "So we do get some insight into Mrs. Gates' cognitive status. You will also notice she watches us for a reaction. She observes. Please continue, Dr. Saxton."

Continue where? Saxton thought. There were so many loose ends, and Mrs. Gates had told him nothing over the past five days. The only information he'd received was from her husband. "Since Mrs. Gates couldn't cooperate with a present or past history," Joel went on, "it was obtained from her husband."

A wiry man in his sixties, still firm of jaw, with a military-trim mustache, Mrs. Gates' husband had come while Joel was still fumbling with ways to obtain a coherent medical history. "She won't tell you anything," he'd said. "I'm Mr. Gates. I'll try to fill you in."

"Glad to meet you. I'm Dr. Saxton. I've already read the Emergency Room notes, but I'll need some more background. She had some kind of operation. What was that?"

"They took some blood clots from the right side of the brain."

"Was that after some kind of accident?"

"Oh, yes, a truck hit her, and she dented her side of the car door with her head."

"Could she walk after the accident?"

"Not well. She couldn't move her left side at all, and the right wasn't good either. That's why they had to operate."

Sounded like a subdural hematoma, Joel had thought. "Did she walk after the operation?"

"For a while. But then she stayed in bed more and more..."

"When did she totally stop walking?"

"A year later..."

"She's been in bed ever since?"

Mr. Gates nodded.

"Do you know why that happened?"

He shook his head. "It happened so slowly...she gained weight..." Mr. Gates pulled a wrinkled photo from his wallet. "That's her, before the accident."

A blonde woman with short curly hair smiled with a rabbit grin and eyes to match. She looked like a ballet star taking a bow. "She was very pretty," Joel said truthfully, trying not to look from the photograph to the patient on the bed.

Mr. Gates said nothing. He replaced the photo carefully within the wallet.

"You've been taking care of her by yourself?"

Mr. Gates nodded. "We moved from Ohio a few months ago. She could still sit up, and I could turn her from the bed onto a commode. The last few weeks I couldn't."

"When was the last time she saw a doctor?"

"About nine months ago. That was to fill her Dilantin and phenobarbital."

"How much of each does she take?"

"Thirty of phenobarbital, and three hundred of Dilantin."

"When was her last seizure?"

"Three years ago."

"Any seizures since then?"

"No."

Dr. Saxton continued relating the history, irregularly punctuated by various obscenities from Mrs. Gates. Through it all, Dr. Morrison remained still, hands clasped and resting below his chin. He turned to Lucy Carlton: "Dr. Carlton, we've heard a fairly complex history. What would be your approach now?"

"The patient's problems center on neurologic, respiratory, and endocrine systems. At present, I see no obvious unifying disease entity, so I would look at each system individually."

"Begin with one," Dr. Morrison nodded.

Dr. Carlton had a high-pitched voice that became even more so when she was nervous. "Well, neurologically, Mrs. Gates could have significant problems from three sources: The past M.V.A. head injury, the subsequent surgery, or a separate disease process affecting the brain. Complicating variables are Mrs. Gates' history of seizures, and her anti-convulsant medication of Dilantin and phenobarbital, which could contribute side effects to her basic condition." Lucy finished, resting her shins against the edge of the bed.

Dr. Morrison nodded. "Thank you, Dr. Carlton. Now would you please not lean against the patient's bed? It may seem a trivial matter, but patients pay dearly for those beds. While they're in the hospital, those beds are their property. I'm not against appropriate familiarity with patients, Dr. Carlton, but out of respect for them and their property, a simple 'may I?' before leaning or sitting on their beds would suffice. Otherwise, a basic erect position is adequate."

In Mrs. Gates' case, Joel thought the reply to such a question would be interesting. But his back, along with the others', stiffened enough to make a marine D.I. proud. In the process, Joel observed that the more Lucy tried to stand straight after Dr. Morrison's remark, the more her lower back curved and accentuated the round rise below.

Joel's exploration of geometric patterns was cut short: "Dr. Saxton, could you give us examples of endocrine or respiratory system problems that could affect the neurologic system, or be part of a 'unifying disease entity' as Dr. Carlton stated?"

Joel's glandular visions crumbled. "In the endocrine system..." Dr. Saxton paused, "hypothyroidism would slow mentation, and exacerbate other neurologic disorders." He fingered the patient cards in his pocket as if they were Braille, hoping such tangible medical proximity would clear his mind.

For some perverse reason, Joel's mind refused to comply in an orderly fashion. As in frustrated erections, the harder he tried, the worse things got: His mind hovered in reverse, travelled to last night's dreams, or to Lucy Carlton's blue blouse stretching with her breathing. Just as Dr. Morrison turned to Dr. Cameron, Joel came out of his stall-dive: "Oxygen, of course. Any severe pulmonary disease, such as the asthma Mrs. Gates has, would decrease available oxygen, and further compromise cerebral function."

"Could you give us a more complete list, Dr. Saxton?"

"Pneumonia, although her X-rays were negative..."

Dr. Morrison closed in: "Just give us a possible, not necessarily probable list, Dr. Saxton."

"Ah...yes. Pulmonary embolus would be high on the list, due to prolonged immobility; tuberculosis is possible, but not likely, although this could also bring on central nervous system T.B." Joel felt his brain-lock finally subsiding: "Also any of the fungal or viral pneumonias, emphysema, chronic bronchitis, bronchiectasis, and even tumors," Dr. Saxton paused, pleased with his extended list.

"Good," Dr. Morrison nodded. "Any others?"

"Not at the moment," Dr. Saxton answered. He doubted he'd missed many, and was ready for the bell marking round's end, and a deserved rest.

But there was no bell or round's end. "Dr. Cameron, would you care to expand on that list?" Morrison asked.

"Along the lines Dr. Saxton developed," Cameron tried to make his Intern look good, "immobility and central nervous system dysfunction predisposes to aspiration pneumonia or aspirated foreign body; there could also be work-related pneumoconiosis, asbestosis; and the connective tissue disorders and vasculitis of Lupus, Wegener's, or Goodpasture's. Vasculitis also reminds me of disorders of the heart which could result in vascular changes of the lungs, cor pulmonale, and pulmonary hypertension."

"Any others?" Dr. Morrison directed the question at all of them, and waited. "Well, along the lines you've already developed," Dr. Morrison smiled, "parasitic pneumonias should be added to viral, fungal and bacterial. And of the medications Mrs. Gates is on, diphenylhydantoin could rarely cause a lupus -like vasculitis, or pulmonary fibrosis. There are also other diseases of unknown cause, such as amyloidosis and sarcoidosis." Dr. Morrison paused: "Dr. Carlton, would you give us a brief explanation of the mechanisms of connective tissue and autoimmune disorders?"

Dr. Carlton stared ahead. How could she briefly explain C.T.D.'s—the Connective Tissue Diseases—and their mechanisms? Comprising a wide range of disorders and illnesses, they were also known as autoimmune diseases, because a major common element was the immune system's misguided attack on the body's own components. How and where the attack occurred determined the specific C.T.D. process. The severity of the attack decided life or death.

Lucy tried to picture it in her mind: It began in the fluid highways of the bloodstream. Their most numerous inhabitants, "erythrocytes" (from the Greek <u>erythros</u> red), were saucer-shaped red cells that ferried oxygen through a maze of arteries, arterioles, veins, venules, and a labyrinth of 50,000 miles of capillaries—from the humblest cells of a toenail, to the highest of neurons trickling electricity. In size, erythrocytes were one of the smallest creatures in the bloodstream—7 micrometers, or 100 times smaller than a human hair; in number they were the largest—2.5×10^{13}, or over 100 times more numerous than all the stars in the Milky Way Galaxy.

Interspersed among the oxygen carrying red cells were the "leukocytes" (from the Greek leukos, white), whose task it was to defend the body against invasion. This White Army, 1,000 times less numerous than the red cells, was composed of multiple fighting units of complex and varied strategies. Bacterial or fungal foe? The "polymorphonuclear" and most numerous group of the White Army—"polys" or "PMN's" for short—tracked the enemy down with a guidance system called chemotaxis; then, with a size twice that of a red cell, grappled in hand to hand combat with bacteria and fungi, usually engulfing them. Even the most fearsome of bacteria, such as staphylococcus aureus—"golden staph"—usually succumbed to the poly's search and destroy missions.

At times when the battleground was tipped toward the bacterial invader, as in burns and crushed tissue with poor blood supply—meaning longer supply lines and fewer reinforcements for the polys—bacteria such as staph could double their numbers every hour. Once entrenched, bacteria deployed concentrated enzymes and toxins, and against their forces and superior numbers, the White Army's polys were reduced to fighting a rearguard action. If the polys slowly lost ground, the war ended when the enemy reached the main superhighways – the blood vessels—from where invasion spread rapidly to other organs, as in toxic shock syndrome. And more formidable bacteria, such as bubonic plague's pasteurella pestis employed not only toxins but even more exotic and unknown weapons, bringing in its wake the Black Death.

At times like these, when the White Army's polys littered the battlefield, when no heroic acts were left to save the day, one weapon still remained: Antibiotics. Derived from a variety of natural and synthesized substances, antibiotics were like artillery: Blasting, bombing, and poking bullet holes into bacterial hearts. Even so, since some bacteria resisted many antibiotics, and a few resisted most, in the age-old wars between microbes and men, battle outcomes were never entirely certain.

While the White Army's polys formed the core legions of foot soldiers deployed for hand-to-hand combat against bacteria and fungi, the next most numerous battle group, the "lymphocytes"—smaller than polys and only a little larger than red cells—comprised complex fighting units that battled all invaders, including viruses. Some lymphocytes served as scouts to identify and label invaders; some commanded polys to the attack; others brought up the mortars of interferon and howitzers of antibodies to the attack. Nor were lymphocytes above some close combat themselves, or activating the White Army's tanks—macrophages / monocytes.

The "Macrophage/Monocyte" battle group was less numerous, about 10% of the White Army, but in size each reached nearly 10 times the size of a poly. Huge, but not lumbering, macrophage/monocytes basically crushed their adversaries, though they also wielded more sophisticated weapons as well.

Rounding out the smaller specialized White Army's battle groups were two more: The mysterious "basophils", containing intensely blue granules and large amounts of histamines; and the flashiest of them all, the "eosinophils", resembling commandos with red and orange satchels of explosives within their cells, directed largely against parasites.

All in all, the White Army's immune systems posed a formidable array, from hand-to-hand combat, to chemical and toxic warfare. Though not invincible, it seldom gave quarter and always fought to the death. By its very might, vigilance, and aggressiveness, the white Army was finely balanced between defense and attack—which made it dangerous when it missed its target. For example, in certain strep infections, the bacterial coats of strep bore a resemblance to portions of heart valves and other areas of the body, such as joints. In vigorous combat against strep invaders, the White Army also unwittingly wounded the innocent bystanders of heart valves and joints, producing Rheumatic Fever.

And so it was with other Connective Tissue Disorders: Though none of them were yet thoroughly known and explained, it was likely that elements of the White Army had misread their orders, and pursued hidden invaders too far and with too much zeal. And in duly obliterating the microbial invaders, the White Army also left behind a battleground of inflammation and scarring—the C.T.D.'s, as collateral damage.

Dr. Carlton finished her rendition of C.T.D's as best she could, then stared down at her reflection on the marbled polish of Dr. Morrison's shoes.

Dr. Morrison clasped his hands under his chin: "Now that we've listed some of the hypothetical possibilities, Dr. Saxton, how did you proceed?"

"Due to the multiple complexities, a Neurology consult was requested. An electroencephalogram (E.E.G.) read the patient's brain waves as showing no potentially epileptogenic foci. So Neuro advised stopping the Dilantin first, then tapering the phenobarbital."

"What do you think, Dr. Carlton?" Dr. Morrison asked.

"Well," she cleared her throat for time to think, then resumed with her usual high, crystalline pitch: "In a patient with multiple problems and medications, it does make sense to remove some medications, and observe whether some of the problems clear. I agree with that decision."

"Sound principle," Dr. Morrison nodded. "But since Mrs. Gates had seizures in the past, she must have had epileptic foci. Whether they're healed and gone remains to be seen. I wouldn't be totally surprised if her seizures returned. Anything else, Dr. Saxton?"

"Her lung problems, mainly asthmatic wheezing, are being treated with smoking cessation and standard combinations of anti-asthmatics. She is responding well." Joel moved to the bedside to listen to Mrs. Gates' lungs. She waited until the stethoscope was firmly planted in his ears before yelling: "Medicines, medicines, medicines! I want to go home!" Dr. Saxton finished the exam with his ears echoing like Gregorian chants across a mountain top.

As they left the room, Joel tried to forget about his ears, and watched Lucy's walk: It was a peculiarly dainty gait for her tall frame, as if more motion went into rolling her hips than covering forward distance. In other girls it would have appeared artificial, or a product of high heels. But that was the way Lucy always walked.

Dr. Morrison asked Joel a question, waited exactly fifteen seconds for signs of intelligent life, then called an end to rounds.

"Damn," Joel muttered. "What did he ask, anyway?"

"The symptoms and signs of Cushings'," Lucy disdainfully shot back.

"Easy, too—obesity, hypertension, hirsutism, personality disorder, weakness..." Joel rattled off.

"Too late now, Joel," Cameron smiled. "Next time pay attention to your own ass: it might be the one you save."

"I thought Morrison was going to turn purple or something," Lucy began to laugh, "when Mrs. Gates started in: Mr. Squeaky Clean Professor meets Mrs. Expletive Deleted!"

"All right, party's over," Cameron tried to look serious. "Let's finish rounds."

Today was their "short" day: No admissions, no call, no evening clinic. They were done by 5:50 p.m.

"Questions, observations, or other burning quests for knowledge?" Cameron asked.

Their silence spoke eloquently.

"Then bright and early tomorrow, same time, same station. No hangovers, coffee jitters, or past or future daydreams. Good day, doctors."

Lucy and Joel looked at each other, wondering whether Cameron was serious, or the condition terminally led to Dr. Morrison's style and a professorship.

· · · · ·

Cameron took off his shoes and rubbed his feet. Choices for the rest of the evening were dinner at the hospital cafe before going to the research lab, dinner outside before going to the library, or any combination thereof. There was also a gym at the Intern/Resident quarters, and the nursing school and dorms were within walking distance. The lack of a date at the nursing dorms made the decision easier, and Cameron replaced his uniform with sweats.

There was no urban overcrowding at the gym tonight. It was empty. Cast iron barbells from 20's to 75's (except for the 65's, which were missing) sat racked alongside one wall. A chin-up bar, mirror, and scattered barbells, collars, and weights lined the rest of the walls. A triangular steel rack held individual slabs of 5's to 45's, next to a bench-press with worn padding. The bench was topped with a black 45 lb. bar. In a corner, an ancient radio resembling a toaster with knobs rose like a pimple over algae-green carpet.

Cameron slipped 45's on each end of the bench bar, leaving the collars off. He centered the bar and slipped between bar and bench. Gripping the bar two feet wider than his shoulders, Cameron pumped it upwards five times. Successively adding slabs of 10, 25, and 35 to each side, he repeated the lifts.

Cameron rested, then added two more 45's, and slid under the bar again. Bar and weights initially wobbled atop his grip, like leaf-springs over a bump. Gravity's mysterious downward force faced a defiant will pressing up. Muscles tensed and coordinated automatically. In fractions of a second, the wobble disappeared. Four more and Cameron thudded the bar back onto its upper bracket.

After adding two tens, Cameron took some deep breaths and slipped beneath the bar again. Gravity accelerated the 245 lbs towards his chest. Air swept into the lungs, muscles contracted over ribcage to break the fall. On full descent, the elbows were forced below chest level. Tendons' living glue held taut muscle onto bone. Chest and limbs disregarded gravity's insinuations of pain. Muscles coiled like explosive springs to blast the weight upward. On the third lift, initial surge turned to hovering slow motion. The bar wobbled atop, until Cameron locked his arms straight.

One more: He took a deep breath, let it out, and inhaled again during descent, timing full chest expansion to meet falling weight. The surge carried through the first five inches, stalled at the sixth. For seconds it remained immobile—weight and will locked dead on. All motion ceased. Muscles remained taut a while longer, then slackened. The bar accelerated down, reaching Cameron's chest with a thud and exhaled grunt.

Cameron had enough power remaining in his right arm to tilt the collar-less bar. Weight slabs clattered onto the floor like an engine block—first on the left, then without counterbalance—more suddenly on the right.

Cameron sat up and thought he heard hands clapping. Max walked in.

"You alright?"

"Sure. Help me set up again. What are you doing here, Max?"

"Just hanging around. Almost in time to save your ass."

"That? Doesn't happen often, but that's why I leave the collars off. Just in case."

"Hey," Max laughed, "where I come from only uptown wimps did that."

"Hey," Cameron imitated, "you either always had spotters, or not enough weights to lift."

"No spotters. You either lifted the weight, or you didn't."

"Sounds like where you come from some must not have made it."

"Some didn't," Max replied.

"Sorry, didn't mean to revive bad memories."

Max shook his head. "Not all of us can have Ivy League pasts like Joel. Say, that's a fair amount you lifted, Cameron."

"Well, around here I can't run as much as I'd like without cars' tire treads climbing up my tennies. So, I lift instead."

"How much weight you want?"

"I'm pyramiding down—two thirty-five; two twenty-five, two fifteen."

"Want a spot?"

"Not if it makes me an uptown wimp."

Max shrugged: "Hey, we had our own way of cheating—on the last lift we'd arch to get it up." Max helped with the last few inches of the lift, adding one finger to the bar. "So you don't run anymore?"

"Sometimes. You know, running and lifting are basically similar—you run, you lift—just you and gravity. No complex diagnoses to figure, no treatments to tailor. Just straining against one predictable force. If you push hard enough, all the rest clears out of your mind."

"Bet it does," Max laughed, "especially when that weight rests on your chest, about to roll on your neck, or your groin."

"It has its interesting moments. And you, Max?"

"I've got no bone to pick with gravity. Lifting's just carry-on baggage from my past. Do it about two or three times a week."

"Your turn. How much weight?"

"Same's OK."

"Collars?" Cameron smiled.

"Leave them off," Max grinned, "To tell you the truth, none of us had thought of doing that. Besides, you're still my Resident, and I've got to do things your way. How's that for an excuse?" He pumped several reps, changed weights, and pumped again. "How good are you at figuring women, Cameron? I mean, we've talked about likes, dislikes, and all that before..."

"Sure. But that's just theory. Understanding women—now that's something else. I doubt anyone's an expert on that. 'Course, they probably say the same about us. So, what's this about, Max?"

"Six more," Max gripped the bar.

Cameron helped with the last one. "Well?"

"Nothing. Just wondering if I'm doing the right thing."

"Sounds like plenty to me. Can you be more specific?"

Max pumped weights again. "So how can you tell... about the right thing, I mean?"

"Well, in difficult cases, think of it as being at your deathbed: If no regrets, it was probably right. But if you'd want to change it, it was probably wrong."

"A bit morbid. Sir William Osler again?"

"No, my dad."

"What if the final outcome depends on many things, so you wouldn't know now if there'd be later regrets or not?" Weights clanged as they changed them.

"Ah, so often the case," Cameron looked at him. "Then maybe primum non nocere—first do no harm."

"How do you measure harm or pain—that of others," Max exhaled while lifting… "and your own?"

Cameron eased the last two lifts. "Don't know. I suppose by walking in another's shoes, as well as your own. Hey, how did simple lifting turn to such heavy stuff?"

Max wiped the sweat with his T-shirt. "Tammy Clarendon," he finally said.

"Ah, the Sports Illustrated swimwear girl."

"Look, it's not what you think. I understood where she came from, and wanted to help."

"Nothing wrong with that. It's our job."

Max tightened his work-out gloves. "Our job of lavaging her stomach and getting her detoxed wasn't going to keep her alive in the long run. It would just happen again, until she succeeded in killing herself. We were treating symptoms, John, not causes."

"I suppose we were. Sometimes, that's all we can do."

"Sure. But what if we can do more? Shouldn't we even try?"

"All right, Max—suppose we can, and maybe we should. Go on."

"Her 'disease' involves a misconception of herself: In her eyes, she's no longer a worthwhile human being. I tried to return a measure of that to her—held up a mirror of the unique person she is, still with her own future, regardless of any past."

"Makes sense, Max. But why not leave that to the psychiatrists?"

"Look, I read the Psych consult report: Slam, bam, you're depressed, get off those drugs, straighten your life, and maybe you'll get better. Clinically correct. But that advice came with little understanding and no dignity."

"You're probably right," Cameron nodded. "But you know, the shrinks are no different from us: They can do their job as well as we do ours. Don't forget, they've been there many times before, with others like Tammy. They get tired of giving it the old college try, and seeing no results. Just as we get tired after the third or fourth O.D: We wash them out, but inwardly write them off for the long run. It's not right, nor the best we can do. But it's human nature: We see defeat coming, and become more detached. And sometimes, just sometimes, that detachment keeps us functioning and sane."

"That detachment wasn't going to help Tammy Clarendon."

Cameron inclined his head. "What, then?"

Max took a few breaths and dove under the bar, pumping six lifts. "Your turn."

Cameron locked his wide grip, and heaved the weight five times. On the sixth, the bar slowed in mid-air, then hung motionless a foot over Cameron's chest. A small added lift from Max' two fingers was all it needed to resume its upward journey, and rest in the brackets.

"See? That's all it took, Cameron. A couple of fingers to help your lift. That's all I did for Tammy: Helped her when she was down."

Cameron glanced at Max and smiled. "All right. If that's all there is, there's no need to talk more about it. How 'bout ten pounds less, and another set?"

"Coming up." Max was silent after his set.

Cameron finished his set, then Max sat down. "Maybe we should talk more. It did start that way. But now we're more involved."

"So, there you were, spotting her—and lo and behold --instead of a chest like mine, there was hers, fresh off the pages of <u>Sports Illustrated</u> and Hawaii beaches..."

"I've got to admit, Cameron, hers is definitely more my type than yours…"

"Thank God! Go on."

"Well, I guess we just liked each other. There's something about her once you get to know her. I mean, there's a complex person inside, more sensitive than most. She became trapped...I guess really, I should say allowed herself to be trapped. But not because she was a bad person. At a certain place and time, she allowed a cascade of events that later went beyond her control."

"Like both of you now?"

"Maybe. I suppose once a train of events is set in notion, it's difficult to reverse."

"Let's not worry about reversals for now, Max. Let's take it from the beginning, the top."

"The beginning can't be reversed. I took care of her medically first. And medicine got her out of the frying pan. But it wasn't going to keep her out of the fire: She needed someone to be interested in her as a person, not a medical case."

"So out went medical detachment, right?"

"Medical detachment would protect us from whatever outcome she'd eventually have," Max said slowly, "but that wasn't what Tammy needed then."

"You make it sound like medicine would have failed her if we simply treated her O.D., gave her advice, and a follow-up appointment."

"Maybe so."

"Wait, Max. Treating her O. D. gave her another chance to look at life, reflect on things. A new chance, and new choices to make. Medicine can't make those choices for her. Though sometimes it may seem like it, we're not in the miracle business."

"We can't make choices for her. But she could sure have used any help we could give while she was making them."

Cameron nodded.

"But you're going to say," Max continued, "that it's okay for someone else to do that, to provide a shoulder to lean on, but not for me, since I'm a doctor."

Cameron shook his head. "No. But as a matter of fact, you're close. You're not only a doctor, but _her_ doctor. And as her doctor, you did your job. Nothing else was required of you."

Max remained quiet, and began to put away the weights. "So, you think it was right or wrong that I did more?"

Cameron thought about it. "I don't suppose being her doctor prohibits you from doing more. But that's a fine line. You both have to realize that whatever else you do, it's not as her doctor, but as a person—a friend."

"I didn't do anything...I mean, inappropriate, Cameron. I want you to know that. Whether she accepted me as a friend or not was one of her choices."

"Maybe that's it," Cameron paused. "If Tammy accepted your help, your friendship, uninfluenced by your status as her doctor, then I don't see an ethical problem. But that's the fine line: In her position as patient, and yours as doctor, she's the vulnerable one. You carry the power of medicine, which makes her choices more vulnerable in your relationship."

Max took the weights he'd just put away, then began piling them, and more onto the bar. "You talk of vulnerability, power? What about the power of money, drugs? They used both to control her. Did you know how she'd get her money for drugs?"

"I have an idea, yes."

Max slid under the bar's 305 lbs. An upward thrust released the bar from its brackets. The bar bent and swayed. Max let it fall towards his chest, caught the fall, and in one continuous motion heaved the weight back up. Once more he let it fall onto his chest. It hit like a kick into a punching bag. Max heaved upwards again. The weights responded in slow-motion this time. Back arched and arms shook, but the slow-motion carried to the top. The bar rested in its brackets. Max breathed heavily and clenched his fists.

Cameron placed a hand on his shoulders. "So how involved are you, Max?"

Max was silent awhile. "Maybe the real thing."

"I see."

Neither of them said anything. Cameron got up to remove the weights. "Why do I feel there's something else you're not telling me?"

Max didn't look up. "They beat her, Cameron. They went to the rehab house and beat her. She was lucky she got away, this time." His fists remained clenched. Cameron was glad he'd put away the weights.

"We've got a problem," was all Cameron said.

He hadn't said anything about Max and Tammy, or whether he'd thought it right or wrong. But he'd said "we," and the way he'd said it, Max knew he wouldn't have to be alone. Sometimes, two fingers on a bar made all the difference in the world.

CHAPTER 11

A THIN LINE

"Half of what we're about to teach you, will someday be proven wrong. Unfortunately, we don't know which half."

—*Sir William Osler*

When Dr. Morrison arrived at 07:15 it seemed as if nothing unusual had happened. Dr. Carlton carried her stack of charts nestled above her arms, Dr. Saxton had already wiped the perspiration from his brow, and Cameron wore his usual pensive look. Dr. Morrison met them at the nurses' station. "Good morning, doctors".

Their reply was brisk as usual, but not in unison. Dr. Morrison noted Lucy Carlton tapped her fingernails on her charts as she glanced south down the hall, and Joel Saxton's white coat had already lost its morning starched stiffness. Moreover, Joel had failed to glance even once at Lucy's breasts resting over the charts. Cameron simply brooded, but that wasn't unusual for him before rounds. Dr. Morrison looked about some more.

"Shall we begin with Mrs. Gates?" Dr. Morrison offered. "I'm afraid you won't be able to concentrate on the rest until we go over her seizures."

Joel's mouth gaped, and Lucy's eyes widened. Only Cameron didn't seem surprised that Dr. Morrison knew.

"Did Dr. Cameron call you about Mrs. Gates?" Lucy asked.

Cameron shook his head.

"There's a used O-P airway on the nurse's desk," Dr. Morrison explained, "and a vial of unused diazepam, and half-used phenobarbital. We don't have that many patients that would have status epilepticus, and make you all look like you've been through the wringer. Also, Respiratory Therapy just walked into Mrs. Gate's room with suction apparatus, which makes it likely she was intubated. How's she doing?"

"We've stopped her grand mals, but a few twitches still continue." Dr. Carlton was still fascinated by Morrison's conclusions. "How did you know it wasn't for someone else in the room, or intubation for respiratory failure instead of seizures, for example?"

"Phenobarbital and diazepam would be poor medicines for respiratory failure, but good ones for seizures. Shall we visit Mrs. Gates?"

Lost in the puffy pallor of her face, her eyes were closed; sweat trickled like rain over a pumpkin. A respirator worked rhythmically, pushing oxygen mixtures along tubes into her lungs. Occasionally, Mrs. Gates shook the endotracheal tube from side to side; it dangled from her mouth, precariously taped to her perspiring face. A slow twitch still rippled across her features at irregular times, raising a corner of the mouth in a brief sardonic grin. Moments before, and for over two hours, her entire face had curdled, eyes rolled, teeth clenched shut, bubbling with foamy saliva mixed with tongue's blood. Her arms and legs had flailed like a frog's jump. Finally, after enough diazepam, diphenylhydantoin, and phenobarbital to change a thoroughbred into a turtle, the *grand mal* seizures abated. So had her breathing. A respirator took over. Her tired body reposed at last.

Dr. Saxton recited the events and medication amounts from memory.

"What do you think happened here, Dr. Saxton?" Dr. Morrison asked.

"Neurology advised us Mrs. Gates wouldn't seize if we stopped her diphenylhydantoin and phenobarbital. We even continued the diphenylhydantoin just in case."

"I'm not blaming you, Dr. Saxton, or Neurology for what happened. The patient was evaluated, and a reasonable decision was made. Unfortunately, it didn't work as expected. Now we need to find what we could have done differently." Mercifully, he gave Joel time to compose himself. "What do you think, Dr. Carlton?"

"One would reason that perhaps in stopping the phenobarbital, it may have been tapered too quickly, leading to rebound seizures."

"You may assert yourself, Dr. Carlton. There is no need to hedge 'one would reason,' but say 'I think.' Isn't that what you meant?"

"Ah...yes."

"And you are correct. That may be a factor. Let's observe the data: How was the phenobarbital tapered?"

For once totally concentrated and untouched by any positioning of Lucy's anatomy, Joel jumped in without glancing at chart or patient cards: "The phenobarbital was tapered over eight days, and a residual level of four still remained at the start of the seizures. We tapered slowly, just for such an eventuality, even though Neurology didn't think it was necessary."

"I'm glad you did so," Dr. Morrison reassured him. "Let's go over some other possible factors. Dr. Carlton, what other medicines was Mrs. Gates on?"

Dr. Saxton wasn't through yet. "She was on theophylline, sir. Her levels had been in a solid normal range—eight to eleven, out of twenty, sir. Since phenobarbital enhances the metabolic clearance of theophylline, as we tapered the phenobarbital, we also decreased the theophylline dose by one-third, to avoid any rebound rise. Still," Joel swallowed hard, "today's level was twenty point-seven, in the possible toxicity range." Joel was silent.

Cameron broke the silence. "As Dr. Saxton stated, the patient's level was twenty point-seven. While toxicity begins at twenty, it usually consists of nausea and tremors. Epileptic toxicity doesn't usually begin until a level greater than twenty-five. However, the level was high, and that responsibility was mine, Dr. Morrison."

Dr. Morrison noted everyone's somber moods. "We'll never be certain whether tapering the phenobarbital or a small rise in theophylline contributed to the seizures, or whether Mrs. Gates simply has a potent epileptic focus not seen on the E.E.G., or even had a stroke—or any combination of these. Now, in view of what's happened, what's our course of action? Dr. Saxton?"

"We'll be following Mrs. Gates in Intensive Care. After the massive doses of phenobarbital she's received for her *status epilepticus*, we'll be backing off, and monitoring what levels keep her seizure-free. We'll also need to observe levels of arousal in relation to phenobarbital depression, versus any possible neurologic damage from prolonged seizures. This distinction may be difficult to make. We've already lowered theophylline dose, and will be observing whether her asthma breaks through. All these factors will be evaluated to determine how long she'll need to be on a respirator."

Dr. Morrison nodded. "I agree."

The rest of rounds passed in Mrs. Gates shadow. When Dr. Morrison was leaving, Cameron followed him to the stairwell. "May I ask a question, Dr. Morrison?"

"Certainly."

"Did you know this would happen to Mrs. Gates if we stopped the phenobarb?"

"I had a feeling. Call it a hunch."

"Why did you let us do it, then?"

"I think you know the answer to that, Dr. Cameron. The alternative of not stopping it, and perhaps adding years of a bedridden existence from the side effects of phenobarbital was equally dismal. The result might well have been the opposite—no seizures, and a more normal patient. Besides, there's one more thing you forgot, Dr. Cameron?"

"What's that?"

"I'm not always right, you know." If there was a smile on Dr. Morrison's face, it was not in the way of excuse or resignation, but recognition of a fundamental principle, at once easily perceived, but often unrecognized in situations of stress.

Cameron understood the smile. "I guess I just expected you to be, Dr. Morrison."

"No one can fill the shoes of perfection, Dr. Cameron. We can only learn how to do our best, then give it our best."

Cameron nodded. "I suppose when there's uncertainty, we'll always look to higher authority. Interns look to Residents, Residents to Attending Professors..."

"...And attendings to books, and other professors, and the latest articles. Yet despite 'higher authority,' certainty at times still eludes us. The fact is, Dr. Cameron, it may take decades, even centuries, to resolve some questions, or provide some particular certainty. Such is the nature of medicine. And while we continue to push back those frontiers, we shouldn't blame ourselves, nor accept the blame, for what isn't yet within our certain understanding."

"It just seems so futile at times," Cameron looked down. "I'm not just talking about her seizures. Even otherwise she just doesn't look right—hypothyroid, Cushingoid, or something else—yet we can't find any such abnormalities in her lab testing. It's as if there are things unknown, that we can't yet test."

"You are right. There probably are. That's where research and people like you come in. Perhaps a fellowship for you next year?"

Cameron wondered how much Morrison knew about his research, how many others knew. But sometimes results seemed so far away. Mrs. Gates' old photographs sat on her bedside table—with a smile, and different eyes, kind eyes. Here their job was to change things back, even a little, to the way she was before. But there were times when they had no art, science, or research to do that. She and others like her would wait for a magic they couldn't provide. Cameron inclined his head. "Thank you for your time, Dr. Morrison."

Morrison paused before leaving. "You spend your time in the academia of medicine, and that's as it should be. But there are storms brewing. Has Dr. Atwood talked to you?"

Cameron nodded.

Morrison continued, "oddly enough—or perhaps not—the pressures of political and economic changes swirling about medicine today, to cut costs, has only added non-medical and medical entrepreneurs to milk these changes. They view Medicaid as bankrupt, and Medicare going that way. They may well be right. They're positioning to take the best and brightest, to care for only the most—what's the word—cost-effective patients.

"All I can tell you is we'll still need doctors like you to care for the most difficult patients, and those no one wants to pay for. For now, all that care will offer is a challenge, and sometimes maybe a thanks." Morrison wasn't given to dwelling on other than academic matters, so Cameron pondered his words carefully. Neither of them knew how prophetic those words would be.

Evening Medicine Clinic brought a welcome change from hospital rounds. Instead of major overhauls, minor tune-ups generally sufficed. Near closing, Cameron went over the list of no-shows.

"Mrs. Wilson didn't keep her appointment?" Cameron asked Joel.

"She just showed up, late. Shall we reschedule her for next week?"

"Better see her, since she's already here."

"I've still got two more to go," Joel didn't mention closing time had been ten minutes ago.

"I'm about done. I'll see her." Cameron ushered Mrs. Anna Wilson into a room, noticing she was unusually pale. And though wheezing wasn't unusual for her, at least on her good days it took a stethoscope to hear it. Half-way through taking her vital signs, the thermometer dropped out of Mrs. Wilson's mouth, and she fell limp onto the exam table.

No further sounds. No pulse. No wheezing. No breathing. Cameron thumped once on her chest. "Code!" he yelled.

A thump provided the equivalent of five joules of electrical energy. Sometimes it was enough to restart a heart.

Still no pulse, no sounds. Technically, the brain could remain alive another three minutes. After that, without additional oxygen or blood pressure to circulate it, brain cells would irrevocably die. Technically, Mrs. Wilson wasn't dead. Whatever it was technically, her soundless, pulseless, motionless body looked as dead as anything Cameron had seen. It was as if a lighthouse had been quenched in an instant by a nocturnal storm's giant wave. Whatever technical distinction remained between life and death, it was about to take place before his eyes.

The thump hadn't worked. The room filled with Joel, Lucy and a nurse.

"Joel, mouth-to-mouth; Lucy, chest compressions," Cameron gave the instructions crisply. "Sally, get me an IV, and EKG leads on."

Cameron threaded in an IV line, then charged the defibrillator to three hundred joules. He watched the EKG monitor come on the screen. "Coarse V. fib! Ready to defibrillate!" Cameron checked the settings for a D.C., asynchronous three-hundred joule discharge. "Ready? Stand clear!"

The metal paddles administered a shock to the heart, to terminate its random electric activity. Once all the regions of the heart became electrically neutral from the shock, it could resume organized electrical animation, directed along the heart's normal conduction lines. Or not.

Joel checked the carotid artery's pulse at the neck, then shook his head. He'd attached an Ambu bag with oxygen to replace mouth-to-mouth. Joel and Lucy worked methodically, thirty chest compressions to two breaths. The breaths contained enough oxygen to keep the brain alive. Lucy's sharp strikes downward, compressing the heart within its ribcage, provided enough blood pressure to continue circulation to the brain. Technically, they could continue this for hours. In reality, chances of recovery dimmed greatly with time.

Cameron stared at the EKG monitor. Still coarse ventricular fibrillation. The heart's muscles followed the disorganized electrical activity, quivering like a water-filled balloon, rather than contracting as one pump. Choices were to administer drugs to make the heart more responsive to the shock, or increase the current. Cameron raised the defibrillator setting to the maximum of three-hundred and sixty joules.

"Ready? Stand clear!"

Cameron placed the palm-sized paddles along the chest's center and left side. He pushed the paddles' red buttons simultaneously. The patient's arms flapped in a spasmodic embrace.

Cameron watched the E.K.G. monitor. A flat line... "Asystole," he muttered. "Wait! Back to fib again!"

Cameron checked the pulses and breath sounds Lucy and Joel were generating. He nodded. "You're perfusing." He turned to Sally: "One to ten-thousand of epinephrine—one amp of ten cc's." He pushed it IV. Electric activity on the EKG, though still fibrillation, coarsened and increased.

"Ready to defibrillate? Stand clear!"

Three-hundred and sixty joules of electric energy flashed though the ribcage. Muscles convulsed once, arms rose briefly, as if in prayer, then fell limply like a rag doll's.

Cameron stared at the EKG: "We've got sinus rhythm!"

The heart had resumed its normal electric activity: Pacemaker cells, from their focal point the size of half a light-switch—in the "Sino-Atrial" area atop of the heart—had once again taken over direction of the heart. Pulsed bursts of electricity of one-tenth of a volt, or about twenty times less than the mini-batteries driving a camera's flash, coursed like a waterfall from this "S-A" pacemaker area, into rivers of specialized nerve-like cells. These cells, the "Purkinje" system, branched like riverine bundles into the heart. Electricity pulsed and flowed along them, contracting the heart's muscle like fingers into a fist.

"We've got a pulse," Joel nodded, without smiling. Time elapsed had been two minutes and twenty-eight seconds. He kept his hand on the pulse, as if life's spell might be broken, and the heartbeat might escape again.

During the next few minutes, they secured all lines, drew blood for chemistries, oxygen concentration, and drug levels. They observed the heart rhythm constantly for irregularities. An irritable electric focus fired off a salvo of premature contractions, and was silenced with IV Lidocaine. Mrs. Wilson began to breathe on her own.

In a soft, calm tone that came only after brushes with death, Cameron gave his last instructions: "Let's get an I.C.U. bed."

Only then did smiles go all around. While Joel wheeled Mrs. Anna Wilson to I.C.U., Cameron browsed through her bag of medications. He shook his head.

"What's the matter?"

"The usual: She didn't take her medications. This bottle of a hundred theophyllines was filled two months ago. At three per day, there should be none left—but it's half-full. Same with her albuterol and her inhalers."

"Think that's why she arrested?"

Cameron nodded.

"Strange how a slightly high level of medication may have contributed to Mrs. Gates' seizures, and not enough would have let Mrs. Wilson die."

"We often walk a thin line, don't we Dr. Saxton?"

· · · · ·

After a morning visit to his canine charges, Cameron stuffed the mail in his pockets, and began rounds in the I.C.U.

Mrs. Wilson leaned forward on her elbows, wheezing like a slow-starting steam engine. "He...hello, doctor...Cameron."

"Good morning, Mrs. Wilson. How long have you been wheezing this time?"

She held up four fingers.

"Coughing?"

She nodded.

Cameron checked the IV's. "Any chills or fever?" Mrs. Wilson shook her head.

"Any chest pain?"

She shook her head again.

Cameron listened to her lungs and heart. He was fairly certain she hadn't thrown a blood clot from her legs to lungs, and probably didn't have pneumonia. "Have you been taking your medicines, Mrs. Wilson?"

"Some..."

Cameron glanced at the theophylline level—4.7. It was about a third of what she needed. It confirmed his suspicions that nothing had changed except she hadn't taken her medication.

"How much theophylline have you been on?"

"Which...color...is that?" After six years of taking (or often not taking) the same medicines, Mrs. Wilson knew more about the cosmetics she used than the medication that kept her from becoming a graveyard statistic.

Cameron said nothing. Now wasn't the time to belabor the point. As if reading his thoughts, Mrs. Wilson leaned forward, her lips pursed in effort to breathe. "I felt...fine...just dandy...you know. I didn't think...I needed...keep taking...all time."

Cameron patted her hand. "No need to talk now. Just take it slow, hang in there with us. We'll get the medicines restarted, and you better."

"I had...a close call," she said. "I'm glad...you answered it."

· · · · ·

Max called after morning rounds. "I heard about Mrs. Wilson. How's she doing?""

"She'll be all right."

"Let's take a break. Continental this evening?"

Cameron thought about all he still had to do. "Let's."

"Was that Max on the phone?" Barbara Davis asked. "Tell him I said hi."

"Sure." Cameron noticed Barbara had been unusually quiet all week. Also, no make-up. "Anything wrong? You've been quiet lately."

"Not really," she shrugged. At the same time her face went from neutral to annoyed.

"Sorry, didn't mean to pry."

"No, it's not that. I mean, it's not you." A trace of dimples floated below crescent-moon cheekbones. "It's nice of you to be concerned."

"Let me know if it's anything I can help with."

"Just usual girl stuff, you know. And keeping the wolves at bay. I think I can handle it."

"We're not talking about anyone we know, like Joel?"

"No. You medical types are really pretty tame. And Joel's been on best behavior lately. I'm almost worried about him. Can't say the same for the surgical types, though—seems some of them have a fast approach to everything."

"A chance to cut is a chance to cure," Cameron intoned the surgeon's maxim.

"And any other chance is a chance to score," Barbara laughed.

"Who's been leaning on you?"

"You're not going to make a federal case out of it?"

"Of course not. Out with it."

"Well, Roger Taylor can be quite persistent."

"Roger Taylor, the Surgical Resident? Roger, of the square jaw, curly dark hair, and blue eyes that leave girls swooning—for the rest of us to revive with amps of ammonia?"

"That's just it: I don't think he's used to getting no for an answer. A 'no' in anyone else's language translates into a 'maybe' for him."

"Hmm. Probably none of my business, but have you tried the really direct approach—one that even he might understand?"

"I haven't slapped him yet."

"How about something short of that? Differential diagnosis: 'Number one, I don't really like you like that; number two, I don't really like you in any other way either. Prognosis: The condition is chronic, and won't change."

"That's not bad. I hate to be that direct, but I doubt it will hurt his ego much. Thanks, Cameron, I'll use it." Her face lit up, then her lip curled into a pout. "Why is it the ones we don't want to notice us always seem to, and the ones it would be nice to be noticed by never do?"

"Ah, anyone we know?" Cameron looked around him.

"Maybe closer than you think," she smiled.

Cameron looked around again, perplexed. "Well...hmm."

"See what I mean? You only notice me when I'm without make-up, or feeling down."

Cameron found himself suddenly off guard, looking into her blue eyes and sailing into a twilight of shooting stars in their reflection. "Who says I haven't noticed?"

"Then you're very quiet about it."

"Maybe that's my style."

"Or another way of playing it safe."

"You're right. Beautiful women basically turn me into a fumbler."

"You, a fumbler? You always seem so calm and collected."

"That's because I don't spend much time around you, Barbara."

"A real compliment?"

"See what I mean? I can't even say that right. But maybe you'd like to join us—Max and I are going to the Continental..."

"A real date?"

"See what I mean?"

"Will you still notice me if I wear make-up?"

"I'll try hard not to—so I don't fumble." He saw her bright eyes upon him, and sensed he should begin trying not to notice right now. "So, the Continental, about eight?"

"See you there."

He fumbled anyway. "Should I invite the rest of the crew? Lucy and Joel?"

"If you'd like."

Lucy later begged off, saying she had to finish polishing Ahrend's medical records system. And Joel had just received a call from Jody: "Something about her test," he said. "Either she's depressed about it, or she passed it. Couldn't quite tell over the phone. Anyway, I better see her this evening."

· · · · ·

Max had two beers waiting on the table. Cameron sat down, and listened: Sound of voices rising and falling, drumbeat cadence, laughter. Lights curled in spiral reflections from the ceiling.

"How's Tammy?"

"Fine." Max didn't say more.

Their tall, leggy waitress came over. "Well, Max and Cameron: Came over for a fare of beer, genetics, and evolution? Anything more I can get you?"

"Double ours, Elaine. Thanks."

"Twist of lime?"

"Sure."

"How's work in the lab?" Max asked after she'd left.

"The canines and hybrid implants are doing fine. Got one more going."

"So why are you shaking your head?"

"I'm surprised by it. I mean, I want more answers why it's working. There's gene splicing involved, and I've got a couple of ideas how and where, but I need confirmation from the gene mapping boys. That may take a while."

Max decided to test whether there'd been any results from Track Sullivan's grant application plans. "Have you thought about grants yet?"

"No, not right now."

Elaine returned with their orders. "There you go, you guys look lost in laboratory shoptalk again."

"That's close. And a long story."

"Maybe I'd like to hear it sometime."

Max looked after her as she left. "Know what I was thinking?"

"Clue me."

"Only Track could match legs like that."

"Track Sullivan?"

"Why not? Let's bring him here sometime. Then he can tell her about the lab, and we can watch your genetic theory at work."

"It's a little more complex than matching long legs, Max."

"Just kidding." Max glanced up in surprise: "Is that Barbara over there?"

"I invited her. Hope you don't mind."

She'd walked in with jeans and a fluffy white sweater on, leaving in her wake a visual gravitational field. Cameron pulled out a chair for her.

"Don't let me interrupt. I always wondered what you guys talked about on boys' night out."

"It was quite scientific, really" Max grinned.

"Sure it was. And here I thought you guys just talked about sex," she coyly nestled her chin in her hands.

"I guess we shouldn't disappoint you, then," Cameron kept a straight face. "We were—but scientifically, of course."

"Since it's so scientific, don't let me stop you."

"Well, Cameron has this theory that our genes talk to each other—that's right, converse, as it were—by the reading and decoding of some traits and physical characteristics. That is, and correct me if I'm wrong, Cameron—genes encode and display information about themselves within detectable individual physical traits, and are similarly able to decode information about the genes of other individuals."

"If that's the way you guys talk about sex," Barbara laughed, "it certainly is scientific!"

"That's before a few beers, Barbara. We confess it changes afterwards."

"Now we're getting to it. Go on. This is going to be educational!"

"Well, it does explain likes and dislikes, and how everyone's are different."

"So, give me some examples. Your theory does have examples, doesn't it?" Barbara prodded.

"You want the before beers, or after beers versions?"

"Both."

"The before beers, scientific version example: In some bird species, brightness and coloration of plumage depend on their ability to fight off parasitic infections. Their plumage is an outward indication of a portion of their immune system."

"Interesting. Now, the after beers example?" Cameron and Max looked at each other.

"Come on now, let's get down to the bare details. I'm a nurse. I've heard it all before."

"Then you don't need to hear it again."

After Elaine had returned with another round, Barbara leaned forward: "For instance, how does she fit into your genetic theory?"

"Well, there are many details: Color of hair, eyes, length of neck, legs..."

"I'm glad you didn't overlook that," Barbara quipped.

"And of that multitude of details, some may have a story to tell of the gene-directed biochemical, physiologic, and immunologic capabilities of their owner."

"So, evolution then wouldn't be totally hit or miss," Barbara inclined her head, "but aided by the ability of genes to check each other out."

"Something like that—maybe evolution with a guiding hand."

"You mean a guiding gene. And here all along I thought we're the ones doing the checking out, while actually our genes were doing all the work. I don't know whether to be glad or disappointed, Cameron!"

"Actually, we still do the work. Genes may communicate in their own ways, but we have to do all the follow-up work for them."

"That's not quite fair, though, you know. I mean, if that's all there is," Barbara's chin jutted forward, "then it's all just reduced to 'skin-deep.' What about those that are just plain or homely? Not everyone can be ruggedly handsome, or ravishingly beautiful. Does that mean they're less genetically capable, less fit?"

"No!" Cameron slammed his mug on the table. "There are probably thousands of different details in each individual that we couldn't consciously comprehend. We see them in terms of what we ourselves are made of: So, the spectrum of beauty is not only 'in the eye of the beholder,' but in the beholder's genes."

"But you can't deny there's a spectrum from plain to pretty, to beautiful, to just perfect," Max put in. "And in real life, this seems to confer an unjust advantage."

Cameron thought about it. "Probably not. It's likely neither just nor unjust, but simply all comes out in the wash. Sure, there's what we term 'beauty' in eyes, lips, curves, muscle, and myriad other features. Yet for all these there are infinite variations. For instance, some might like a distinct curvature of the lips, or an arch; others might prefer a certain fullness; still others a particular coloration or outline. It would take the better part of a day to describe all the possible favorite variations just relating to lips, and in the end, there'd be no 'ideal beauty' we'd all agree on. Extending this to other characteristics, it's obvious 'beauty' can assume many forms: Beauty in motion, beauty that just glides; beauty in energy, beauty in reflection; beauty in a walk, beauty in endurance; beauty in the tilt of a head, or wink of an eye."

"That's nice to say, Cameron, and not without some truth," Barbara nodded. "But you have to admit there exists also that beauty that eclipses, overpowers everything else. Sort of leaves plain folk awash in its wake."

"What of it, Barbara? Often it does so only to the detriment of other traits that involve not only appearances, but behavior. The race isn't won until it's over, and it's not won at the starting blocks on appearances alone: It's not even won by the sum total of what an individual potentially has. The finish line is for those who can realize and use all potential they've been endowed with. If, as Hemingway once said, courage is grace under pressure, then perhaps beauty is the elegance with which each individual builds and gives of all that's within."

"Maybe you're right," Barbara stared nowhere in particular. "We've all seen patients that were sick, maimed, with bodies sometimes broken and shriveled. Yet they grow on you: Because inside them live Princes and Princesses, and they begin to look like what they are inside, rather than how they appear on the outside."

Max nodded, and looked away. They were silent awhile.

"Hey, c'mon," Cameron finally said. "We're not in an ER or a ward now. We'll be there soon enough. For now, we're in a bar, remember? Another round?" He searched his pockets and brought out two bills and the morning's crumpled mail.

"Paying with hospital mail?" Max asked. "Looks official enough." The mail was from the Director's office. Despite his own declaration of being in a bar instead of at work, Cameron opened the letters. He stroked his chin, then threw the letters on the table.

"What's going on?"

"Read it, Max."

"Looks like three incident reports: The first one's on Mrs. Gates. Seems her theophylline level, at twenty point-seven, was too high by 0-point-seven—even though standard doses were used." Max shook his head. "They're blaming you for her level, the level for her seizures, and therefore you for her seizures."

"That could be true," Cameron said quietly.

"But the doses given were actually below normal for her weight. And it was Neurology that recommended stopping the medicines that would have protected her from seizures, not you."

"True. Still, her theophylline level was high, and she did have seizures. Whether or not they were causally related, we'll never know. But it should have been lower, and that is my fault."

"The next one's about Mrs. Anna Wilson—also an elevated theophylline level, from months ago." Max whistled: "I remember that! The on-call team had increased her dose, and three of our orders to decrease it or stop it were ignored. That wasn't your fault! Why would they report that against you?"

Cameron shrugged.

"The last one's on Mr. Lester Brown. Says here his treatment to dissolve fat emboli was experimental, without sufficient merit, and not to be used without Pharmacy Committee referral and approval. As if any committee," Max muttered, "could decide anything in time to save anyone's life. Who was it that said committees are formed by those who do nothing on their own, but together can decide nothing can be done?"

"You know, it's odd the incident report on Mrs. Gates came through so quickly," Barbara remarked. "Usually they take weeks to process. What's even more incredible," she set her glass down, "is how you sure got nailed, without mention or whisper of how you'd really saved Mr. Brown's life, and just got through saving Mrs. Wilson's."

There was that thin line again, Cameron thought: No matter how often they walked it and came out to the good, the score was kept only on the bad.

"What are you going to do about this?" Max asked.

"Answer them, I guess."

Elaine returned with another round. "I see she perked you both up," Barbara commented. "So sometimes you guys are even normal. How can you be such regular guys here, yet so professional at work? I mean, you work with all kinds of patients, some that are pretty, and even knockouts. But you just do your job, with studied detachment, like wearing scientific blinders. How do you do it? How do you keep your normal, non-professional side under control?"

Max looked at Cameron, then away. Cameron had understood his look, but said nothing.

Barbara pressed on. "So, what is it? How do you do it?"

"I haven't thought that much about it," Cameron shrugged. "I suppose a lot of it is simply discipline. Our first clinical exams felt awkward, and most awkward under the circumstances you mentioned. But after several years of a hundred-hour weeks—whether studying in the library, on clinic rotation, or internship—medicine becomes something you eat, drink, and sleep. Emotions and personal problems learn to come in second."

Cameron paused and thought: "Besides learned discipline, there's also motivation. In all patient encounters, from the difficult patient to the centerfold model, our primary motivation is to make the patient's health better. That simplifies our outlook and choices."

Barbara looked dubiously down her empty glass. "It makes it sound so simple: Motivation makes your work come first, and discipline gets you used to doing it right. But isn't there ever any wavering, any conflicts of interest?"

"It might be difficult to understand," Cameron replied, "but after a while, motivation and discipline become automatic. During work, I'm Dr. John Cameron—doctor first, because that's what I trained to be and must be—and John Cameron second. The rest of the time, I'm just me."

Max hesitated, then raised his hand like a schoolboy. "It's not always that simple for all of us," Max fidgeted. "I guess I recently overstepped that boundary, between doctor and personal self. Maybe you, Barbara—as a woman, and a nurse—can give me your opinion on this." Max told his and Tammy's story, leaving her name and certain parts of Tammy's life out.

Barbara let him finish, then touched his arm across the table. "I remember Tammy, from the ward. She did look like a lost soul—lost soul, with a sad beauty still within." Barbara shook her head. "It is her, isn't it? That's quite a situation you've got. Medically, I suppose it's overinvolvement. But," she kept her hand on Max's arm, "personally, I'm glad you were there for her. I'd want the same done for me. Whatever involvement and romance grew, seems to me, was a secondary event."

"Thanks for the vote of confidence."

"Max, in this situation, I'm more concerned how all this might affect you. I think it's sweet of you to help, but I'm going to worry about you."

"Some vote of confidence." Max attempted a smile.

"I wish you luck, Max. I do."

Flakes of snow floated past the window. Some came to rest like crystal flowers with roots of light on the glass. Then melted slowly like teardrops, rolling down a pale, transparent face.

"Going home for Christmas?" Barbara asked. Cameron shook his head. "Not enough time off. Christmas at home has been a rarity the last few years."

"And you, Max?"

"Wouldn't know where to go."

"Then I wouldn't mind fixing Christmas dinner for a couple of guys, if they aren't on call. What do you say, Cameron? And you, Max, please bring Tammy."

"If we're off call, we'll be there," Cameron inclined his head, "thank you."

Max nodded agreement and stood to go.

"And now," Cameron threw on his coat, "it's time to take Wildwolf in."

"Who's Wildwolf?"

"Long story. I have to return him to Dr. Sullivan's lab."

"Can I meet the fearsome puppy?"

"He's in the back of my car."

A light, fluffy snow continued to fall, like down feathers floating in a wind-drift. The parking lot was a blanket of white on the quilt work colors of cars and pavement's night.

"Why do I get the feeling Max didn't tell me everything about Tammy?" Barbara asked. "Could there be some trouble he left out?"

"Maybe he'll tell us when he's ready."

Barbara opened her hand and felt the snowflakes. "Somehow snow always makes me sad."

"Why?"

"Don't know. Maybe it's because it eventually melts, and then all the jagged edges become uncovered again, like before. Make sense?"

"I think I understand," Cameron reflected. "You know, I've carried this image inside, I'm not sure why, of coming home in the snow, after a long journey. It's night all around and snow, and a home lit up with Christmas, and I'm finally coming home."

"What kind of journey?"

"I don't know. Strange, isn't it? But it seems far away, and for a long time. Then I come home in the snow for Christmas."

"Then the journey ends well."

"My image of it ends well. How journeys really end, I don't think we're given to know beforehand."

"Maybe they end...in the same way we travel them."

Wildwolf slept curled up in the front seat, tail over one eye, paw covering the other from the parking lot lights.

"I thought you said he'd be on the back seat," Barbara laughed. "Is he really part wolf?"

"Probably not."

"Part of your lab experiments?"

"More than that now."

"What do you do at Sullivan's lab, anyway?"

"Tinker, I guess."

"You can bring him along."

"Who?"

"Wildwolf, for Christmas."

"Deal. Good night, Barbara."

Outside, the snow had stopped falling: Christmas would be at Barbara's; far-away journeys were only in his imagination, and the promise he'd made would be simple enough to keep. After so many thin lines, solid ground felt good underneath.

CHAPTER 12

TWO ROSES

One rose:
 Love on one-way street.

Two roses:
 Paths join, climb a mountain,
 to the sunset on the other side.

At the appointed time, Jacob Werner waited, as usual, in the anteroom. Today the door opened before Jake even had a chance to open a magazine.

"Come in. Do sit down." Terrance Liverpool pointed to a chair but did not extend his hand. He remained behind his desk, perusing a file. Terrance finally looked up. "Glad to see you. How's the project coming?"

"All the basics are in place. Subject is being undermined in the usual ways. He's made some mistakes that are helping us as well. It shouldn't be a problem."

"How much longer?"

"Three to four months more, to do it neat and clean."

"That may be too long. Let's stay within our original estimate."

"It can go faster. But I can't guarantee it won't get messy." Jacob Werner sometimes laid out his plans with a double edge. This would be one of those times. The warning was also a future disclaimer, for whatever edge would be the cutting one.

Terrance brushed it aside. "What about the idea? The project's idea itself? When do we get our hands on it?"

Jake feigned surprise. "I didn't know that was as much a priority."

"You had your instructions: Neutralize the subject, and place his idea in safe hands. They're both priorities." Terrance sounded annoyed. Someone had to be putting pressure on him as well.

Jake had known it was a priority. But he wanted to keep Terrance on edge. It sometimes helped tip Terrance's hand, forcing him to reveal more of his plans than he'd intended. "Along with the rest of the work," Jake stared calmly ahead, "I've already come across some of that information."

Terrance perked up: "How soon can you deliver it?"

It had been difficult enough to prepare the rest of the groundwork unnoticed, so Jake hadn't really begun the information gathering. But since he'd obtain it eventually, in a sense he wasn't bluffing. "I have to double-check sources, make sure they're not false leads. I should have something within a month—not complete, you understand."

Jake seldom bluffed, and at those times that he did, he himself wasn't certain whether it was a bluff or not.

"Don't worry about completeness. Just give me what you have."

Keeping Terrance on edge was working. Unwittingly, he'd just given Jake permission to drag it out. "How do you want it?"

"Original copy. That'll go directly to the lab boys. We've already profiled two responsible enough to handle this. Neither you nor I will keep a copy. It'll all go directly to them."

Made sense that Terrance wanted to limit copies. But it wasn't something he could enforce. Jake nodded, "Of course."

"Three weeks, then." Terrance came from behind the desk and extended his hand. "Thank you, Jake. I know I can count on you to serve the best interests of our society."

· · · · ·

Cameron glanced at the chart: Mr. Miroslav Mojic, 89 year old with an ER. diagnosis of pneumonia. "First admission of the day. You're up, Dr. Carlton." He gave Lucy the chart. "He's also been here ninety-one and ninety-three, and a few ER visits. That ought to provide enough work for your new charting system."

Dr. Lucy Carlton settled down with the fist-thick, three-pound chart. Each Emergency Room visit had generated over ten pages of paper: The ER entry sheet and record, in triplicate; an overflow medical record for additional doctors' notes; one consent form sheet; one advice and disposition sheet; and two billing forms in duplicate. Of these ten pieces of paper, only one or two contained anything that could improve Mr. Mojic's health. The rest went to satisfy bookkeepers, bureaucrats, insurance companies, and lawyers.

In fact, upon hospital admission and before a single antibiotic could sail forth on its bacteria-bashing and patient-saving mission, another nine pages would be tossed into the fray: Quadruplicate admission sheets; nursing assessment forms; a nursing flow sheet form; and doctor's treatment orders, in triplicate.

Mr. Miroslav Mojic's latest medical portion of the record began:

"C.C. (Chief Complaint): 89 y/o Yugoslavian male with cough and shortness of breath of 6 days duration..."

Lucy Carlton pondered. What did this really mean? "Yugoslavian:" Had Mr. Mojic been a mountain-entrenched federal partisan during World War II? Or had he been an independent-minded Croatian nationalist? Or perhaps neither, and disenchanted with both, had uprooted his family to come to America? "Eighty-nine years old:" What was his physiologic age compared to his chronologic age? Did he still bounce grandchildren or great-grandchildren on his knee, or did they visit him in a nursing home once a year?

Lucy Carlton read on into Mr. Mojic's past admissions. Three years ago, he'd fallen off a ladder while building a tree-house and broke his arm. Family history: The father of five children, he'd been widowed at eighty-five. How much of his life had departed then? Did he believe death would reunite them? Did he feel that reunion was overdue? Or perhaps he still saw his absent but not disappeared mate's smile and eyes in a long line of generations, from children to great-grandchildren, as the latest of the line sat over the old roots of his knees, and listened with eyes full of wonder to enchanted tales gathering magic over passing years.

Lucy paused and closed her eyes. There was a danger here, she knew. A danger that those treating any patient would begin to believe that files, forms, and charts could explain and contain one person's lifetime.

She continued reading. Social history: "Laborer"...Had he been a blacksmith watching red iron take shape under his hands? A construction worker setting roofs to retain home's heat and keep out the rain? A lumberjack who'd felt the earth tremble at the fall of hundred-year trunks?

Perhaps none of this would matter in the treatment of Mr. Mojic's pneumonia. Then again, it could. Perhaps it could even explain how he'd gotten it in the first place, or whether he'd take his medications, or simply ignore them and go chop wood in his backyard. But no summaries, charts, or files could contain all that, Lucy realized. And the answer wasn't to increase the size of the charts, or add to the weight of papers or e-files. A realization was needed that some "important" documents were not so important for healing after all; and of matters that were important, not all could be reduced to the written nor electronic page. A realization was needed that medicine primarily treated individual people, who happened to have a certain disease, rather than applying a protocol to a disease attached to a "case." Otherwise, Mr. Mojic would remain the "pneumonia case" of Room 509B, with a three-pound chart of papers that attempted to satisfy all the different parties that wanted something from Mr. Mojic's file: Accountants, administrators, employers and/or insurers, review groups, lawyers, and electronic records that were even easier to ignore when the computer was shut off. And those dedicated to healing the patient would simply never be able to please them all.

Dr. Lucy Carlton cut short her musings to finish summarizing Mr. Mojic's past chart history onto her new recording system. The best part of the three-pound bulk was distilled onto two pages of bright pink that stood out from the rest of the chart. With three pounds, and two pages under her arm, Dr. Carlton set out to Room 509B.

Mr. Mojic smiled shyly as she came in, then a puzzled look came over his face; he stared at the sheets as if wondering what he was doing in bed in the daytime. His eyes blinked at the bright lights and white walls; then he crossed his arms, looked down, and waited. Square jawed, with smile-wrinkles twinkling about a weathered face, and a mane of wavy gray hair, Mr. Mojic looked like a misplaced walrus, cast adrift on an ice floe in an unfamiliar sea. The hospital gown, with its open back, was a comical on him as a grass skirt on a bull-walrus.

His son, a tall man in his forties or fifties, arranged a woolen scarf around his father's neck, snugged the bedcovers around him, then sat back on the edge of the bed.

Dr. Carlton decided to start from scratch. "Hello, Mr. Mojic, I'm Lucy Carlton. What can I do for you?"

Mr. Mojic glanced up: "I was just swimming last week, and then…" a cough rattled his deep ribcage. His torso convulsed in an effort to suppress it—he considered it impolite to be ill. "May I get up?"

"Of course."

He stood, walked alongside the bed, then sat down again. He patted his clothes neatly folded on the bedside table—a V-neck button-down sweater, checkered flannel shirt, and old but still pleated trousers.

"Now, can you tell me what's bothering you today?" Lucy tried again.

He looked bewildered: "It was cold swimming then…"

"When?" Lucy asked.

Mr. Mojic looked at his son: "When was it?"

"Can't you tell her, dad?"

"It was the same place as usual, the same—where was it…?" His lips pursed like an absent-minded storyteller at a campfire. The voice carried a trace of a lisp, and a heavier accent. "In Yugoslavia, you know, we went to visit about two weeks ago."

Lucy was trying to imagine where in Yugoslavia it would be warm enough to swim then.

"No, dad. That was over two months ago, remember?" The son's voice carried a more distant accent; its tones wove a soft cocoon around the old man. The comfortable, clean clothes also bespoke of the same kind of care.

But Dr. Carlton still hadn't gone past the chief complaint. She turned to his son. "I'll ask Mr. Mojic first, but if he can't answer it, or doesn't answer correctly, maybe you could fill in. Agreed?"

The younger Mojic extended his hand. "I'm Alex Mojic. I will be pleased to do so."

Mr. Miroslav Mojic nodded towards his son, then smiled, wanting to make clear he still wished to be of help. Another spasm of cough neutralized Mr. Mojic's face.

At this point, it would have been easy to simply ask Mr. Mojic if indeed the cough was bothering him most, thus finally obtaining a "chief complaint." But it would have been just that—a prompting—that perhaps Mr. Mojic, in his eagerness to please, would agree to even if something else bothered him more, such as chest or abdominal pain. Dr. Carlton resisted the temptation. "So, Mr. Mojic, can you tell me what's bothering you?"

"Hmm," he inclined his head. "Maybe a little cough."

"He's been coughing for five days now, with yellow phlegm," his son added. "Not bad in the daytime, but at night he has choking spells and gasps for air."

"Any chills, or fever?"

"About hundred plus one temperature, and several chills," the younger Mojic answered.

"Any chest pains or wheezing?"

The older Mojic was about to say something, then lay back against the pillow, silent.

"I don't think so," the son answered.

"Nothing hurts," the father now put in.

Dr. Carlton went on to the "Past History" and "Review of Systems."

"Have you had any operations, Mr. Mojic?"

The elder Mojic tugged at his mustach like a pirate pondering distant booty, but remained silent. It occurred to Lucy that perhaps Mr. Mojic simply couldn't hear well. She was about to repeat it louder, when Mr. Mojic decided to field the question. "I don't think any operations, no."

"Dad, remember you cut your left leg with a chainsaw?"

"That was a long time ago..."

"And how about when you lost the ends of those two fingers, Dad?"

Dr. Carlton noted it. "Anything else?" she asked.

Mr. Mojic shook his head.

"Any hospitalizations, besides a year ago for palpitations, and a half year ago for congestive failure?" Lucy had already reviewed them from the old chart.

"No. He's been very healthy most of his life," the son added.

Dr. Carlton tackled the "Review of Systems" next: Detailed questions about symptoms in each organ system of the body. Sometimes these correlated with the "Chief Complaint" and "Present History" to help clarify the main diagnosis. At others it uncovered different problems that needed follow-up. With this new array of questions, Mr. Mojic's smile gradually faded into bewilderment. He lay back against the pillow, at a seemingly uncomfortable angle, and didn't look up.

"That's all right, Mr. Mojic. We're done with the questions. May I examine you now? Then we'll see what we can do for this cough." Mr. Mojic leaned forward, burly hands on his lap. On both inspiratory and expiratory phases of deep breathing he had rhonchi—bronchial sounds similar to the way the word "rhonchi" itself sounded. Some deep breaths brought with them rattling spasms of cough, followed by diminution of the rhonchi, and the appearance of fine rales at the bases of the lungs.

During the neurologic exam, despite moments of confusion, Mr. Miroslav Mojic named off seven out of ten cities, colors, and animals. Given enough time, he was able to name three more to complete the list of animals: A bear etching its claws on a tree; a deer leaping a fence; a hare bouncing along a field, only its ears above the grass. Mr. Mojic's eyes regained some of their twinkle as he embellished his task with descriptions. He smiled like a child who'd just completed his first crayon stick-sketches of the numbers 1 through 10.

Dr. Carlton finished the exam: On the surface, it was a basic case of pneumonia, to be treated with antibiotics. A routine chest film, sputum gram stain and culture, and blood count would do. The government DRG for pneumonia, #89 was simple and not as expensive as other possibilities and complications. Accountants would appreciate the simplicity of billing; the hospital would be happy that expensive lab tests and exams not covered by the pneumonia DRG payment would be avoided; and lawyers would find the edges neatly trimmed and rounded with a few "defensive" lab tests. Surfaces could always be polished to resemble the truth, when the deeper truth wasn't as important as the underlying economics.

What about his past congestive failure and palpitations? That was of the past, and not of concern here. What of his intermittent confusion? Probably senile dementia—at his age, why look so hard for something else? So, the main diagnosis fit, treatment matched diagnosis, the paperwork would be in order, and everyone would be satisfied.

Dr. Carlton looked at Mr. Mojic: He sat more relaxed now, curiously glancing around him, thick white eyebrows moving like soft large moths dancing around the firelight of his eyes. He wasn't quite certain why he needed to be here, nor entirely sure he wanted to be. Then his eyes settled on Dr. Carlton, and he smiled.

Yes, Dr. Carlton thought, everyone would be satisfied. Everyone, except Mr. Mojic if he really knew, and Lucy Carlton herself. She shook his hand, then left to formulate a more thorough diagnosis and treatment plan.

In the lab room, she lined up the old chart, new chart, and pink-sheet summaries. Her eyes and brain searched for bits, pieces, and clues to a puzzle that didn't yet seem whole.

"Ready to finish rounds, Dr. Carlton?"

"Give me a few more minutes. I think I almost got it."

· · · · ·

By late afternoon there had been twelve admissions. Mr. Mojic was the most stable, so Cameron saw him after the rest. He shook Mr. Mojic's hand, noting the firm grip around his, minus the two fingertips. The palm was leathery from decades of manual work, but without the signs of "clubbing" of the nails or fingertips to indicate chronic lung disease. "You've got a good grip, Mr. Mojic. I'm Dr. Cameron. I'll be helping Dr. Carlton take care of you."

His son gone, Mr. Mojic tugged at his mustach and apprehensively looked around.

"I understand you're from Yugoslavia."

"Croatia," Mr. Mojic answered, pronouncing each vowel, in the European way. "You've been there?"

Cameron improvised. "No, but I hear it has a beautiful coastline and mountains."

Mr. Mojic warmed: "That's right. Once a year they have festivals in mountain villages. City people climb small paths to the villages, and drink the new wine, and dance by cliffs over the Adriatic sea."

"What did you do when you came here from Croatia?"

"Many jobs," Mr. Mojic reflected, "anything I could."

"How'd you lose those two tips?"

"That was streetcars. Worked them twenty years. Crawled underneath, to all the wires and cables. We weren't supposed to do that. But I knew the wires," his hands bobbed up and down with excitement, and the fingers moved like a guitar pick: "No, wires never hurt me...but the brakes blew one time," he held up the two cropped fingers.

Mr. Mojic's recollection of his medical history wasn't nearly as vivid. Cameron was glad Lucy had obtained that information before him. But as uncomfortable as Mr. Mojic was during the rest of the history taking, he was quite cooperative with the exam. By this time, Mr. Mojic had figured anyone interested in listening about streetcars was also probably interested in him.

After finishing, Cameron extended his hand, and received a wrap-around grip in return. "Thank you," Mr. Mojic said. The smile on his face was so wide that it curled his walrus whiskers.

Cameron looked at his grizzled countenance. "You're very welcome."

Back in the lab room, Lucy and Joel were catching up on their charts.

"How's Mrs. Wilson doing, since we transferred her out of I.C.U.?" Cameron asked Joel.

"Doing well, now that she's back on her meds. That chest pain when she moves could be from a broken left rib."

Lucy raised her hand: "My fault, I pressed too hard during CPR."

"Something bothers me about Mr. Mojic," Cameron sat down and looked at the diagnosis he'd written:

1. Probable pneumonia, RML.
2. Probable Congestive Heart Failure, early.

3. Possible C.O.P.D.
4. Intermittent dementia/organic brain syndrome—unknown cause
   a)   ? hypoxemia due to # 1 and 3.
   b)   ? metabolic
   c)   ? Alzheimer's.

"He doesn't fit the usual Alzheimer's dementia pattern. And he doesn't have the 'magnetic' glued-to-the-floor walk of normal pressure hydrocephalus, or the rigidity of Parkinson's. So neither of those is likely to be causing his memory lapses."

"Since when do things fit neatly in medicine?" Joel chimed in.

"You're right there. At times I feel like we're tilting at windmills. Lucy, I noticed you put 'pneumonia' down for diagnosis. Got anything else?"

"Right here," she smoothed a sheet of paper:

1. Respiratory: a) pneumonia
2. Cardiovascular: a) history of arrhythmia 1 year ago
                        b) history of congestive failure half year ago
3. Neurologic: a) intermittent organic brain syndrome, cause unknown.
4. Endocrine/Metabolic: a) R/o hyperthyroidism causing #2 and #3 and above.

How did you do that?" Cameron asked.

"What?"

"Get to the 'Endocrine/Metabolic: Rule out hyperthyroid' part?"

"I know I jumped to conclusions," Lucy was apologetic, "and he doesn't really have any signs of hyperthyroidism, but the old cardiovascular history fits in with his new confusion problem, don't you think? So I..." she bit her lip.

"No, go on, that's great! How did you derive it?"

Lucy smiled now, and brought out her pink summary sheets. "I just plugged in all I knew about him from the old charts, plus what's happening now, and arranged it by organ systems into this summary. When I came to the empty Endocrine/Metabolic section, it suddenly struck me that could tie in the rest. I mean, if you think of hyperthyroidism there, it would explain both his past heart problems, and his present confusion. But," her enthusiasm dampened, "if he's really hyperthyroid, and had congestive heart failure from it in the past, then he should also have some C.H.F. now."

"He does!" Cameron placed his list beside hers. "It's mild, and his few faint rales are almost hidden by the sounds of pneumonia. But he also can't lie down flat—keeps sitting up to breathe better. Besides, I already looked at his chest X-ray: Pneumonia infiltrate right middle lobe, and early vascular engorgement of congestive failure."

"What's this?" Joel's interest perked up. "Some new approach to 'instant' diagnosis?"

"Not exactly 'instant', and let's see how those thyroid tests turn out." Lucy tried to decrease expectations that might later prove embarrassing.

"Regardless of how the tests come out, your idea is a good one," Cameron encouraged her. "The point is, hyperthyroidism is a definite possibility. I missed it, and perhaps it was missed before. But your summary system brought it out."

"Lucy, if the thyroid tests return high, will you show me your system?" Joel asked with a dubious smirk.

Lucy shrugged. "Sure." She was uncertain whether to be happy the system was generating such interest, or be dismayed that it rested on the superficial aspect of a lab test's outcome.

. . . . .

Cameron met Max at the Cafeteria for dinner. He hadn't touched his food.

"What's wrong, Max?"

"I don't want you to get involved, and I hate to ask. But I have to."

"Go ahead, ask."

"It's not for me, Cameron. It's for Tammy. She's overdue in leaving the rehab home. Tom's been watching out for her there, and he tells me two guys have been hanging around close to the place. Probably waiting to see where she'll go."

"Yes?"

"She's worth a lot of money to them on her back." It was the first time he'd actually mentioned Tammy's past. Max glanced out of the corner of his eye at Cameron for a reaction.

There was none. "It's going to be a thing with them to find her, and get her back." Max paused. "And I just can't let them do that."

"I understand that. I wish it wasn't you involved, Max, but I understand."

"She's got no job, no place to hide, no place to go, Cameron. I've thought about this many different ways."

"And?"

"She needs to leave with no tracks behind. They don't know I'm in the picture, but I can't take her to my place directly, because that'd be too easy to follow. She could take a taxi to the hospital instead—nothing suspicious there. Then she disappears here, for a few days, until I pick her up. She needs a place to stay until then."

Cameron scoured his pockets. "Here's my key. You've discussed this with her?"

Max nodded.

"Anything else I can do?"

With suddenly regained appetite, Max dove into the hamburger in front of him. "That'll do fine, Cam."

"Have you thought about where all this might lead?"

"We've both thought about it. Sometimes, when I'm not sure she's going to be all right, I can't think of anything else..."

"I see," Cameron nodded. "So, it's love, or as close as it gets?"

"That's good," Max grinned back. "I think you're finally getting the picture."

"Hmm..."

"Don't say it like that."

"I didn't say anything."

"You should be happy for us," Max' feet bobbed under the table.

Cameron was silent.

"So go ahead and say it, Cameron."

"Have you...I mean, did you... No, it's none of my business."

"You're asking what I think you're asking? Did we go to bed together?"

Cameron nodded.

"You can ask. I realize that might seem important. But it's not, you know. Not that important. We care for each other beyond that. And the answer is no, we haven't."

"Max, what happens to you matters to me. And the same goes for Tammy, since you care for her. I'm going to back whatever decision you make. I just want you to think about some things, maybe feel something you haven't yet felt."

"Like what?"

"I saw that look in your eyes once, Max: The look of a battle-scarred wolf, alone without his wolf-pack, without even a moon's light to guide his steps out of deep canyons of a heart left elsewhere. You know, guys like us don't fall often, but when we do, we fall hard. I don't want to see you like that again, Max." The other time he'd seen that look, Cameron remembered, was in a mirror.

"What are you trying to say?"

"Something that will hurt you now. And for that I'm sorry. But I'd rather it be now and less, than later and a hundred times more."

"Go ahead." Max placed both hands open on the table.

"What's going to go through your head, Max, when you do? What will you think of then? How will that past affect you?"

"You mean when Tammy and I go to bed?" His hands tightened shut, but remained on the table, like iron fists bound by chains beyond earth's gravity.

Cameron nodded, aware of the chance he was taking.

"I've thought about it, yes." Max' fists loosened. "It hurts at times. But they've taken her body, not her soul, Cameron. No one has taken her body and soul."

Cameron looked at the fists. "I wanted you to feel that now. Because a time will come, sooner or later, that it will be worse. There may even be times, when the better she tries to make it for you, the more you'll wonder how much of it is from the past."

The fists clenched white, but remained still. "I know that," Max said quietly. "But I care for all of her, not just one part."

"You'll need to remind yourself of that often, Max."

"I have," Max finally smiled, "and I will. It hasn't been that difficult." His hands relaxed.

"Then I do think you really love her. Hey," Cameron extended his hand, "I'm happy for the both of you. I wish you the best. Anything more I can do, let me know."

· · · · ·

Days later, Max knocked twice on Cameron's door. "It's me, Max." He'd come to take her.

Though it wasn't cold, she shivered as she laid her head on his shoulder. He enveloped her within his arms and held her and rocked her gently.

"I almost feel free...new," she said.

"You are."

For the first time, Max saw Tammy really smile. Dimple-pools danced alongside the half-moon corners of her mouth, like a girl accepting her first prom's corsage. "I have something for you," she said. The smile continued as she held out a white flower, perhaps a rose, now crushed from their embrace. He took it and kissed her.

"There's nothing I could get you, Max, nothing I could think of, that would show how much you mean to me."

"That smile on your face is enough."

"I've never been so happy! I've got you. And," she looked at the room, "you've got good friends that'll help you."

"That will help us, Tammy."

"You've told him, about us?" The pools faded as her mouth lost the half-moon.

"Of course I told him."

"Oh," she raised her hand to her mouth. "What did he say?"

"That he was happy for us."

She stared ahead. "But doesn't Dr. Cameron know? I mean, who I am... Or maybe he doesn't remember?"

"He knows who you were, and it's not as important as who you are now."

"He said he was happy...for us? He really said that?"

"He did."

The dimple-pools returned. Her hair fell over his shoulder as she snuggled her chin between his neck and chest.

"Ready to go?"

She nodded, looking back at the room, with piles of books, scattered notes, a few pictures, and a worn pair of spiked track shoes.

"What do you make of it?" Max smiled.

"Interesting character. Runner's worn shoes—guts; books—not afraid to keep learning; mess of notes—maybe working on something others might learn. But," she grinned, "he does his own laundry, and doesn't have a girlfriend now."

"Pretty close. All you left out is a very big heart."

"Goes without saying, since he's your friend."

· · · · ·

Max took her bag, and made sure they weren't followed. He'd parked his truck by the laundry entrance. Checking the rear-view mirror frequently, he took several detours and side streets. Tammy remained curled up on the seat.

Max pulled into his driveway. "You asleep, Tammy?"

"Just dozing. It feels so good with you, I feel safe. I could fall asleep like that," she snapped her fingers. "But I'm so excited too! Didn't sleep a wink last night!"

"You can sleep in," he turned on the lights. "Sorry this place is so small. You'll be getting cabin-fever before long."

She took in the studio, with a kitchenette and bath beyond. "It's just fine," she hugged him. "And I'm getting up to make you breakfast."

"You don't have to."

"I want to!" Her tone was final.

Near a single bed, on a nightstand, was a neat mound of towels and clothes. A single pink rose lay atop. She cradled the rose in her hand. "We both had the same idea, Max!"

"Go on, look at the rest. I figured you'd need some clothes, p.j.'s, and stuff..."

She unfurled a nightshirt, socks, jeans, sweater, and a dress. She placed the dress against her waist and whirled. "Right size! Now the socks," she added laughing, "wild colors! But I still love them, 'cause they're from you!"

"For waist size, I told the lady this," Max held his hands as if around her waist. The socks—I figured the colors would keep you from getting bored. There's more."

Between the towels was a bag of undergarments. She took them out. "Now these aren't too wild," she remarked.

Max cleared his throat. "That was the hard part. Sure got me some weird looks."

She hugged him, and sat on the edge of the bed. "What a day! Thank you!"

"Any complaints about shape, size, or color, and I'll go exchange them."

"Ah," she smiled, "You should know you still can't keep a lady from shopping."

"Not for a while, Tammy, until the heat is off."

Memories returned. She glanced at the small, single bed, and said nothing.

"You're tired, Tammy. Let's call it."

"Okay." She began to take off her clothes.

"Wait a minute," Max blurted out, "my bed's in the kitchen. There's a door in between, and I'll knock."

"You mean we're not sleeping in this one?" She said it in a flat, uncertain voice.

"You're here because I want to help, Tammy. I don't want to rush you, or get something in return. I know this may be a temporary place for you, until they stop looking for you. I want you to feel free, and make whatever plans you want."

"They'll never stop looking, Max."

"All right, then, when they're looking less. Then you can change your appearance—an alteration here and there, in hair style, color, clothes. Maybe a different town, and you'll have a brand-new start."

"That doesn't bother me, Max. I believe all that might work. I know I can change my looks. But I can't change what happened, Max, change what I was. Just tell me if that's what it is, what's bothering you."

"Tammy, to me you're you, and nothing else. The rest doesn't matter."

"Don't tell me it doesn't matter. It matters to me too." Her head dropped with her voice, to a whisper: "Every night I go to bed thinking about it, about us, wishing none of the before had ever happened; hoping

I'll wake in the morning, to find all the bad parts were just a dream. Then there'd just be you and me, and nothing in between. But each morning I wake, and it's the same—just a dream, that never comes true."

Max sat next to her, felt her crying. "That part is not a dream, Tammy," he put his arm around her. "About you and me, and nothing in between: That part is true."

"How can you mean that?"

"I love you." It was the first time he'd told her. She rested her head on his shoulder, and he could feel the tears on his neck. "So you see, there's no need for those," he wiped her cheek, brushed the hair from her face, and hugged her. "Now get some rest." Max went to his makeshift bed in the kitchen.

In the morning, when the alarm rang by Max' bed, he showered and got ready for work. Tammy was still asleep. A dimpled smile like dawn's sun rested on her face. On the nightstand, in a clean glass, two flowers were entwined—one pink and one crushed white rose.

CHAPTER 13

HOLDING THE LINE

Four years of Medical school: Eight thousand hours in classrooms, clinics, and hospitals; nearly five thousand hours in books, libraries, and labs. Yet after it was done, when it was all over, and graduation added an M.D.—Medicinae Doctoris—to one's name, it had just begun.

Because now, the battles against disease and death were given no quarter. Like soldiers, they'd been taught to place victory above all costs. Surrender wasn't an option. Medicine and war were waged in surprisingly similar ways. And to win, one could believe only in victory.

Yet, unlike soldiers' wars, defeats at the hands of disease would become an inevitable part of their battles. At those times—with victory impossible, defeat imminent, and surrender unthinkable—all that was left was holding the line.

Dr. Lucy Carlton sifted through the morning's stack of lab results, pulling out Mr. Mojic's thyroid function results. The basic panel of thyroid tests included the T_4, T_7, and T_3 uptake. T_4 was the total thyroxine—both free and protein-bound forms of thyroid hormone—responsible for speeding or slowing metabolism, acting as a thermostat for the body's furnace. In Mr. Mojic, T_4 was high at thirteen point-five, the normal being five to thirteen.

The T_7 portion—or calculated free (non-protein bound) fraction of thyroxine—indicated the active amounts of freely circulating thyroxine hormone. In Mr. Mojic, it was ten point-three, only slightly high, the normal being three point-five to ten point-two.

Joel looked over her shoulder. "Found what you wanted?"

"You bet," Lucy grinned.

"That chart summary thing really helped you?"

"Works for me."

"Show me how to use it?"

"Sure, after rounds."

"Good morning, doctors," Cameron walked in. "Do I detect an eagerness to probe the mysteries of the thyroid gland today? Perhaps Mr. Mojic's? Let's begin rounds here. Our gentleman might become unduly alarmed during discussions about a gland that's so small, does so much, and isn't completely understood—especially since that gland happens to be his.

"Dr. Saxton, could you run down the basic thyroid hormones, as we know them today?"

"The thyroid gland's principal hormones are thyroxine, or T_4 and triiodothyronine, or T_3. Since there's so much more of T_4 than T_3, T_4, is the main controller of the body's metabolism."

"Dr. Carlton, if as Dr. Saxton suggests, T_4 and to a lesser extent T_3 direct our metabolism, what assurances do we have that this little one-ounce gland, stuck on the front of our necks like a bow tie under the skin, is making the right amounts of T_4, and T_3 for our bodies? What controls the controllers?"

"In keeping with the brain's role as the seat of all higher functions," Lucy smiled and continued in her high-pitched drawl, "the pituitary gland from its position in the center of the brain, produces the regulating hormone T.S.H.—Thyroid Stimulating Hormone. If the thyroid gland's function is decreased, the pituitary increases TSH to stimulate it. Conversely, if the thyroid's producing too much T_4 or T_3, the pituitary will react by decreasing its Thyroid Stimulating Hormone, signaling the thyroid to shut down."

Joel gazed at Lucy, contemplating her seats of higher and lower functions.

Cameron dampened Joel's contemplations: "Sounds pretty simple, Dr. Saxton. Now why is that so important?"

Why was what important? Higher or lower functions? Joel sifted through his haze, then remembered Lucy had mentioned T.S.H. "Autoregulation—feedback loops, as we call them—are important because...without them different organ systems couldn't communicate how much they need of a particular chemical, enzyme, or hormone. For any organism, all its parts must work in step with each other. An organism out of step eventually falters and dies."

Cameron had to give credit to Joel's ability to recover. "Anything out of step in Mr. Mojic's thyroid function, Dr. Carlton?"

Lucy recited the results.

"What do you think, Dr. Saxton?" Cameron asked.

"While the T_4 is high, the T_7 isn't convincingly high to make the diagnosis of hyperthyroidism."

"What else would you like, Dr. Saxton?"

"A T.S.H. would help," Lucy offered.

Since she'd chosen to answer for Joel, Cameron volunteered her again: "What other tests could also be confirmatory?"

"A highly sensitive T.S.H.: If it's low, that would mean the pituitary's reading the thyroid hormone status as too high, and is attempting to decrease it with a lowering of Thyroid Stimulating Hormone. Additional tests would be a T.R.H., and a Reverse T_3."

"Dr. Saxton, which would you chose?"

"That's a lot of tests," Joel commented, "I mean, how many do we need to accept a diagnosis of hyperthyroidism? They don't come cheap."

Cameron wasn't certain whether Joel was playing for time, or was really concerned about costs.

Joel realized Lucy had the subject well cased, and decided to go with what she'd already ordered. "Adding a T.S.H would probably be sufficient."

"Very good, Dr. Saxton. Though diagnostic certainty is necessary before treatment, you're right, we don't need overkill testing. Now, what types of treatment could we offer for hyperthyroidism?"

"Surgical removal of the gland would be curative, or we could use anti-thyroid drug therapy, like P.T.U. or tapazole."

"Other alternatives, Dr. Carlton?"

"Radioactive iodine, by shrinking the thyroid, would be the medicinal equivalent of surgery."

"Since he's your patient, Dr. Carlton, which would you chose for Mr. Mojic?"

"The problem would be which Mr. Mojic would allow. Surgery would seem drastic for his age, and any mention of radioactive iodine would probably make his mustache curl. He could perhaps be talked into using drugs."

"You're correct in tailoring the treatment to the patient, Dr. Carlton. The problem is anti-thyroids often don't work well in older people, and surgery has the possibility of removing the tiny parathyroid glands along with the unwanted thyroid, creating a problem worse than the one we'd cure. Radioactive iodine will be his best bet, but you're right, we'll have an uphill convincing him."

"You said 'will'—don't we have to await confirmation with the TSH?" Lucy asked.

Cameron pulled a slip from his pocket: "Low at zero point-two Just got it this morning. I ordered it two days ago because I figured the others would be borderline. Being sick usually decreases the T_4 and T_7, so while being acutely ill Mr. Mojic could have borderline values and still be hyperthyroid. Now, shall we go talk with our patient, and see if we're curing his pneumonia as well?"

Mr. Miroslav Mojic blinked at the three white coats assembled, then smiled at Lucy.

"How are you this morning, Mr. Mojic?" Lucy asked.

"Not so bad. I cough less, I walk more...every day I feel more good."

Lucy read off the 172/82 blood pressure, 98 pulse, 26 respiratory rate, and 99.2 temperature. "May I listen to your lungs?"

The rhonchi and sounds of pneumonia had diminished, unmasking the few fine rales at the bases.

"When can I go home?" Mr. Mojic asked.

"You're doing better, but we still have a touch of pneumonia to clear up. Also, your thyroid gland is overactive."

"Thyroid? What's thyroid?"

"A small gland in the neck," Lucy pointed it out. "It makes hormones telling your body how fast or slow it should go. Yours is speeding your body up."

"Sure," Mr. Mojic's eyes twinkled, "I like to go fast. That's good."

"Not so good sometimes," Dr. Carlton shook her head for emphasis. "It makes your heart go too fast, and other things that can be dangerous."

"Hmmm ..." Mr. Mojic stroked his mustache with the hand of the two missing tips.

"So, we'd like to take care of that for you," Lucy offered.

Mr. Mojic was dubious that something else had to be fixed in a body that had served so well for so long. He tugged at his mustache and said nothing.

Cameron sensed that things were moving too swiftly for Mr. Mojic. "Mr. Mojic, your cough and pneumonia are getting better with our antibiotic treatment, and you'll be able to go home soon. But like Dr. Carlton said, we also found your thyroid is set too high.

"The thyroid is like your body's thermostat, controlling how fast things go, and how much fuel you burn. If it's set too high, several things happen, some of which you may feel, and others not—until it may be too late. For example, if you keep a stove too hot, you'll slowly burn it inside out, and you may not notice it until a hole wears through. You understand, Mr. Mojic?"

He continued to tug at his mustache, but nodded.

"One of the ways it burns you out is by speeding your heart constantly, without a rest. This backs up some of the blood the heart's pumping, as extra fluid in your lungs. This is called congestive heart failure. You've had that before, and have some now. That's why at times you like to sit up rather than lay down to breathe."

Mr. Mojic remembered he did that, and nodded.

"It can make you lose weight, feel more nervous, not let you think straight; it can also make you weak." Cameron summed up, calculating that weakness was something Mr. Mojic would least tolerate.

Mr. Mojic listened intently, plucking one side of his mustache even more vigorously.

Cameron could sense the foot in the door, but didn't press hard: "The important thing is, Mr. Mojic, we can fix your thyroid problem. And we can do it while you're getting your pneumonia treated. Why don't you think about it, and talk it over with your son? Dr. Carlton will later explain how we can slow your thyroid to normal."

Out in the hall, Joel objected: "Why not cure his pneumonia and send him home? I mean, that's all the Medicare D.R.G. will cover. Then he can return for more treatment later," Joel grinned, "under the DRG for hyperthyroidism—which would cover these extra hospital costs."

Cameron looked at him: "We could divide the patient into DRG parts," Cameron said softly, controlling his voice to a calm-before-the-storm edge, "and treat likewise. Now, who said 'an organism out of step eventually falters and dies'?"

"I did," Joel claimed it.

"Ah, so you did. You were speaking as Doctor Saxton then. You also just spoke as Accountant Saxton. To be in step with your own self, eventually you'll need to decide which master to serve: Will it be a hospital? A mega-clinic? Government? Medicare? HMO, PPO, or some other insurance company? Or will it, perhaps, be the patient?"

Joel fidgeted with his patient cards, wishing he'd kept his mouth shut.

"Then again, maybe you believe you can serve all at once? The simple answer is you can't. These masters have different goals. While the patient's aim is to be cured, whatever the cost, that of the others is the 'bottom line'—solvency, or profit. The others can look out for themselves. The patient can't. The others already have accountants, lawyers, administrators; and the patient pays for them as well. But the patient has only you, the doctor, for an advocate. If you try to please them all, you'll succeed with none.

"You'll need to be clear on your path," Cameron's voice had lost its edge, and only the calmness remained, "because the world is not an impartial place. It favors money and power. And unless you make an effort not to serve them, you will. And if you do, you won't do much else well."

Joel's gaze looked to Lucy for sympathy, then to the floor.

"As for Mr. Mojic," Cameron finished, "after he leaves here, he may never again return. You may not have another chance to treat him." He paused. "Lucy, please prepare information on the efficacy and safety of the alternative hyperthyroidism treatments for Mr. Mojic. Joel, you may accompany her to the library. Rounds are over, Doctors."

Barbara interrupted him: "Dr. Cameron, call from Med 3. It's about Mrs. Ellen Samuels," she said outside. "She's been readmitted. Med 3 wants to know if we'll take her as a 'bounce' from them. She gave your names as her doctors."

"Tell them yes. I'll go see her right now."

Back in the lab, Joel panicked: "What does he mean 'rounds are over'? For the rest of the day? We just got started."

Lucy shrugged. "Think about it."

Cameron returned: "Continue rounds without me. I'll catch up." He was in time to see Mrs. Samuels wheeled into her room. Her heavy-lidded eyes watched the ceiling pass above her gurney, like white sky interrupted by luminescent neon clouds. Her hair, totally white, lay straight and thin as silk upon the pillow. Cameron watched her, and realized hospital ceilings would probably be the only skies she'd see again.

"Dr. Cameron... " It was an effort for her to talk. Her dry lips parted like tiny fish out of water, gulping thin air. "I'm so afraid..." The words formed slowly, like clay over the pasty pallor of her face.

Cameron searched for words. "Don't be afraid," was all he could find to say. "We're here to care for you."

"Thank you for taking me back." It was the most she'd said. The effort showed with perspiration on her face.

Cameron finished his exam. A lump-studded liver filled nearly the entire abdomen. Fluid from the tumor—ascites—further distended her torso to grotesque proportions in someone so emaciated. Shiny veined skin, like a gossamer jellyfish, stretched over the growing lumps, unable to hide them.

After the exam, words were even harder to come by. "We'll keep you comfortable," Cameron said. "Let us know if there's anything else we can do, Mrs. Samuels."

"Thank you," she uttered with a small nod.

"The other doctors will also be here to see you."

"Max and Joel?" She remembered them by name.

"Yes."

"That's good..." she smiled briefly, like a child going to sleep. It seemed as if there'd be more words coming, but there weren't.

Cameron touched her hand.

Rounds were at Mrs. Anna Wilson's bedside when Cameron returned. Joel presented the normal vital signs, which for Mrs. Wilson was a definite improvement: At times of severe asthma, not only did her respiratory rate increase, but also her pulse and blood pressure; as her asthma improved, so did her vital signs. On exam, she still had a few scattered wheezes, but they were confined to the ends of exhalation rather than taking up her entire inspiratory and expiratory phases. Her present brief wheezes also had a looser quality than the past tight ones, which had sounded like a choked-off siren. A complete clearing of wheezes, however, after forty-five years of smoking on top of her asthma, was a luxury Mrs. Wilson would never have again.

"I feel just dandy," Mrs. Wilson announced. "Never felt better in my life! When do I go home?" She smiled that I-knew-I'd-win, now-give-me-the-roses smile.

One had to admire her tenacity, optimism, and undaunted smile—like some improbable flower, blooming on high craggy cliffs near oxygen-starved clouds.

"No problems, then?" Dr. Saxton asked.

"None."

"No shortness of breath, no chest pains?"

"Well, maybe a little pain, when I move like so," and she pointed to her chest.

Joel was puzzled. Her chest had sounded clear for her—no pneumonia...maybe angina? Or a blood clot? "Maybe we'll need an EKG, or a lung scan," Dr. Saxton thought out loud.

Mrs. Wilson frowned at the mention of more tests. "It's just a little sore, not even all the time," she protested.

Cameron leaned over and palpated the ribs and sternum. She winced at one spot on the left chest. "You're tender over the costochondral junction," he explained, "that's where your ribs and cartilage meet. We probably strained that area during CPR chest compressions. Likely a strain, but maybe even a broken rib."

"Without the CPR I wouldn't even be here, would I, dears?"

"And if you'd taken your medicines, you wouldn't have needed the CPR," Cameron added.

"Now you're getting serious on me, dear." She paused and reflected: "I've had time to think about it. I realize I didn't take care of myself like I should, and that's why I'm here. I've been a bunch of trouble for all of you, dears. And I promise to take all my medicines from now on."

"Good," Dr. Saxton nodded. "We'll see how you're doing this afternoon, and if it's all right with Dr. Cameron, maybe we can send you home after evening rounds."

In the hall, Joel wrote on the chart, then looked at Cameron. "What shall I put down for the chest pain?"

"What do you think?"

"I think it's what you said – c.c. strain or broken rib. Guess we'll have to list it as a complication of CPR. All incidents and complications are being tracked now, you know, for Joint Commission hospital accreditation purposes. It's like the National Data Bank on doctors, keeping tabs on all malpractice lawsuits—win, lose, draw, or settle for even one dollar. And both have in common that once any information is in, even if proven to be erroneous, it can't be removed. It's cast on the hardest tablet of them all—the bureaucrat's computer."

"Interesting. Sounds like we better not take care of the sickest patients," Cameron smiled, "they'll always have the most complications." Cameron had said it in jest, but Joel didn't take it that way.

"Makes sense: Look at Mrs. Wilson's case," Joel continued. "Nothing goes into any computer about how many times we saved her life. Only that one high theophylline level goes in under our name, and now the bruises or fractured ribs."

"You're serious about that Data Bank stuff?"

"Sure."

"And no correlation is made for severity of cases, or how many we save?"

"Nope."

Cameron shook his head. "Odd way of rewarding those caring for the sickest patients." Cameron looked away. "By the way, Mrs. Samuels is back. I took her from Med 3. She asked for us, Joel."

"I'll go see her now."

When Joel returned an hour later, he looked at Cameron: "She's dying."

"I know."

"She'd like to see Max, too. Seems to reassure her we're all here for her."

"I've already called. He'll come."

"Thanks." Joel turned to leave, then stopped. "There's nothing else we can do, is there...." It was not so much a question as a remark on the present futility of all they had learned.

"No," Cameron said gently. "But I think what you're doing will help."

"Not enough."

"You going to be all right, Joel?"

He nodded.

"Let's get back to work." Cameron felt he should say something more. By the time he'd worked up to it, Joel had gone. Cameron felt that same helplessness. That end of the line. Finish line with no victory. Life's races all ended the same—with little to tell good endings from the bad. Or maybe not the same: Cameron knew of endings as much as anyone. But he couldn't answer that. Perhaps life's endings, like life's starts, were only a small part of it, and didn't really matter much. Either could be good or bad, just by chance. Just as birth conferred on one title and wealth, and on another a genetic accident, so also death bestowed corporeal finality in any number of unpredictable ways. But neither the starts nor the endings, Cameron began to realize, made the race, though sometimes it appeared that way. The real race was in between, and what one did with what one had.

In that sense, Mrs. Samuels final days were not a destination or an end, but a small part of her journey. Cameron suddenly realized how ironic it was that this part of Mrs. Samuel's journey, dying of gallbladder and liver cancer, was on his medical service, at the same time his own research on organ regeneration—also on the liver—finally came to fruition. The extension and application of that research to human treatment involved essentially the same concepts. Given the chance, he could attempt that procedure on humans tomorrow. Or today.

The possibility made Cameron shudder. His research had only been a "what if" theory, a puzzle, a dream. Now the dream had come true. Between the dream and reality's practical use came more confirmatory testing, committee approvals, state and federal regulatory agencies, and likely more paperwork than there had ever been in the research itself. Cameron knew he couldn't push the piles of forms to satisfy everyone. He also realized that without them, no one like Mrs. Samuels or anyone else, except his lab mutts, would benefit from what he'd found.

・・・・・

Max came to see Mrs. Samuels after evening rounds. Afterwards, he found Cameron in the lab room. "I'll be stopping by in the evenings to see her, if that's all right."

"She'll like that," Cameron said.

Max looked down. "Why is this so hard?"

"Because she's here with us, for her last few days, and there's little we can do to change what will happen."

Max shook his head. "So this is why we're supposed to remain objective, and not get involved?"

"Trouble is, the same part that makes it harder for us, makes it easier for her."

"Track thinks your research could help people like Mrs. Samuels."

Cameron looked away. "Maybe it could."

"He wants to get together. I suggested maybe this evening, the Continental, if it's all right with you."

"I've still got some work at the lab…"

"Can I help? I'll tag along, and we'll go after."

"You already told Track, didn't you?"

"Nine o'clock. And I checked—Elaine's also working tonight. So, you can't let your coach down."

Cameron smiled. "Let's go."

It was already dark outside, and patches of light from the research buildings flickered in the evening mist. Cameron unlocked the outer door, and they walked one flight down to the basement. The barking of dogs greeted them half-way down the corridor.

"So how many pooches are there now?"

"Wildwolf and M.R.'s seven to twelve. Haven't named those yet." Cameron stopped at a slate-gray door with white lettering:

HEPATOLOGY RESEARCH CENTER
M. Sullivan, M.D. Biochemical and Genetic Research
Authorized Access Only

Dogs barked and wagged their tails. Wildwolf showed off by standing on his hind legs, forepaws on the bars, cocking his head after each bark, waiting to see if he was understood. Cameron released them all, and prepared to feed them.

"Sure these guys won't bite?"

"Only if you don't pet them," Cameron grinned. Seven there," he pointed to a black-and-white hound mix, ears covered with fur like sheep's wool, "prefers chest rubs. Now M.R. Nine," a gray and white terrier tugged at Max' pant leg, "likes the neck above the collar scratched."

"How 'bout naming the rest?"

"You name 'em, you'll have to feed 'em. Eventually, I suppose they'll need a home, too."

"So I'll name two—one for me, and one for Tammy. For M.R. Nine, how about Misty? And that one," Max pointed to a large dusty-white shepherd dog, "will be Shadowfax, after the Wizard Gandalf's steed, in Lord Of The Rings."

"I'll give you a key, and show you what we feed them. But first, it's exam time."

Initially, Wildwolf had resented the presence of the new M.R.'s. But by now he shouldered the situation with bored equanimity. At exam time, he trotted from his rug and onto the carpet-covered exam table, from whence he viewed the rest of the pack with the air of one who'd been through it all before. One by one the dogs followed, after their exam waiting for their food and Milk Bone treats. The last, M.R. Twelve, clearly would just as soon skip directly to his treats.

Max followed Cameron into another room, made small by a refrigerator and freezer on one side, the other completely lined with steel and glass incubators. A simple desktop built into a wall carried shelves with stacks of papers above. A dissecting microscope and a light microscope sat on the right side of the desk, while the left gathered files and binders in various states of disarray. The remainder of the room was cramped with steel sinks, steel worktables, shelves of chemical reagents, and a chromatograph and chemistry analyzer backed into a corner.

"Chemistry, stains, and light microscope slides I do here. Genetic recombinant analysis is across the hall, or sometimes sent out to one of Track's colleagues. Electron Microscope work I sneak in with Track's batches at the university." Cameron followed Max' eyes around the room. "That's just the glamour stuff, though. The tedious part is just keeping the cultures going in pure form, checking for genetic drift, or any contamination."

"What exactly goes on here?" Max wondered out loud.

Cameron opened a case of slides from a drawer. "Let's look." He adjusted the microscope's aperture and filters. Light pierced darkened nuclei, gray and pink cytoplasm, and multi-colored granules. Cameron adjusted the focus. It looked like a miniature tide-pool, frozen in time. "Here you've got neatly layered, regularly organized, evenly shaped normal cells."

Max looked through the dual viewer, nodding.

"Now look at this." Cameron slipped in a new slide. "Cells with bizarre cytoplasmic whorls and edges, patches of nuclei dark as coal, and clumps of cells tacked on each other. Not too difficult to see malignancy here: Cells appear bizarre, without regularity, and no boundary growth inhibition."

"Odd looking, aren't they?" Max commented.

"Think about it: What's even more strange is that the previous 'good' normal cells are doomed to accomplish their work, then die. But these 'evil' looking cancerous cells are, for all practical purposes, immortal. Behind that paradox lie many factors: Cancer cell 'laziness' or lack of work such as other bodily cells have, increased aggressiveness, and endless replication. To be sure, there's still work going on in the cancer clump as well—but work only for itself. Immune suppression factors are produced, blocking antibodies, growth factors, angiogenic or blood-supply recruiting factors, and probably many more. They're the result of millions of years of blending of oncogene, chemical, and infectious components. You see," Cameron changed filters to contrast different areas, "cancer cells have also evolved, slowly and meticulously, carving out for themselves an ecological niche in the universe's rainbow, just like any other species of life."

Max peered through the microscope, then shook his head. "Thinking of it that way, cancer's a highly evolved, parasitic form of life."

"Exactly. Now, more by accident than anything else, I managed to cleave out the final genetic messages that transform these cells into complete cancers, but still maintain the beneficial expression of rapid fetal-like growth. Here is the resultant hybrid, in various stages of growth." Cameron changed slides again. "There's still aggressive growth at the edges, and more activity in cytoplasm and nuclei, but only during initial stages of growth or tissue implantation. See what happens with time," Cameron slipped another slide next to it.

"I don't see any difference now, from the normal."

"Precisely. If you observe fetal cells growing to adulthood, you'll observe much the same changes as in this series of hybrids. Normal hepatic cells, incubated with pre-selected cancerous genetic material, behave at first with the same vigorous growth characterizing fetal development, paralleling it immunologically as well. Then maturation tones the process down."

Max looked up and rubbed his eyes. "Basically, you're saying you've separated the 'good' from the 'bad' in cancerous genetic material, to maintain organ growth and function."

"Something like that."

"So how long did this 'accidental development' take?"

"Over four years." Cameron's voice became a whisper. "I'm afraid of the possibilities."

"Why?"

"These hybrids are at least partially derived from immortal cell clones. After genetic splicing and differentiation, they become mortal. But so far, the rate of decay and renewal of these hybrid organ cells have been altered. If my initial calculations hold over time, their life expectancy could nearly double."

Max stood on his tiptoes and whistled. "You know what you're saying?"

"Afraid so."

"This could change a lot of things."

"I could be wrong. It's still early, and the numbers could change with time. Or maybe it's just a quirk in my calculations."

"What if it isn't?"

Cameron shrugged. "Then I stumbled onto something maybe big."

"Big? You call this 'maybe big'? It's sensational!"

"Not sensational: Sensational is black holes, splitting the atom. This isn't unraveling the genetic code, only tailoring it a bit. It needs more work."

Max looked at him. "What are you afraid of?"

Cameron sat down. "My final month on call, peds rotation, a boy of five came in peeing blood. The little guy was calmer than his parents. They figured he was going to die; got so they even had him scared. Acute glomerulonephritis is what he had," Cameron continued. "I knew we could get his kidneys back into line, or as a last resort even transplant them. So I told them. It was like a weight lifted off, like he was already cured. And he was. The bleeding stopped that week." Cameron paused. "…He died a few days later. Sudden, fulminant staphylococcal pneumonia. Pneumonia, you know? I mean, not even some exotic disease." Cameron looked away. "I just don't want to make promises I might not be able to keep."

"I think I understand. It's not an easy burden to carry," Max looked at him. "The future changes, not always in ways we plan or want. I suppose some awe and reflection at the brink of innovation are better than blind speed ahead. Anyway," Max paused, "there'd at least be poetic justice in it, extracting good from bad. Taking one of the scourges of man – cancer – and repurposing it as a basis for organ regeneration and longevity."

Cameron didn't answer. He put away the slides. "Track's probably already at the Continental. Let's go."

· · · · ·

The Continental crowd was thinner than usual, and they could see Track's long legs stretched out under the table.

"Hope he hasn't been waiting long."

"Track's never just waiting. There, he's going over some notes."

"Welcome." Track grinned, putting his notes away. "I finally get to see my nighttime lab ghost."

"C'mon, it hasn't been that long, coach."

"Long enough. The place is getting overrun by pooches."

"Just named two more of them."

"I'm glad you're naming them. What else is happening at the lab?"

"Well, for starters, the pooches are alive."

"I've noticed that." Their banter was casual and relaxed. Beyond coach/athlete, professor/student, Max sensed a deep friendship, almost brotherhood, between Track and Cameron. Any reservations Max had that Track's grant application might have been for his own personal gains were dispelled.

"I've been checking on liver regrowth patterns with biopsies. Looks good."

"What does that mean?"

"The pattern is consistent: When implanted, there's fast regrowth of the incubated hybrid tissue with no traces of tissue rejection, and good organ function."

"I already knew that."

"Well, that was the theory. Now it's actually working." Track nodded, as if expecting no less. "Any glitches?"

"Crossbreeding native cells with the research line to produce hybrids can be a bit tricky. Incubating and harvesting's routine. Actual implantation into damaged tissue can pose a few technical problems, but if my hands can do it, then others could do it even more easily and consistently. What's left now is analyzing the exact nature of the hybrids, and follow-up for long term results. We sent some stuff to that genetics lab you thought might help us. What did they say?"

"So far, they haven't come up with any obvious differences. Whatever difference exists between native and hybrid cells is either hidden, blocked, or so small it bypasses usual tissue rejection mechanisms, right?"

Cameron nodded.

"Another thing's puzzling to the lab: Besides their initial rapid growth pattern," Track's eyebrows rose, "hybrid cells don't seem to age at the same rate as comparable native cells. They'd like more information and tissue samples."

"As soon as I have more, I'll pass it on, coach."

"What do I tell them in the meantime?"

"Their guess is as good as mine," Cameron smiled.

"So, you're probably holding out on me, but that's all right. I've backed you since this was a pipe dream, and I'll back you the rest of the way. I do need to know, though, if there are any reasons this wouldn't work on humans."

Cameron shook his head, adding quietly: "It should work."

"So what's the next step?"

"I need to enlarge the data base, more experiments, maybe then I'll be closer..."

"Closer to what?"

"Eventually we need to hybridize bits of human liver tissue – then clone and observe it, as I've done with the rest."

"How much tissue do you need?"

"Depends on how well it works."

"Would a needle biopsy sample be enough?"

"I could try it."

"Good. Then you've got one sample already," Track settled back in his chair, "mine."

"Wait. Hold it. I can't do that."

"Why not? Don't you believe it will work?"

Cameron's search for an answer was interrupted by Elaine. She gazed at their new companion: With distinctive angular features, in crew-collar sweater and jeans, Track looked more like the stroke in an eight-man racing shell than a research and teaching professor of medicine. She forgot to ask what they wished to order.

"A round of beers?" Max asked.

"Oh, sorry, of course." She turned to Track. "Which kind will you be having?"

It wasn't that Track hadn't noticed her long legs, rising like a spiral staircase to the curve of her hips. But his speed on the ground didn't always match other areas. "Guess I'll have the same these two are having, if you recommend it."

"One, or two?"

"Two...I mean one."

Cameron sensed perhaps it was time for introductions. "Track, this is Elaine Mathiesen. Elaine, we decided to bring our friend, Track Sullivan."

"I'm glad you did." With a twist of her hips, she waded back into the bar's crowd.

Track followed her walk. "You guys planned this, didn't you?"

Max and Cameron gave each other the "who, us?" look, and shrugged.

"Now, where was I?" asked Track.

"Your liver biopsy," Max reminded him.

"I thought about it," Cameron announced, "and I can't let you do it."

"Why?"

"Unless I do it on myself as well."

"Better make it three then," Max added. "Wouldn't want to be left out of any round-robin' liver biopsy tournament."

"I don't know, Max..."

Elaine returned with their rounds.

"Sure you do, Cam. So, let's give our livers one more round while we can. Seriously, will alcohol make any difference on our liver cell biopsies?"

"To play it safe, off alcohol for two weeks."

"Then it's resolved!" Track exclaimed. "That'll be the start of our protocol: The subjects, having forsaken beer and all manner of alcoholic sustenance, for a period of two weeks before biopsies, and after properly informed consent, do hereby donate biopsy slivers of their livers to project...Project Hybrid!"

"I'll drink to that!" Max seconded.

"What are you toasting?" Elaine asked.

"Research project. Maybe we should let Track tell you about it."

Track shrugged. "Not my project. It's Cameron's. I'm just background."

"You could tell me anyway," Elaine said in a soft voice.

"Let's see: It's about cloning organ cells, and from them, regenerating an entire organ."

"They say each bodily cell has the same complete genetic material as the entire body," she reflected. "So theoretically, from one frozen live, say, mammoth skin cell, all the rest of the animal's cells could be derived."

"True: A theoretic possibility. All cells are really multi-potential, but express only a fraction of that potential by turning on or off some of their functions. They specialize or differentiate, in this way, from other cells in the body."

Elaine nodded.

"You understand it, then?"

"Of course I understand," she countered in a mock-offended voice. "I may not have as much specialized knowledge, but I've got the basics down."

Track cleared his throat. "Biology major?"

"No. More esoteric—Botany. Do you realize the complex genetics of plants? With typical animal chauvinism, we think of trees and plants as all basically the same—wood and leaves—right? But all woods are different, and leaf varieties run into millions. The eucalyptus family alone has nearly five hundred species. The Coastal Redwood has twenty-seven billion base pairs in its DNA, while humans have three billion DNA base pairs. And what about the genetics that go into different kinds of fruit? The colors and flavors of grapes, the skin of peaches and apricots, the sweetness of plums, the hardness of apples, the smell and taste of limes in your drinks..."

"True. Not to mention that your flora practically invented chemical warfare," Track added, "using a multitude of toxins in leaves and sap, to ward off insects and fungi."

"You understand it, then?" she mimicked.

"I might not have as much specialized knowledge," he smiled, "but I have a few basics down," he mimicked back.

"Say, I take it they call you Track for obvious reasons."

He nodded.

"High school or college?" Elaine asked.

"Both, and still some nowadays."

"Maybe we could run sometime. But I wouldn't want to be left far behind," she added.

From his casual slouch, despite his height, Track had to look up to her hips. He overcame his shyness and came up to speed. "I don't think I'd want to leave you behind."

"Your track or mine?" she asked with a sparkle.

"Should we let Max or Cameron pick one, and join us?"

"I could bring one of the canines. Wildwolf likes to run."

"Sounds like Wildwolf will put speed into our run," Track commented. "What about you, Max? Don't you have a girlfriend?"

"Ah, not exactly..."

"Let me know then," Elaine smiled and returned to her work.

Track eased back into his chair. "You guys planned this. I know you did."

"We didn't exactly have to twist your arm."

Track shrugged. "Well, it's not easy to find someone good to run with."

Max and Cameron looked at each other and grinned. "Right, Track."

On the way back, Max was quiet. Cameron finally asked: "You haven't said much about Tammy..."

"She's doing fine. But they're still casting a wide net for her."

"How do you know?"

"I've got my ways. Besides, for now, they don't know me, and it's easier for me to keep tabs on them." Max changed the subject: "You going to ask Barbara for the run?"

"I'll call. But seems whenever I'm off call, she's working, and when she's not, I am."

· · · · ·

It was past midnight. Max went home, and Cameron went up to the ward. Mrs. Samuels' nightlight was still on, and the sheets crumpled under her chin, as if she'd been restless right up to her moment of sleep.

Cameron realized she'd probably never leave the hospital alive. Whatever they did would ultimately end as failure and a loss. The loss was so great, that most families couldn't cope with seeing the dying day to day. It was assumed that hospital people could. Since they dealt with it more often, it was supposed to be easier for them. Yet suffering and death were intimate processes, bringing those involved closer. So however it appeared on the outside, the loss was never routine. The loss was always of someone who mattered.

The fact was those who worked in a hospital hadn't been trained to accept death. Quite the opposite: They'd been trained to fight for life.

From beginning to end, medicine was taught as all out warfare against disease and death. When the inevitable came, rather than acceptance, hospital halls became one more, final battleground. Perhaps that was rightfully so, since if ever thought was given to compromise with disease and death, then future battles might not be as tenaciously fought.

But a time did come, when finally all medical counterattacks only prolonged agony, with little hope for relief. Perhaps with defeat inevitable, yet retreat or surrender equally medically unacceptable, a reasonable alternative was holding the line. At times, that line became very fine: Had one done too little? Or had one begun to do too much?

No matter how well the line was held, when those words were finally said, or thought—"nothing more can be done"—they were felt as a failure. Death, the enemy, had won, and the patient was lost. Perhaps there were ways to prepare for the failure. There were no good ways to prepare for the loss.

CHAPTER 14

FATE GYPSIES

Far away,
By whispering trees
A gypsy campfire sparks;
They sing and dance
Into deep of night;
When embers fade
They talk of love,
They talk of fate:
Do not seek either
From a rich man's heart,
Find it rather,
In a gypsy's soul.
                —*Lithuanian Folk Ballad*

It had been Jacob Werner's briefest conference with Terrance Liverpool, lasting the short end of fifteen minutes, and terminating with Terrance slamming his previous report down as if it were a cookbook in a kitchen on fire. "It's not enough," Terrance had said.

Of course Jake knew that. He usually obtained the information, then fed it to Terrance in bits and pieces. So long as it was finally complete, and not unusually delayed, there was no fuss. There had to be a lot of pressure on Terrance this time to break their routine.

Trouble was, this time the information really had come by bits and pieces. Sure, he could simply take what he needed from the lab, and pass it on. But it was one thing to destroy the man, and another to destroy the work the man believed in. Men made their own mistakes—their fumbles and turnovers in life—and Jake simply ran them in for his own touchdown. It was quite another matter to destroy the things they had done right. Still, the information would have to be obtained.

· · · · ·

Somehow morning rounds weren't the same today. It wasn't just that Dr. Atwood's rounds weren't the most edifying. They were all used to that. But Joel and Lucy weren't quite themselves either. Perhaps it was simple coincidence, or perhaps it was the sudden turnover in patients. Mr. Mojic had finally consented to RAI treatment of his hyperthyroidism. By his grimace one would have thought he was being asked to chew on a nuclear reactor core, instead of swallowing radioactive iodine, I-131, just strong enough to knock out his over-revved thyroid gland. Mrs. Wilson, after many entreaties to continue taking her prescribed medications, with her Christmas-light smile and as many nods and promises that indeed she would, finally went home. Mrs. Ellen Samuels had died yesterday evening. Joel had been called to "pronounce" her—officially certify her death. The word evoked dreadfully solemn, dramatic, and perhaps even religious overtones. Reality was different: She was dead whether he "pronounced" her dead or not. Joel noted the date, time, and lack of pulse and respiration. Then, trying not to look too closely, he drew the sheet over her face.

Compared to some other things, perhaps rounds with Dr. Atwood weren't that bad, after all. When they were over, Dr. Atwood reminded Cameron of his Moderna Clinic offer; again Cameron politely declined.

By now, Joel had left for lunch, and Lucy was in the lab room, staring at a pile of charts.

"Your charting system is working well," Cameron sat down. "Looks like Joel and Max like it too."

Lucy was silent.

"I think Dr. Atwood liked it also."

Lucy broke the silence. "He didn't say anything."

"Precisely. He would have found something bad to say if he didn't like it." On the other hand, perhaps he hadn't even noticed it, Cameron thought.

Lucy didn't comment.

"Lunch?" Cameron asked.

"Not hungry," she shook her head.

"Anything wrong?"

Lucy looked down at her coffee. "No."

Cameron could see her eyes were puffy. It didn't look like from lack of sleep. "What is it?"

She didn't answer.

Cameron tried to lighten up. "I know Dr. Atwood's rounds are not the best, but they're nothing to cry about."

That didn't work either. Lucy remained quiet.

"It's me, your Resident, remember? You can tell me about it."

"Not something like this," she said slowly.

"What do you mean, 'not something like this'?"

"It has nothing to do with you. And nothing you can do about it."

"Try me."

"You don't understand, it's not something that can be changed, or fixed, or returned to the way it was..."

Cameron was silent. He tried to understand what was happening, but his usually sharp intuition failed him. He refilled Lucy's coffee mug, and waited.

"You promise," she finally said, "this will stay between you and me?"

Cameron nodded.

"I was raped." She said it fast, looking away.

"What?!...When?"

"Last night..."

Cameron was speechless. He tried to be rational: "Do you want to get checked? I mean I could go with you. I could get an Attending to take over here. Dr. Sullivan would do it."

"Go to the ER.? Get checked for lacerations? Acid phosphatase stain for sperm? Pubic hairs combed for the presence of other hairs? No, thanks. I know the route. I've worked there."

"Doesn't have to be our ER. We could go to another hospital."

"See? You don't understand. It would be just as humiliating."

"I just thought, you know, to make sure you weren't hurt."

"It's not that kind of hurt..."

Cameron shook his head. "Did you call Security? Let someone know?"

"And tell them what?" Lucy's voice came with a screeching laugh: "That another doctor raped me? That he followed me to the sleeping rooms, saying the men's dorm was full, and could he sleep in this one? Only he didn't, you see. There was no one else, and he locked the door, and..."

Cameron sat there, numb, unable to comprehend. "Who was it?" he finally asked in a hoarse voice.

"Nothing you can do," she shrugged.

"Maybe not."

"If I tried to do anything about it, I'd just be dragged through the mud. I have an idea of how things go. And you'd just get into trouble over me, Cameron, if you got involved. No good would come of it."

"Lucy, I know what you should do is up to you. But I still want to know who it was."

She shook her head, but Cameron persisted: "I won't do anything rash. There's no room for that here. And no one else will know. I promise." Cameron reflected. "It wasn't Joel, was it? I know at times he's a walking hormone..."

Lucy shook her head. "Not Joel. He's been on best behavior lately. The poor thing's been so down over Mrs. Samuels death." She hesitated. "You promise?"

Cameron nodded.

"It was Roger Taylor," she blurted out. "There, now let me forget about it."

"You can take the rest of the day off, Lucy."

"I'd rather keep working. Please." Cameron didn't say another word.

In the evening, after rounds were done, Cameron made a phone call and picked up his mail. Two official-looking envelopes had arrived from the Director of Medical Education's office. Cameron opened them both. They were from the Quality Assurance Committee, and had been routed through the Medical Education office:

> To: Dr. John Cameron.
> Re: Anna Wilson, File # 090456,
> Medicare # 512-09-3913 A,
> PIN # OT 2407900
>
> A physician-related incident report has been received. It has come to our attention that your patient, case # 090456, underwent recent CPR on your service. As a result, she suffered chest pain, and a broken left fifth rib.
>
> At your earliest convenience, or within ten days, please explain this patient complication, and breach of CPR protocol.
>
> Chairman,
Quality Assurance Committee

Cameron folded it, and read the second letter:

> To: Dr. John Cameron
> Re: Ellen Samuels, File # 083165,
> Medicare # 512-07-4401 A,
> Pin # OT 0024079
>
> A physician-related incident report has been received. It has come to our attention that your patient died as a result of carcinoma of the gallbladder, metastatic to the liver.

At your earliest convenience, or within ten days, please explain your failure to diagnose same (diagnosing gallstones instead), and failure to have this operated and removed prior to the patient's demise.

Chairman,
Quality Assurance Committee.

Cameron rubbed his eyes, blinked, and replaced the letters in his pocket. He turned off his call-light, and went to the gym to see the results of his previous phone call.

Roger Taylor was already waiting. "You said it was something personal and important," Roger stood next to the chin-up bar, his extended arm reaching it like a surfer leaning on his board.

"More than personal, definitely important. I'll cut through the crap. Lucy told me all about it, but she doesn't know I'm here. I just wanted you to know you won't get away with it."

"Ah! That's what this is all about! You're going to take her word over mine?"

"As a matter of fact, yes. Seems you knew about this without my even saying it."

Roger Taylor realized he'd fallen into the trap. "You can accuse anyone of anything. Proving it is another matter."

"There are forensic ways of doing that."

Taylor began to sweat. "Look, it's not like I really forced her. She could have gotten up and walked out."

"If she could have, she would have."

"There aren't forensic means to prove that," Roger Taylor regained some of his composure. His tone slowly became more arrogant. "There's nothing to prove I forced her. Why didn't she scream, kick the door, or me? There aren't any marks on her, and none on me. Forensics can't prove I forced her. So what are you going to do about it?"

Taylor barely finished the sentence. It turned hoarse in his mouth. He doubled over neatly at the solar plexus—around Cameron's fist. Taylor fell back against the wall, then slid off Cameron's fist, down to his knees.

"That won't leave any marks either. Difficult to prove I did it forcefully, eh? You see, it works both ways. How unfortunate we couldn't discuss this in a more civilized way. I would suggest your future conduct around Lucy Carlton be beyond any shadow of reproach. Or I will hold your balls personally responsible."

Taylor couldn't catch his breath, much less reply. Cameron looked to see if more was necessary to get the point across, then left.

He wondered if eventually this would become an incident report as well.

· · · · ·

The truck's heater whistling past his ears, Max almost nodded at the wheel after a day and a night and a day's work. Snow slid under his headlights like Christmas-tree tinsel. After the final turn for home, a gray four-door sedan turned, sliding in the snow, then disappeared into the night. Max' somnolence suddenly left. Strange, he thought, how one's adrenalin reacted sometimes. After all, the gray sedan's snowy slide had been too far away to pose any danger.

Max pulled into the driveway. As he fumbled for his door keys, his hands suddenly began to shake: The sedan image took on a new meaning. It had been like the one staked out for Tammy at the recovery house. Coincidence? Max managed to get the key into the door. "Tammy!" he shouted.

As he shouted again, Tammy came from the kitchen. "Sweetheart, what's the matter?"

Max lifted her and hugged her. "Nothing," he said. "Nothing at all." He pressed her head against his neck.

"You sounded so worried..."

"Just a coincidence."

"Tell me this coincidence."

"It can wait." He hugged her again.

"You're right it can. I've got dinner for you. And I've missed you."

"I'm sorry you've been cooped up like this. We'll see what we can do for your cabin-fever, get you out a bit."

"I'd miss you even if I wasn't cooped up. You're still all tense—what happened?"

"Like I said—coincidence. Say, dinner smells great. Where'd you go shopping for that?"

"You got most of it, last week. I just went to the corner deli. In two sweaters, muffler, and a small pillow under the coat. See?" She puffed out her cheeks, until her pouting lips were almost erased. "I looked like a cross between a bow-legged duck and a turtle. Totally unrecognizable."

"You sure you haven't gone anywhere without that stuff?"

"Wig and everything. Even colored the eyebrows, and dental wads between the cheeks to puff them out. I like the idea of getting away, though. Can you get the time off?"

"Maybe a weekend afternoon off call."

"I also want to talk to you about something else."

"Sure," he nodded.

"You already know I have cabin fever. I can live with that. But it's time I made plans, I mean, for what happens later. I've had time to think, to look at myself, and outside myself. I've got to do something with my life. I think now maybe I can. I hope you won't laugh at me."

"Why would I? I always knew you could."

"Don't look so sad, either. I don't have any plans without you."

"It wasn't that. I was thinking about something else."

"You wouldn't miss me if I left?" She drew a teasing finger down his arm.

"Course I would. Where are you going?"

"Nowhere, really." She sat on his lap. "Not anywhere you wouldn't want me to."

"I want what's best for you."

"And what's best for you is letting you finish your dinner." She drew a chair next to him. "Anyway, I know I've been seeing the world through one tiny corner of a very clouded looking glass. For the first time I see, and I realize how little I do see and know. I mean, I understand we're little dots in a huge universe, and not very important that way. But in a way, each little dot makes a difference. I want to learn how to make a good difference.

"I know I tried to make my dot disappear in the past, and it wouldn't have been missed. But things have changed. I've watched you work, I've read, I've seen what goes on around me. I know now, no matter what happened or will happen to me, I'm not the most unfortunate. There are others even I could help: The handicapped who try so hard; the retarded who don't understand but still feel like us; the children who don't look like the rest and no one wants. They're all innocent of the cards life's dealt them. I don't have that excuse," she smiled. "But I don't need excuses anymore. I can learn more, do whatever it takes to do that work. You might laugh, but I've always wanted to do that." She paused: "What do you think? Now am I certifiably crazy?"

"It's worthwhile, and it's what you want. What I think doesn't matter. But if you want to know, I'm really proud of you." He drew her by the waist and hugged her.

"It's not a sudden thing, you know. I always thought it would be nice working with people who need you: Who look you in the eye, smile, and mean that smile... So many don't. In the past I guess I've been too weak for it; and later too full of self-pity." She pressed his hands. "You made me realize what I was doesn't need to be my future. Do you think I can do it?"

"I know you can."

"Thanks." She returned the hug. "Now, I have a list of books for you to get. Or do I go to the library myself?"

Max laughed: "I guess that's one place they wouldn't look!" The telephone rang. "What have you been doing about the phone, Tammy?"

"Haven't been answering it. Only the way you ring, like we agreed. It's been ringing a lot today, though."

Max picked it up.

"Hello..." the voice was muffled and vaguely familiar: "Max, I'm sorry. I want you to know that. But I have to tell you..." there was fast breathing, as if the caller had been running.

Max recognized the voice. "What's the matter, Tom?"

"Got a little roughed up... That doesn't bother me. Then they began talking about my daughter...I knew they were serious. They knew where she was, school, everything. She's only five, Max...I told them what I knew."

"Wait a minute, Tom: Who's 'them'? And when?"

"The gorillas after Tammy. I had to tell them, Max..."

"What did you tell them?"

"Just what I knew. That she'd left the recovery house without anyone knowing where, but there'd been an Intern visiting her. Your name they already figured. I called because I figured they'd put a tail on you to get to Tammy."

Max pondered quickly: As he'd suspected, Tom still didn't know where Tammy was. That bought more time. "You going to be all right, Tom? You don't sound so good."

"Just a few bruises, a couple of loose teeth. Nothing's busted except maybe the nose. Max, I wouldn't have told them anything, except..."

"I know, Tom. Don't worry. The bastards will get theirs. When did it happen?"

"This afternoon, 'bout four-thirty."

"Give me a number I can reach you."

"Same place. The recovery house."

"Stay put. Don't try to do anything about them. You might want to call the police about protecting your daughter."

"They can't protect her twenty-four hours a day." He paused. "I know if those guys don't find Tammy, they'll be back."

"You want in on those guys, Tom?"

"You think you can go after them, Max? They're big time."

"You know what General Patton once said: 'They've got us surrounded, the poor bastards.' So they have. And they've left us no choice."

There was a pause on the line, and what sounded like a spit. "I'm in. For me, it's got to be all or nothing."

"What do you mean?"

"It's got to work totally, so this business is ended, or I'm a goner. I can't leave this unfinished, or me unfinished, for them to return for my daughter."

"Tom, you don't have to do anything. I understand the spot you're in. You can pull out, no questions asked."

"Don't mind doing it," it sounded like another spit, "just got to be done right. Hell, I'm in."

"Feel the same way. I'll get back to you."

Tammy stood with her mouth open. "What was that all about? Is Tom okay?"

"He'll be fine."

"What's going on?"

"Mob's getting too close. We'll have to do something about it."

"They know I'm here?" she began to shake.

Max sat her on his lap. She wrung her hands nervously, fingers moving like rabbit's ears. He took her hands in his. "There's no way anything will happen to you." She laid her head on his shoulder. "They don't know you're here yet, otherwise they would have been here. They'll case the place, check me out, tail me. They figure I'll lead them to you. We don't need to do anything different tonight, other than pack for tomorrow."

"What? Where are we going?"

"I'm not going anywhere. But you're going to Cameron's."

"Wait a minute! For one thing, I don't want to. I don't want to leave you. For another, Cameron probably doesn't want me there either."

"It'll be the safest place for you. Cameron's already promised help when needed. He won't back down on his word."

"I can't stay there forever, Max. I can't hide like this forever."

"You won't have to."

She heard the tone in his voice. "Oh no... what are you going to do?"

"Not much. Just send a message they can all understand. Now you pack your things. We'll need to get them all out—no trace left behind." Max stood up and went to the next room.

Tammy followed him. "This is all so sudden...so mixed up..."

"Sudden, but not mixed up. I've thought it out before." From a gym bag, Max pulled out a sheathed knife and a .357 revolver.

He opened the steel chamber, loaded it in order with three types of bullets, then clicked the chamber shut. Max filled a speed-loader with magnums only, and replaced both in the gym bag. "I'll be seeing you," he touched her gently, "not as often or as long as I'd like. But you'll be safe. This will be over soon, I promise."

Tammy's eyes widened. Instead of calming down, the veins of her neck pulsed like a bird's breathing; her teeth pressed the lower lip blood red. "Over? What are you saying? All that'll be over is you! You're going to tangle with those guys? This isn't a movie; these guys aren't special effects! In the backstreets they don't care about broken bones, or lives. They enjoy that part of it like you enjoy fixing people. It's not close to an even match, Max. Don't do it!"

"There are things I haven't told you, Tammy. I didn't get to med school by direct transfer from Ivy League suburbia. I know those backstreets myself. They didn't beat me then, and they won't beat me now. This time there's even more at stake. You."

Tammy was silent. She watched Max collect her things on the bed, and pack them. "You're going to do it anyway," she shrugged, "no matter what I say."

Max nodded. Tammy said nothing more, and helped him pack. "Let's get some sleep, sweetie." Max had taken her bags into the truck, and pulled out his trundle bed.

"Not tonight," she pulled him away. "We've waited long enough. I'm not the tramp you met back then. If I'm still not good enough for you, tell me. Otherwise, you stay in my bed tonight. I may not see you again."

Max lifted her chin with the palms of his hands, as if holding a wounded bird. "If I've waited, it's not because you might not be good enough, but because you're good enough to wait for. It was my way of showing my help was a gift to the woman I love, not a trade..."

Tammy placed her hand over his mouth. "I haven't loved anyone before. I do love you. This is so different, and feels so good..."

Afterwards, with her body pressed along her entire length against his, Max thought about what he needed to do to make his promise to Tammy come true: That he'd never let anything bad happen to her. He thought about it many times, in many different ways. Finally, after all plans and details were in place, he knew the rest was up to fate.

Tammy waited until he was asleep. Watching his face, she thought perhaps she could leave him, walk out of his life forever. She got up without waking him. But the plans he'd made, Tammy realized, he'd still keep. Leaving now would only complicate those plans, without changing them: Afterward, he'd also try to find her, and it would give him more to do rather than less.

She looked at him, resting miles away from any tomorrows. The gym bag with the gun was by the bed. His hand was near it, fingers open just enough for a pen or a scalpel, not the butt of a revolver. She wondered what she could do to keep it that way.

Tammy went into the bathroom. Her makeup, lipstick, comb, brush, few pieces of glass jewelry, chrome bracelet and a small oval, faded bronze St. Christopher medal, were still there. She gathered a few of them into a little pile on the sink. Dim moonlight filtered through the frost-covered window. It had stopped snowing. Reflections touched the bits of glass, metal jewelry, medal like a gypsy's bundle of dreams, living only in tales by campfire's dim embers of night, never really coming true.

She bowed and prayed.

CHAPTER 15

SOUL SEARCH

"To harm is easy;
To heal, much more difficult."

—Chinese proverb

John Cameron finished work at the Hepatology lab and locked it for the evening. Being on call every third night, and at the lab the rest of his evenings left Cameron little time at the Intern/Resident quarters, and gave Tammy plenty of time for privacy, to the point of boredom.

Though it was late, Tammy was still up this evening. "Been reading some of your books. Hope that's all right."

"Sure. Help yourself, Tammy. How are you doing so far?"

"Not bad. I miss Max. I'm sorry we're putting you out like this, you know, me just moving in and all." She laughed, "I mean, what if you wanted to bring a girl to your place?" They had placed a folding metal-framed divider in the room, like those between ER beds. Tammy's robe and a nightshirt draped over it.

"I guess I'd have some explaining to do," Cameron smiled, looking at her things on the divider.

"That'd be a lot of explaining. Listen, I could just go down to the laundry room or something, or hang out someplace else in the meantime."

"Thanks, I'll let you know," he chuckled. "For right now there doesn't seem to be any pressing need for that. Did Max call today?"

She nodded. "He was supposed to come by, but said he couldn't today."

"I'm sure he had good reason. I know he cares as much for you as you do for him. He wouldn't have missed seeing you otherwise."

"It's just, you know, from seeing him almost every day, to maybe once a week..."

"He's working to change that situation, Tammy."

"What can he do? You know what he's up to?"

"All I can tell you is not to worry. Max is a big boy, and can take care of himself."

"Thinking that can get him in over his head."

"Medicine teaches us to be careful, Tammy. I think he's learned that."

"I fixed you a snack. I'm used to fixing one for Max, so I hope you're hungry. He's been eating like a horse lately, says you two have been running and working out together."

"A bit. Thanks for the snack."

"I don't suppose you'll tell me what he is up to."

"Even if I knew, I probably wouldn't," Cameron smiled. "So don't worry, and good night."

"Easy for you to say," Tammy pushed the partition into mid-room, and opened the sofa-bed.

Lights went out. Cameron could hear the rustling of clothes as Tammy put on her usual sweatshirt in place of any nightgown.

"Cameron?"

"What?"

"Thanks for letting me stay here. I know you're in the middle of some hard work and all. But you've been really nice."

"And I'm not complaining about the evening snacks, either. One thing, though—you've got to stop doing my laundry."

"You don't like the way I do it?"

"I don't want you to feel like you have to do it, like you owe me something. You and Max are my friends, and that's why I'm doing it."

"Seriously? We're both your friends?"

"Of course."

"It doesn't matter that I...?"

"You're not going to give me that stuff about your past and everything—that's history."

"But history matters."

"Sure. And you learned the hard way. Now you also know that part of your history is over."

"Cameron?"

"Yes..."

"You know, I've never had a brother. But, well, I mean...you sort of feel like one for me..."

Cameron looked up into the darkness. "I never had a sister." If someone had predicted that during his Residency Cameron would be manipulating organ regeneration through hybrid genes, and sleeping in the same room across a partition with his Intern's girlfriend, Cameron would have taken a million-to-one odds against it. But sometimes long odds won. "I suppose that's fair enough," Cameron replied. He paused, "...but don't brothers have to be more strict or something?"

"That's only when they're little—when brothers can be mean and tease their sisters. Later they look after them, like you're doing."

"Right. But I'm still supposed to check on all your boyfriends and stuff?"

"Sure….So, how about Max?"

"Hmm... So, all right, Sis, we'll pass him…."

"Good. Hope I see him soon."

"You will. Now get some sleep. Good night."

· · · · ·

The telephone shook him from sleep, like a tree-limb crashing at the foot of his bed.

"It's a go," said the voice on the telephone. Cameron rubbed his eyes: "It's a go?"

"It's now, Cameron. Are you awake?"

There were times he'd woken up, only to fall asleep again, dream-weaving an elaborate plot, far away from any reality.

"You awake, Cameron?" Max repeated.

This time the elaborate plot was real, though even Cameron didn't know all the details. "Yes, I'm awake."

Max went over brief instructions.

"I'll be there," Cameron replied. "Fifteen minutes." He checked his watch.

Tammy was awake. "Where are you going?"

"Out a short while." Cameron didn't need to turn on the lights. His whites were folded near the bed beforehand.

"I thought you weren't on call."

"I'm not. They've got a crunch in ER. I've got to help out a little, is all." Each statement, taken separately, was true enough. "Be back soon." Cameron closed the door behind him.

· · · · ·

Max made two more calls—one to Tom, the other to Carlos Schmidt. Afterwards, he pulled on skintight leather gloves, and checked the revolver's loading order. Satisfied, he snapped the chamber shut. The rest of what he carried tucked in his shirt pocket was designed so the first wouldn't need to be used.

It was four a.m. Max crept up behind the gray sedan—it had been there since late evening. Inside, the one Tammy called Gopher was asleep; the other, Gator, was probably awake. They'd left the driver's side unlocked. Max had already confirmed Gator's hair whorl was on his left side—that made his left brain hemisphere dominant, and therefore Gator was right-handed. Max moved up quietly, and jerked the door open. As Gator's elbow slipped down, Max caught the wrist, and cleanly rotated Gator's right arm behind his back. Before Gator could even twitch, Max had released the contents of an injection into his right deltoid.

"Shit..."

In response, Max pushed up on Gator's twisted arm, until wrist reached the shoulder blade's scapular spine. "I'd keep still. It could break."

Gator gave a grunt of exhaled air.

Max saw Gopher stir from slumber. "That goes for you too. Any moves, and this arm is history. One more thing: The injection was a neurotropic poison. First it paralyzes, then it kills. Without an antidote, in five minutes you can't breathe. If I'm not here to give the antidote, Gator's dead. Nod if you understand."

Gator nodded more quickly than Gopher.

"You can still breathe, right?" Max massaged the injection site to speed uptake of anesthetic into the bloodstream.

With a twisted face, Gator nodded, then cursed under his breath.

"We've got four minutes," Max tugged upward on Gator's arm. The joint crackled, Gator's knees drew up, and his lips curled with pain and another curse. "You can keep swearing," Max continued, but you'll be using up time. Better listen instead." Max massaged the injection area slowly, then went on in a voice calm as a bedtime story: "Everything will go numb and paralyzed. The last thing to go will be your breathing. By then you'll have received and understood my message, and I'll give you the antidote. There will be no next time. I only give an antidote once.

"Now here's the message you need to understand. First: No one put me up to this. I'm doing it because I like doing this. I came from the streets myself. I know your kind: You're the scum that flows into sewers. I know you and what you do. You're going to stay scum until you stop what you're doing.

"Second, you're not going to have a choice about one thing you're doing—that's looking for Tammy. You, your pals, and your bosses are going to get out of her life. You can choose to remain scum, do whatever else you're doing, but her you're not going to touch. I'll tell you why.

"I've dealt with your kind before, and got off the streets just fine. I don't need much of an excuse—not a big one, not even a little one—to finish what I started then. Looking for Tammy, being anywhere near her life, that'll do it. Since my backstreet days, I've acquired more refined ways of dealing with people like you. More refined," Max jerked up on Gator's arm, "but less pleasant." The arm went slack in his grip as Gator's paralysis deepened. A groan issued from Gator's mouth. "Back then, I dished it out same as you guys, and more. But now it's different. I can touch Gopher here, and nothing happens," Max drew his gloved hand across Gopher's forearm. "Then I take a little water—plain water—see?" Max first drank from a vial, then sprinkled it over Gopher's arm. The same water Max drank made Gopher scream in pain.

"You see the difference now? I can make plain water burn like a cat o' nine tails. And you, you're not even breathing so well, are you?" Gator's eyelids were closing, paralyzed. Gopher looked in horror at crimson welts like scalded pig's skin spreading over his arm. "This was just a little demonstration. For your sakes, I hope you can convince your bosses. Your bosses, well, you're princes next to them. So if anything at all happens to Tammy, they'll never know what hit them. It may be the food they eat, water they drink, even the air they breathe. It might be a chemical, a virus, or neither. Or any one of ten thousand items in the medical dictionary. I've got thousands of ways of doing what I need to do, and I'll do them without batting an eye.

"Just so the message is clear: Nothing on earth will cure that arm. It won't kill you this time, but will stay like that for two weeks. Show it to convince your bosses. Your lives will depend on it."

Gator went limp on the car seat, against Gopher's shoulder.

"Oh, almost forgot—the antidote." Max brought out another injection, gave it near the same area, and waited for Gator's eyes to open.

"In case you have a misguided idea that getting rid of me might solve all your problems—think again." Max reached into the car and turned on the headlights. Three figures in white, their faces indistinguishable in the distance, stood at the end of the street. "There are more of us. Many more. Any one of them would be glad to finish my work."

Max suddenly released the arm, and disappeared into the night. After a few minutes, the gray sedan was also gone.

Cameron returned after five a.m., took off his whites and jumped into bed for barely another hour of sleep.

"Everything all right?" Tammy asked.

Cameron wondered if she'd just woken up, or had remained awake the entire. "Sure. Except you're still awake. Goodnight."

· · · · ·

That evening, Cameron met Max at the Continental for follow-up rounds.

"How did it go?" Cameron asked.

"Right on the button."

"Think it will work?"

Max shrugged. "It was a good show. We'll see soon enough."

"You know, I never asked what kind of show you put on last night."

"And I didn't say. That way, if something went wrong, you guys weren't involved. I can tell you now: I took the driver out with a sub-anesthetic dose of vecuronium I.M., enough to paralyze him, but still keep him breathing, and listening. Before leaving, I gave neostigmine as an antidote. The other gorilla I neutralized by first sprinkling dry jellyfish pneumatocytes..."

"The ones I got you from marine lab toxicology?"

Max nodded. "Then I simply added water to the nearly invisible pneumatocytes, and presto! In contact with water, they uncoiled like miniature poisonous blow-darts! He got a jolt of welts that ought to last a while."

Cameron looked away. Elaine didn't seem to be working tonight. The dance floor was starting to get crowded. "So, you think this will be the end of it?"

"I don't know yet."

"And what if it isn't?"

Max shrugged and stared ahead. "I'll do whatever I have to do."

"I was afraid you'd say that. How far do you plan to carry this?"

"As far as necessary." Max' stare didn't change.

"That worries me, Max. Not just for you, but for Tammy's sake also. There's a limit to what you can ethically, and legally, do."

"I think I understand you, Cameron: As a physician, I shouldn't be using knowledge of the profession to cause harm. I agree with that. I haven't done, and don't intend to do, anything that might cause permanent harm that way."

"What if your semi-paralyzing dose had for some reason paralyzed his breathing also?"

"There was the antidote, and I could also have intubated him. I had all the equipment on hand."

"Still, cutting it a bit close, don't you think, Max? I know it was meant just to scare them. But does the end justify the means? And what if it escalates? What's next then?"

Max continued to stare ahead. "That's where we differ, Cameron: In your Ivy league world of libraries, research labs, and track fields you can measure win or lose by published articles, a finish tape, or a stopwatch. You can ponder your philosophies of intentions, means, and ends.

"Where I came from, win or lose meant one's life. I've dealt with the types of last night and their bosses up close: In that world there aren't libraries or labs to escape to, no finish lines to signal the end of friendly competition. There aren't any values at all by which you live or you die, or stay trapped in a living nightmare. Their philosophy is greed and pleasure; their ethics power and money—obtained through fear, force, and exploitation.

"You know, they've got at least seventeen girls," Max hadn't touched his beer, "seventeen lives of prostitution, drugs, and fear. They've got no way out, no finish line this side of life. That's what this is all about. Not just some statistics, but involving me and Tammy. I sent them a message, Cameron, in the only language they understand. What I did was self-defense. Antibodies rising to fight a disease."

"I know how you feel," Cameron reached for Max' shoulder. "But the message you sent included the use of medical and scientific knowledge in ways they weren't intended."

Max pondered it. "So scientists have split the atom, and from it created instruments of destruction on a scale unimaginable. Where's the difference?"

"I don't know," Cameron stared down at his beer. "I suppose a very simple and incomplete answer is that we took an oath not to do so. Another might be that they shouldn't have created that evil from good, and are responsible for it."

"Are you saying I should wait, let them strike first? Tammy would be a goner then."

"I'm saying we should be careful with this, Max. Neither the Ivy league, nor the school of hard knocks has all the answers on this one."

"Something like the old question, isn't it? If you were Attila's, or Hitler's, physician, and knew what he was doing, would your first duty be that of a physician for his patient, or to the rest of humanity?"

Cameron smiled. "It's not often the ethics of a physician might conflict with those of humanity. I guess we're human first, physicians second. In a situation of ethical conflict, maybe we're left with the choice of the most good, or the least harm. That's not something anyone can tell you how to measure. Each of us has to search his own soul for the answer."

"Fair enough," Max replied. "And I thank you for being there."

"I said I'd help if you needed it. I just wish you'd leave the doctor stuff out of it."

Max bobbed up on his tiptoes and grinned: "You want to hardball it instead, then? All right. We can do that if we have to. Workouts at the gym from now on, three times a week."

"Sure." Cameron laughed, "if we also run three times a week."

"Deal. How's Tammy holding up?"

"Fine. I think she suspects something came down last night, though. You should give her a call tonight."

"I don't want to tell her anything she'll worry about."

"I think she's worried enough already."

"Thanks for letting her stay, Cam."

"No problem. She's never had a brother."

"So?"

"I've never had a sister." Cameron paused. "You know, I would never let anything happen to her either."

Max put his an around Cameron. "By the way, do you know that girl there?"

"Who?" Cameron asked.

"Light blue dress, white belt, blonde hair, classy looking…"

"Don't think so."

"Then maybe you should. She's been looking at you."

Cameron glanced again. "No, don't think I know her. Maybe she's been looking at you."

"The human eye may seem very small from a distance, yet somehow we're quite well programmed to follow exactly where it's looking. And she's looking at you, Cam."

"No way!" Cameron shook his head.

"Suit yourself. I think she just smiled at you."

"I suppose I could stretch my legs awhile…" Cameron got up enough courage to start walking in her direction. She had appeared to be looking directly at him, though he was equally certain he'd never seen her before. He would have remembered eyes like that: Light blue like an early spring morning, sparkling like sea-waves. Her features were well defined, with soft, wide eyebrows, prominent cheekbones, small bob of a nose, angular chin, and a sensuous mouth, with lips curved like a long-winged bird gliding in spirals. If Cameron had seen her before, it had been in his dreams.

As he approached, his initial resolve began to dwindle, then just a few steps away from her, totally vanished. Cameron veered off towards the bar. He felt foolish just standing there, and ordered another beer. He figured it had been a case of mistaken identity, or maybe she'd been looking at someone nearby. Perhaps on the way back he'd ask and clear up this mistaken identity. At least he'd be cushioned for the fall.

Cushioned for a fall? Cameron pondered: Was that also the way he ran? The way he did research?

Cameron was jump-started from his musings. The spiral-winged smile was before him: "Would you mind ordering a drink for me? The bar's getting crowded, so I thought since you're standing there, maybe you could…"

"Certainly… ah, what will it be?"

She told him, and he ordered it.

"I thought before, when you were walking toward me, maybe you were going to talk to me." Her voice carried a melodious, almost Southern lilt.

"It was my intention."

"Why didn't you?"

Cameron hesitated. "It seemed like maybe you knew me—I mean, perhaps mistook me for someone else."

She looked at him with her blue eyes: "I guess, in a way, maybe it does seem I know you."

"But you don't, right? I'd remember it if we'd met before." Cameron felt himself blowing it, right from the starting blocks.

She laughed, in that same melodious voice. "Who's to say we haven't? Haven't you ever felt as if you're standing in a place long ago, sensing what happened then; or touched a future that's yet to be?"

"Maybe..." Cameron tried to decide if such beauty had simply been bestowed on someone who believed all she read in the Enquirer, or on a rare soul not defined and confined by the boundaries of earthly beauty.

She searched his eyes and replied for him: "Maybe...maybe once."

"How did you know what I was going to say?" She shook her head, and her voice began a poem:

> *"From far riverbanks they gazed,*
> *At each other, from separate shores,*
> *Unbridgeable in those ordinary ways*
> *Of life, that we all know.*
>
> *But they saw with eyes anew*
> *Rainbows in the grass, birds a-wing,*
> *Melting chains, space, time,*
> *With the magic in their souls."*

"Wordsworth? Shelley?" Cameron asked.

"No. Me."

"That was good. Does 'me' have a name?"

She extended her hand: "Sonia Palmer. And yours?"

He took her hand. "John Cameron." He didn't want to let her hand go.

Her eyes were still on his, with all the blue hues under the sun. "Glad to meet you."

"So, Sonia, what do you do in your spare time, when you're not reciting poetry?"

"Depends on where I am."

"How's that?"

She paused. "I'm a lobbyist. You know, someone who takes the cause of various interest groups to legislators, and tries to convince them of the merits of such causes.""

"I bet you're good at it." It was Cameron's turn to pause. "Are all causes meritorious?"

"No. I try to pick the few that mostly are."

"Do you have much choice in the matter?"

"Not always. Sometimes there's a downside to what I do."

"Maybe that's why you do poetry."

"Maybe..." She looked away, then her gaze returned. "Shall we dance?"

It was a slow dance. His arm on her waist felt the rhythm echoing through her hips. Hips smooth, high-curved, tapering suddenly to her narrow waist.

"Now that you're perhaps disappointed in the conflicts of interest of what I do, how about you?"

"I suppose no one is immune from conflicts of interest."

"I suppose."

"You still haven't answered. What do you do?"

Cameron shrugged. "Try to help people feel better."

"That certainly narrows it down," she nodded. "Let's see: Could be a giveaway-TV show host, car salesman, TV evangelist, even a drug dealer..."

"Do I get to pick one?" Cameron smiled.

"If you want. Or you could be serious."

"I'm a medical Resident."

"And in your spare time?" She teased as he had.

"I guess I do research."

"A hobby, or work?"

"Maybe I haven't decided that yet," he shrugged.

"Is it something really important to you?"

"Maybe like poetry for you."

She appeared saddened by his reply, and pressed closer to him.

"What's the matter?"

"Nothing. I guess I was thinking..."

"What?"

"I was thinking…maybe I'd like to see you again. But you sound pretty busy…"

The dance ended. They walked off the floor. Their hands were still together.

"Not if you don't mind joining me for feeding time at the lab, for the canines."

"As in feeding dogs? Poor little bow-wows?... You do research on them?" She placed her hands on her hips, mimicking him: "And are such causes meritorious?"

"There may be conflicts of interest," Cameron smiled, "but you can come see for yourself."

"I'd like that. When?"

"I'm on call tomorrow. How about day after?"

"Sure." She had a way of pulling him closer when they talked. The proximity of her eyes sent chills down his spine.

"Well, I suppose Max and I should be going. We're both on call tomorrow…"

"Would you mind walking me out first? I have no reason to stay." Her eyes settled on him, perhaps knowing what effect they had on him.

The night received them with a chill wind and frosty halos around their breaths. He could still feel her hand in his. "I guess," Cameron began, "I'm not very good with words sometimes…"

"What did you want to say?"

"That I want to see you soon."

"I'll be there the day after tomorrow, remember?"

"Yes, the lab…I wish it could be someplace else."

"That'll be fine, believe me. And you know," she paused, "I also want to see you again soon."

Walking back to his car, Cameron recalled holding her again, and her words like a kiss upon his lips.

CHAPTER 16

HIGH CLOUDS

Winter's storm came from the sea, towards the mountains.

Clouds hung back as if deciding whether to pass over the high peaks, or slam their fury against the mountainside.

As the storm's gray slate hesitated, a compact V-line of geese flew high, near the cloud heads.

Something strange happened: two more squadrons of geese appeared, from different compass points, converging upon the same slate-gray backdrop. The three squadrons flew each their own individual formations: One a compact V; another with a long arm loosely trailing into the horizon; the last curving like a boomerang.

When the three tribes met, their greetings echoed over the thunder. Squadron formations dissolved into a flurry of swirling wings. For a long time, their spiral dance continued, against the gray clouds, oblivious of the storm and lightning.

It was an average on-call evening, with fifteen admissions before midnight. Just after, Dr. Cameron received a call from Emergency Department.

"Cameron, I need your help on this one."

"What's up, Alex?" Alex Dawson was an Emergency Medicine Resident. He was as intense as his chosen field in medicine. Before ambulance sirens faded at the ER.'s doorstep, he was already in the shoes of whoever was being brought in, his mind racing out from the blocks of radio-relayed information. His tempo, but not his temper, was volcanic—always at a constant simmer, and ready to burst with energy when needed.

"I've got one here that needs admission, but is refusing it."

"Don't I have enough admissions already, Alex? You're trying to talk me into another one?"

"I'm calling you because I think you could do it."

"You're working on me, Alex."

"Sure, I'm working on you. But it's true."

"Fill me in."

"A Mr. Ted Gardner, in his sixties, used to be a college professor—English, I think. His daughter died in a fire about two years ago. He's been going downhill since. Looks like a hermit who hasn't come down off his mountain, hasn't washed, shaved, or seen the light of day."

"Sounds like a psych case to me—I don't mean it in a bad way, Alex, but they should be better able to help him."

"That's the catch—Psych already came and saw him, but he still had enough right answers, so they couldn't put a seventy-two hour hold on him. He's got bad emphysema, though, and maybe a pneumonia."

"So maybe I'll take him."

"Not that simple. He won't go. Doesn't trust docs much."

"And you want me to convince him to stay?"

"Look, I could just sign him out A.M.A., Cam. But without medical care he'll die just as surely as some of the others would have that you admitted tonight."

"I'll talk to him."

"'Atta boy!" Alex exclaimed. "I owe you one."

"By now, more than one," Cameron chuckled.

"'Atta boy! 'Atta boy! 'Atta boy!..."

As Dr. Cameron turned the corner to the Emergency Department's basement entrance, hospital life seemed to change. It changed from Lab Microbiology, to Nuclear Med; from Pathology to Physical Therapy—within the hospital's universe, each department was a little world of its own. Just as Surgical wards were tuned differently than Medical wards, so Emergency Departments marched to their own particular beat. Approaching the ER.'s orbit, lights seemed almost too bright; movements more accentuated and hurried, like a scrimmage; noise levels varied as unpredictably as earthquakes. Where Surgical wards and Medical wards were usually busy and occasionally stretched to limits of disarray, the ER. was always in constant turbulence. Trying to maintain steadiness and predictability in the ER was like keeping a foothold on a surf-swept ocean shore: The sand always shifted, forcing a state of constant reaction. Unfolding events controlled those who worked in an ER, and they had to be at their best within storm's chaos.

There was also the singularity of encounters in an Emergency Department: A variety of patients came at different times, most out of need, some for convenience. Since physicians also rotated through different shifts, chances of a patient -doctor encounter more than once were rare. Patients and doctors thus remained intimate strangers.

In medicine, first encounters retained the dubious distinction of being more raw, and therefore perhaps more real than society's other encounters. Though at times harsh and painful, this reality left little room for small talk or pretense on either side. First impressions dictated to the doctor the manner and speed with which to proceed; first impressions gave the patient his chance to size up his doctor under fire.

Dr. Cameron pushed aside the white curtain separating patient cubicles, for his first encounter with Mr. Ted Gardner. Strands of clumped hair almost hid a face pale as waxpaper; under unshaved mustache and beard, the lips were an unearthly concord grape purple. As Mr. Gardner breathed and coughed, his chest quivered like the pleats of the curtain suspended around him.

His color, labored breathing, and respiratory rate quickly told Cameron there would be only hours, not days left for Mr. Gardner's life, unless there was improvement soon. Mr. Gardner's ghostly appearance of depression also told Cameron that Mr. Gardner would be unlikely to allow any treatment that might yield such improvement.

Cameron looked beneath the unkept hair. In the frantic eyes, waiting for death, he saw something still alive. A far away pain. If there was pain and loss, perhaps there was also still a glimmer of love alive. Though not much, it gave Cameron something to work with.

"Hi, I'm Dr. Cameron," he extended his hand. "I'd like to take care of you while you're here."

"I don't want anyone...doing nothin'," Mr. Gardner replied. "I just want to go home." Strange talk from an ex-English professor. A sneer crossed Mr. Gardner's face—a sneer of endured agony, not contemptuous distance.

"I know," Cameron tried again, "I want you to go home too, but we need to get you feeling better first."

"How are you going to do that? There's nothin' wrong with me... don't even know why I'm here." A cough like tires over a gravel road rattled his chest.

The ex-student who'd brought her ex-professor to the hospital stood by: "He's been coughing like that for over a month, only worse now. The groceries just pile up at his place—he won't cook, he won't eat."

"Caliban," Mr. Gardner managed a smile, "Paradise Lost..."

"You should have seen him," the ex-student continued, "he was a great teacher—the best. Oh, he made worlds come alive in front of your eyes! Not like notes from dusty pages, but a wrap-around screen in front of your mind's eye!"

Cameron nodded. "Mr. Gardner, all I need is a couple of days here to get you better, then send you home." Cameron usually told the truth. This time he knew it would take more than a few days. But if he could just get started, get some results so Mr. Gardner felt improved, then maybe the professor wouldn't be in such a hurry to get home.

"No...no...no..." Mr. Gardner choked up, then coughed like a backfiring exhaust muffler.

Cameron listened to his chest. The muffler acted up again with a cacophony of wheezes and sounds that would have done a dragster proud. Heart sounds were totally unheard under the rest of the noise. Cameron had to feel the pulse to count the accelerated rhythm of the overburdened heart. Afterward, Cameron went straight to the point: "I think you ought to stay here, Mr. Gardner, if you want to live. You see, you have emphysema, with severe asthma, and probably pneumonia also.

You're moving little air through your lungs, and the lack of oxygen is draining your system."

"No," he sputtered, "I don't need that. I don't need to stay."

"Mr. Gardner," the ex-student joined in, "why not let them take care of you here awhile? You can't do it alone. And I can't be there all the time to help you."

"What do you think?" Cameron encouraged again.

"No...no..." Mr. Gardner held out his hands in front, as if blocking a tackle.

But Cameron persisted. He listened, cajoled, entreated, listened some more, warned, bargained, and finally after one hour—endured. Professor Gardner turned to him: "You think it's really necessary, I mean, the hospital...?" He hastily corrected himself: "No, I can't do that. I have matters to take care of."

"What matters? You can do that from the hospital phone."

"No, I just can't..."

Cameron sensed an opening and hung on like a bulldog, but with soft jaws and filed teeth. Most cases were saved by medical expertise; some by sheer doggedness of will. "Sure you can," Cameron replied.

Whether Mr. Gardner simply got tired of saying no, or perhaps his breathing didn't allow for more words, he finally muttered something like "... a few days." Arrangements to transfer him to Dr. Cameron's ward were swiftly made.

Cameron watched the orderly fluff the blanket and arrange it around Mr. Gardner. It was done carefully and unobtrusively. That was the thing about orderlies: No one noticed them until they were needed.

Then they were there, with soft hands, strong arms, and usually a smile no matter the time of night. In Mr. Gardner's case, a rough orderly could have blown all of Cameron's work. But most orderlies sensed things without being told. They got the job done, then anonymously disappeared until they were needed again.

Lucy met Cameron on the ward: "I'm up next. You want me to take the new admission, Mr. Gardner?"

"Please. But let me see him first. It took me an hour just to get him to come in."

"Why?"

"Why what?"

She looked at him: "Why did you do that? I mean, not everyone will go out of his way just for the reward of admitting a difficult patient."

Cameron shrugged. "That's what I trained for—to help those who need it most."

"Just checking. I was wondering how many of us crazies are left."

"A lot, Lucy."

"And how long will it take for insurance companies, government bureaucrats, and paperwork to do us in? How long 'til we all become McDoctors at a local McHospital?"

"Depends on how soon people come to realize patients aren't the same as hamburgers. What brought this on, anyway, Lucy?"

"There's a letter on your desk. Special inter-departmental delivery. I meant to tell you earlier."

"So?"

"It's from Quality Assurance, and Q.A. called earlier in the day. They wanted you to call back. From their tone I figured they were probably leaning on you about something. What is it?"

"I'm not sure I know."

"Look, if you were any better at what you do, you'd raise the dead. Those of us in the trenches, who aren't pushing paper, know that."

"Thanks," Cameron pocketed the letter, and went to begin Mr. Gardner's work-up.

After midnight, admissions kept up a steady pace, elbowing out any thoughts of sleep. Morning rounds were subdued despite a caffeinated breakfast. Halfway through morning rounds, Cameron remembered he still had a letter in his pocket to read, but it would have to wait until the end of rounds. Before that happened, Max arrived with questions on one of his own patients, and to talk to Lucy about her charting system. As Cameron went over Max' questions, a policeman showed up at the nurses' station, asking for Dr. John Cameron.

When Cameron identified himself, the policeman brought out an official-looking legal folder. "Please sign here," the uniformed messenger said curtly.

"What am I signing?"

"You can see for yourself—a summons for malpractice."

Cameron was too bewildered to ask anything else. What was the proper response in this situation? *Thank you? Glad you stopped by? What the hell is going on?*

Cameron signed. There were no parting pleasantries. Cameron was left with yet another enigmatic document.

Cameron retreated to the lab room, followed by Max. He waited until Cameron had finished reading. Max didn't want to pry, but finally asked: "What's going on?"

"Happened during my internship, Pediatric rotation," Cameron reached back into his memory almost ten thousand patients ago. "I was in Peds clinic, the ER was jammed that evening, so they sent their non-emergency ones to us. This boy was shy of six years old. I remember him because he actually seemed healthier than the rest of the sore throats, runny noses, and coughs we'd been seeing all week. Mom had brought him in for a red left eye, which turned out to be a garden-variety subconjunctival hemorrhage in the outer quadrant—the sort of thing you see from rubbing the eyes in the allergy season. There was no eye pain, and visual acuity was normal."

Cameron paused, setting down the summons papers. "As I examined the retinas, I caught a glimpse of blood in the opposite eye, the right—but not of the superficial conjunctiva—this was near a retinal vein. Then I found one more speck of blood. At that point, I also noticed a burn scar on the boy's arm. This began to bother me, so I examined more of the face, then chest, ribs, and long bones for any fractures or injuries. I asked the mother how the burn got there. I forgot what she said."

Cameron looked past the closed lab room door as if the child were standing there in front of him: "The thought of child abuse crossed my mind. I decided to observe how child and mom interacted, and did so unobtrusively, as I wrote the history and physical findings. It eased my suspicions that he didn't seem afraid of her, or of other adults, but I still called the other hospital where the burn had been treated. Their chart was clean—nothing suspicious of abuse.

"So I had on my hands a child with an initial presenting problem of left eye redness, which was subconjunctival trauma of minimal significance, and the incidental findings of two tiny retinal vessel bleeds in the other eye, and a burn scar on the arm. I ordered x-rays of the face and ribs just in case injury was a common denominator, and a CBC with platelets and a protime, to check for infection, bleeding tendency or even leukemia.

"I wrote up two pages, called the Resident, and then waited for the lab while I finished taking care of the other patients. The lab came back normal. The Resident found me staring at the x-rays, and I told him the story. We saw no fractures, old or new. He'd also seen the two in clinic before, and vouched that the possibility of abuse was unlikely.

"At that point, I told the Pediatric Resident I wasn't sure what was going on, and I'd be uncomfortable sending the boy home without knowing he'd get adequate follow-up. The Resident rechecked the boy's eyes and vision, and tried to call an ophthalmologist. But clinics had been closed for an hour, and there weren't any ophthalmologists around."

Cameron stared ahead, as if the scene was still unfolding before his eyes. "I remember the Resident stroked his chin, looking from the lab work on his desk, across the open door to the boy in the exam room: "Well, we certainly can't hold him for possible abuse—that's highly unlikely, and doesn't warrant police swarming in here. And he's in no distress, and with normal vision, so it doesn't make sense to keep him for that. So how 'bout I get him an ophthalmology clinic appointment within a few days, and make sure they keep it?"

"That seemed fair enough," Cameron continued. "I rotated off Peds that same week. When I called back, the boy was in the hospital—his sight was nearly gone on the right—diagnosis of papillophlebitis or chorioretinitis, cause unknown. I came close," Cameron muttered, "but not close enough to save his eye."

Max interrupted the silence that followed: "So what's chorioretinitis or papillophlebitis?"

"A very rare inflammation of the retinal blood vessels. Treatment consists of immunosuppressant steroids injected in the eye. Even then, chances are eyesight will be lost. In this case," Cameron added, tossing the summons in front of Max, "the boy was even more unlucky. Within six weeks, he lost sight in the other eye."

Max picked up the documents:

SUMMONS

NOTICE TO DEFENDANT:

John D. Cameron, M.D.; Does 1 through 30; Doe Company and Roe Company

YOU ARE BEING SUED BY PLAINTIFF:

Dennis L. Renner, a minor, by and through his Guardian Julia Renner.

You have 30 calendar days to file a typewritten response at this court.

A letter or phone call will not protect you; your typewritten response must be in proper legal form if you want the court to hear your case.

If you do not file your response on time, you may lose the case, and your wages, money and property may be taken without further warning from the court.

You are served as an individual defendant.

Endorsed
S. Trevors, Clerk

1.	SUPERIOR COURT
2.	
3.	No. 68324, complaint for Medical Malpractice
4.	
5.	
6.	Plaintiff Dennis L. Renner complains of Defendant
7.	John D. Cameron; and Does 1 through 30; Doe Company; and
8.	Roe Company, and for a course of action alleges as
9.	follows:
10.	
11.	The true names and capacities, whether individual,
12.	associate, corporate, or otherwise, of Defendants Does 1
13.	through 10, Doe Company, and Roe company are unknown to
14.	Plaintiff who therefore sues said Defendant under such
15.	fictitious names, and hopes and prays they become known to
16.	him. Plaintiff believes and thereon alleges that each of
17.	the Defendants is responsible in some manner for the
18.	events and happenings referred to and caused injuries and
19.	damages proximally brought to Plaintiff as herein alleged.
20.	
21.	Defendants did negligently, carelessly, and
22.	maliciously diagnose, treat, and care for Plaintiff,
23.	including but not limited to the failure to diagnose
24.	Plaintiff's condition so as to cause Plaintiff Dennis L.
25.	Renner to suffer permanent blindness and further injuries
26.	and damages as hereinafter alleged.
27.	
28.	As a proximate result of the intentional negligence
29.	and carelessness of Defendants, Plaintiff was injured in
30.	his health, strength, and activity, sustaining injury to
31.	his body and shock and injury to his nervous system and
32.	person, all of which have caused and will continue to
1.	cause Plaintiff great mental, physical, and nervous pain
2.	and suffering and have permanently disabled him, all to
3.	his damage in excess of the jurisdictional minimum of this
4.	court.
5.	

6.   As a further proximate result of the negligence and
7.   carelessness of Defendants, future earning capacity will
8.   be severely curtailed. The exact amount of said loss of
9.   earning capacity is unknown to Plaintiff at this time, and
10.   Plaintiff will ask leave to amend his pleading to set
11.   forth the exact amount when same is ascertained.
12.
13.   Wherefore, Plaintiff prays for judgment against
14.   Defendants as follows:
15.   1. General damages in excess of the jurisdictional
16.   minimum of this court..."

Max dropped the paper like a letter from hell. "Sounds like you invented the disease, rather than trying to cure it," Max commented. "And there's enough of lawyers 'hopes and prayers' to include them in a monastic order with God on their side."

Max' comments went unanswered.

"You're not actually blaming yourself for this, are you?" Max asked. "You did your best. Someone else wouldn't have even looked beyond the conjunctival changes of the left eye, let alone detect the bleeds in the other."

"That's the problem," Cameron said somberly, "I was so close, yet not close enough to help him." Cameron gathered the papers, and walked out of the room.

· · · · ·

Next day, a different sort of summons arrived: The Medical Director, Dr. Neuhaus, requested D. Cameron's presence. That was on top of the other letter he'd held in his pocket: A new incident report on Max' altercation with the surgeon, Roger Taylor, over the disclosure of Mrs. Samuels' cancer.

> "...The lack of proper discipline of a subordinate Intern in-volved in a heated argument with a Resident of the Surgical Service is a serious breach of a teaching Resident's responsibility. Not only was the lack of discipline improper for patient care, but also for the inability to instruct an Intern under your care in the

proper ethics of dealing with colleagues. We view this matter with utmost concern..."

Appended was a letter from the Quality Management Committee (its name had recently been changed from Quality Assurance to Quality Management) declaring an immediate need for consultation and report to the Q.M. Committee. It was slated within the week.

After such correspondence, Cameron was not expecting good news from the Director's office. He'd at least managed to review the boy's records, and confirmed that events were as he'd remembered them. Though his drawing of the boy's burn scar was as primitive as Neanderthal cave paintings of thirty millennia ago, and much less graceful, the rest of the scientific observations were there—over two pages long—far exceeding the usual brief clinic notes. Still, volume would not take the place of reasonable thinking. So Cameron reviewed his work line by line. His final diagnosis had been:

"Impressions:
1. Subconjunctival hemorrhage, L eye.
2. Small retinal bleeds, R eye, cause unknown.
   - no evidence of leukemia (CBC normal)
   - no evidence clotting abnormalities (lab normal)
3. Burn scar, R arm - no evidence abuse at this time.

Plan:
1. Eye rest; do not rub eyes.

2. Reviewed and discussed with Pediatric Resident Dr. Warren Holden: After examining patient, he found no supportive evidence of child abuse, and no need to hospitalize at this time (visual acuity normal). Follow-up with ophthalmology clinic (per Dr. Holden), within a few days.
3. Recheck if vision worsens.

J. Cameron, M.D.
Intern, Pediatric Rotation"

What happened afterwards was not totally clear: Somehow the clinic appointment was not kept, and then events quite unrelated to the initial left eye redness ended in the boy's loss of sight.

Cameron again went over the sequence of events in his mind, and was relieved to realize he'd done his best. Probably nothing, including earlier treatment, could have changed the cascade of events that followed. Still, he'd been so close, and stumbled—stumbled just before the finish line.

Cameron entered the Medical Director's office.

"Dr. Neuhaus is expecting you," the secretary ushered him in. Dr. Neuhaus remained seated behind his desk. He tried to keep his countenance neutral, but as he lifted the rather thick file from his desk, he appeared troubled. "Can you tell me what's been happening, Dr. Cameron? A few months ago, your file was nearly empty. Now..." he let it fall with a thud upon his desk. What the file held inside didn't appear to matter as much as the weight of its accumulated papers.

"I'm not sure, sir..." It was the truth. Cameron had no explanation of how the paper's growth had spread like a malignant process. And now the lawsuit. How would he explain that?

Dr. Neuhaus broached the subject for him. "Seems we have a real problem on our hands. Now there's also a lawsuit against you. It will likely involve the hospital as well."

"I know, sir. I read the summons and reviewed the chart."

Dr. Neuhaus clasped his hands, and was silent.

"Dr. Neuhaus, I believe I can give a very reasonable defense..."

"We'll leave that for the lawyers, shall we, Dr. Cameron? In the meantime, stay away from that record. And don't dream of altering anything in it."

Cameron recoiled at that statement. "Sir, there may be many things in those files. Whether or not they're true remains to be seen. Until then, I don't believe I should be treated as if my integrity is questionable."

"Actually, if I'd been told something like this would happen to one of my Residents, you'd have been the least likely in my book." Dr. Neuhaus paused. "And yet," he pointed to the files, "we have to answer to these..." perhaps he was about to say "facts," but trailed off without saying anything more.

"I believe I have written adequate answers to all those incident reports, Dr. Neuhaus."

With the impatient tone of someone who had more important daily matters to deal with, Dr. Neuhaus brushed his comment aside. "You'll have a chance to present them to the Quality Management Committee." It was dubious whether Dr. Neuhaus had actually read any of Cameron's responses.

"Yes, sir. I will be glad to do so."

Dr. Neuhaus turned his back, and looked out the window. "In the meantime, due to this epidemic of incident reports, I must relieve you from your double-duty as Resident for the Carlos Schmidt and Max McDaniel team. I'll get another Resident to supervise them. Maybe the extra time will help you."

Cameron knew time wasn't the issue. He was being demoted, even before his meeting with the Q.M. Committee. Cameron didn't reply, and sensed no reply was awaited.

"I hear you've been working on some lab projects as well. It's nice to see someone with initiative," Dr. Neuhaus gave a wry smile. "But Residency is more than a full-time job. Maybe you're spreading yourself too thin."

Cameron didn't reply to that either. The silence became uncomfortable. "May I go now, Dr. Neuhaus?"

"Think about it. You had a lot of potential."

The past tense still ringing in his ears, the office door slammed shut behind him. For once, Cameron didn't know where to start. It was one of those times when inner senses of direction failed, as if finding oneself alone on a moonless night, adrift at sea.

Cameron called Max.

"What is it?" Max immediately knew from Cameron's voice something was wrong.

"I've been pulled off being your Resident. I wanted to tell you myself."

"Why?"

"Incident reports, the lawsuit..."

"That's insane. You're the best Resident this hospital has. I'm not the only one who thinks so."

"Apparently others don't agree, including the Medical Director. I have to make an appearance before the Q.M. Committee also."

"This is getting out of hand. I'm not sure why, but something tells me there's more than medicine involved. Even that cop didn't seem quite right to me: Uniform too crisp, everything too shiny. I know a cop when I see one, and that wasn't a regular cop."

"Why would anyone go through the trouble of dressing up as one, just to deliver the summons?"

"Why indeed? Especially since malpractice summons aren't usually delivered by police. I checked. Apparently, someone is trying to shake you up. Why don't you call Track and find out if he's got any ideas?"

"Will do. Thanks, Max."

"Hey, you going to be all right, Cameron?"

"Nothing that can't be fixed."

"That's right. That's our business, isn't it?"

By the time Cameron called Track Sullivan, he was beginning to calm down. After all, he'd have a chance to present his side in person at Q.M., and that would probably be the end of it.

Track sounded concerned, however, that it had reached this far. "I agree with Max; sounds strange. Listen, we should talk. I've got a run planned with Elaine this evening. Join me? Bring someone if you like, so she can keep Elaine company while we run ahead a bit and talk."

. . . . .

Despite the half-inch of snow on the ground, Track was already in his running shorts. He always ran feeling the wind on his legs—gave him cadence, he said. Cameron made the introductions, being careful to avoid Sonia's sensitivities about animal research, and leaving out any references to Track's hepatology research. "You already know Wildwolf," Cameron concluded, tossing a frisbee into the air for canine, and his own, warm-up.

Sonia and Elaine stretched, ran in place, and talked.

They must have reached a similar notion on not being outdone by the males, as they also bared legs from their sweats after warming up. The curves presented were like a sleek chorus line. In the ritual of dating and courtship, the leg power and muscle of the two males had been amply matched, and perhaps upstaged, by the more frail structures of Sonia's sacroiliac dimpling and swaybacked pelvic tilt, and Elaine's gracefully curving legs.

Elaine strutted forward. "I've stretched enough."

"I'll say," Track smiled.

"Maybe one loop around the park?"

"That should keep us warm."

The girls set the initial pace. Wildwolf ran alongside, on snow-shod winter grass, his thick coat making the barelegged humans seem out of place.

Neither Track nor Cameron appeared to mind letting the girls run ahead. Cameron's stride, usually broken only by someone behind and gaining, now experienced a few lapses as he watched Sonia run. Technically, she was mildly knock-kneed. Aesthetically, it was easy to forgive, as instead of the streamlined, economical lines of a runner, Sonia's were more ideally suited for the boundaries of a bikini. Below a waist that narrowed as if by an invisible belt, the rest of her curves were full, round, taut, and smooth. Whatever Track may have been thinking as he watched Elaine, Cameron didn't even want to guess.

After a valiant smile, Sonia's knock-knees took their toll, and she dropped pace. "Go on ahead. I'm going to slow down a bit."

Elaine pulled up. "I'll keep you company. Besides, I wouldn't want to make the boys feel bad if I went on," she smiled.

"We can give it a rest," Track replied.

"No. I can see it in your faces," Elaine glanced at them. "Go ahead. We'll meet you around the loop. Go!"

The word had an instant effect on both. Track and Cameron were at speed like deer leaping over a fence. Wildwolf followed. Track's gait was a long, effortless glide. Cameron's stride was more like a reckless cavalry charge. It was a mystery how the two different styles held pace, along a snow-bordered track, at dusk.

They could have talked of many things: About the girls, about the lab, of their daily work, of the incident reports. They did not. They simply ran, into the colors of a winter evening, gathering around them like mist.

Just short of finishing the loop, they went into a full-out sprint. After nearly a quarter-mile abreast, their strides synchronized into a slow lope.

"I thought of what you told me," Track began. "Can't remember anything like it happening over stuff like that. I've kept my ears tuned to any rumblings or clues, but found nothing. If anything, consensus is everyone speaks very highly of you. So beats me what's going on."

"Maybe we're being too paranoid, and the Q.M. Committee will clear the air."

"Maybe," Track mused. "But committees consist of many different heads without necessarily adding up to a single mind. So don't assume anything. Document everything three times over, from every angle. And be careful of Dr. Atwood, he's the committee's vice-chairman."

"Right."

"If you get anything but a clean bill after this, let me know. We'll have to put our heads together and see what's behind this."

They finished the loop at an easy glide, Wildwolf panting beside them. Sonia and Elaine had already put on their sweats to ward off the cold.

"You guys must be hungry, after all that showing off," Sonia commented. "How about dinner at my place? I'll throw something together."

Track and Cameron glanced at each other. Their stomachs were willing. But Cameron begged off. "Raincheck? I've still got work at the lab."

"Got another idea," Sonia offered. "Go to the lab, and I'll bring dinner there."

"If you won't be too bored there," Cameron agreed.

Elaine and Track left, and Cameron returned to the lab with Wildwolf. Sonia Palmer brought chicken dinner, with tidbits on the side for Wildwolf.

As usual, Cameron had all the M.R.'s loose while he worked, and they'd gathered around Sonia. Either she—or the chicken—had made an instant hit with the canines. Wildwolf, in a more dignified manner, sat at Cameron's side.

"Would you like to meet the pack on the paw?"

"They don't bite or anything, do they?"

"No. They'll just mob you, like they're doing now."

Sonia's clinging powder-blue sweats—less a feature of the clothes than of their form they covered—made Cameron forget he should have been watching more carefully for canine overexuberance. One was already settled in Sonia's lap.

"How cute!" She exclaimed. "What's this one's name?"

"That's Shadowfax."

"Strange name for a dog."

"Just a few have names. Wildwolf's special—he was the first. Max named the others. Well, I'd have to say they're all really special."

Another M.R. rose to the occasion by presenting paw. "This one's so cute!" Sonia read the collar: "Misty. Can I adopt this one?"

"Already adopted." Cameron knew it would be difficult to explain its adoption by Tammy. "You can pick out another one, though."

"And you actually experiment on these doggies? What do you do to them?"

"Did," Cameron corrected, "they're all done. Two were part of another lab's experiment to see how certain chemicals affect liver metabolism. The rest were hungry pooches who ingested 'death-cap' mushrooms, forwarded to us by vets when nothing more could be done. These dogs were going to die, but regrew new livers..."

"Those first two...why would you want to do that in the first place?"

"I didn't have much to do with that—just inherited the doggies as they were, and regrew their livers. But there was good reason to do those first experiments also."

"None of those reasons would matter, if you were a dog."

"It would for humans, though."

"Isn't there some middle ground? Some way it can be done in a test tube or something?"

"Maybe. You're the lobbyist and expert in middle grounds. In our field, nothing new was ever achieved without some initial risk. Life itself is a risky experiment."

"Sorry. I didn't mean to pressure you about the research. Besides," she observed, "other than being cooped up, they don't seem to be suffering."

"I do try to minimize any suffering. They're anesthetized for all procedures."

"I sense I'm making you nervous while you work. Why don't I leave you alone, and I tend to the doggie menu? Where's their food?" After he'd shown her, Sonia hesitated again. "One more thing," she added sheepishly. "None of this research is dangerous, is it? I mean, you mentioned virally transformed livers..."

"No, there's no whole live virus left, if that's what you mean. Just bits of genetic material that's been incorporated in a certain way in tissue culture. Initially, there was a cell line purposely infected with Rous sarcoma virus, then accidentally reinfected and modified with an influenza virus. Neither of them remains in its original, active form."

"Isn't this like gene splicing? Brave new forms of life? And therefore, illegal?"

"And how do you know so much about this stuff?"

"As a lobbyist, I dabble in legalities, remember? But I'm only interested in this because you're doing it." She paused. "I also wanted to know if it was safe—you know, since I don't understand what's going on here."

"It's safe," Cameron replied. He was about to add a qualifier—that nothing at the edge of a new frontier is guaranteed, and no one really knew what lay ahead.

"I trust you." She looked at him with her blue eyes, beside which any other shade of blue looked faded.

"Technically," Cameron tried to explain, "it's not really gene splicing. I didn't purposely open up a gene sequence and insert genetic material to create a new bacteria or virus. I did alter mammalian cells, but that's routinely done—for example, inducing tumors with Rous sarcoma virus. That's a naturally occurring process anyway, not an artificial one. And the superinfection with influenza virus is also a natural process. Satisfied?"

Sonia nodded. Perhaps there were still remnants of questions in her eyes. Cameron had an idea. He took a box of slides from a drawer.

"Let's take a look. These are liver cells departing the land of the living." In an instant light broke through a miniature landscape that even to the untrained eye was as desolate as a cratered lunar surface. Amid the debris of disintegrating cellular walls, globules of lysosomes formed dark pools; spirals and tendrils of fibrous collagen twisted like remains of tangled wire; broken mitochondrial engines lay scattered like rusting gears across a wrecking yard. Cellular life had been extinguished like exploding stars in a vanishing galaxy.

Cameron changed slides. "Now check this." His eyes gleamed as he adjusted the microscope: previous inflammation and death gave way to regenerating healthy tissue. New cell/stars marched into the previous chaos, like terraced green valley farmland, viewed from a mountaintop.

"You did that?" Sonia gazed through the microscope eyepiece.

"I helped."

"Then get back to it, I'll manage to keep myself and the doggies entertained."

Beauty, intelligence, and she wasn't even bored on their first date with a run around a snow-covered park, and a lab full of dogs. When she left, Cameron tried to finish more work, but his mind circled in clouds far above the lab.

CHAPTER 17

GOLD STANDARD

- Average Chief executive Officer salary (1998) for 708 executives at 304 top firms: Over $2 million per year. Top CEO salary: Over $40 million per year (including benefits).

- Top 10 Wall Street earners (1998): Median Income over $15 million per year

USA Today

- Average projected National Basketball Association player salary for 1999, based on increases since 1983: $10 million per year.

Sports Illustrated

- Average physician salary (1998): $144,700 Per year (median $120,000 per year).

American Medical News

- Two-thirds of countries spent more in the 1980's on the military than on the health needs of their citizens.

"World Military and Social Expenditures, 1989"

- All the children in the world could be immunized against six fatal diseases for $1.27 billion – the cost of one U.S. Trident submarine.

"World Military and Social Expenditures, 1989"

- Estimated cost of Stealth Bomber: $1.058 Billion. At that price, the 70-ton B-2 oz.) would cost more than its weight in gold.

Time

Jacob Werner thumbed through a copy of Executive Magazine while he waited. The cover, featuring a merchant king who sold cars, smiled back at him. The article that followed was a "How To" story. Since Americans spent more on their cars than on health care, there were many more kingdoms like it waiting to be established. Another article covered the world of advertisement: A 15-second TV commercial had cost one-half million dollars to make. Jake wondered about that sometimes, how fortunes were made: A few well-placed real estate deals (perhaps after a few key people had been influenced to change zoning regulations), and millions were created; a sports team won a national championship, and they became overnight heroes, with million-dollar ad contracts; entertainers earned thousands of dollars per minute of work, yet asked for more; politicians pointed their fingers at the earnings of doctors, then themselves retired from government work to become "corporate advisors" at twice the amounts they'd previously wagged their fingers at.

And yet, Jake pondered, what did these photogenic faces really contribute to the productivity of this earth? Was the ability to act, place a ball through a hoop, or advise corporations on how to find loopholes really more valuable than the ability to grow food, build homes, bridges, and dams that would last centuries, or teach the minds that built them, or create a vaccine that would save millions of lives?

And now Jake was in midst of destroying someone precisely because that someone was successful, but in the "wrong" field—medicine. Money spent on other areas was not a problem—but when spent on health care was for some reason considered either too expensive, or wasteful, or both.

These were strange thoughts for Jake, but not exactly second thoughts. He wasn't responsible for making policy, Jake reminded himself, but simply helped implement it. If he didn't, someone else would. There was enough money in the system for that. Not that Jake wanted to change the system. He liked what he did—most of the time—and had no illusions about that. He lacked the perseverance of a farmer, the patience of a researcher, and was absolutely lost in the rows of figures of engineering calculations. But manipulating people and events was his great challenge. If the events were beneficial at times, so much the better. If not, so be it also.

In the empty waiting room, Jake smiled. None of that would change his immediate, or more distant objectives. The immediate one—the John Cameron file—was proving to be one of his most interesting cases. As such, perhaps he'd give its subject the chance to defend himself. Besides, contests that were too unfair bored Jake. As for his more distant objective, there was no rush: There was still much to learn from and about Mr. Terrance Liverpool.

By strange timing, the reception door opened. Terrance Liverpool ushered him within, in much better spirits than previously.

"Do sit down, Jake. Your last batch of information was quite an improvement. Gave the lab boys something to sink their teeth into."

"Thank you, sir."

"Getting him to send samples of tissue directly to one of our 'front' labs was a bit of brilliance, Jake."

It was interesting how they avoided names, and used 'him' instead: Those whom they wished to destroy, they first rendered nameless. Jake wondered why he didn't feel better about it. Perhaps it had been too easy.

"As good as your information was, I gather your 'disinformation' is going even better," Terrance commented.

"Ahead of schedule, sir." Whatever their motives were, Jake had found enough weaknesses and bias in the medical personnel field, to exploit to his advantage. Again, it had been almost too easy. But he didn't want Terrance to think he was getting too good at this. "Bit of luck, sir," Jake concluded.

"See if that luck extends to obtaining more information on how this 'hybrid' was initially produced."

"The lab boys haven't been able to figure that from what I gave them?"

"Something about 'differentiation and dedifferentiation,'" Terrance shrugged. "Just passing on what they told me. Anyway, they're close, but not quite there."

"I'll do my best, sir. Will there be anything else, sir?"

"Your bonus," Terrance scooted an envelope over the desk towards Jake. "Check in within a month. My office will set up the time."

"Yes, sir," Jake nodded. As he left, he looked back towards the desk. Whatever was on it would soon be cleansed, by being passed through a shredder. Terrance's desk would always remain clean and empty.

Just then, if Terrance had looked closely, he might have observed Jake's trigger-gunsight eyes.

· · · · ·

Lucy went through Mr. Ted Gardner's chart for rounds. "Mr. Gardner's doing much better. He's put on a few pounds along with new pajamas, combs and shaves himself, talks more, and even smiles sometimes. Still," Lucy paused, "his status seems to fluctuate wildly at times. One moment he may be fine, then the next, back to his former self—silent and confused, not even able to feed himself." Lucy tapped on the chart. "I've tried to correlate these fluctuations, positive or negative, with certain times of day, or the taking of his medications. But there doesn't appear to be any pattern."

Cameron turned to Joel. "Any ideas?"

"A fluctuating sensorium..." Joel pondered out loud. It was difficult to ascertain whether Joel actually thought in those terms, or was merely employing long words as a delaying tactic. "Medication side-effects would indeed seem a good bet. I'd go over those again. If not, maybe it's something he's doing, or taking by himself, that we don't know about. Not many diseases manifest like that, with such sudden changes."

"You're both probably on the right track. Follow it a bit more," Cameron added.

Lucy read off Mr. Gardner's medications, including vitamins, and acetaminophen for pain, and their timing. She shook her head. "Checked them all, even combinations of medications, and no patterns fit his sudden alterations."

"Joel?" Cameron asked.

Joel Saxton shook his head as well.

"I believe you've left one medication out of the list. Perhaps not exactly medication, and as common as the air we breathe," Cameron hinted.

"Oxygen!" Joel exclaimed. "Sure! He's got emphysema, and if he's marginal at times with the oxygen supply circulating to his brain, the emphysema could starve his brain of enough oxygen to trip his mentation on and off. To test it out, we just run a few serial arterial blood gases at different times."

"Problem," Lucy interjected: "We could, but he's very squirrely when it comes to lab tests. If he doesn't like what we're doing, he'll just sign himself out. It won't do us any good to be right, and lose the patient. I've been doing his labs bit by bit, to give us time to work with him."

"There's one more way," Cameron added. "Giving oxygen during Mr. Gardner's 'off' times should improve his condition. It's not the same hard-numbers data as ABG's, but we can document our observations, while slowly collecting arterial blood gas samples to confirm them."

The idea was accepted with nods all around. By late morning, Mr. Gardner had one of his spells of withdrawal and confusion. Within ten minutes of inhaling an extra two liters per minute flow by nasal cannula of a colorless, tasteless gas we call oxygen and take for granted, Mr. Gardner was discussing the plot structure of Tom Clancy's Red Storm Rising.

· · · · ·

After a while, Cameron excused himself from Mr. Gardner's literary discussion to attend the noon medical conference. Besides Joel and Lucy, Cameron also rounded up Max and Carlos.

"What's it on?" Carlos asked.

"The Inca's Curse."

"What?"

"It's a curse on anyone who doesn't hear this lecture," Cameron chuckled. "Now let's go. There aren't many speakers like Thomas O'Neil."

While they had their lunches, they listened to a lesser-known history of the Old World and the New World, and how it crossed paths with medicine, and the twentieth century.

The story began in ancient times, with what were still ancient puzzles: Although an abundance of merchant ships and galleys from Greek and Roman times had been recovered from shipwrecks and reconstructed, not so with warships. This made ancient seafaring puzzling. How, for example, did the Greeks accommodate nearly one hundred rowers on a trireme—literally three tiers of oars, stacked one upon the other—without the lowest oar's portholes being too low and taking on water, and the highest portholes still being within a long oar's effective reach of the water? How did the Romans, in the space of a few prodigious months, build an armada of warships for their expeditions against Carthage, in an output that rivaled any modern-tooled shipyard?

Max and Carlos glanced at each other, ate their sandwiches, and relaxed, wondering what this had to do with their internship. Joel's thoughts, whenever out of gear and coasting in neutral, immediately turned into a nap's suspended animation, or daydreams about Jody. Lucy summarized another thick patient record onto her condensed charting system.

The historical footnotes went on: Merchant ships carried cargo in their holds, which doubled as ballast. When shipwrecked, their cargo left mounds bristling upon the seafloor, which divers could spot long after the hull's timbers had come apart. This made the recovery of old merchant ships easier. Warships, on the other hand, sailed lean, with only men, armaments, and perishable food. With no bulky cargo to leave traces on the seabed, warship wrecks were rarely found. When one was finally discovered, at the site of a Mediterranean naval battle—where at least a few ships on the losing side would have failed to stay afloat—one small mystery was solved: The cushioning of the ballast of lead and stones from the hull was provided by a flora of plants and leaves. Analysis of that flora revealed an abundance of Cannabis sativa—marijuana. Since its mood-altering properties were well known even in those ancient times, it was likely the ship's sailors were fairly laid back when they were laid to rest on their final journey to the bottom of the sea. The warship was Carthaginian. The Carthaginians lost that Punic War. And the next. Once their sea power was broken, their cities were razed to the ground.

<u>Cannabis sativa</u>, indigenous to many populous inner-city areas of the twentieth century, had been making its reappearance as part of the cast of characters in the play of life for nearly three millennia.

A fine historical point perhaps, but nevertheless oft repeated. Nearly two millennia later, when Pizarro eliminated the Incas from the map of modern civilization, he was forewarned: "You may take our silver and our gold, but our coca will destroy the white man."

It probably didn't help the Incas much either. They chewed the coca leaves with a mixture of lime, which yielded about one percent cocaine. Their European conquerors didn't improve on this yield for centuries, probably because the coca leaves transported back to Europe were improperly dried and preserved, and so lacked the active ingredient—benzoylecgonine. The Inca's curse had to wait for the persistent efforts of an eighteenth-century Frenchman, who'd inherited a marginal vineyard. Somehow, he found a way to bring back preserved coca from the Andes and into the hands of Chateau de Vin Mariani.

With a stronger solution of cocaine under its cork, Vin Mariani definitely had "good years," and its popularity soared. On the western side of the Atlantic, not to be outdone, the New World introduced the "Real Thing," and "a tonic for the brain." It was indeed, the "Real Thing"—laced with cocaine.

But by 1903, strong sentiment began to build that perhaps something was amiss with cocaine. Coca-Cola announced it would remove all cocaine from its colas.

Despite Coca-Cola's move, cocaine use continued to grow, its expansion ended only by World War II. And in the "flowering sixties," it began another resurrection. Now Colombian processors, by developing the more concentrated white "bazuco" paste of 30% cocaine, had eliminated the carrying of one hundred pounds of coca leaves down the Andes to obtain one pound of cocaine. The "bazuco" was then further purified to 80% cocaine hydrochloride—more pure, easier to transport, and with more kick per gram. Also more expensive, and more profitable.

A large industry was born. And the markets were ready. They were found in the ghettos, born of despair. They were found in middle class suburbia, born of credit-card play now, pay later values. They were found in the upper crust, born of boredom, and the need to flaunt affluence with a golden spoon and a line inhaled through a hundred-dollar bill.

But what goes up, must come down—what's true of gravity is also true of cocaine. One of the characteristics of cocaine is that its "high" is followed by an even deeper and devastating "low", for which the answer seems to be—more cocaine. But the next "high" is never as high as the one before, while the "lows" for some reason continue to plunge. The cycle—and curse—is complete. More coke upon coke, and still no end to that post-coke depression.

The Incas, in their pre-technical state, remained content with their 1% mixture. Perhaps some at times received a higher dose of cocaine—since its metabolism is highly individual—and then seized in fits of epilepsy. Indeed, Inca skulls bore evidence of trephination holes in the skull—what better reason for these, than to let out the "evil spirits" of a seizure? Or perhaps trephination was simply a coincidence, as was the loss of the Inca empire and its never having invented the wheel. We will never know.

At any rate, modern yuppiedom, in its technological quest for thrills and a way out of the vicious post-coke depression, was not likely to be interested in reviewing Inca history for guidance. For their part, suppliers and dealers were more than happy, and technologically ready, to provide the answer: Even a purer form of cocaine, "free-base" in the form of "crack" or "rock" of 92% pure cocaine. Now it could be injected directly into a vein. And instead of waiting the five to twenty minutes for the "high" from intranasal use, it took only twenty to thirty seconds circulation time to provide the drug from the blood vessels to brain. Better yet, in heated and vaporized form, it could be inhaled directly into the lungs, bypassing the peripheral circulation to go directly into heart and brain—in a mere seven seconds. The time from addiction potential was also reduced from several times use, to perhaps only once.

But cocaine's truism, like gravity, remained unchanged: The higher the high, no matter how fast, or by what route, the deeper the low. The vicious cycle continued. Kids waiting outside a dealer's "crack house" made their purchase, used the drug, then rejoined the line again—their "high" having already worn "low".

A comedian once called cocaine "God's way of telling you have too much money"—not to mention too little brains. In perhaps a less poetic vein, medical pathologists were able to microscopically recognize the hearts of dead cocaine users from those dying of other causes: Regardless of age, "contraction band necroses" were found only in the hearts of cocaine users. Their hearts were dying while they were still alive.

Pizarro was dead. The Inca's curse lived on.

In a less historical, but more amusing vein—the lecture went on—California yuppiedom had sponsored its own entrant on the scene of "recreational drugs." It posed more marketing problems, however, than the aforesaid poppy seeds, cannabis, or coca leaves. Nothing that a good P.R. campaign couldn't overcome, though. Something like: "Leapfrog into a higher consciousness," or "wet, wild, and chant the night away" would probably do. Although "croak" would be more appropriate than "chant," since the object of desire was none other than an abundant tailless amphibian, that blessed California's coastal highways and byways—Bufo Americanus—or giant American toad. It seems Bufo's abilities extended to secreting a slimy substance on the outer surface of its body that was a powerful hallucinogen. The active ingredient, bufotenine hydroxyindol alkylamine, was apparently responsible for extremely vivid visual and auditory hallucinations.

The marketing problem: One had to lick the toad. One wonders how the first intrepid discovery of Bufo's secretory powers was made. Then again, California was noted for many firsts, proving no horizons were unreachable for the truly inquisitive mind.

Lucy had long stopped her charting summaries, and by the end of the presentation couldn't suppress her laughter. Joel wondered whether bufonamide-induced hallucinations would be as vivid as daydreams of Jody. For Max, who'd been exposed to the more immediate street-reality version, the subject didn't hold any comedy.

"Another Resident showed up for rounds with us this morning," Max told Cameron on the way out of the conference room.

"I told you they would take me off rounds with you and Carlos. Anyway, give the new guy a break. He's just trying to do his job."

"Well, *our job* is not the same without you. Heard anything from Q.M. yet?"

"Now that you mention it," Cameron browsed through his pockets, habitually forgetting to open his mail. "I think this is it. Came this morning. From Q.M., and sealed with a tap water enema."

"Can't be that bad. What's it say?"

Cameron read it once, then over again. "It is that bad:

FROM: QUALITY MANAGEMENT COMMITTEE
TO: Dr. John Cameron
RE: REVIEW OF INCIDENT REPORTS

"We hereby acknowledge the presentation of your views on incident reports #IO 7239, IR 6523, IM 0527, LS 3105, RD 0591, TR 1702, BQ 0331, RD 0056 (EXHIBIT A), and malpractice action 68324 (EXHIBIT B). Your answers have been appended to the above reports (EXHIBIT C).

"After prolonged deliberation in executive session, it is the view of a majority of this committee that such a quantity of reports cannot be ignored.

"While your present medical privileges will not be currently abridged, the committee confirms the curtailment of your teaching assignments to two Interns at a time. Furthermore, in order to maximize protection of patient care, and minimize hospital and staff liability, a focused review of all your charts has been instituted, retroactive for two months, for the rest of your Residency year. This will take the place of, and supersede, any routine reviews.

"Furthermore, if there is any employment outside the scope of your usual duties as Medical Resident at this hospital whether "moonlighting", research, or any other such employment activity, medical or non-medical— because of its possible bearing on your ability to make appropriate use of your time as Medical Resident, this committee requests a written detailed description and report of the nature of such work and hours scheduled or therein spent.

"This committee has the utmost confidence that if your practice of medicine is of standard quality, the above requirements will not be burdensome, and in fact will avail you of every opportunity to clear up these matters.

"Your presence for an interval Quality Management Committee hearing is expected in two months, for the purpose of updating your file, and interval review.

> Sincerely Archibald Atwood,
> M.D., Chairman

Three other signatures trailed Atwood's. Cameron was speechless: Surely after his careful explanations there couldn't have been such doubts left as to his patient care. Yet there it was: Not only was he being demoted from Resident duties for Max and Carlos, but now all his charts were subject to review. Cameron knew what that meant. Since reviewing hindsight was always better than working foresight, any number of things could be found "wrong" through the retrospectoscope, limited only by the imagination and bias of the reviewer. Focused review of all charts could make the previous incident reports look like a picnic.

They'd also just mandated to provide what he'd sought all along to avoid—reams of administrative paperwork about his research. Cameron knew no matter how many papers and forms he'd fill out, they'd always want more, to the point he'd soon be producing more paper than work. Such was the nature of the bureaucratic beast. It was the reason he'd never applied for a grant. He felt no different now: What he did in his own time was his own business. There would be no report now; and none until his work was finished.

Cameron glanced once more at the "Sincerely", followed by four signatures. Something struck him as odd about that, but he couldn't place his finger on it. Cameron shook his head, tucked the letter in his pocket.

Max glanced at him. "Track mentioned we better put our heads together if it's bad. The Continental, nine p.m.?"

"I suppose so. I sure don't have any more answers."

· · · · ·

By mid-afternoon, when Barbara Davis came in with the nursing p.m. shift, she immediately sensed Cameron's somber mood.

"Hi." She paused. "So what's wrong? Why the downcast look?"

"Some...problems." Cameron was deliberately vague.

"Anything to do with incident reports?"

"Not a bad guess."

"Let's have dinner downstairs when you're done. You might be interested in what I've found out."

The cafeteria was less crowded in the evening, and they landed a corner table.

"So what's happening with these incident reports?" Barbara asked.

"I thought you were going to tell me something about that," Cameron replied.

"Have they been rather strange?"

Cameron nodded. "Not much meat to them, but they keep coming. An example would be a patient's high theophylline level, after the on-call team increased the dose. I ordered a level afterwards, which wasn't done, and then ordered a decrease in dose, which wasn't done either. In fact, it took three written orders to get it done. Luckily, no harm was done. But I'm not sure how these errors wound up on my scorecard, or why I should be writing letters of explanation for them."

Barbara nodded. "Exactly. Why do you think that is?"

"I'm not sure."

"It wasn't considered because someone didn't want to consider it. Just as someone didn't really care about why the lab wasn't done, or why the orders weren't carried out. It's not meat or substance they're after, but the appearance of substance. And if they can't get facts to support substance, then they try to create some, by means of frequency and repetition."

"I see your point. But why? And who's 'they'?"

Barbara shrugged. "I don't know. All I can tell you is none of the nurses I know on the ward originated those reports. One told me someone new, someone she didn't recognize, approached her with a handful of charts. She was asked to 'confirm' these incidents happened. They appeared out of context—like the theophylline level you mentioned. She was to 'confirm' it had been high, but there was no interest in any surrounding information. She was told it was just a routine audit and verification formality. She thought that a bit odd, and later told me about it. She recognized your writing on the charts."

"A handful of charts, you say?"

She nodded.

"That is odd. Sounds like someone is deliberately fishing for problems. If you look hard enough, you'll find them, or be able to construct them. I don't believe more in my charts than anyone else's, though."

"Less in yours, if anything, Cameron."

"So, the question, again, is why?"

"Can't you place it, Cameron? What about the signatures on the reports?"

"Could be anyone, or no one. In the world of medical committees, such things are shrouded in anonymity, rules of evidence don't apply, and I'm finding one isn't presumed innocent until proven guilty." Cameron pondered why or who would orchestrate something like this—if indeed it had been orchestrated. Enemies? He didn't have any who would go to such lengths. Roger Taylor, after he'd punched him? But Roger didn't have this kind of orchestrating reach. Cameron shook his head at the lack of plausible explanations. "I don't know what to make of it, but thanks for the info, Barbara."

"Are we still on for Christmas dinner, with Max and Tammy?"

"We're both working call Christmas eve, so we should be off Christmas afternoon."

"Great! You'll talk to Max?"

"Tonight, as a matter of fact."

"Just be there Christmas," Barbara looked at him, "and I won't ask why I haven't seen much of you lately."

. . . . .

After dinner and work in the lab, Cameron and Wildwolf drove to the Continental. Cameron ran into Joel at the entrance.

"Decided to come tonight," Joel said. "Who knows? Sometimes even someone who's a pain in the ass with figures might help."

"Glad you could join us," Cameron said.

Max and Track were already there, with a pitcher from Elaine. Track filled the mugs: "The meeting's called to order."

"Sorry I'm late. Had to tie some loose ends at the lab."

"So we'll write you up for that too," Track quipped.

"Don't need any more of those. I'm already feeling the squeeze."

"Sorry about that. Now let's get this straight: The case against you is built on a couple of high theophylline levels, which you did your best to prevent; on a life saved, albeit by the unorthodox means of IV alcohol; on a death from cancer developing in a gallbladder which you had previously recommended be removed; then you were held responsible as *Respondeat Superior* for an altercation between your Intern and another Resident regarding the patient's notification of cancer. More recently, you were also held responsible for broken ribs caused during CPR by another Intern, never mind that the CPR was successful, and the patient's home and well. Lastly, you are held accountable before a malpractice trial is even underway, for what really appears to be another Resident's decision not to hospitalize, and for a disease whose outcome could not have been changed anyway. That about sums it up?"

Cameron nodded.

"Max filled me in on the Q.M. Committee's sanctions. Seems they landed on you like a rock. Can I read the letter?" Track asked.

He was pensive as he read it. "I haven't seen anything like this before. We've had a rare bad apple now and then, but the cutoff was swift, and not via incident reports. This sounds like someone's trying to nibble and chew you to death." Track paused: "The docs on Q.M. aren't that dull. If we followed these guidelines, there wouldn't be any doctors practicing medicine, including the illustrious members of Q.M. And I'm sure they know it. Wait a minute!" Track raised his hand. "This is unusual. There must have been some dissent within the committee over this: Only four signatures appear on the bottom," Track placed the letter down, "but the committee has seven members. That means three refused to sign it, and it passed by a narrow majority. It's interesting that even in criminal and civil trials a unanimous vote is required. At any rate, Dr. Morrison, who was Chairman with his term to run another two years, also refused to sign. He's just too principled to let something like this go through. Dr. Atwood, who was vice-chairman, now signs it as chairman! There must have been some bitter political infighting to replace Morrison with Atwood over this."

"But why? What's so big about this?" Max wondered.

"Could be a coincidence. Just something that maybe got out of hand," Cameron put in.

"Coincidence? No," Track shook his head. "Examine any of it—the malpractice summons, for instance. Usually, a whole roster of docs are included, and the hospital as the 'deep pocket' pay-off. Instead, in this case only Dr. Cameron is specifically named. No one else is forthrightly listed, so we can assume it's Cameron they're after."

"I don't think it's coincidence either," Max nodded. "I remember something else about the summons incident: The 'policeman' delivering it wore his holster on the right, but he was left-handed. It was all done as a setup for intimidation!"

Joel hadn't spoken so far. "I don't think this is personal," he began, "and with all due respect, I don't think Cameron's that important for these extreme actions."

Max was about to give an offended rebuke, but Cameron beat him to the draw. "I think Joel's right. All this sounds too far-fetched for a personal vendetta. Anyway, on a brighter note, I do have some good news from the lab. Remember those liver biopsies we did on each other? All hybridized and cloned without a hitch."

"What's that about?" Joel asked.

"Part of Cameron's project," Max explained. "He's been regenerating dog livers anew after they've been lethally injured. Now, since he's worked with slivers from our livers, theoretically, he could regrow one for us, in case we had a fatal case of hepatitis, for example. Isn't that right?"

"In humans, theoretically so."

"You mean you've already done this in dogs?" Joel asked, his eyes widening.

"Nine dogs altogether."

"That reminds me," Track added. "I've put in calls to the Vet school to extend your work to simians. You can start any time. Dr. Jack Wekell is your contact there. You'll be working in his lab. Besides," Track chuckled, "I've got to get you out of mine before it's totally overrun by canines."

"What about the requirement by Q.M. to list all your extra-curricular activities?" Max asked. "How will they take that?"

"No problem," Track interjected. "The letter states you need to report any outside employment. You're not getting paid for any of this, so it's not employment."

Cameron took a gulp from his mug. "Good. I wasn't really planning to fill out any paperwork on this."

Joel asked a few more questions about the project, which Max filled in. "...That's far out!" Joel exclaimed after he understood.

"Certainly is," Track nodded. "And I don't understand why I haven't heard from the NIH yet," he thought out loud.

Cameron gave him a quizzical look.

"I meant to tell you: I sent them a grant proposal. You deserve one, and it will speed things for you. But I figured you'd never get around to applying. So, I put one together. I might as well say it: What you're doing in the lab is more far-reaching than anything I've got going there, and you're working on a tenth of the funds. But you'll need more for your next step—human application. I'm surprised the N.I.H. hasn't responded yet. Not that it has anything to do with your present problems."

"Did you use your name, or Cameron's?" Joel asked.

"Cameron's, of course."

Joel paused. "They may really have responded," he said quietly.

"What do you mean?"

"Look, someone big wants Cameron's ass, and wants it bad. And like I said, I don't think it's a personal matter. What does that leave? You've all been looking at this from your own ethical, moral, and medical points of view—assuming your standards prevail. You've assumed, for example, that research making progress against disease is automatically good, and will be welcomed and rewarded by all. But altruistic standards don't usually run everyday reality. Reality runs on the gold standard."

"Meaning?"

"I'm afraid the reply to your grant proposal has already been sent. This research could revolutionize certain aspects of health care, one of which is increased longevity for many patients. But its very strength holds the key to your problem: The project's success would be too expensive. In fact, the better it works, the more expensive it becomes for today's medical health budget. More and more older people would get older and older, adding to a Medicare budget the feds must pay for."

Track's mouth dropped. "So you're saying..."

Joel nodded: "What you see as a breakthrough to help people, others—probably even before it reached NIH researchers—saw as an unbearable expense."

Cameron and Track looked at each other; Max stared ahead. "I know it sounds horrible to you," Joel continued, "but regardless of what the Constitution says about life, liberty, and the pursuit of happiness, if you upset Washington D.C.'s budget standards, you'll quickly find yourself in danger of extinction. Their response was termination of your career, Cameron."

There was silence around the table.

Max finally broke it. "You know, I'm afraid that makes sense, and explains a lot of things."

"A few others also fit now," Cameron pondered. "Barbara Davis told me someone's been rummaging through charts, for the incident reports—someone no one else seems to know. And at the lab I've received at least two requests for tissue samples from another lab I don't recall working with before."

Track put his head down: "You know, I was just trying to help. I'm sorry."

"You didn't mean anything bad, coach."

Elaine came by and placed a hand on Track's shoulder. "Oh, my! You boys look so glum; like you've just been to a funeral. Ah, maybe I shouldn't have said that…"

"It's not that grave," Max managed a smile. "But I think we could use another pitcher just the same."

"Coming up, and it's on me."

"Well, now that we know, what can we do?"

"All right. Joel's idea is the most plausible," Track began, "and we'll need to act accordingly. I'll talk to Dr. Neuhaus, and sound out what he knows about all this. Nothing I can do about Q.M., but it was a close split there, and they still don't have enough to do you in."

"I'll track down whoever's been snooping around the charts here," Max added, "and get a fix on who sent him."

"Meanwhile, I can play along with the 'rogue labs' that have been requesting samples," Cameron said, "see what they're up to, and who their puppet master is."

"Doesn't leave me much," Joel commented. "But if my theory is correct, and the malpractice suit is part of it, you'll need a lawyer that's working for you, not for the hospital or insurance company. I'll keep tabs on that."

"The rest of what you have to do," Track raised his glass, "is dig in at the starting blocks—and run your own race, Cameron."

"Sounds like a relay to me," Cameron smiled. "Thanks!"

"To Project Hybrid!" Four mugs rose a toast into the air, in a smoke-filled midtown bar.

CHAPTER 18

CHOICES

"... such questions of life and death seem to us to require the process of detached but dispassionate investigation and decision that forms the ideal on which the judicial branch of government was created. Achieving this ideal is our (the court's) responsibility and that of the lower court and is not to be entrusted to any other group...

"... we take a dim view of any attempt to shift the ultimate decision-making responsibility away from the duly established courts of proper jurisdiction to any committee, panel, or group, ad hoc or permanent. Thus we reject the approach ... of entrusting the decision whether to continue artificial life support to the patient's guardian, family, attending doctor, and hospital 'ethics committee'."

—Massachusetts Supreme Judicial Court, full opinion handed down November 1977, fourteen months after the patient's death in July 1976.

B etween heaping tablespoons of breakfast cereal, Max looked at the brown bag on the cafeteria table. "What've you got in there, Cameron? Another experiment?"

"Rest of breakfast." Cameron ceremoniously opened the bag and took out cupcakes and blintzes. "Actually, they're for you, from Tammy."

"So have some, too."

"There's also a note for you."

Max dispatched a cupcake, and opened the note:

"Dear Max,

Hope Cameron hasn't eaten all the blintzes and cupcakes. Miss you lots. Need more books—some of Cameron's are too stuffy. Need spring schedule of classes. Also need you!

Love,

Tammy"

Max smiled and placed the note in his shirt pocket. "She's getting restless."

"Like a caged bird."

"Maybe she won't need to be caged much longer. Nothing's been happening with her past acquaintances. Still, " Max paused, "they're birds of prey."

"Isn't it strange? The predators aren't caged, or declawed. Instead, she's the one really imprisoned."

"Hope she's not much trouble for you."

"I'm hardly ever there, anyway. That reminds me: Barbara asked us for Christmas, remember? Are you going to spring Tammy for that?"

"I think so. Things have been quiet enough."

"Maybe they've forgotten about her, or your warning paid off."

"I suppose it's possible. But wouldn't bet on that yet. Speaking of what's possible—did you get started at the simian lab?"

"The first implant, in a chimp, just passed the critical part. Seem to be doing well."

"When will you be ready for the next step?"

"What next step?"

Max paused. "Human. I mean, you cloned our liver biopsies with no problem, right?"

Cameron looked away. The question was inevitable, but he hadn't come to terms with it. It had always remained something far into the future. Something that despite getting ever closer, somehow he'd never have to deal with. "I don't know," Cameron replied. By that he meant "if ever," not "when."

"It's one thing to work within the safety of a lab experiment, on canines you haven't named yet; and without a family in the waiting room." Cameron shook his head. "It's scary, Max."

"Of course it brings responsibility. But we carry that everyday already."

"We carry it, but within mainstream medicine, Max. In things you and I have answers for, or if we don't, we can ask someone else. There's always someone else to turn to, someone to divide the responsibility with. But you're talking about uncharted seas, which no one else has navigated."

"I don't blame you for being spooked, Cameron. But you know something the rest of us don't. That carries its own kind of responsibility. It doesn't mean you're always going to be right, or that you'll never fail. It does mean if you don't try to work with what you know, no one else can do it for you. Maybe someone could, eventually: But how many lives would be lost waiting? How many lives would have been lost to smallpox if Jenner had waited with his vaccine?"

"There's something else," Cameron hesitated. "I guess this business with Q.M. and the incident reports is making me lose my nerve." Like shadows running behind him, Cameron thought—strides nearing, breaking his own. "Anyway, with what's going on, getting approval for human procedures will be next to impossible."

"Like Track said: You're going to have to run your own race." Cameron didn't reply. It was time for morning rounds.

· · · · ·

While at one time Mr. Ted Gardner had been a source of extreme concern during their rounds, today he provided their high point. His hair was neatly combed, his pajamas were pressed, and a kerchief was jauntily tucked in his breast pocket. On their approach, he put down the book he was reading, and peered at them from above his reading glasses. "Gentlemen, and ladies," he gave Lucy a nod, "fine morning, isn't it?" The sound of Christmas carols jingled from the nearby radio.

"Sure is, Mr. Gardner," Lucy looked at his chart. The last arterial blood gases showed a pO2 of 62 and a pCO2 of 44 on room air. For optimal functioning, Mr. Gardner needed an additional one to two liters of oxygen flow per minute. "Any problems, Mr. Gardner?"

He adjusted his thin oxygen tubing. "Not at all. I'm feeling just dandy."

Lucy listened to Mr. Gardner's lungs and heart, then recapped his hospital stay. "Mr. Gardner's lungs improved with a combination of theophylline, beta agonists, prednisone, and inhaler medications. We added digitalis and diuretics to reverse his heart failure, and oxygen to improve his overall function. Antidepressants helped his sleep patterns and mood, and in turn, Mr. Gardner helped us by stopping smoking. Mr. Gardner is now functioning normally, and" she closed his chart, "is ready to go home."

"I'm a changed man," he smiled. "I owe you my life."

The English Professor was indeed a far cry from the depressed recluse with claw-like fingernails, stained brown from tobacco smoke, and hair and beard that would have done justice to Bigfoot. He'd appeared like a ghostly remake of the emaciated Howard Hughes in his final days—the shell of what once had been. But in Mr. Gardner's case, the shell had reversed into a cocoon, spinning out new life.

"We're all glad to have been able to help, Mr. Gardner. I'll have a list of medicines ready for you, and a prescription for oxygen to use at home, same as here. We'll be seeing you in clinic in about one week."

"I confess, after being so well cared for here, I face the prospect of leaving with some trepidation. Of course, I realize I must go. I thank you all." Mr. Gardner gave a small, polite nod.

Outside the room, his former student waited to take him home. With a look of astonishment at Mr. Gardner's recovery, she listened to Dr. Lucy Carlton's home care instructions.

Even Joel, despite Mr. Gardner's stay of seven days past his allowable DRG's, was buoyant. "Not bad for someone who didn't even want to come to the hospital, eh?" Joel commented.

Cameron wondered whether Joel had forgotten that results for Mr. Gardner had been achieved not only with medications, but with patience; not only by medical technology doled out according to numbers, but by a watchful eye and a helping hand, dispensed by a caring heart.

But, ever the numbers man, Joel hadn't forgotten the fine points of DRG's. "What are we going to do about Utilization Review's notice that Mr. Gardner exceeded his allowable stay by five days?"

"We already documented in the chart, and for U.R., that Mr. Gardner had special, individual circumstances that required the extra stay," Lucy replied.

"What did U.R. say to that?"

"They haven't, yet."

Cameron had remained silent. He realized that what seemed obvious to treating physicians on the scene, for whom all patients were special, was not necessarily so for the Utilization Review Committee, whose job it was to oversee patients' hospital days used, and so viewed all patients as standard "cases."

At any rate, as usual in medicine, they didn't have much time to bask in their success. In the next room, 503B, Mrs. Edna Dwyer had been in the hospital for three days, with severe back pain of several months' duration. X-rays and nuclear bone scan showed bone cancer. They had ruled out liver, female organs, and breast as possible primary sources, and found it had begun as a small nodule in the right upper lung. Mrs. Dwyer was a smoker. And her skin sign of Laser-Trelat that might have been an earlier tip-off had previously been missed.

"How are you, Mrs. Dwyer?" Joel asked.

"Real good. I feel pretty good." She smiled. It was the smile of one who hadn't won many battles in her life, but was willing to try again.

Dr. Joel Saxton went over the vital signs, and wrote down the lab results. He cleared his throat. "We've found the primary, Mrs. Dwyer. That is, we found where the tumor in the bones came from." Tumor didn't sound as bad as cancer. At the time, it was one of the few breaks in life Joel could offer Mrs. Dwyer. "It came from a small spot in the lung. We could barely see it on the chest X-ray, but the C.T. scan confirmed it." Joel let that sink in a little before going on. He didn't mention there was also widening of the mediastinum—the central area containing the chest's great vessels, lymphatics, and heart—which meant there was likely spread to the lymphatic chain.

Mrs. Dwyer's shoulders sagged as if heavy from the newly added weight of the cancer. But her face still looked up, with her same shy, retiring smile.

"Do you have any questions?" Joel asked.

In a life like hers—first abused as a child, then beaten by an alcoholic husband—she'd answered life's questions also with alcohol. Since she'd never received normal answers, she'd become used to not asking questions. She shook her head.

"We'll need to decide how to treat this," Joel continued. "It may not be easy." A far shot at best, Joel knew. He had to remind himself he'd signed up to fight all the battles, not just the easy ones, like three-day hospital stays for patients that left as good as new. His mouth felt dry as cotton, but he tried to keep his voice upbeat. "It would help to know what type of tumor we are dealing with. We've gone over this in conference, and we think the tumor in the lung can be reached by a fine-needle biopsy. Any questions?" Joel asked again.

With a tremor around her lips, she maintained her smile, battling for hope.

Cameron took her hand. "The fine-needle biopsy is usually painless, and we can give you medication if needed. It's a procedure during which, under X-ray guidance, we place a very thin needle into the tumor, and retrieve a little of it to study under a microscope. The kinds of cells it has will help us decide which type of treatment could be more effective. Then we'll have two more doctors see you afterwards, specialists in radiotherapy and oncology-chemotherapy, to give you some treatment choices. We'll talk more later, Mrs. Dwyer, and answer any questions you might have."

Mrs. Dwyer looked up. "Thank you." As they left the room, a far-away smile remained on her face.

· · · · ·

Hands in his pockets, blowing haloes of frost in the cold winter evening, Tom Barnes browsed along shop windows. He was happy today. He'd been off alcohol and drugs for over a year, and held a job at the

Rehab center. He had changed his life around. Of course, he'd have to do even better, he thought—but it was a start. He'd even saved up enough to buy Christmas presents this time—real presents—to make up for all those other times.

What would she like? Probably everything, and anything, as little girls usually did. She'd be six soon. He hadn't seen her for nearly a year and half. Ponies had been her favorite: Along with the little pony with long tail and mane, she'd liked "My Little Pony" shoes, and "My Little Pony" hairbrushes. "Rainbow Brite" had been another favorite. On summer nights, she'd gazed at the stars, and wondered how far they really were, and how they stayed up in the sky. He'd tried to explain about stars, moon, suns, and light years—it seemed so long ago now.

But he'd been no good for them like that—most of the time stone-drunk, or spaced-out. When he'd realized that, he left. And tried to change it. In a way, no matter how much he'd changed, he would still feel a part of him wasn't good enough for them. But he had to start somewhere.

Tom Barnes stopped suddenly at a store window, looked intently, then went in. He emerged a while later with a grin, and a small, gift-wrapped box. The first Salvation Army Santa that Tom saw received a crisp five-dollar bill as Tom moved swiftly past. He'd just remembered today was Wednesday --the day they used to go to Chuck E Cheese! Salvation Santa, playing his bell, thought he saw the fast-moving donor click his heels.

The walk to Chuck E Cheese took Tom through a musical Christmas tour of the city: Two Jingle Bells, one Silver Bells, one Tannenbaum, two Little Drummer Boys (the second of which he finished himself), and assorted others, blending into Silent Night as he reached his destination.

That much hadn't changed: C.E.C. was still the same cavern full of mechanized trains, planes, ponies, helicopters bobbing up and down, and spaceships that spun. Kids, dressed in as many hues as the colors of the abundant toy machines, clambered atop the rides to try their joysticks, toggles, and push their control buttons. Tom Barnes walked to the adjacent banquet and stage area. Balloons adorned tables, and two long rows of seats were packed end to end with the laughter of urchins attending a birthday party. Others sat in the round, watching an animated cast of characters from childhood fantasies. Tom's heart sank:

Though the show included Amy's favorite bears, she wasn't anywhere in the crowd of smiling children.

Once again Tom searched the crowd's faces, but Amy's wasn't among them. Tom's hand clutched the little gift box he carried. Was it possible after all this time he might not recognize her? Or she him? He shook his head and placed the gift box in his pocket. He should have seen them earlier, kept in touch. But he remembered: They had seen him down and out often enough. Part of what kept him going was they wouldn't see him like that again.

Tom Barnes began to walk out. A yellow plastic ball, from the "ball-crawl" pool, rolled by his feet. He bent over to retrieve it, when the corner of his eye caught a glimpse of a ponytailed little girl doing a back flip into the pool of plastic balls. It was Amy! Often she'd jump in like that, almost doing a cartwheel. Her mother, Lisa, stood at the soda fountain with her back to them. Tom's pulse skipped a beat.

He picked up the plastic ball, and walked towards the ball-crawl pool. Amy did another cartwheel, and landed smiling in the middle of it. Tom wanted to call her name, but couldn't. What if she didn't recognize him? What would he say? That he had a job now? That he was straight? His legs felt heavy, and his pace slowed.

Tom realized now that he'd come to rehearse what he had to say: To run it through his mind, get himself used to walking up to her, to be able to hold her hand, and place the gift within hers with the certainty of a father's touch. Perhaps it was strange that he needed to prepare himself beforehand. But Christmas Eve was meant to be happy, and he didn't want her to see him cry.

Tom stopped, staring at the plastic ball in his hand. He was afraid to tell her that sometimes people, even daddies, didn't live up to what they should be. He replaced the ball quietly and left.

· · · · ·

Snow clung to Cameron's shoes on his way to the lab, gathering in clumps like his thoughts. The canine experiments had become routinely predictable, and his primate work was going well. It was strange how dark clouds of incident reports hung over him in the hospital, while sunshine hovered over his lab ventures. Still, in a way they had become linked now, and failure in one could bring failure in the other.

Cameron entered his usual lab notes, then prepared more slides for microscope work and radionuclide testing. Wildwolf's ears perked up, and periscoped towards the door. There was a knock.

"Come in. It's open!" Perhaps it was Max or Tammy. They were all going to have dinner later at the apartment.

Sonia Palmer shook the snow from her coat and removed her gloves. "Figured I might find you here. What's going on? You look so serious."

"Probably nothing that can't be fixed."

"Can I help? Maybe fix dinner later?"

"It'll take me another hour here. Sure you won't be bored?"

"Came to see you, didn't I? I'll just steal one of your doggies in the meantime."

"Sure you're not gathering information for some anti-experiment, animal protection group?" Cameron laughed.

"Maybe I should be," she grinned. Now get to work, then we'll relax, and forget about labs and lobbies."

"What did you have in mind?"

"Tell you later," she pressed a finger to his lips. "Better yet, I won't tell you."

"I better make a call about dinner." Cameron dialed his room twice. "Hello, sis. Max there? Look, why don't you two have dinner without me. Save me a piece of that apple pie."

Sonia's eyebrows rose questioningly. "Didn't know you had a sister."

"It's a long story."

"We'll have plenty of time this evening," Sonia smiled.

"Better yet," Cameron matched her, "I won't tell you." He continued his work, only slightly distracted by Sonia's sinuous presence. An hour later he turned off the microscope, and made his finishing entries in the notebooks.

Sonia had been reading one of them. "You know, I almost understand some of this. What you're doing seems like it might be a big thing if it works out. Will it?"

"Might."

"What will you do then?"

"I'll try to keep mind an old saying: 'Those whom the gods wish to destroy, they first grant their wishes.'"

She looked away, pondering something.

"Don't worry," he added, "so far, my wishes are far from being granted."

"Will it really help people," Sonia looked at him, "or just let them suffer more?"

"Why do you say that?" Cameron asked.

She hesitated no longer the composed, persuasive lobbyist but simply someone uncertain and frightened. "I remember my grandfather, dying that way," she said quietly. "He had Alzheimers, or a Parkinsonian dementia—they couldn't tell which. He spent his last year's life stiff as a board, and the last two months on machines, IV lines, tubes coming in and out of every orifice." Sonia stopped, looking away. "He was a gentle, but proud man, always kind. He paid his taxes to the last dime, because he figured other people needed it more. He never walked by someone holding a cup, hat, or hand out on a streetcorner, without placing something in it. I remember him taking us kids on hikes, and when we got tired, he'd just lift us on top of his backpack. He'd patiently explain the 'whats' and 'whys' for his childhood chatterboxes, and he'd show us riverbeds, and nests, and odd rocks that became entire toy-worlds in his hands." She shook her head with a distant smile. "In the hospital, what I saw—that wasn't my grandpa..." she began to cry. "But then, it really was him, too..."

Cameron dried her cheeks with microscope lens paper.

"Why couldn't they let him die...just like he had been? A proud, kind man?"

"Perhaps there aren't any 'kind' ways to die, Sonia."

"But there are choices, aren't there? To do this, or not do that? Put in IV's, or not, to use or not use a respirator? Tell me, aren't there choices?" She shook all over. Cameron reached for more lens paper.

"Sometimes there are. But we, as doctors, don't usually make those choices anymore." Cameron paused. "Relatives make them when they ask that 'everything possible' be done, regardless of how terminal the situation may be. Society makes them when it allows government to control and ration care. Government and insurances make them when they do ration that care, for example by not paying for terminal care in a hospital unless it's accompanied by IV's and similar paraphernalia.

"Bureaucrats make them by tracking morbidity and death statistics, without caring whether the patient's interest was served first and foremost, or there was simply a multi-machine effort to keep someone alive, without regard for quality of life saved, or suffered."

"I don't remember that we made many choices," Sonia dubbed her eyes, "and my grandfather couldn't. It seems it would have been kinder to keep him warm in bed, keep him bathed, spoon-feed him if he wanted it, and let the rest pass as it may."

Cameron reached for more lens paper, then gave her his handkerchief instead. "There," he wiped her cheeks, "now blow."

She complied, then smiled briefly. "I'll wash and return it."

"I know what you've been saying," Cameron looked at her. "None of us are good at the dying part. Even when we work with it every day. Most of the time, we can tell when death is near. But sometimes patients fool us, and go on to live another good one, two, or more years. Our job as doctors isn't to predict death, but to fight it, on behalf of the patient."

"I thought it was to alleviate suffering as well."

Cameron nodded: "*Primum non nocere*, first do not harm. To cure sometimes, alleviate often, comfort always," he recalled an old saying.

"Then why not do that—keep a patient comfortable, with as little suffering as possible when there's so little hope of returning to a near-normal life? Why fight a hopeless battle with death, at the patient's expense of suffering?"

"That's when choices become complicated, Sonia. What's hopeless? In a sense, nothing ever is. Part of medicine is hope. I'm a scientist, but at times I sense there may be forces other than science involved in healing." Cameron closed his notebooks. "And what's near-normal function? Or a worthwhile life? Some quadriplegics may wish to die, while others with the same problem adjust to their injury, and go on to do things we'd consider impossible. Chemotherapy may be risky and painful, but with it many are cured. Likewise respiratory and endotracheal tubes are miserable, but also save lives. So, when do we do these things? When do we tie patients' hands so they don't remove the tubes through which they breathe? Or the tubes that feed them? How do we judge beforehand an individual's spirit and capacity to adapt? How do we know the amount of suffering a patient will endure for a chance of improvement, or cure?"

Sonia dried her eyes. "Wouldn't that be up to the patient to decide?"

"Of course," Cameron nodded. "As doctors, we work for the patient, and within the choices the patient gives us. But even then we may face problems. What if a patient with unsteady gait, but of sound mind, wishes to walk despite his infirmity? Even if the patient accepts the risk of falls and fractures in order to walk, present laws are such that the hospital could be found liable to the tune of millions. So now we find patients tied down on all fours, against their will, for legal rather than medical reasons."

"But that's not right!" Sonia exclaimed. "They're being tied down same as animals!"

Cameron nodded. "Even animals get to move around more than some patients. Of course, the same legislators and lawyers who set up such liability concepts in the first place, finally found the idea of people being tied down or 'restrained' distasteful. So a new legal euphemism for hospitals and especially nursing homes has been coined: 'Postural supports' instead of 'restraints.' They're still tied down, but now it's called something different and more socially acceptable. The end result is the same: Those elderly people who still retain an instinct for freedom, despite whatever infirmities they may have, and who wish to continue walking and exploring life until its end, are tied down more for ease of care and to prevent liability, than to prevent injury." Cameron shook his head: "It's amazing how many lies will pass for truth with just a little change in wording."

"… Like children, aren't we all, young or old?" Sonia mused. "We all begin and end the same—weak and helpless—yet still trying to reach for all the edges of life."

"Zivi zivot."

She looked at him questioningly.

"An old Yugoslavian toast—live for life," Cameron explained. "We don't tie down children to keep them from falling. And if elderly patients so wish, we should grant them the same dignity. I'm a doctor, not a jailer, and if society or the law wish to tie patients down for non-medical reasons, they should get someone besides the medical profession to do it. I guess my beliefs don't matter much, though, in today's corporate-medico-legal complex. Liability concerns override patient freedoms, and legal decisions are more important than a physician's judgment. Doctors like me are becoming the dinosaurs of the medical profession. Soon there won't be any of us left."

Sonia looked away and was silent. "How did it get this way?" she finally asked.

Cameron shrugged. "It didn't happen overnight. A little law change here, a word alteration there, a little insurance restriction there, a new Medicare edict yonder. Society has forced two schizophrenically opposite pressures on medicine: One force, through malpractice lawyers, holds that everything must be done to its medical and technologic perfection, and cost and efficiency don't matter. Penalties for transgression include risking all of one's possessions, even after a lifetime of saving lives, over a single malpractice case—say, an unpredictable vaccine reaction in a child.

"The other force, driven by government and insurance companies, is cost control. Despite society's demand for ever more perfect care, less money's left for direct patient care, and more is spent on middlemen and bureaucrats trying to control it, regardless of consequences. As one businessman put it: 'It's just like developing specifications for assembly lines. If you can do that with assembly lines, why not medicine?' But patients don't respond to either disease or treatment in assembly-line fashion, which makes medicine a profession blending art and science, not an industry. That's why bureaucrats' projected 'assembly-line' savings don't materialize, and never will. In fact, costs usually go even higher, since any legitimate savings are eaten up by more red tape and administrative costs. Unless, of course, the patient dies in the process, which produces the ultimate in cost savings."

"What about socializing medicine?" Sonia inquired.

"The same applies. Savings come from rationing, and from patients dying while waiting their turn for costly procedures, like dialysis, or transplants. What good is it then, to have a free-market economy providing the best of cars and homes, but a socialized medicine allowing only mediocre care for health? Simply put, the incentive motive drives the quest for improvement and excellence in any field. Take that away, socialize it, and excellence is gone. While 'you get what you pay for' isn't always true, 'you don't get what you don't pay for' eventually becomes true. And once excellence is gone, all the money in the world won't bring it back overnight. Send the message that in the U.S. other fields will be free, but medicine socialized, and following the laws of human nature, the best and brightest will go elsewhere. Now, you might at times get by without the best and brightest. But sometimes you will not.

"So you see," Cameron stood up, "medicine today is in the same shape your grandfather was—all tied up to tubes of red tape, bound down by machinations of legalities, and no way out."

Sonia blew her nose one last time and put the handkerchief away. "I think we could both use a drink in hand, have each other close, and our feet in front of a fireplace."

"Fireplace sounds nice. Talked me into it."

"And here I thought it was me," she pouted.

Cameron smiled and bowed: "Hearth's fire will thaw body's ice, fire in your eyes melt soul's snow."

"Nice recovery."

Cameron locked the lab, and Wildwolf followed them into the car. It wasn't until they got to the old part of town they found a cafe with a stone hearth, licking fingers of melted frost across a windowpane.

"Shall we?"

They settled on an old couch, the fire casting its radiance like a necklace of heat around them.

Sonia looked at him: "You finally seem relaxed."

Cameron closed his eyes. "It feels like…we're resting on thick furs, a fire before us, in a prehistoric cave, at the edge of the glacial ice… I've returned from the hunt, empty-handed this time. But tomorrow's another day. And tonight's quiet and warm, the storm miles away outside…"

"Ice age cave, ha? You're not going to drag me by the hair, are you?"

Cameron smiled. "Would I have to?"

She looked back with a gaze from her blue eyes that unsettled him. Had the jukebox changed songs, or was he imagining a new melody to match her eyes? He looked into them, and the fire: He saw himself far away, outside boundaries of time, returning…returning from what? From a snow-journey's end, or an endless blue sea… the melody of her eyes was the same, waiting for him beside the hearth's fire, or by shore's sand still warm at dusk. Cameron felt warm inside, melody and eyes, wrapped around him like an arm's hug.

Her hand touched his. "What are you thinking?"

"About your eyes."

"I know a lot about what you do," she kept her hand on his, "the lab, the hospital—but not really about you. Like your running; you and Track; whether you've had a serious girlfriend."

"The running part is simple enough: We both like to run. Track runs for the pleasure of it, and for a certain perfection he finds in it that parallels life. I run because it makes me feel free. So I ran, and Track coached. One time, towards finals, something happened. I had my usual bad start, but just ran—for the freedom of it, for the fun." Cameron closed his eyes. "I didn't care about the start. The stride felt high, light. Before the final turn I pulled up even. I passed on the outside, feeling nothing but the wind. Then, before the finish line, there was no one in front of me. That was good, but not important. Freedom and the rush of the wind were important. Yards before the tape, my ankle tipped. I'd been above the ground, not watching the earth. So I met dirt instead of tape…" Cameron's eyes opened. "I didn't want to face anyone. But Track walked up, dusted me off, and smiled. 'You ran your own race,' he said.

"A few years after building a solid rep in Sports Medicine, Track left that field for other research. He'd been torn between running for its own sake, and running that was becoming an automated science for winning races—with chemical analysis of oxygen extraction, muscle biopsies of fast and slow-twitch fibers, and performance altering drugs. He'd been at the forefront of that science himself. But he couldn't bring himself to use it in an ice-cold way to replace the beauty of running, the unexplained flash of energy that sometimes burst more fiery than science. Deep down, he couldn't help the physiology of science defeat the flame of spirit."

"And you?" Sonia asked,

Cameron shrugged. "Like I said, I was never a great runner. Sometimes I ran a good race. I guess the rest doesn't matter that much to me."

"You won't get out of it so easily," Sonia persisted. "What about the rest? Girlfriends and such?"

"There was one serious one, as you put it."

"So what happened?"

Cameron shook his head. "Long story, but short in the telling:

'I loved my friend.
She went away from me.
There's nothing more to say.
The poem ends,
Soft as it began
I love my friend.'

"I don't know where that came from. But she had eyes like yours. When they were gone, she left a void."

Sonia looked on without blinking, as if unafraid of a memory. She took his hand and stood up. She stopped by the jukebox. "Let's write down the name of this song."

"It's in Greek, and Greek alphabet," he smiled, "no subtitles."

She copied it anyway. "Maybe we'll get lucky and find it."

He watched her copy letters and words neither understood, and wondered if his images from the song were true—whether the melody came from some universal place that bypassed words, and directly found heart's dreams.

"Let's go," Sonia led him out, her hand in his. Wildwolf stretched himself out on the back seat, ears perked up to the tune of Christmas carols. Under Cameron's hand, Wildwolf's throat issued a hoarse canine equivalent of a cat's purr.

On reaching Sonia's apartment, Wildwolf trotted up beside them. A small Christmas tree blinked its lights from a corner of the room. Sonia brought a hot toddy, threw off her shoes, and put her feet up beside Cameron's.

"Your turn now," Cameron nudged her, "what makes you tick?"

She hesitated. "Between my work, at times I stop and think—to see if it still all makes sense."

"And does it?"

She tossed her hair back and laughed. "Seldom does it all make sense. When none of it does, then I play, or I dream. And sometimes," she looked at him, "the unexpected happens and I meet someone like you." She fixed him with her blue eyes: "I don't want you to go tonight."

Cameron averted her gaze, to regain his footing back on earth.
"Wildwolf looks comfortable here," he finally said.
"You will be too."
Cameron put his arm around her waist and drew her close.
"Tell me, what did you hear in that song?" Sonia asked.
"Let me show you instead."

CHAPTER 19

A CHRISTMAS JOURNEY

"…The woods are lovely, dark and deep.
But I have promises to keep,
And miles to go before I sleep,
And miles to go before I sleep."

—*Robert Frost, 1875.*

HYBRID

The fine-needle biopsy on Mrs. Edna Dwyer had shown malignant cells rolling like granules of gunpowder-black lava onto a meadow of normal cells. The invaders were small, round, and deadly looking like blood cells, but wearing black. The nuclei of their dark activities packed cells to the brim with machinery for destruction rather than life. Under the microscope, small inkblots advanced like chaotic whirlwinds of Black Death. It was an "oat-cell" carcinoma of the lung.

Joel felt a knot saying it, though to Mrs. Dwyer's ears the name wouldn't carry the same meaning. Not until he explained it. Even in its early stages, I and II, the 5-year survival rate was between 3% and 30%. That was with the combined treatments of surgery, radiation, and chemotherapy. Mrs. Dwyer had Stage 4. Without treatment, her life expectancy was 6 to 17 weeks. With treatment, it went up to a year.

For now, Joel was able to leave out the statistics. They had more immediate problems to deal with. The same tool that had provided their diagnosis and would guide treatment—the fine-needle biopsy—had also punctured the lung and produced a pneumothorax. Although the lung nodule had been superficial, the biopsy needle had caused an air leak. When the air-leak didn't seal itself soon enough, extra air leaked into the chest cavity causing a pneumothorax, partially collapsing the lung. If the collapse was large enough, re-expansion of the lung had to be accomplished via a chest tube, venting the extra air pocket outside the chest cavity.

Mrs. Dwyer, a clear chest tube securely taped below her armpit, and snaking into a sealed vacuum system, tried to smile. Through no fault of her own—or anyone else's, for that matter, since even in the most expert hands a pneumothorax was a statistically unavoidable complication in 20% of cases—Mrs. Dwyer's losing streak continued. Her smile told she was used to it. It also told she would go on fighting, as long as she wasn't alone.

Before going over Mrs. Dwyer's chart, Joel looked at her chest tube, and wished he could change her luck, reverse what had happened.

"It doesn't hurt," Mrs. Dwyer said.

He realized she expected less than that—perhaps nothing more than kindness. Joel looked at her. What would Cameron do? Sit down, and touch her hand? Joel couldn't bring himself to do that. His rectangular patient cards came out, and with them, their insulating distance. He spent Mrs. Dwyer's rounds going over the science of the case, rather than holding out the possibility of hope, and risk losing. He wasn't as strong at it as Mrs. Dwyer.

After morning and evening rounds, Lucy, Joel, and Cameron went for a cafeteria dinner together. It was Christmas eve. They had the duty for the rest of the night. Lucy pulled a note from her pocket. "Mr. Gardner wrote us. He's doing well, and will see us in clinic."

"How'd you rate getting a letter, and not even a note for us?" Joel asked.

"Actually, he also needed a form filled out so Medicare would pay for his oxygen."

"Didn't you write a prescription when he left the hospital?"

"Sure. But I guess that wasn't good enough for Medicare. Their form is a two-pager, and at the end has a declaration:

'I certify that other forms of treatment have been tried and have not been successful in eliminating the need for oxygen, and therefore, oxygen therapy is required. In addition this oxygen equipment is medically indicated and, in my opinion, is reasonable and necessary for the treatment of this patient's condition. I certify that the foregoing information is true, accurate, and complete and understand any falsification or concealment of material fact may be prosecuted under Federal Law.'

"I already filled it out," Lucy added. "Maybe it'd carry more clout if a Resident instead of an Intern signed it."

Cameron looked it over and signed it. "Pretty soon we'll need five doctor's signatures on five forms, in triplicate, to fill a laxative prescription for Medicare." Cameron made up a jingle:

"Always a better way to go slow ...
Dam up the flow...
The Medicare way."

Joel chuckled: "Whatever happened to Utilization Review's beef about his 'extra' hospital days?"

"Received an incident report on it a couple of days ago," Cameron answered. "Seems it was my fault he was kept longer than needed. Medicare review didn't allow the extra days."

"We sent him home when he was ready, not before, or after," Lucy interjected. "He'd been back within a week if we'd sent him out earlier."

Cameron sighed: "I suppose they would have sent me an incident report about that, too."

Joel's eyebrows rose. "He was a smoker with emphysema, and not enough oxygen to even think straight; he looked like a pre-historic hermit on the verge of death. With T.L.C. we got him to stop smoking, to take his medicines, and extended his life as a normal human being. And now they're writing you up because it took five more days, and an extra inflated ten or twenty grand to save a person's life?" Joel paused, "as I recall, a previous hermit, Howard Hughes, wasn't so lucky. While we spent a few extra days and a few of K's to save a life, lawyers spent years and charged eight million dollars to settle Hughes' estate, after his death. This amount was staggering enough to let a court decide if it was reasonable: The judge deemed it was, indeed, 'reasonable. Not an unreasonable point of view for a judge, since he's also a lawyer himself. So, I guess the medical work to preserve life is less important than the paperwork after a person's death."

"And I wonder if they worked their Christmas eve nights?" grumbled Lucy.

"Well, we do," Cameron smiled, "so let's finish dinner and get on upstairs."

The ward was festooned with renditions of Santa Claus, cherubic papier-mâché choirboys, and even reindeer became airborne on the glass partition of the nurses' station. In the evening, the wax candles with haloes drawn on frosted glass looked almost real, alternating with boughs of holly. Each ward created its own Christmas away from home.

No two evenings on call were ever alike. This Christmas eve began at an average pace on the ward, but the Emergency Room soon became a runaway train. Cameron answered Dr. Alex Dawson's call for help, and went downstairs to lend a hand.

All exam rooms were full, stretchers trailing into the hallway. Of countless patients coming through, some had the sniffles, some had the runs, some had pneumonias, others cuts and bruises, others broken bones. Some with viral flus looked very sick, but would get better with little or no medication. Others looked well, but had appendices already burst. Some had migraines that looked like strokes, others headaches that were simply nagging, but turned out to be meningitis. At times serious diseases masqueraded in benign appearances, at others mild illnesses presented themselves with dramatic symptoms. One had to fly by intuition, as well as science. Those in insurance and government fields that insisted on writing "guidelines" for medical practice (which already existed in medical libraries) would also need to ensure all patients came from the same mold, to fit those "guidelines."

Cameron remained in the ER until past midnight, when the corridors were no longer blocked stretcher-to-stretcher. Dawson brought Cameron a cup of coffee. "Thanks, I owe you one."

"Sure," Cameron gulped it down. "I better head upstairs, and catch up there." They'd admitted seven from the ER. to Med Ward I, most of whom Cameron had already seen.

"This is Unit 16," an ambulance radio crackled in formal, dispassionate tones, "come in Base Station I."

Dr. Dawson bounded towards the radio, with Cameron following. "We're rolling Code 3, repeat Code 3, with stab wounds to chest and abdomen. No pulse. Chest wound leaking blood, air...We're starting IV's."

"This is Base Station 1. We read you, Unit 16: John Doe, coming in Code 3, with multiple stab wounds. We're standing by. Give us your E.T.A."

"Base Station 1, this is Unit 16. E.T.A. is three minutes."

"They must be close," Dawson turned to the nurse: "Get the surgery team, tell them we've got a thoraco-abdominal inbound... Lord, that's not much time."

"I'll stay," Cameron said.

"Good. Open the Trauma Room's crash cart. Two I.V.'s up—one normal saline, one D5/Ringer's Lactate." Dr. Dawson gave the orders calmly, without hesitation. "We'll need endotracheal and chest tube sets. Type and cross for type specific blood first. If not available within five minutes, then ten units of O-negative, either packed or whole." He turned to the orderly: "Cut away all clothes and get MASTS on him."

The siren sounded like the screeching brakes of a locomotive, changing pitch as it cut through the night. Like some unearthly creature, the stretcher telescoped its legs/wheels onto the ground and was galloped into the Trauma Room.

Under the glaring lights, Cameron inserted the first IV—a large 14 gauge needle into the right arm then positioned himself to place the endotracheal tube. Dr. Dawson placed the second IV, while the ambulance paramedic continued bag-to-mouth ventilation. Between bag ventilations, John Doe didn't breathe on his own. Dark blood with bubbles oozed out the left chest, leaving a ghostly white body behind.

Cameron felt the neck's artery: "Got a pulse with compressions. I'm ready to 'tube him."

Dawson nodded and stopped CPR for the eight seconds it took Cameron to position the laryngoscope into mouth and throat, find the inverted V of the vocal cords, and slip the endotracheal tube into the trachea. He connected the E.T. tube to oxygen, and listened to the chest.

Dawson continued CPR.

"Tension pneumo, left chest," Cameron took off his stethoscope. "Chest set!" Dawson called out. "Get portable X-ray here!"

In less than two minutes, they'd placed a large pleurovac tube into the left chest to remove blood, clots, and free air. It would allow the lungs to expand and receive more oxygen. Meanwhile the heart received closed chest compressions to pump blood throughout the body, especially the brain, until the heart recovered from shock and could continue on its own. Crystalline solution, though not as good as oxygen-carrying blood, dripped intravenously as a temporary substitute for the volume of blood that had been lost.

Type-specific blood wasn't available yet. "Get 0-negative!" Dawson called. "Feel any pulse?"

Cameron turned pale himself.

"What's the matter?" Dawson asked.

"Can't get a pulse." In midst of keeping John Doe's heart and brain alive, Cameron had missed one observation: "This isn't a John Doe," Cameron said. "Get Max McDaniel; tell him his friend Tom Barnes is in the ER!"

"Tracing shows V. fib."

"Give me three hundred joules, non-synchronous." Two round palm-sized silver paddles pressed against the middle and left chest.

"All clear!"

As the two red buttons atop the silver paddles were simultaneously depressed, the electric burst flailed both arms upward like a wounded bird flopping upside down. Then the body was still again.

"No change. Fine fib." Tiny spider-web lines raced across the EKG monitor.

"One amp of one-to-ten thousand epinephrine, IV," Dr. Dawson said evenly. "Follow it with one amp bicarb."

The spider-lines became coarser and thicker.

"Now give me the max, three hundred and sixty joules, non-synch. All clear!"

All hands, including those performing CPR, fell away. The endotracheal tube quivered like a rattle, the arms twitched their inverted bird-flap. Everything stopped, frozen in time.

A momentary rise and fall of the chest... sounds of air rushing out the endotracheal tube... "He took a breath!"

"Monitor shows sinus rhythm!" Across the olive-dark screen, jabs of light marched evenly like a torchlight parade. Before there was time to rejoice, the torches bumped into each other, trailing sparks of spider webs again.

"Run of V tach. Now he's back in V. fib. Lidocaine, seventy-five milligrams bolus, IV. Follow with a one milligram drip. Give me three hundred and sixty joules again. Stand clear!"

The arm-flop left IV lines swaying like rain in gusts of wind. The tiny wake of spidery fireworks coalesced into a march of torchlights again.

Max came in. The question, hanging curve-like on his lips, drew taut. He saw Tom's face above a body white as a sheet, slashed with stab wounds like red exclamation marks.

Cameron studied the lines on the EKG monitor, and was silent. The lines were slowing. He felt the neck pulse, then the groin: "Too weak for all the blood and fluid replacement we've pumped in."

"Let's add one amp of calcium gluconate."

"Dr. Dawson," a nurse called in, "we've got a patient in the Cardio room with chest pain, pale, and clammy. His monitor's showing all kinds of aberrant beats!"

"You all right in here, Cameron? Or you want the one in Cardio?"

"Max and I will stay here. Get loose when you can."

"Surgery team's on their way. They'll be ready in O.R. in minutes."

Cameron's fingertips found no pulse. The lines on the EKG were thinning. Tom Barnes didn't have a few minutes. "Zero- point-eight of atropine, one-to-one thousand, IV. Max, get a CVP in, left subclavian."

"Zero-point eight of atropine in," the nurse repeated.

Heartbeats sped up on the monitor, but without achieving a pulse. Cameron checked the rise and fall of the chest during CPR, and the pale pink color of Tom's lips, like a rose's frosted bloom.

"Continue CPR."

After feeling the small 'pop' as if going through saran wrap when the needle entered the vein, Max threaded in the subclavian IV catheter.

"CVP?" Cameron asked.

"About fifteen—that's odd." Central venous pressure measured the resting venous pressure of the heart: With the apparently poor cardiac output and blood loss, it should have been lower.

Cameron understood it: "Electro-mechanical dissociation, from cardiac tamponade. Get me the pericardiocentesis tray."

Tamponade was a collection of fluid or blood filling the space between the heart's muscle and the relatively stiff pericardial sac that surrounded the entire heart. Like a wet-suit too tight around a diver, it took only a small amount of blood or fluid trapped within the pericardial space to quench the heart's contractile force. When that happened, the heart's electrical impulses continued, but heart's muscle couldn't generate enough force to produce a pulse—a condition called electro-mechanical dissociation.

A stab wound had penetrated Tom's heart, leaking blood into the pericardial sac. Cameron readied the thin, long needle used to reach the pericardial sac, and draw off the tamponading blood. "Interrupt chest compressions." He slid the needle slowly from the xiphisternal notch towards the left shoulder. A syringe-full of blood returned.

"Non-clotting. It's tamponade. Any improvement in pulse?"

"For a few beats only."

"It's filling up too fast. He'll get minimal brain perfusion, unless..." Cameron didn't finish his sentence. The lines on the monitor disappeared. Tom's lips turned from frosted pink to snow.

"Scalpel!" In one curved motion along the left chest, Cameron opened a cavernous gap from breastbone to side. Soft pink lung floated up like foam against non-bleeding wound edges. Cameron's right hand disappeared into the wound. He held the ribs apart with his left. "Keep ventilating!" In less than thirty seconds from the flash of the scalpel, Cameron's hand held the heart, and squeezed back life. The pericardial sac met his fingers like a softball full of jello.

"Scalpel again."

Max passed the instrument. Then he held Tom's right hand, clenched bloodlessly pale.

IV lines pumped blood. Respirator hissed like a leathery sail.

Monitor screen remained empty.

Cameron opened a thin vertical slit in the pericardial sac. A thin column of dark blood spurted warm against his glove. It passed frothing along the rib edges. Cameron cupped and squeezed the heart rhythmically.

"Pulse?"

"Yes!"

"Tamponade released. I can feel the heart." Between contractile squeezes, one finger probed inside the pericardial sac. "Found it," Cameron said calmly, with the control of one who might have broken the tape in record time, yet waited for the official announcement. "Got my finger in the hole. Pulse?"

"Good!"

With Cameron's hand squeezing the heart, Tom's lips pinked up, and the chest wound began to trickle blood. Circulation was being restored.

"We need A.B.G.'s, lytes, a surgical CBC with PT and PTT. Any other bleeding sites you can see?"

"One near the liver. Nothing near the spleen. Stomach's not distended," Max answered.

"Heart's starting to beat on its own!" Cameron exclaimed. "I can feel it press against my finger in the hole!" There was an unusual beauty in being able to wrench life from death's grasp.

"I can feel it! I feel a steady pulse!" Max held Tom's clenched fist in his.

"That's not me anymore! It's his own heart!" Cameron kept his hand loose around the heart, little finger wedged within the hole caused by the stab wound. Heart muscle quivered and pumped blood like a stream past snowmelt.

"CVP?"

"Nine."

"Surgical team's ready!"

One of the surgeons came in. "What've you got here?"

"Multiple stab wounds. One through the heart, left ventricle I think. Got my finger in it. Had initial standstill and tamponade. I opened him up. Also had a left tension pneumothorax. Maybe a wound in the liver."

The surgeon, Dr. David Hulse, looked at even blips crossing the monitor screen. "Good job. Let's do the rest. Keep your finger there, real easy, while we move to the O.R."

· · · · ·

Two hours later, Cameron left the O.R., tossing his sweat-drenched surgical cap aside. He met Max in the hallway.

"Lucy and Joel are handling call okay upstairs," said Max.

Cameron said nothing. From his face, Max already knew.

"He's dead," Cameron finally said.

Max slumped back against the wall.

"Seemed like he'd make it at first," Cameron stared away. "But the stab also went through a coronary artery."

Max remained silent. Then began walking towards the O.R. Cameron put an arm around his shoulder, and joined him.

Tom's body was still on the table. Tubes led to and fro, but nothing moved through them. IVs hung frozen like icicles.

"He'll be a coroner's case," Cameron said slowly. "They'll be here soon with the police."

Max didn't reply. He'd stopped by the body, and looked at Tom's clenched hand he'd held during CPR. The fingers were still locked shut. Max shook his head. "I know who did it. Tom called me earlier tonight. He wanted me to know," Max looked away, "that he had a gift for his daughter, for Christmas."

His gaze returned to the locked grip. Max caressed the hand once, then slowly pried it open. Inside rested a brilliant gold star, cradled in a half-moon encrusted with diamond dust. Max turned it over, and read the inscription. Then his own fist clenched around it.

"What does it say?"

"'For Amy: May this be your lucky star. Dad.'" They were silent.

"She will need a gold necklace, to go with it." Max nodded.

They walked back to their night call on Christmas eve.

After dawn, their night call was done. Max and Cameron met for breakfast. Neither had slept.

"I know who did it," Max repeated.

Cameron poured the coffee.

"They're still looking for Tammy. And they put the pressure on him. Too much pressure."

"How can you be sure?"

"That's their style. Tom was tortured before he died. Ritualistic. When he called last night, he said he expected trouble from them." Max paused. "But I was on duty..."

Cameron placed a hand on Max' arm. "Don't blame yourself. What about Tammy?" Cameron added. "Is she safe for now?"

"Tom never knew she's at your place."

Cameron thought a while. "Has it occurred to you, if they want her that bad, that you might be next?"

Max' voice didn't hesitate. His eyes didn't blink: "They're going to be next." He finished his muffin and coffee.

"Are you in?"

Cameron looked at him. "Let's finish today first, shall we? After work we have a little girl that needs a gold necklace for her gift. And we have a dinner to go to. It's Christmas."

. . . . .

After early afternoon rounds, they checked out to the on-call team. Cameron walked to his quarters, wondering how he'd tell Tammy. He'd notified plenty of families and next of kin before. But each time was different. And just as hard. He knew Tom had become like family to Tammy.

He knocked as usual, then unlocked the door. Tammy came into the living room, and twirled once: She'd already dressed for their Christmas dinner.

"How do I look? Think Max will like it?"

"He'll be absolutely floored. I'll have to hold him up." The dress was dark blue, with white highlighting ruffles along the shoulders and hem. The space in between was sleek and streamlined along her waist and hips.

"Made it myself, just adding here and there."

"You look beautiful, Tammy." Cameron took her hand. "Now sit down, please. There's something I have to tell you."

She shivered a little, then sat very still.

"Tom died last night." He told her quietly and quickly.

"We took care of him in the ER, Tammy. Max was there. Tom left his last wish with us, and we will see to it. Nothing more could be done."

Tammy remained very still, like a child used to bad news. She looked at Cameron, then turned away.

"Come here," he held her shoulders. "You can cry if you want to."

"I'll get make-up all over your shirt."

He held her while sobs shook her body. He held her tightly and didn't let go until they quieted. "You're not alone, Tammy. We're still all together."

She looked at his soaked collar, tried to straighten it. "One of us is gone now."

"Tom left his love behind. That part of him is still with us, and will never be gone."

She gave a faint nod.

"Now finish drying your eyes, and I'll take you to Barbara's. I have something to do for a bit, but don't want you to be alone."

"Anyone tell you, you make a great brother?"

Cameron thought of a distant past. "You just did, sis. Now let's go celebrate Christmas. It's a rebirth."

· · · · ·

Though late afternoon, downtown's skyscrapers were as silent as mountain peaks devoid of trees or wind. An eerie calm had descended on the city on Christmas day. Flanked by high-rise cement and glass, rectangular patterns of sky overhead were crisscrossed listlessly with birds, flapping wings like figurines against a computer screen. Down below, deep within the canyons of the deserted city, there were few signs of life. Papers, old and new, drifted in gusts of wind, coming to rest on corners and gutters.

Evening approached. One after the other, all shops were closed. Cameron was beginning to wonder where he'd find a gold necklace. The high-rises gave way to the older part of town. A few souls wandering into a bar provided the first few signs of life. Two blocks later, in blinking blue neon, a pawnshop proclaimed itself open.

Cameron was surprised when the door opened, as if the sign could have been left on by mistake. With long Einstein-like gray hair, the pawnbroker stooped over his wares, shining them intently. After a moment, he looked up at Cameron, studying him with the same attention he'd used at his previous task. "What can I do for you?"

"I'm looking for a gold necklace. Delicate, but strong."

"Ah..." Lines creased across the pawnbroker's face, as if he understood the meaning behind this simple request. "I do not have many such," he said with the trace of an accent—Slavic, perhaps? Cameron thought.

The pawnbroker brought out two from behind the counter. One appeared too long, and the other too thin. Maybe the long one could be shortened, Cameron thought. "Do you have any others?"

The old man had been watching Cameron pick over the necklaces like a gambler watches a table—with distant yet keen scrutiny. "Mind if I ask what it is for? I mean, not everyone comes looking for a gift on Christmas day. I presume it is a gift?"

"It is."

"Ah, then," he nodded, "it may be important for whom." The questions and slow cadence of his voice made it obvious he wanted to prolong the encounter.

"It's for a little girl. The daughter of a friend." Cameron found himself following the slow cadence.

Creases returned over the old man's face. He made an effort to conceal their pained look.

"Now it's perhaps my turn to ask," Cameron tried to break the silence that followed, "why you are working on this day."

The old man looked around his shop. There were some photographs on the walls. "It is a difficult thing," he began, "for a parent to see his child die before him." He looked to find a chair to sit on, but remembered he'd removed them to force himself to be up and busy. "My daughter had lymphoma—the doctors said that was like leukemia of the lymph glands. They worked on her for two years. But near the end, it was better for her to go to another place, than stay here." He stopped looking at the photographs, and shuffled behind the counter. "This is why I am here today. To have something to do, and forget... But we never forget. Do we?"

"Forget?" Cameron shook his head, "we're all God's creatures, remembered best for the love left behind, that lives on."

The blue neon sign continued blinking its message in the window. Clocks in the pawn shop chronicled the passage of time, each with its own different ticking. The two of them were caught in a silence that spoke no words between minds, but hearts understood.

After a while, the pawn broker collected the golden necklaces and nodded.

Cameron hesitated, wondering if he should choose one even if it wasn't quite right, rather than chance not finding one at all. "Wait. Could we not shorten this one?"

The old man put them away. "If it is important, then it should be the right one."

"But..."

The pawnbroker raised his hand, requesting patience. He went into a back room, returning with a dark velvet case. He placed it upon the counter and opened it. The necklace was made of thick gold, elaborately woven and heavy in Cameron's hand. The clasps at the ends were entwined hands of gold.

"Maybe this is what you've been looking for."

Cameron nodded, and the pawnbroker replaced the chain carefully within the velvet box. "Shall I gift wrap it for you?"

"No. It will be very fine as it is."

The old man placed the box carefully in Cameron's hands.

"Thank you," Cameron said, and waited.

The old gentleman looked up at the photographs on his walls. "You're welcome."

"Aren't you forgetting something?"

"No. Remembering."

"But..."

"It is a gift," the gentleman pressed Cameron's hand around the box. He smiled for the first time. "A gift from my daughter, to your friend's daughter."

Cameron shook his head, dumbfounded.

"Accept it, please. You came here for a reason. Now it is done. It will bring some happiness to all of us."

Cameron knew he could not change his mind. "Accept then, please, my thanks, and the thanks of two others." Cameron extended his hand.

They shook hands. "Joseph Lapinski."

"John Cameron. If I can ever be of service to you." Cameron left a card on the counter.

Mr. Lapinski gave a slow bow of his gray-topped head, and the door jingled closed behind Cameron.

· · · · ·

Above the city's canyons, as dark thick clouds swirled to block the sunset, the few remaining patches of blue sky seemed out of place. Billows of chill winds began to gust, curling clouds like giant waves of smoke, twisting and melting with the fire glow of sunset.

As an onrushing storm embraced the empty city's man-made megaliths, something became strangely clear: Man was ever under siege. Cameron had just returned from waging microcosmic battles against bacteria and viruses, in worlds where man evolved to better antibodies and more antibiotics, while microorganisms evolved their own ways to overcome them. Outside, the macrocosm of nature swept the streets clean with howls of wind. And snowflakes began their slow but unstoppable descent. Yet neither micro nor macrocosm was really man's worst enemy: Man filled that role himself.

Strange to think then, that above a deserted city, blanketed by snow and storm, two souls from different worlds had managed to exchange gifts. Cameron wrapped the velvet box within his coat. He turned his collar up against the wind and watched the snow. It was time to make a Christmas journey home.

CHAPTER 20

A FROG, A PRINCE, A KNIGHT

Frogs, Princes, and Knights—they come and go
  at times unnoticed
  at others unneeded
Cloaked in the garb of everyday existence,

Until a day when Fate plays tricks
  and gives choices:
Between doom, and a fairy tale ending
  is when you will see them.

Seeing Tammy again was like a breath of fresh air—air that Max needed to breathe, for his life. Tom's death made her seem so vulnerable: Standing there under the mistletoe, in her blue dress with white borders the color of her skin, pallid from sadness. When he hugged her, she squeezed herself against him as if two bodies could melt into one. Her head rested on his shoulder for a long time.

"I feel like it's my fault," she finally said, "like Tom died because of me."

Max held her in his arms, without letting go. "The people that killed Tom have killed and hurt many others before, and will do so again. That you're involved is an accident, and doesn't increase or decrease the toll they take." He lifted her chin up, brushing her cheeks with his hands. "You understand?" His hands shook feeling her tears.

She nodded.

"Then don't think like that again." Max lifted her in his arms, and carried her next to the living room fireplace.

Before Christmas dinner, they talked of family, friends, and the events that had bound them together. Cameron brought out thin wafers of white unleavened bread, and passed them around the table. "An old Lithuanian custom," Cameron explained. "They're called 'plotkeles,' a tradition of Christmas sharing."

"Lith...what?" Barbara asked.

"Lithuanian. You know, one part of the Baltic trilogy of Lithuania, Latvia, and Estonia. That's from my grandfather's side: He was a burly old bear, with the chest of a blacksmith, and voice like thunder. When I was little, it felt like I could fit in the palm of his hand. But when I was sick, he'd tuck me in, and his voice became softer, telling bedtime stories. Sometimes he'd sing. Once when I asked him what the songs meant, he took my hand: 'I could tell you many things about the songs, and about <u>Lietuva</u>,' he said with his accent. 'But most of those things you won't remember. If nothing else, remember this: There are no swear words in Lithuanian, and the worst thing you can call anyone is a toad. And wherever you find more than two Lithuanians, they will sing. Whether happy or sad, they will sing."

They brought out dinner, and when they sat around the table, Max' and Tammy's chairs touched. Though eyes were on Cameron when Barbara suggested grace, Cameron looked towards Tammy: "You know, my words would probably sound like the wishes and thanks of a differential diagnosis list. I think Tammy might speak better for all of us tonight."

After dinner, Cameron gave Max the velvet box containing a gold necklace with delicately carved cupped hands for clasps, to hold the gold star cradled in half-moon encrusted with stardust - - Tom's final gift for his daughter. Max guarded it within his hands, and left into a snowy Christmas evening.

. . . . .

Max liked seeing the snow. It made everything seem clean and soft, covering the sharp edges of life. But some of those would always remain, in places inside that snow's softness would not soothe, or its thick blanket cover. Of those places Max bore sad tidings, that even a starlight's gift would not erase. A cluster of low-profile apartments came into view. Through the snow, Max matched their numbers to the address on his notes.

There was no doorbell. Max knocked.

"Who is it?" asked a hesitant voice from within.

"Tom's friend."

"...Why didn't he come with you?"

So they didn't know. They *didn't know*. The snow outside just turned colder.

"Tom left a gift for his daughter, Amy. He...he couldn't bring it himself." Max choked on the last words.

"Why couldn't he?" The voice from inside insisted. Max felt being watched through the peephole.

"Tom was doing well. He worked as a counselor. He wanted to prove himself before he came back. Ma'am," Max continued slowly, "he proved himself. But he won't be back. I took care of him in the hospital last night."

"Oh, my God!" She unbolted the door. "How is he?"

Max didn't answer. He saw a little girl, maybe five years old, playing under a small Christmas tree. "May I give this to your daughter?" Max walked to the little girl, knelt next to her. She was quiet and shy, with the same deep-set eyes as Tom.

"It's Christmas," Max said. "You daddy wanted to give you this very special Christmas present. Take good care of it. It comes from your father's hand, to you." Max opened the velvet box, with the gold star and necklace, and she touched the star. Then he placed it gently around her neck. "Your father loved you so very much."

Max got up to go. He turned to Tom's wife. "I'm very sorry. We took care of him in Emergency last night. The gift for Amy was in Tom's hand when he died. I can tell you his last thoughts were of both of you here." Max looked at them. The little girl remained in the corner, touching with tentative fingers a legacy that maybe later she'd understand. Max dug a card from his pocket. "If there is anything I can do, please let me know. Tom was a friend." Max bowed slightly and left.

Outside, the snow felt cold. It fell thickly upon the city.

· · · · ·

After Tom's death, Max had two things left to do: The first was done. The other already planned. If it was true that retribution was best left as God's work, prevention still rested in the hands of man. When the two coincided, distinctions between work reserved for Providence, and that left for the hands of man, became blurred.

Despite all his thinking and planning for prevention, Max realized retribution burned in his brain. He tried his best to keep it out of the planning, but used it for motivation to the hilt.

He used it now: The long bar hovered atop his arms, on his eleventh bench press of 245 lbs. Just a moment he wondered if he should go for a twelfth. He did. Max let the bar plummet towards his chest, hit the ribcage, then drove arms and chest upward against a bar that sagged at the weighted ends. But the arms didn't bend. They continued their motion upward, though slowing with every inch. A few inches from the top, Max arched his back. The bar responded by moving slightly, but not enough. down. Max closed his eyes, and kept the weight from coming down. He heard a bark. When he opened his eyes again, the bar seemed to be moving slightly upwards.

Cameron stood with one finger under the middle of the bar. "C'mon, Max."

The last two inches took ten seconds. Max finally racked the bench press bar, and sat up.

"Not bad for a guy in shirt and tie," Cameron commented. Max looked down: His shirt was drenched. He removed the tie and unbuttoned his shirt. "What's Wildwolf doing here?"

"Same as you – training."

"Seriously?"

"Seriously. I've been running them, and working the pack with whistles. Wildwolf likes it 'cause he's the lead pooch."

"You all set then?"

At first, Cameron didn't reply. "How can you be so sure?" he finally asked.

"I've checked out their *modus operandi*: I know which guys used what knife, and where. That night, from Tom's hands I also saved blood and skin that didn't belong to him. I matched it up by DNA fingerprinting to two of our future customers."

"What lab did you use for that?"

"Yours."

"You've been a busy boy, Max. That makes me feel better."

"So?" Max waited for a decision.

Cameron stalled. "So Tammy's worried about you. She thinks you might be next."

"But if something happens to me, you'll take care of her, Cameron. Please."

"Great!" Cameron smiled. "You ask me to take care of Tammy, and she sent me to take care of you…" He looked at Max: "When's the day?"

· · · · ·

The day seemed like yesterday, but it held far more of their future within its time-hands. Max and Cameron looked at each other. "Stick to the plan, to the schedule, to the letter," Max said. Don't do anything crazy."

"You same," Cameron added.

"I mean it. At least one of us has to come back, for Tammy."

Cameron nodded.

"Let's get it over with."

Cameron and Carlos went to position themselves. Max left to pick up his shadows. That wouldn't be difficult, since they predictably followed him on certain days and places.

Gator and Harry were eating hamburgers when they began trailing Max. "He's not following the usual route today," Gator commented.

"Nope."

After a while, Gator looked at Harry. "Hey! Where's he going?"

"Looks like he's moving in with us. Boss will like that!"

"We better cut him off!"

They did.

Max expected it: He'd taken the easiest way in, through the front gate. "Came to make a deal," he told them, "with your Boss."

"You're nuts!"

"I'll make it worthwhile."

"What if Boss doesn't want to see you?"

"Let him decide that. He wouldn't be happy if he lost a great deal because of you."

Gator thought about it. "Let's take him in. Frisk him, Harry." Max obliged, putting his hands up behind his neck. Harry patted him down. "Clean."

"Let's go." Gator put a gun's muzzle into Max' ribs.

That Boss wasn't going to be particularly happy seeing anyone was immediately clear: "What'd you guys drag in here?"

"You wanted him, Boss. We got 'im."

Max sized up the situation quickly. "Boss" reclined in a massive swivel chair, behind an equally huge desk. One of his lieutenants—this one had to be Don, with quick-moving steel-blue eyes—sat on a corner couch. The two that had brought him remained near the door. Max's eyes surveyed the scene without blinking or moving, his vision focusing diffusely around the room.

"Not interested in 'im," the Boss waved his hand. "I want the girl."

"That's why I'm here," Max said. "I came to make a deal."

"He wants to pay for the girl, Boss."

"You've got a half minute to talk, boy." Boss looked at Max, then his watch. "I better like what I'm hearing."

Max remained relaxed, his gaze looking past Boss' corpulence—which wasn't easy—and reviewed his options.

"It's a simple deal. Your boys killed a friend of mine, on your orders. So you let Tammy go, and any other girls that want to, and never bother them again. That'll make my friend's death not quite so worthless."

A deep belly-laugh rumbled through Boss' cavernous gut, slowly rising like the belch of a choked-up volcano. His face was a mirth-pink color. "I don't think you have that much money!" Boss laughed.

Max remained calm. "As far as you're concerned, I have all the money in the world."

Boss' color became ruddy, his patience worn thin. "No more games, boy. She's yours—for three mill." The rumbling belly-laugh returned.

Max smiled. "I've got a better one for you: Your life, for Tammy's and the other girls. Considering the little yours is worth, that's a bargain." Max didn't have time to watch Boss' face turn shades of deep purple anger. From the corners of his dilated pupils, Max caught sight of Don rising from the corner couch. Max spun a razor-tipped boot kick, opening with near surgical precision Harry's quadriceps muscle and tendon. Harry crumpled to the floor. Following Don's gaze and aimed gun, Max dropped down and behind Gator. Shots rang out, impacting Gator gun in hand, between Don's muzzle and its target, Max. Gator sprawled backwards over Max.

With one hand Max retrieved Gator's gun, with the other he ripped out his own from the sole of his boot. It was a thin gun, mostly handle and barrel. In one jump, Max had both guns pointed at Boss' face. Boss' hands came up from his desk drawer, and he eased back into his chair.

"Drop it!" Max watched Don. "Or your Boss is gone."

Boss' eyes went from Max to his lieutenant. "Do what he says, Don."

The clang of metal followed. "Now kick it toward me. Hands slowly over your head."

Outside, several "pops" like uncorked champagne went off somewhere in the courtyard. Sounds like a pack of barking wild dogs followed. Max didn't have time to smile.

"Get up and turn around," Max ordered Boss.

"What are you doing?" Boss' arms flailed above his head. "Let's cut a deal! Anything..."

"Shut up and listen. I won't kill you. Your life isn't worth enough." Max had one barrel trained on Don, the other on the Boss' corpulent butt. The second gun went off twice.

"You shot me! God, you shot me!" Small bursts of blood soaked along Boss' wide-bumpered wool pants like red poppies over a meadow.

"Listen carefully. Your life depends on it." Max kept both guns trained on their targets, and his eyes scanned the room for Harry and Gator, still on the floor. "I shot you with pellets. Some are metal, some are not. Some are too small to be seen by the naked eye. Some are time capsules with the AIDS virus." Max paused to let that sink in. "From now on, every time you sit, you'll remember an AIDS time-bomb ticking in your butt!"

"No!..."

"Listen up! Only I know the time-release schedule. Only I know how to special image to get the pellets out. Anyone else will just release them ahead of time. Follow so far?"

"Save me, please! Don't let that happen..."

"Relax, Boss. Your butt will heal. And so long as Tammy and the other girls that leave aren't bothered again, I'll return to save your ass." Max saw Don moving: "Not a twitch, Don, or I've got the same for you."

"I'll let them go! Promise! Just save me now, please!" Whether from pain in his buttocks, or a belated attempt at piety, Boss went to his knees.

Max shook his head. "Not yet."

"Then when? How will I know? How do I find you?"

"You don't find me. I'll find you. I'll check on you—every six months. In the meantime, you're safe unless someone tampers with the time-capsules."

"What if something happens? What if you're too late?" The blood was beginning to congeal on the wide-pleated trousers.

"You can pray I won't be." Max backed away towards the door. Gator lay in a pool of blood, cut down by Don's bullets. Max wasn't about to stay for CPR. He threw open the door. A thick mist of smoke poured in. As he closed the door behind, nothing could be seen in the courtyard. Sounds of barking mixed with waves of smoke.

Cameron had checked and rechecked his watch. The shots had come unexpectedly, and Max still hadn't come out. Cameron made a decision: He'd thrown the smoke bombs ahead of schedule. He hoped that Carlos, seeing the smoke, would also release the dogs earlier. Cameron pulled out his high- frequency whistle and blew. Barking at the other end of the compound followed.

Under the cover of hovering smoke, and the howling of an unseen ghostly dog pack crisscrossing the courtyard, Max was to make his exit.

But he hadn't. Seconds ticked by. Cameron approached the main entrance, listening to the barking pack scattering under the clouds of smoke. Soon he'd have to call them back, and the element of surprise would be lost. Cameron made a second decision. And went in.

Max felt his way along the courtyard, counting out steps he'd memorized. He knew he was behind schedule. To gain time, when he reached a steel-grated window, Max hoisted himself to the roof. From the rooftops, he could see areas where the smoke had begun to clear. Then Max froze: For whatever reason, Cameron had entered the courtyard. He was moving deeper inside, without realizing someone behind him had drawn a gun. Max reached for his own. "Frog! Behind you!" Max yelled.

Cameron dropped to the ground, while Max stood on the rooftop, and took aim. "It's like frogs, princes, and knights," Carlos had remarked about what they were going to do, "I hope it works." The phrase had stuck, and they'd used it for their codenames.

Now Knight was on the roof, unarmed Frog down below. Boss' henchman hesitated over the two targets. Then chose the rooftop.

Instead of gunshots, a growl came from the clouds of smoke, and the whirling of Wildwolf's fangs connected somewhere into the henchman's posterior.

Cameron dispatched him of his gun, then recalled his dogs, and broke into a run that needed no starting blocks, towards the gate. Max disappeared over the rooftops.

Cameron counted the canines as they leaped back into the van, and Wildwolf climbed in beside him. Cameron stroked the muzzle that had saved his life. Then stepped on the gas and peeled out.

Outside, someone still harbored persistent desires to follow them.

A storm-blue Cadillac emerged from the smoke and into the driveway. It made it a little past the gate before a scarred ancient battlewagon, set in motion by Carlos, made its final cruise into the Cadillac's shiny flanks. Peeling paint shook off the yard-wreck, followed by steaming geysers from burst radiators.

Carlos returned to the getaway car, exchanged grins with Max, and they accelerated away from the blocked exit. In the van, on the way back

HYBRID

to the hospital, Wildwolf placed his muzzle on Cameron's lap and slept. They had all left the swamps safely behind, for fresher air.

They rendezvoused back at the lab, and checked the canines for wounds. Shadowfax had a small cut on his paw, and the only other casualty was a chipped right fang on Wildwolf.

"Must have laid into someone with gluteal sclerosis," Carlos chuckled.

"Or a gun in the back pocket," observed Max.

Cameron fed the pack extra rations. He examined Wildwolf's chipped fang and stroked under his neck. "These guys saved our lives today."

Max nodded, then looked at Cameron: "What was the big idea? Why'd you walk in?"

Cameron shrugged. "I heard shots, and you were taking longer to come out. I promised Tammy."

"So what would you have accomplished, besides getting yourself killed?"

Cameron grinned: "I guess I would have announced there's a doctor in the house." Cameron paused. "What about those shots? What happened in there?"

"One of the boys had an itchy finger. And he scratched it, getting Gator instead of me."

"It was that close? I thought you had it all planned out, Max."

"I did," Max smiled. "But it's like a race, Cameron: You never know the finish until you hit the tape. A number on a T-shirt, a team name or codename, being one of the good or one of the bad guys, doesn't guarantee a win or a loss. Life's not like that."

"I know. Research and medicine are also the same—but we don't have to lose our lives over it."

Max shook his head. "I didn't know another way to save Tammy."

"The way I see it," Carlos interrupted, "you were both damn lucky. That's all that matters now."

"Yeah!" Max bobbed up and down on his tiptoes and grabbed Cameron by the shoulders. "And thanks for coming in after me, Cameron, even if it was against the plan."

"You think it's over now?" Cameron asked.

Max told what he'd done with the pellets, and what he'd said to Boss. "I wouldn't be surprised if he sent a bodyguard to protect me now," Max added.

Cameron looked at him: "Did you really put anything in that buckshot, Max?"

Max smiled, said nothing.

"Go see Tammy," Cameron said quietly. "She'll want to know from you that everything went all right. I'll spend the night in the lab."

· · · · ·

Rounds the next day went on as usual: Meaning nothing was ever the same, and there was always something new. It kept Cameron from dwelling on the events of the evening before, and whether they had really succeeded in ending their problems. The morning was completed with another incident report:

> "Dr. Cameron:
>
> The Quality Management Committee has received another alarming incident report. It concerns your performance of C. P. R. on an Emergency patient, Mr. Thomas Barnes.
>
> After initially carrying out routine CPR, it seems that for rea-sons unknown, you thereafter resorted to open-chest CPR, without a back-up surgery team being present. Mr. Thomas Barnes subsequently died.
>
> We are currently actively investigating this incident, and would like your response. While we can possibly overlook your presence in the Emergency Department, and absence from the Medical wards during duty hours, your performance of surgical procedures that you are neither qualified nor ap-proved for is viewed with great concern.
>
> We will be awaiting your reply within three days."
>
> —QUALITY MANAGEMENT

It was as if an elevator had just dropped under Cameron's feet. Tom's death flashed back into his brain like an arrow. The incident report heaped insult upon a raw wound. But for CPR, Tom Barnes would have been dead long before the Surgery Team was ready. There was also no question routine CPR couldn't have plugged the hole in his heart: Tom's only chance had been what Cameron had done, and the Committee members knew it. But regardless of that, they were going to hit him with technicalities. For Cameron, Tom's death wasn't a technicality. The letter crumpled in his hand.

Joel approached with charts under his arm, and a smile on his face. He'd missed the crumpled letter's trajectory to the wastebasket. "How's it going, fearless Resident?" Joel was obviously excited about some good news. Cameron did nothing to dampen his spirits.

"Fine," Cameron replied.

"You seem a bit down. Anything happen?"

"No," Cameron shook his head, "nothing unusual. But thanks for asking, Joel. What about you?"

"It's not about me. It's Mrs. Edna Dwyer! The chemotherapy got rid of most of her pain, and we're now thinking about Radiation therapy."

"Sounds good," Cameron was surprised at Joel's enthusiasm. "How's her weight holding up?"

"She's gained a pound, and I've added vitamins and minerals. Anything else you can think of?"

Cameron smiled. "I think you've got it under control."

He was happy for Joel's exuberance. At the same time, Cameron hoped Joel wasn't headed for a fall. As Max had said, there were no guarantees for plans in life, nor medicine.

CHAPTER 21

REQUIEM

Runner,
Guardian,
Friend.
*   The race is done,*
*   Your work is over.*
*   Locked deep inside*
*   Heart's home,*
*   You'll remain*
*   Forever my friend.*

Jacob Werner didn't have to wait long for his appointment with Terrance. That probably meant Terrance Liverpool was under pressure as well. From Jake's point of view, he could allow timing and pressure to build, to force Terrance into a mistake: A mistake significant enough to sink him, but not take Jake along with him. It would be a delicate matter. But Jake liked it that way. It wasn't that he disliked Terrance. Dislike was an emotion Jake could ill afford in his business. Jake reminded himself that anything but absolute impartiality sowed the seeds for possible mistakes. Nor did he view Terrance's skills lightly: on the contrary, he had the highest regard for Terrance's cunning. It was simply that things had come too easily for Terrance. Not that Jake's concern was with morality or righteousness, but with a more elemental form of ethics: Earned versus unearned success, and payback time. And Terrance hadn't earned it all.

Jake had already pondered the various methods of rising to the top. The common way was slow, but fairly simple: Staying within the shadows of the fast-climbers and doing their bidding also provided the pull of their wake. While such a rise was tedious and undramatic, it did reap its eventual rewards. Furthermore, it was a strategy of little risk for a fair gain. And if the star of a fast-climber faltered, one could—with a little footwork—detach at any altitude unscathed, and resume ascent with another.

At one time, Jake would perhaps have considered such an option. But for one thing, Terrance's shadow didn't suit him. For another, Jake preferred the fully earned, "all the marbles" approach, to the low-and-slow pull of a star's wake.

As usual, Terrance sat back in an impeccable gray cashmere-blend suit, and motioned Jake to sit down. "Your report?"

"Our subject's a tough one, but pretty well wrapped up. I've accessed most of the key people for the job. The web's in place, and all we need is to shake it a bit."

"Timetable?"

"I would advise another two to three months to finesse it more. As the pressure increases, our subject should make a few more mistakes, and tighten the web himself."

"That would put us behind schedule," Terrance reminded him. "Like I said, he's a tough one. We've had to use a magnifying glass and do microsurgery to get the job done. I could hurry it up, but it wouldn't be as tight as I'd like it." Jake watched Terrance's reaction: He'd just given Terrance a choice, and himself a disclaimer, in case matters didn't go as planned.

Terrance didn't bite. "It depends on how soon the second part of our project can be completed. We still don't have enough information for the lab boys to piece his ideas together."

Jake gave his best surprised look. "Didn't you get my report on that?"

"On time," Terrance nodded, "but not enough. Our lab boys couldn't make enough out of it to take over where he left off."

"You trust them?" Jake asked disingenuously.

"I have to trust them." Terrance loosened his guard, becoming irritated. "Anyway, we need more data."

Now there was something he could work with, Jake thought. He already knew which labs were receiving his information. Setting things up from within would be difficult, but not impossible. Probably a great deal easier than his task had been with Dr. Cameron. "I've got additional microfilm," Jake continued without missing a beat. "I've already arranged for a pickup."

"How soon?"

Two days, Jake thought. But he didn't want to give it away that soon, nor in its entirety. And since he didn't know enough of the science to supply only non-critical information, Jake would need other lab sources to check it out. That would entail its own time, and danger. "Two weeks," Jake replied.

"Why so long?"

"I don't have direct access to some of our field operatives, particularly this one. Outside prearranged intervals, I can make contact only with some difficulty. But what's lost in timeliness is made up by discretion. I think you can appreciate that, considering our positions."

"So be it. On my desk, fourteen days."

· · · · ·

Cameron studied microscope slides from his last simian experiment. Regeneration of hybrid cells had progressed at an astonishing rate, roughly corresponding to the growth of simian fetal tissue. The hybridomas had taken as well in simian tissue as they had with the canines, and no new problems had arisen. In fact, the only significant difference had been dealing with the various simian personalities. One of which, Mutation Simian III—otherwise known as Toto, had learned to throw temper tantrums as well as the best of humans. The tantrums could easily be stopped by the administration of apples or figs. More than once, staring at an empty bagful of what had been apples, Cameron wondered whether Jack Wekell's choice of Toto for his experiments had been purely accidental: While Jack fully supported Cameron's project, it was also within Jack's sense of humor to pick Toto to underscore the Alice in Wonderland nature of the project.

Cameron finished checking the slides and turned off the small beacon of white microscope light. Whatever the odds, "Alice" was doing well, Cameron thought. It was only his own status as Resident that was in jeopardy. Cameron turned to go and shut off the lab's lights.

Sonia Palmer waited in the hall.

"What are you doing here?" Cameron asked. "How long have you been waiting?"

"Not long..."

Cameron recalled Wildwolf's ears standing at attention nearly a half hour ago. "Why didn't you come in?"

"Didn't want to bother you. I mean, I suppose creative creatures need their solitude at times."

"At times, it helps." Cameron looked back into the darkened lab: "Free associations, ideas, connections—they are like night dreams—stars floating about a quiet night-sky, never landing, forever moving, but always appearing to stand still. They can only be caught, if ever, within the spiderwebs of stillness and solitude."

"Poetic," Sonia pressed his hand. "You add a touch of poetry to everyday life, to the way you do things."

"Maybe that's because there is poetry in everything, and nothing's just ordinary."

"Sometimes what I do feels very ordinary."

"Nothing's ordinary if it's done well."

"So maybe I don't do things well enough."

"Do you enjoy what you do?"

"Sometimes, no," Sonia replied. "Maybe lots of times no."

"Then change it."

"I believe I'm trying to. It seems so easy for you," she looked away. "What am I saying? I know you work hard. You just make it look easy."

"Something's bothering you," Cameron said. "What is it?"

"Nothing, really," Sonia shook her head. "What about you? How are your battles doing?"

"You mean the incident reports and Q.M. stuff? Same as before, with a few new ones added. Research's doing fine, though, and so are the patients. But I suppose I should get busy, and answer some of those reports."

Sonia kissed his cheek. "Do it. Don't let them stop you. I've got to go now. I've got some work to do as well."

Before Cameron could say he'd missed her, she was gone. His luck with blue eyes hadn't changed: They disappeared as suddenly as a sunny day eclipsed by thunderclouds borne on a north wind.

· · · · ·

Jake's phone rang just before midnight. Stroke of luck, he thought, when he recognized the voice. "Hi, honey. I'm glad you returned my call."

"I was planning to call you anyway. And I would prefer it if you didn't call me 'honey.'"

"Certainly. I can understand that. Do you have the package? I'm under a deadline."

"That's why I called. We may have a problem here."

"What kind of problem?" Jake paused to collect his thoughts. "We retained you because you were the best for the job."

"I agreed to do it. But I didn't know what it would all entail."

"Let's not talk over the phone. How about tomorrow, usual place, about six. I would appreciate it if you brought what you have. Like I said, I've got deadlines. And I'm sure we can solve any problems you might have."

"We'll talk. I'll be there."

Jake cradled the phone and stroked his chin. Most reservations on the part of his contacts centered on money. He suspected this would be no different. It was not an unpleasant solution—except it usually diminished his own share. Still, it was a solution he could live with. Another choice would be to ransack her apartment for the microfilm. Searching for tiny exotica, however, was not one of Jake's favorite pastimes, even if he might finally find it tucked between folds of scented lace lingerie. He decided to keep next evening's appointment instead.

Jake waited at La Veranda for his contact. She didn't keep him long.

"Good evening, Miss Palmer." He kept it formal. That usually helped when it came time to negotiate payoffs. Familiarity only inflated the final price tag. Not that he was oblivious to Miss Palmer's charms, or would have minded an extra dose of familiarity with her. But business was business, and this business dealt in high stakes.

She sat down and remained silent.

"Shall we order?"

Sonia Palmer wasn't interested in dinner with Jacob Werner. It had simply been a business arrangement from the start—another government mission. But it wasn't turning out so simple anymore, nor could she be proud of it. She realized, however, that her pride and other concerns were of little interest to Jake. She'd need to remain on her guard and watch her step. Her cards would have to be played exactly right to salvage any chance of straightening this out. "Of course," she replied, looking at the menu. "Antipasto with prosciutto, and linguini with white sauce."

"Bottle of Verdicchio?"

"A glass."

Jake ordered. After the waiter left, he glanced at Sonia. "You mentioned some problem about this?" Jake hoped the suddenness of his opening would bring the price down.

"I first took the job, Mr. Werner, because I was told it might accomplish some good—restrict experiments with peoples' lives and curtail the expansion of mechanized medicine at the expense of its humanistic side."

So the broad could think—why was he so surprised? He'd given her that recruiting pep talk himself. But he'd never thought she'd fall for it, or even understand it.

"I remembered my grandfather, with that look in his eyes," Sonia continued. "Tubes dangled all around him. He couldn't move. His look begged me to stop them. I loved my grandfather. I was only a child then…I couldn't stop them…" Is that why, she pondered, she'd initially taken the job? To stop "them"?

Jake felt uncomfortable about the grandfather part. He'd used Terrance's computer-based psychological profiles, which had shown that to be her salient weakness. But it was one thing to see it on a computer screen, and quite another to use it for manipulating a human being. Jake loosened his tie and shirt's top button. Certain types of sentiment still made him feel uneasy, even in his work. Jake wondered whether somewhere, some computer would list that as his weakness. That was his job, of course: To make use of vulnerabilities, as well as abilities. At the outset, he'd thought of her as a bimbo: A classy one, but a bimbo just the same, who needed a fashionable cause for her work, if only for appearance's sake. It was rare nowadays to find someone involved mainly for principle. When that happened, even Jake had some reservations about using people unscrupulously.

Sonia hadn't touched her plate. "I found Dr. Cameron wasn't like that. When he places those tubes, uses them for life support, it hurts him to watch people suffer. He does it because he believes there's a chance they might leave those tubes behind, to a normal life again. Sometimes some of them do."

Jake became even more uncomfortable, and tried to cut the topic short. "I can see that could be true. What's that got to do with the microfilm?"

"Here's what: I know you want it. I know I agreed to get it for you. But here's your money back." She placed a white envelope beside him on the table.

Jake managed to cover his surprise. "You know it's not that simple," he shook his head, "I can't do that. We both work for a higher authority. I can't go back empty handed, just after I've told them the job was done."

Her initial gambit had failed. Sonia tossed her head back. "I didn't agree to be a part of Dr. Cameron's destruction."

"What do you mean?"

She continued in a voice as flat and as ordinary as possible, trying not to give herself away. "He's been having—shall we say, certain incidents or difficulties not only regarding his lab, but at the hospital. Not only don't I want any part of it, I want these planned 'difficulties' terminated—if you know what I mean. That's within your power, if I'm not mistaken, just as the microfilm is in mine."

"I do see what you mean," Jake nodded. "I'll do what I can for Dr. Cameron. His ideas will then be safe with us, and his future safe because of you." Whether he could make good on the deal or not didn't deter Jake from agreeing to one.

"If you don't keep your bargain, I will blow it wide open," Sonia said. She dropped a small package beside the white envelope, then moved her chair out.

"What, no dessert?"

"Perhaps another time."

"You're leaving this?" Jake motioned his hand to the white envelope.

"I can't take it."

Watching her go, Jake felt something strange, perhaps sadness. He also felt fairly certain what she'd left behind would make up for it. He slipped the package with microfilm, and envelope with funds inside his coat pocket. And busied himself with a new opening to undo Terrance, with the possibilities behind her threat.

. . . . .

Joel Saxton couldn't believe the report:

"Edna Dwyer
Inpatient #EED6502

There is a suggestion of enlargement of the previous right upper lobe mass. Blunting of the right costophrenic angle may be due to small pleural effusion. Chest X-ray remains otherwise unchanged, with no definite evidence of further hilar or mediastinal enlargement." Joel stared at the chest film and shook his head. "What do you think?" he asked Cameron.

"I'm afraid I agree with the report. It does seem a little bigger." Cameron had come down to the Radiology Department with Joel because he was worried about him. Joel had placed so much of himself into treating Mrs. Dwyer's illness that any setbacks took a personal as well as medical toll.

"Don't you think maybe it's just underexposed a little so the edges look bigger?" Joel traced with his finger the outline of a half-inch shadow, appearing on the X-ray film like a compact snowball remaining on a field of melted snow.

Cameron had already taken into account the differences in film exposure, by comparing areas of variable densities in old and new films. The result was the same: Enlargement of the primary cancer nodule.

Seeing Cameron's reluctance to answer, Joel looked away. "Could we call Dr. Don Guttman for his opinion?"

"I already did," Cameron replied.

Dr. Guttman's comments were the same: The enlargement of the cancer mass was real, and not an artifactual change in appearance due to technical differences in exposure. "The central hilar and mediastinal areas don't seem more enlarged, though." Guttman had measured them, and had compared the ribcage measurement ratios. "So there probably isn't any greater lymph node spread."

Joel nodded, but remained silent. They returned to ward rounds. "What am I going to tell her, Cameron? We may have to change chemotherapy, and she'll ask why. She's been doing so well otherwise..."

"We'll tell her what we have to tell her, the best way we can."

There was no mistaking the resignation in Mrs. Edna Dwyer's eyes when Dr. Saxton told her. She had asked, and he had to tell her. Despite Joe's couching of the bad news within all the positives he could muster, perspiration collected on Mrs. Dwyer's forehead, and her hand trembled with apprehension. She folded them together on her lap, to decrease the tremor.

Cameron touched her hands. "Oncology will probably recommend a change of regimen in the chemo- therapy," he began quietly. "How do you feel about that, Mrs. Dwyer?"

Joel watched her. A smile returned to Mrs. Dwyer's face, tentative at first, but peaceful. Joel realized it was the peacefulness that came from the ebb of a will to fight. As Cameron talked, the smile changed slowly, becoming brighter. But resignation still predominated over the quest for life.

"I guess that's all right," she smiled at them, agreeing to the changes in therapy. "I think I'll be okay."

Out in the hall, Cameron caught Joel's look. "She's lost the will to fight. We need it back. She needs it."

"How do we get it back?" Joel asked.

"All we can do is be there when the patient needs us. And never give up hope."

· · · · ·

Jake had already prepped his laboratory contact with the need for secrecy. The Importance of the project he'd figure out by himself. The local McDonald's would have provided them with an inconspicuous place to meet, if Bill hadn't arrived in an old Army jacket over a bright Pendleton and several decades old bellbottoms. Bill was as inconspicuous as a pink panda promenading outside a zoo. Jake smiled: There were things unlisted on a computer profile. Among them, having known Bill for many years, was that despite appearances, Bill was reliable and loyal. In fact, Bill was the kind of person who, if you placed your trust in him, would return that trust unconditionally back. Jake was about to put that quality to use.

"What do you think?" Jake inquired about the information he'd given Bill from the microfilm. "Can you figure it out?"

"Not all of it," Bill shrugged. "I'm a molecular biologist—the basics and all that. You know we look upon M.D. researchers as rather plebeian: Instead of solid, step-by-step scientific theory and research, they tend to function on a trial and error basis. If something works, they are happy. How it works is not particularly important to them. Now for us, *how* it works is the key."

Jake was getting impatient. "So what did you get out of it?" Bill appeared lost in another train of thought.

"Bill?"

"You know," Bill smiled, "I guess it goes both ways. In our research, we look at how something works, and consider that the purest form of science. We poke fun at M. D. researchers because they try to pull rabbits out of a hat. But they look at us and say: 'Do you know what kind of a doctor a Ph.D. is? One that never cures anyone.'"

"So?"

"You asked what I thought about it. This guy actually did pull one out of the hat."

"How did he do it?"

"I don't know. It's not all there."

"What do you mean?"

"The notes are in bits and pieces. I can follow some thoughts. Others are really detailed, procedural stuff. No problem there. But there's stuff missing in between, like he's making frog jumps—big ones. I lose him there."

Did that bitch hold out on him? "You mean there are pages or parts missing? I checked the originals for splicing or tampering," Jake remarked.

"Not necessarily missing. That's what I mean by some of these researchers pulling rabbits out of a hat. Instead of plodding, they hop-skip-and-jump. And sometimes they pull it off. Like he did. The real thing."

"Is it good?"

"Yeah, it's good. This guy's brilliant."

Jake thought quickly. "Can you reproduce it? I mean, with a little more info, figure it all out?"

"I'd need a lot more. Like I said, this guy jumps and does mind pirouettes. A lot of it is just sitting in his head. For example, most of the beginning is missing. And that's the crucial part. Can't get anywhere without it."

"Could someone else, maybe with a lot of computer power, fit the missing pieces and crunch it together?"

Bill stopped in mid-bite and put his double-decker down. "I won't say it can't be done," he shook his head. "Nothing is impossible. But his beginning is key, and that's not on paper, but in his head. Most of the info on his breakthrough, hybridizing new tissues, is recent and complete. But he's been working on the foundation—how the hybrid factor was developed—for years. And that part is missing. Without it, I doubt anyone can duplicate it."

"You sound positive about this."

"Yep. He's going to be mighty hard to track." Bill proceeded to devote his attention to the double-decker and malt shake before him.

Jake thought about it. "I guess that's good and bad news."

"Why?"

"Like I said. This is strictly confidential," Jake began. Bill nodded with his malt shake.

"Most of my work is to promote efficiency, to cut government waste," in his mind Jake was only bending the truth. "You know, dollars and cents stuff. I've got a problem with this project, though, since it might do people some good. But my boss, Terrance L., wants this stuff confiscated, and the researcher discredited."

"Why?"

Jake shrugged innocently. "Has to do with the budget, cost/benefit ratios, things like that. I can only do so much about it," Jake continued ambiguously, "and I've stuck my neck out enough already. Anyway, the good news is that if the information isn't all there, Terrance can't destroy it all. The bad news is I can't preserve it, either." Jake glanced at Bill to see what effects his words were having. "I suppose what we have is better than nothing," Jake reflected. "I'll be turning it in to Terrance L., and plan on retaining a copy for safekeeping. Should anything happen to me," Jake added with a touch of drama, "the information will be in this envelope. Don't open it unless I ask you to, or unless I'm in trouble. I'm trusting you to carry the ball if needed."

"You're asking me to sit on something really big, Jake."

"I wouldn't ask anyone else."

"What about the researcher, Johnny C.?"

"I'll do my best to keep him out of hot water," even Jake knew he'd gone past the point of stretching the truth. "But if he's discredited enough, no one will care what he says."

Bill shook his head. "Damn paper pushers," he said referring to Jake's boss, Terrance. He'd completely lost his interest in the half-eaten double-decker before him.

"Deal?"

"A deal." Bill extended his hand.

Jake knew that part of his plan would be safe. "Thanks for coming, Bill." Now he'd have to stall Terrance a little longer.

· · · · ·

Clutching a breakfast bag with treats for the canines, and incidentally his own breakfast, Cameron dashed across the parking lot for the lab buildings. It was early enough so he could take Wildwolf for a run. Cameron heard them barking down the hall, and wondered whether with the advent of spring the other canines were lobbying for more runs also.

The door swung open. It hadn't been locked. Cameron dropped his treat bag: Three cages were open and empty, and there was blood, urine and excrement over the floor. One of the open cages belonged to Misty; another closest to his workroom, to Wildwolf. The rest of the room was in shambles. Though few things appeared broken, nearly everything had been opened or turned upside down.

Cameron entered his laboratory workroom. On his desk, next to the microscope, he could see the unmistakable golden color of Wildwolf's fur. Cameron rushed over, but there was nothing he could do. Wildwolf's thorax and abdomen lay open. The organs had been removed. Life had long since gone from Wildwolf's eyes. Cameron placed a hand on Wildwolf's mane, and slid to his knees.

The initial shock numbed him. Perhaps it was all a bad dream. In a few hours he'd wake, go to work, and afterwards find everything normal in the lab. Touching Wildwolf's lifeless form, and gazing at the dark spatterings of blood over his desk, finally convinced him it wasn't a dream.

Disbelief gave way to rage. The numbness wore off, and his mind began to race. Who'd do this? Cameron realized the other two dogs were missing because they could be taken alive. That meant they were needed alive, probably for more experiments, or a more leisurely autopsy. Wildwolf had probably given them trouble, and rather than take him, they had dispensed with the trouble by doing an autopsy on the spot.

Wildwolf had guarded his master's place for the last time. Cameron took down his lab coat off the wall, wrapped what was left of Wildwolf in it, and took the body to the cold storage room across the hall. He fed the other dogs, but left the rest of the lab as it was. Outside, a light drizzle was falling. The water trickling down his neck reminded him it wasn't a dream, that he was awake. Streaks of blood on his clothes diffused into pink stains in the rain.

· · · · ·

For the first time in years, Cameron was late for rounds. Joel and Lucy were both startled by his appearance. Whatever vestiges of morning somnolence remained, these now dissipated away. They looked at each other, and at Cameron. He sat down, trying to wipe the rain from his glasses with his jacket sleeve, but the jacket was wet also.

"Sorry I'm late."

"Where have you been?" Lucy asked.

"Went to feed the dogs. It's raining outside."

Joel looked at Cameron. "Well, it's not raining blood, is it?"

Cameron seemed to see it for the first time. "It's the canines... It's Wildwolf's."

"Is he alright?"

"Someone killed him."

"But why?"

Cameron stood up. "Let's start rounds."

Barbara had come to see why they were late. Appraised of the situation, she got surgical scrubs for Cameron to change into before rounds.

Track Sullivan came up to the ward shortly after. "Lab's a mess," he said quietly.

Cameron nodded.

"Know what happened?"

"Not exactly."

"I'll go over it all: Check the place, examine Wildwolf. Maybe I'll find some clues. I don't think you'll want to be there for that."

"I want to bury him," Cameron said.

"You can do that later this evening. In the meantime, we'll straighten up the place. Max and Joel are helping."

"Thanks."

"Later we'll try to figure this out. You all right for work?" Cameron nodded.

He didn't go to the lab until nightfall. By then, it seemed almost as if nothing had happened. Looking over the clean counter tops, it was only his memory that replayed a different scene. His memory, and three empty cages. Cameron didn't stay long. He lifted the bag with Wildwolf's remains, turned off the lights, and padlocked the door.

There was no place near the lab or hospital to bury Wildwolf. Besides, he hadn't really belonged to either of those. Cameron drove to the park, where they had run. An old oak tree had marked the lap's end of their runs. Its branches were wide, gnarled and heavy with years, like an arthritic arboreal grandfather. Under its arms, Cameron covered Wildwolf in his final resting place.

The moon peered between branches. Cameron carved a few words on the tree.

> "Wildwolf -
> Runner,
> Guardian,
> Friend..."

He felt like a child doing it. Yet when children buried their little creatures, dedicating to their memory whatever small tokens they had, perhaps they felt a keener sense for the unity of life than adults. Their sense of life knew of no final departures, and maintained memories alive that no death could erase.

It was done. He touched the carved words on the tree.

The ground was smooth under his feet. Cameron felt very tired, and lay down under the oak to sleep.

CHAPTER 22

THE DRAGON

Of many faces
    but one countenance
Of many forms
    but one scourge

Its weapons are smoke
    fire and ice
Its scaly armor
    darkness and fear

It crushes the mortal shells
    of weak and strong alike
Of bold and brave
    of gentle and kind

It kills without dying
    hurts without feeling

But there are things the Dragon
    cannot do

It cannot break the spirit
    of the humblest of souls
Nor stop the tiniest bloom
    of kindness and love.

Max couldn't remember a time when their mood had been this somber at the Continental. Elaine brought a pitcher and exchanged glances with Track.

"Why is everyone so glum?"

"Wildwolf won't be running with us anymore."

"Something happened to him? Your hybrid idea didn't work?"

"Something happened to him probably because it did work."

"I don't understand."

"We're also trying to figure it out."

Elaine didn't ask more questions. Track began with what they had found at the lab: "We categorized everything broken or missing. Here's a list. If you find anything else missing or tampered with, let me know. As for the canines," Track paused, "besides Wildwolf and the two missing, the others are all right. The two missing are by now probably dead. I base this assumption on the remains of Wildwolf, who appeared to have had a hurried autopsy. Most major organs, including the heart, lungs, liver, spleen, and a sampling of regional lymph nodes were removed. Despite the hurry, the procedure had all the earmarks of being done by expert prosectors. The incisions were clean and precise, following anatomical landmarks. One more thing: I also found a small amount of tranquilizer in Wildwolf's blood, along with a scratch on his left hind leg. Wildwolf's long fur probably deflected a tranquilizer dart. Trace of human AB positive blood confirms Wildwolf gave them more trouble than expected." Track looked at Cameron, but there was no comment or response.

Max waited, then began his portion of the report: "No significant clues as to who was involved, but there were at least two different sets of footprint patterns and sizes on the gore. They wore gloves, left no broken locks, and though a lot of things were overturned, the actual damage was minimal."

"In fact," Joel added, taking out his notebook, "the entire damage came to seven hundred and seventy-three dollars, not including replacement cost for the missing canines, which would be difficult to assess. Now," Joel added hastily, "it's not that I'm being insensitive or callous about what happened, but I'm trying to make a point. That has to do with a peculiarity in what happened: Someone went to a lot of trouble to get, search, and then destroy something. But not destroy too much.

What comes to mind is that much of this equipment originates from a previous federal grant—so conceivably any large-scale destruction could technically bring in the F.B.I. My guess is the parties involved were aware of that. They came for samples, and to leave a maximum of chaos, and a minimum of destruction. I'd say they knew very well what they were doing."

Track observed Cameron: He hadn't touched his glass and had remained silent. Though Track had seen him start slow many a race, he'd also seen him too often to doubt his finish. The only question was when he'd begin his kick. "It's safe to assume," Track said, "that this 'expedition' had two purposes: To gather information, and to intimidate. The question is what we're going to do about it."

"I agree about the information gathering," Cameron finally spoke. I found a puncture mark medial to Blackie's right foreleg, over the liver. I believe it was a fine needle biopsy."

"Sorry we missed that."

"But why the intimidation aspect?"

"To keep you off the project," Track stared at Cameron.

"I see," Cameron said slowly. For the first time he sipped his beer. "A few basic questions remain unanswered," Max stroked his chin. "It would be easy to assume the same outfit, the same people, that are behind the incident reports were also involved in this. Now the fellow who's been gathering the chart information and fueling Q.M.'s incident report hunt has been very careful. His credentials, though no one seems to recall specific names or authorizations, apparently involved H.C.F.A./Medicare and N.I.H. documents, supposedly to collect peer review and 'occurrence-trending' information. But through some internal bungling—meaning payoffs—there are no copies of actual authorizing documents. So the trail stops there. But this job," Max continued, "wasn't as smooth, and so doesn't seem to have the same imprint on it. But it may have an 'inside' aspect to it. Who's got access to lab keys, has been around the lab, or knows its layout?"

"Quite a few, actually. The maintenance people, and all of us sitting here."

"Anyone else?"

"Sonia Palmer's come by to see me, a few times. And I'd think Administration would have a passkey."

Max filed that in his memory, but said nothing more. "Anyway, the locks now are all new, and double-locked, and only myself, Cameron, and Albert, the custodian, have keys," Track said. "And Albert loves these animals. He already packed a gun this morning on feeding rounds. Nothing will happen to them while he's around. I extended similar precautions around the simian lab."

"How about an additional protective element? A sign on the door reading: 'Danger—Biohazard H.I.V. (A.I.D.S.) Research in Progress.' It'd give pause to ponder," Max chuckled.

"Not a bad thought. I'll also run Joel's idea of an FBI investigation by Director Neuhaus. Anything else?"

"The trail after our 'incident report' agent is pretty cold, but I'll stay on it for any connection with the lab," Max turned to Cameron. "What about those 'rogue labs' that tried to get info from you before?"

Cameron hadn't given any indication of how, or even whether, he was staying in the race. Track awaited his answer.

"I've been feeding them," Cameron said slowly, "and I've got a fix on them."

"Good, I could use that."

Cameron smiled—visions of a pre-dawn lab raid by Max, under the cover of smoke—crossed his mind. "Don't get too hasty. For now, I've got to get back to my own lab work."

Track grinned at that.

Cameron pushed aside his unfinished beer and stood up.

"Where are you going?"

"To work."

"Now?"

"As good a time as any."

Track extended his hand: "Hey, it's still a relay race, remember? we're all here if you need us."

Cameron returned the handshake, followed by two more. It was strange how a common bond had developed within such an unlikely quartet: A track coach and Professor of Medicine who ran a research lab; a Medical Resident whose unofficial but persistent research had made him a target; an Intern who'd come from the back streets to face the mob once again; and another Intern with a surfer-boy's looks, the mind of an accountant, and struggling on his way to finding the soul of a doctor. Recognition of their bond came to them in ways as varied as their characters. But it arrived with the solidity of iron turned to steel. Accompanied by silence rather than fanfare, its only ceremony was a handshake.

· · · · ·

The next evening Cameron spent repairing and double-checking for damages at the lab. He'd considered moving all his work to the simian lab, but besides the inconvenience, it also wouldn't improve security any, since he could visit and keep an eye on Track's lab much more often. Cameron gazed at Wildwolf's collar still on his desk. The telephone rang.

"Sorry I couldn't make it today, Cameron. I'm still at work."

"I understand, Sonia."

"You sound down. They're still hammering you about the incident reports?"

"That hasn't changed much." Cameron didn't elaborate. "Any new ones?"

"One. Not much I can do about this one." She could almost feel him shrug.

"Why?"

"It's about the new charting system Lucy's using. Apparently, any new forms or data must be blessed for use by the hospital's Medical Records Committee. They're holding me responsible for allowing inclusion of her additional summaries to the charts without prior authorization."

"I remember you telling me about it. But that's been helping patient care, right?"

"Sure. It's a great idea. And her charts are the best I've seen."

"So why are they after you? Couldn't you talk to her, or clear yourself?"

"They're not after her—she's an innocent bystander. Doing something about it would only kill her work in the process, and they'd still be after me with something else. There's no sense in having her pay for my problems."

"You mean you won't try to correct the report, and clear yourself?"

"Her idea is worth it. If I don't stir anything up, she'll be able to take it directly to Medical Records, without getting it mixed up with me."

"I wish you would take care of yourself, Cameron, and be careful with your research project."

"Sure."

"Is anything else the matter?"

Cameron glanced at the collar on his desk. Then he told her about Wildwolf.

There was a prolonged silence on the other end of the line. "I'm sorry," she finally said in a far-off voice. "I really am. I have to go now. There's some work I must do. Don't you give up, now. Whatever you do, don't give up."

It would have helped, Cameron thought, to hear her say when they'd be talking again.

· · · · ·

Anxious as she was, she made it a point to be late for her meeting with Jake. From business suit to gloves, Sonia gave her best impression of seriousness, while avoiding emotional content. "Hello, Mr. Werner." She sat down and took off her gloves.

"Dinner, Miss Palmer?"

"Yes." Sonia ordered for herself, then looked at Jake. She'd decided to take one step at a time. "You told me the harassment would stop, Mr. Werner."

"What harassment?"

"Of that doctor on the research project," she didn't use Cameron's name. "We made a bargain, remember?"

"Ah, Cameron," Jake paused. "Indeed, we did. But it seems you didn't keep your end of the bargain, Miss Palmer. They weren't able to figure much more about the project from the information you gave us."

"I gave you all the information I had. That's what you asked for. If they can't figure the rest, that's their problem." Sonia didn't betray her inward smile. "Our bargain wasn't over whether they could figure it out or not."

"That's true," Jake uncharacteristically admitted. "And if what you're saying is true, it's not your fault. But they're still on my back. And what can I do about that?"

"I don't much care," she looked at him without blinking. "What are you going to do about your end of the bargain?"

"I've done nothing further to harass our researcher friend," Sonia cringed at his use of the word, "since we talked. I'd have nothing more to gain by it."

"Your reasons are more complex, Mr. Werner, than you'd like anyone to believe."

Jake sensed danger, but was nevertheless beginning to like her.

"So what do you suggest we do?" Sonia asked.

"About our mutual agreement?" Jake considered his options. Part of his job was to remain flexible and improvise. And part of the thrill was that at times he could turn the unexpected into something better than he'd originally planned. "You can try to convince my superiors to back off from our researcher, and at the same time confirm you have no more information to give them. That would take the pressure off me."

"What if they're not convinced I don't have any more information?"

"You'll just have to be convincing," Jake smiled. "That's your job, isn't it?"

She inclined her head.

Jake took that to mean agreement. "Good. I can't make it any easier than that." Or any easier for himself, Jake thought: She would take him off the hook for any shortcomings of information; and if anything went wrong, whether initiated by Cameron's unlikely victory, or her going public, there was one more witness to hold Terrance ultimately responsible.

His satisfaction was short lived. "I need a few more things, Jake." It was the first time she'd addressed him by anything but his last name. "I want to know who put you up to it. I want names. And I want everything like what happened in his lab to stop." She smiled. It was a cold and dangerous smile.

Jake tried to remind himself that dealing with the unexpected was still one of the thrills of his job. "Put me up to what? Just exactly what happened?"

"Don't play with me. I'm talking about what happened at the researcher's lab a few days ago."

"Look, that had nothing to do with me. It was a terrible thing to happen."

"Then you do know about it."

"It's my business to know. But I swear I didn't know beforehand—I don't know when it was planned, I don't know when it was done. I found out on my own afterwards."

"No doubt it upset you greatly." Her smile was cold as the disappearing sun.

"I have my orders, and I play my game. I'm good at it, and I usually win. That doesn't mean I follow someone else's game plan. I play by my rules, and they don't include kicking someone who's defenseless. Though you may not believe it, Sonia, I do have some scruples."

"If you didn't, who did?" Though keeping her guard up, Sonia was inclined to believe in at least the possibility of what Jake had said. She was also feeling almost as guilty for initially having had anything to do with it.

"If you want something done about this, the direct approach isn't the best," Jake replied. "You and I would be dragged down and take the fall, while those responsible would walk."

She looked at him without blinking. "If you aren't going to do anything about this, I will. I want names, and I want to know where they work."

Though Jake knew very well his next move, he made a show of pondering it over. "Look, there's no proof available to help you. I would suggest you wait a while, see if things settle down, or some proof becomes available."

"I need the names, Jake."

"All right. Let's cut another bargain." Her demands couldn't have fit the direction of his own plans any better. His only danger would be the possibility she was a "plant" from Terrance. That was as likely as the moon rising in place of the sun. "I'll provide the names you wish. But unless something similar happens again, you'll wait and hold your horses until there's more proof. Fair enough?"

"How do I know the names will be the real thing?"

"When the time comes, if you're still not satisfied with what I give you, nothing will stop you from coming after me with what you know. But," he added, "I wouldn't make haste of that, since it could work both ways." Jake printed just one name on a piece of paper.

Sonia blinked when she saw the address, and decided not to look at the name – yet.

. . . . .

Her color was ashen. Depressions slate-gray as lava surrounded her eyes. Sparse, thin hairs crowned her head, like slender burned twigs atop a desolate mountain after a volcano's fire. Her own fires burned low, except for those of her pain.

Dr. Joel Saxton went over Edna Dwyer's chart: She'd lost another two pounds, down to ninety-six. Blood pressure and pulse sustained a thread of life. Despite combination chemotherapy decreasing the cancer load to her bones, and now slowing the one in her chest, another had spread to her brain. Dr. Saxton would have liked to hide behind the chart longer. But Joel set it aside. "How are you feeling, Mrs. Dwyer?"

She tried to smile at first. The smile went ashen, with a droop on the right side, like a rag doll held too tightly many a year within a child's arms. Something within Joel felt like giving her that kind of embrace—but he could only pretend everything would be better after he let go.

"Oh...not too...bad," she answered his question slowly, hoarsely, with only half her mouth functioning. "My lips feel...thick..." she put her fingers on the side not moving, feeling a cool numbness. She didn't ask why it was happening.

And Joel didn't want to tell her. They'd done the brain's M.R.I. scan last afternoon. He'd seen the small white clump with its spreading spidery tentacles choking off control of the right side of her face. Dr. Joel Saxton gathered his thoughts to say something.

"Hooome..." she said in a low wail. "I want to...go hooome..." Dr. Joel Saxton was too confused to reply. Dr. Saxton wanted to fight with her, for her. Dr. Saxton didn't want to give up. But he was also afraid. And more than fear, Joel felt a pain and sadness, distant yet close, like childhood's memory wrapped in a gathering thundercloud above a playing field.

"You've taken gg..oood care of me," she mumbled with difficulty. "You ttr...ied hard," she extended her hand, "thank...you."

Joel took her hand. It was the most difficult "thank you" he'd ever heard. And one that meant the most.

While Lucy remained silent, and Joel couldn't speak, Cameron approached Mrs. Dwyer's bed. "We can make the arrangements for you to go home, Mrs. Dwyer." As usual for him, Cameron took her hand. "Are you afraid?"

"Yes."

"Of what?"

"Being...alone. The pain..."

"You can think about it, and still decide to stay. Or come back anytime. We're going to put our heads together with the specialists, and see what kind of treatment or radiotherapy we can continue for you as an outpatient. We'll get you home health care as well, and you'll have pain medicines available. We'll be seeing you in clinic every week."

Mrs. Edna Dwyer nodded. And she gave them her best half-smile. After they left, she laid her head back on the pillow. The tears she'd fought so hard to keep back welled up and filled the craters around her eyes. They rolled down her face and head, and when she tried to brush them away, tufts of hair came away in her hand. She left the fine strands clasped in her hand, and was happy she hadn't cried in front of them and upset them.

· · · · ·

After morning rounds and plans were done, including calls to the specialists regarding Mrs. Edna Dwyer, Joel set her chart on the desk in front of Cameron. "You really think she'll make it, Dr. Cameron?" The odds were against her. They seemed against her since she'd been born: Abused as a child, beaten by an alcoholic husband, and now this. Cameron ran his hand over his brow. "Our job isn't to foretell the future, Dr. Saxton, but to fight for and alongside our patient every step of the way. The odds don't matter, and we use every medical weapon at our disposal." Cameron looked at Joel: "But this isn't what it's really all about, is it? So let's have a talk."

Cameron set out two cups of coffee. "You're afraid for her, aren't you? And you're afraid for yourself. You feel more than you think a doctor should, yet personally wish it were less."

Joel nodded.

"We're all afraid, Joel. In one way or another, we are all afraid for our patients. And if we place ourselves too much in their shoes—afraid of what it would be like for us to have the same disease." Cameron paused. "We are taught that to be 'good doctors' we should feel empathy, as distinguished from sympathy. Well," Cameron sipped his coffee, "forget that dictionary definition crap. You've got a heart and a mind, and nobody needs to tell you definitions of how to feel towards your patients. Deep down, and in our own ways, all of us feel for our patients—or else we wouldn't have chosen Medicine. The few that maybe don't—well, they're beyond teaching, with or without a dictionary.

"For most of us, it comes down to simply this: There's fear for our patients, and fear for our own mortality. The fear will be greater for some diseases than others. But in distancing ourselves from the disease, we can't allow to be distanced from our patients. We have chosen to do battle with the dragons of disease—to defeat them when we're able, hold them at bay when we can't. Win or lose, prolonged or hopeless, the patient will have to fight the battle. He or she shouldn't have to fight it alone.

"There will be times, it is true, when the dragon is too formidable and powerful for the medicine we now know. It will destroy our medical swords and shields; dragon's teeth will flash by day, its fire burn in night. Nothing much will seem to stand between the dragon and our patient. It is at those times," Cameron looked at Joel, "that even with broken lance and shield we still can give the patient some moments of comfort and rest.

"To do this, yes," Cameron reflected, "you will close too near within the dragon's grasp. Your fears will return, as you look into the dragon's eye. It is then you will also see your own reflection in it. You will see your splintered sword and broken shield, shattered armor about you. How you bear yourself then, only you will know. But perhaps it will also be the only time, that you'll see a knight in full armor shining back." Cameron's voice trailed off.

"More than most men, we have chosen to face the dragons of disease and death. Indeed, seeking them out is our quest. One day, we will meet our final dragon, the one that has come for us. It will probably be familiar. And if at last we won't be able to defeat it, we will still know the times we snatched our patients from its jaws."

. . . . .

In the evening, Cameron had gone to the simian lab first, to follow up on his four hybrid-liver charges. Their recovery was complete, and if anything, had been even faster than their canine counterparts. Returning to the canine lab, Cameron thought at first that the chorus of barks was due to his later than usual arrival, until he noticed the figure in a slim-waisted overcoat by the door. Even in the distant shadows he recognized Sonia's silhouette.

"It's good to see you," Cameron put a hand near her waist. "Am I that hard to get a hold of so you wait for me here, or you just prefer it that way?"

"I wanted to talk to you many times before," she hesitated, "but I couldn't."

"Come in and get out of the cold." Cameron realized now how awkward the explanation would be if Sonia called him or came to visit while Tammy was there. "You've been away for a while, working and lobbying hard?"

"You might say that," she sat down. "How have you been?...No," she took a deep breath, then stood up quickly again. "Every time I try to tell you, we talk about something else. And now I must."

"So tell me. What is it?"

Sonia felt her legs weak and thought about sitting down. But she continued to stand. "I'd like you to know I'm not telling you this due to a guilty conscience. I mean, I do feel guilty now, but initially I took the job for motives that seemed good at the time. It just didn't work out that way. I decided to tell you because of the way I feel about you now. Even though I don't suppose I have a right to say that anymore."

"Sonia, you're not making much sense."

"I'm not, am I? Well, here it is: I was set up. No," she looked away, "I set you up. I worked for the government, to get information on your project." She stopped, as if the weight of her words paralyzed her tongue.

It was Cameron's turn to decide whether to sit down or remain standing. "Why?... Why would you do that?"

"I guess from my own limited experiences, I had felt doctors, hospitals, the whole medical system had become more technological, and less humane. Your research was presented as another high-tech step at the expense of humanism. I believed it. I realize now, even if that were true, I have no right to hinder someone's work or research. Regardless of beliefs, no one has the right to interfere with your or someone else's work, any more than to seize property, or dictate beliefs. And if further decisions are needed on how such work, research, or technology can be put to individual or societal use, it should be the subject of open discussion, not hidden destruction." She let out a long breath. "I'm sorry, Cameron. I'm sorry for everything I caused." She looked at Wildwolf's empty cage. "I had no idea any of this would happen…"

Cameron was in heart's shock.

Sonia touched his hand. "I realized I was wrong…even before I fell in love with you. But I don't have the right to say that now." She pulled her hand away. "Even though I don't expect you to forgive me, I had to tell you everything."

Cameron stared ahead. "So the night we met was just… just…"

"Was a set up," she finished it for him. "But I won't regret that night—without it, I wouldn't have met you. And the rest of our times together weren't set ups. Though I know I've hurt you where I've touched your life, mine was the better for knowing you. But I hurt you…" she repeated, "so I must leave."

Only parts were getting through to Cameron; bits and pieces scattered in his mind like icicles shattering in an ice-cave earthquake. He saw her leave. Echoes of words and footsteps slashed like ice shrapnel across his chest. When he looked up next, she was gone.

He tried to continue work, but wheels spun wildly, thoughts and movements floundered in thick fog. Cameron thought of retreating to the Continental's watering hole, but it'd be closed by the time he got there. He closed his notebooks, passed out snacks to the sleepy canines, and returned to the Intern/Resident quarters.

Cameron liberated a months-old six pack of beer from the refrigerator, and lay on the bed without turning on the lights. Tammy was asleep. Cameron opened a bottle, stared through the darkness to the ceiling. He heard Tammy get up, felt her take the beer from his hand.

"What have we here?" She sat on the edge of the bed. "What sorrows are you drowning with this hard stuff past your bedtime?"

"What makes you say that?"

"That's for sisters to know."

Though he hadn't planned on telling her, Tammy slowly pried the story out of Cameron. She listened in the dark, her knees curled up under her arms.

"Did you consider she could really be in love with you?" Tammy asked when he'd finished.

Not the "really" part, Cameron thought.

"What if that's true, and she still loves you?" Tammy repeated.

"But she left..."

"You let her go."

"I don't understand," Cameron said.

"You didn't tell her you needed her, that you wanted her to stay."

"I don't want her to stay for my need, but because she'd want that for herself." Cameron replaced his empty with a full bottle. "I shouldn't have to be a success for her to want me, nor a failure needing comforting for her to stay by my side."

In the dark, Tammy nodded. "All the things you say are true. But after what happened, even if she wants to come back, maybe she's afraid."

Cameron reached for another bottle. "Should it be this complicated?"

"Things can't always be that simple either, Cameron. Don't burn bridges just to simplify your choice of roads."

Cameron thought it over. "Thanks, sis."

"How many of those are you going to drink?"

"As many as I need to fall asleep." It was strange how a loss brought back memories from the past, as if an abyss gaped wide with desolate reminders of life-roads that could have been. There was no need to tell Tammy of those... Or of another brother she would have had, about her age now, if his life hadn't been extinguished by leukemia at age five.

Tammy didn't see Cameron in the dark, but she felt his silence. She'd wanted to cradle his head in her arms. But he probably wouldn't want her to know he was crying.

. . . . .

Cameron woke to a shrill alarm. He rubbed his eyes and sat up. "Careful, don't spill your coffee." A breakfast tray was at the edge of his bed. Where the empty bottles would have been, there were only his slippers. Maybe last night hadn't happened, Cameron thought. Maybe Sonia was a government agent in a bad dream, and she hadn't left at all.

"You're also on call tonight," Tammy smiled. "Feel up to it?" The way she'd smiled, Cameron knew all of last night was true. "You know," Tammy buttered some toast and continued, "Max once told me it doesn't matter how many times you're knocked down—just how many times you get up."

Twenty minutes later, Cameron stood blinking under the ward's lights of Med Team I. He looked at Lucy and Joel: "Rounds."

CHAPTER 23

Almost a Good Race

Noise clamors, light flashes, life bursts
Fast or slow, no turning back
Be it to the strong, to the swift?
To those of cunning, bold, or of wit?

Or if that be taken away, or crippled or lame
Can simple courage yet sway?
Strength gained from sorrow, or fear
A smile drawn from a tear?

And if not courage, then kindness perhaps
Not all can be strong, or so brave:
But a hand held open unasked
Gives all it has from the heart.

So who's to say, in the end
Who has won, lost, or finished the race?
Is the victor's raised arm
                for own triumph
Or a salute to the spirit
                of others?
For it could be
                the race is not with others
                        but within.

Though he hadn't gotten used to the idea, Cameron hadn't seen Sonia again. Within the hospital's walls there was enough to do, as well as dealing with the Q.M. committee's seemingly endless stream of letters. He dealt with each one, but somehow another soon followed. And after many delays and postponements, another deposition was scheduled concerning the malpractice summons. Outside the hospital, Cameron flung his energies into his research at the canine and simian labs. But he no longer left his notebooks there.

At times, when even work didn't keep his mind from wandering into painful memories, Cameron ran. He ran mornings, or he'd run at night. Sometimes at the park he'd stop, look at an oak tree's inscription, then gallop off again at blistering speed that sometimes made him stumble in the dark.

One spring day that felt more like summer, Track ran with him. He'd been silent the entire time, as if concentrating on running—or something else. Cameron knew him well enough to realize Track didn't think about anything while he ran. Whatever it was had to be important.

Cameron wiped his forehead's sweat and slowed the pace. "Out with it. Why so solemn? We're not about to run an Olympic marathon, are we?"

"Not we," Track corrected him. "You." Track picked up the pace again.

"Say again?"

"Actually, it may be more difficult than that. A four-year old boy is dying—mushroom poisoning. He's already had one liver transplant. Failed. He's not expected to live past two or three weeks. Another liver transplant won't come in that soon..."

Now Cameron increased the pace. "Are you asking what I think you're asking?"

Track nodded. "You're his only hope. You haven't failed in the last seven canines, four simians, and our own three human biopsies..."

"That was research. This isn't the same."

"This is for a boy's life, Cameron..."

Cameron dug in his feet, and stopped. Imprints of his shoes remained imbedded in the track. "I know what you're saying. But do you know what you are asking, Track? I don't have approval from the state or the hospital for human experimentation. I don't even exist on any research book rosters. And there are those, from some government group down to Q.M. that would as soon have my balls, or see my license lifted, in whatever order."

Track didn't mention any of that. He already knew. "Could you do it?"

Cameron nodded. "I could try."

"His chances?"

"I'd estimate better than fifty-fifty."

"Right now, he's got zero."

"You know, if it fails, or maybe even if it doesn't—I'm finished."

"So's the boy."

That was true, Cameron thought. Whatever his own risks were, the boy's were higher. Cameron looked down and pondered. "It's not possible," he finally said.

"Why not? You just told me fifty-fifty."

"Where will we do it? We can't just wheel him into the lab! We need our i's dotted and t's crossed. We need an operating room, a surgeon I can assist, an anesthetist, and a scrub nurse."

"I've thought of that," Track nodded. "I've got a surgeon and anesthesiologist willing to do it. We'll open an O.R. at night. And I'll be the scrub nurse."

Cameron thought some more. "One big problem: For his best chance, I need to hybridize and clone his own native liver, not the failing transplant."

"I know. He's had a partial adult's liver implant. But he's got bits of his own liver left. We can localize his own native liver, do the biopsy you need, by fluoroscopy."

One by one, his reasons for not doing it were falling by the wayside. "Who's the surgeon?"

"The patient's attending doctor, Walter Ormsby. He's cared for this family for three generations. He's not willing to let the boy go without a fight. How about you?"

Cameron said nothing. His brain was a tangled mixture of thoughts, emotions, and fears. In a way, he'd been awaiting—and fearing this moment for a long time.

"I've got five pages of detailed consent forms all duly witnessed and signed by the boy's grandfather and legal guardian, a Mr. Joseph Lapinski."

"…What did you say?"

"The boy's parents are both dead. His guardian is his grandfather. It's all drawn up and signed. He wants to give the boy a chance."

"What was that name again?"

"The boy is William Clement."

"And his grandfather?"

"Joseph, Joseph Lapinski."

Cameron's face relaxed. Not that he believed in omens. But the confluence of the pawnbroker's name, a Christmas necklace, and a little boy like his brother years ago needing another chance seemed more than coincidence. "I don't suppose," Cameron asked Track, "we have enough time or clout to get approval for this beforehand?"

Track shook his head. "It's either the paperwork, or the boy." Track placed an arm on Cameron's shoulder. "I can't tell you what to do, or how to run this race. But I've seen you run your own race before—a great race. I know you can do it again."

"Almost a great race," Cameron corrected him, remembering the end.

"The finish didn't matter as much as you think."

"It will matter now."

"If it was my own child, Cameron, I would ask for the same."

The ending couldn't be known ahead of time. But the first step was up to him. Without that first step, the boy's fate was sealed. Somewhere between a Christmas evening, and his brother's early tombstone, the decision had been made. Cameron simply nodded.

"When do you want to start?" Track asked.

"Tonight. There isn't much time. I'll need William's chart, and if everything's in order, I'll call you, and we can do the liver biopsy in the morning."

"I brought the chart with me," Track smiled. "The attending and I will be waiting for your call."

Cameron spent the night going over the book that was William Clement's chart: A procession of hospital chapters told the story of his ebbing life, down to the last thin page. Unless another new liver transplant was found within a week, there would be no happy ending.

After that, he'd have one hybrid chance, or need a miracle. Cameron prayed for both, and made the phone call.

. . . . .

As hard as Cameron worked to hybridize and clone the remnants of Billy Clement's poisoned liver, Cameron also prayed. He prayed that a full or partial liver transplant would be found, and that none of his work would be needed. He even had his own liver tested for histocompatibility as a donor, and Track followed suit. But neither matched; and while William Clement's liver biopsy hybridized and cloned rapidly, and healthily, in Cameron's lab, Billy himself languished and lost ground day by day.

Cameron visited Billy daily in the Peds ward, and watched his color turn a deeper dusty yellow as his liver functions deteriorated from bad to critical. Billy hadn't eaten for a week, and only an intravenous line sustained him.

Caught in a four-year old's body that shrank instead of growing, Billy Clement tried to make sense of it all. The hospital seemed huge to him: Like a football field with white bleachers fading into the walls. Rooms and corridors too brightly lit reminded him of the sun coming in through uncurtained windows on mornings he didn't want to get up. It had been a long time since he'd gotten up. As long ago it seemed, as Uncle Steven's birthday, when they'd fished a river's cool, slow-moving pocket at the forest's edge. They caught two silvery fish that danced in the sun like flags in the wind, and Uncle Steve blew out the cake's candles right by the riverbank. They ate cake, waded barefooted where the river boulders came up like giant turtlebacks, and he'd splashed Uncle Steve, who first scolded him, then laughed and carried him on his back, high so he felt he could touch the tips of trees by the ridge under a rainbow-sparkle of clouds.

Billy remembered all that better than some pain he'd had in his belly; that had gone away, and Uncle Steve had shown him a scar on his tummy like his own, where they'd taken a part of Steve to put inside him. Billy wasn't sure why that was done, only that he wanted to get up again. Maybe go to the river again, sit on Uncle Steve's shoulders, and listen to the stream coil around the rocks. But now he wondered if he'd have enough strength to hold on to Steve's neck. Nurses and doctors that came into his room were like many people in a big-screen movie; when they talked to him, Billy wasn't sure what it was about. They tried to be nice, but they couldn't be trusted, because sometimes they poked needles, and afterwards were nice again. Some were nicer than others, but not like Uncle Steve or Grandpa Joe. They came every day, and brought balloons the color of marbles, and stuffed animals that sat around him on the desk and chairs.

Grandpa Joe and Uncle Steve were quieter now, and the nurses' voices more far away. A new doctor came, too. He never smiled much, until he sat by his bed, and brought out crayons or coloring books. He didn't talk much, but taught him how to arm-wrestle, and always messed up his hair before leaving. One day when he couldn't hold up his hand to arm-wrestle, and couldn't hold onto the crayons to color, the doctor read him a story from a coloring book. That was strange, because the book didn't have printed words. But it was a good story about a boy who ran. Afterwards, the doctor said he'd try to help him run. His name was Dr. Cameron. He reminded him of Uncle Steve.

Cameron had gone over the implant procedure with Dr. Walter Ormsby, as he'd done it on the canines and simians. They made charts of anatomical landmarks and went over them until even Track could recite them in his sleep. The procedure would be simpler than either a heterotopic or an orthotopic liver transplant, and easier than a partial liver lobectomy, which it resembled. They finished their drills with a trial run in the canine lab, which took less than an hour and a half. "Track was right about you," Ormsby slapped Cameron's back afterwards. "I'm glad of it for Billy."

Cameron would have been far happier not being needed. "Yesterday Billy wasn't strong enough to color his book. Today he wouldn't talk. We don't have much time left."

"You have enough tissue cloned for him?" Track asked.

"I'd like more. But we'll have to do with what we've got."

"When do we go?"

"Tomorrow night," Cameron said.

· · · · ·

Cameron remembered the pawnbroker's quiet eyes. Mr. Joseph Lapinski and Cameron sat in a small room with a paper between them. Mr. Lapinski's eyes were far away. Cameron was silent. Finally, Mr. Lapinski motioned to the papers. "They're all signed, the consent forms." His eyes hadn't returned from their far away place.

"Did you understand them?"

"Yes."

"Let's put the papers aside for a moment," their eyes met. "I have an idea of what Billy means to you. I've met him. We all want to do what's best for him. As much as we want to do that, I have to tell you the procedure is totally experimental in humans. We can only regard it as a last, desperate attempt. I wish I could give you and Billy more than that. But I can't."

Mr. Lapinski had been hunched over, listening. Then he straightened: "I want to know... one thing: Will it give him a better chance than he has now?"

Cameron's gaze met his. "I cannot foretell the future, Mr. Lapinski. But short of a miracle, any chance is better than none."

"Would you do this for your child?"

"I would."

Mr. Lapinski nodded slowly, then extended his hand.

"I'm sorry our next meeting was like this, Mr. Lapinski."

"I am also. But I am glad it is you."

Mr. Joseph Lapinski's eyes were closed as Cameron left the room. The future before them remained unknown. Cameron longed... for something like the simplicity of a race. Win or lose, in a few years all that would be remembered of a race or game would be that it was run or played, leaving no other mark. But this trust left upon his shoulders would always remain.

· · · · ·

The night halls were as silent as their little patient. He'd been down corridors like this before, and Dr. Cameron had prepared him. But his four-year old mind still wanted to know why. Grandpa, why do the stars come out at night? Grandpa, who lives on the moon? Grandpa, why do birds fly?... "Dr. Cameron, why am I sick?"

Cameron curled his fingers around the boy's dark hair. It was long and smooth and thin. His eyes looked back at Cameron like little blinking pools of light. The question had been muffled and soft, but still rang in Cameron's ears. Cameron knew the statistics: What percentage would get what disease; the prevalence of this or that infection; the chances of recovery. General numbers that meant nothing now. Numbers that one hid behind, without questioning fate. Nothing Cameron knew could tell him why a four-year old boy with dark hair and deep hazel eyes was being wheeled into an operating room at night for the last chance of his life. Nothing in medicine could provide answers to any of that.

Children didn't know sometimes there were questions without answers; so they made up their own. Behind eyes that stared ahead, Billy wondered if all this was because he'd somehow been bad, like maybe when he'd splashed Uncle Steve. Maybe that's why his parents had died, and that's why he was sick—because he'd been a bad boy. Billy pondered it as the corridor's ceilings flew overhead like clouds on a windblown evening. "Dr. Cameron, am I a bad boy?"

"What makes you say that, Billy? Of course not. You've always been a good boy."

"So I am a good boy, right, Dr. Cameron?" His words came weakly, but it was a matter he had to be sure of: "I'm a good boy, really, ha?"

"Of course, Billy. You know what?" Cameron lifted him, light as a doll, onto the operating table. "You're the bravest boy I've met."

"If I'm a good boy, then I won't be sick anymore?"

Those were Billy's last thoughts, before the anesthesiologist began his sleep-work. Body-taut plastic drapes clung over the boy's scrubbed chest and abdominal skin.

"Incision," said the surgeon. Like jaundiced parchment, the skin parted under the knife. The anesthesiologist, Chester Roland, recorded the time on his log. Blooms of red flowers opened within the finely cut crease. "Cautery," Dr. Ormsby's hands moved. Rivulets of blood followed them through the operation, as Billy's clotting factors were compromised by his liver disease. But reversal of his clotting defects also carried the opposite risk of facilitating blood clots. "Clamp," Ormsby requested. Track handed the instruments and counted sponges. Cameron assisted Ormsby.

Their movements were spontaneous and smooth. A thin layer of abdominal muscle twitched open under the electro-cautery scalpel. Instead of the usual glistening reddish-grape hue of a healthy liver, the failed organ transplant was a dull mustard color. Instead of a soft, rubbery texture, the electro-cautery scraped against pebbly-hard tissue. To create a bed for the new implant, they removed portions of the diseased organ, down to viable blood vessels and bile ducts. Blood followed them everywhere: Cut arterioles spurted like miniature angry gooseneck clams, needing ligation or cautery depending on size; venules bled less briskly, but were more difficult to find within their oozing ochre pools.

They cut carefully, cauterized swiftly, implanted the new tissue snugly. Dimensions had been sculpted like a work of art: Too much space, and serum and blood would move in to fill it, creating a nutrient-nest for infection; too constricted a space, and the developing blood vessels would suffocate. When they were done, the new implant rested like a baby in a crib. They irrigated with an antibiotic solution, which remained crystal clear. Even the smallest bleeder would have turned the bathing fluid crimson. They looked at each other. Under their masks, their hopeful smiles went unseen.

"Closing!" Ormsby said.

The anesthesiologist lightened the anesthesia. They went out slower than they came in. Suturing together was slower than cutting: They closed the thin muscle layer, together with the tough fasciae that held connective tissue; then the subcutaneous layer, then skin. By the time the last stitch was spread over the skin like a butterfly's wings, Billy was breathing on his own.

They remained around Billy until his eyelids stirred. Ormsby and Roland had fallen asleep in their chairs.

"Dr. Cameron," the boy said.

"You're okay, Billy," Cameron wiped Billy's forehead, then his own.

"I want to see my grandpa."

"He's been waiting for you."

They left the O.R. a few hours before the day's dawn shift.

Over the next few days Billy's condition didn't worsen, and the deterioration in his liver function tests stabilized. Cameron's evening runs stopped, replaced by vigils at Billy's bedside. Track also began to arrive late in the evenings, to chase Cameron off to sleep.

After a week, there was a slight improvement in Billy's strength, and in his lab tests. Track smiled. "According to your graphs, that's when the implants begin to show function, right, Cameron?"

Cameron nodded silently. That was true, but he didn't want to let his hopes soar.

Improvements continued, including Billy's appetite, to the point Cameron allowed himself the return of hope. When Billy suddenly worsened five days later, it wasn't so much their guards that were down, but their hopes already too high. Ormsby, Track, and Cameron considered the possible causes of setbacks and complications, then ordered the needed lab work and X-rays to confirm.

Cameron spent that evening with Billy, and Billy's teddy bear—a rotund, rust colored bruin with bent ears, black nose, and an eye missing. Billy kept his arms around the bear.

"Am I going to die, Dr. Cameron?"

The question shouldn't have come as a surprise, but it did. Somewhere deep, despite trying to prepare himself for the worst, Cameron hadn't envisioned Billy really dying. "You are a good boy, Billy." Cameron touched his hair, matted from days and nights in a bed.

"Will you tell me a story, Dr. Cameron?"

It was a simple request. And Cameron's doctoring powers were done. Many thoughts crossed his mind, but none that really made sense. There wasn't much sense in a four-year old child's dying. "Sure, Billy," Cameron patted the teddy bear. "Only it won't be an ordinary story, with a beginning, middle, and end. We'll just start it now, and we'll go on with it tomorrow. Okay, Billy?"

Billy nodded, and settled into his covers. Soon he was asleep. Chin tucked under comforter, his pale forehead rested on the rust-colored teddy bear clutched under his arm.

Cameron stood silently. Before reaching the door, he turned and whispered: "You're a good boy, Billy."

· · · · ·

Before morning rounds, Cameron called Pediatrics to leave word he'd be visiting Billy during lunch.

"You won't need to. Billy died this morning."

Cameron's stomach felt like an elevator had just dropped under....

Phone slipped from his hand, breathing stopped, he tried to stand... Billy had been going on the strength of his spirit, on a child's life-instinct to continue. Finally, that hadn't been enough.

Cameron went through the motions of rounds and admissions on their call day. Like a medical computer, a disembodied machine, he visited patients, worked up new admissions, and answered his Interns' questions. He went through the steps—history, exam, lab, diagnosis, treatment, as before—the computer was plugged in and functioning, but no one was home.

In the early afternoon, a call came for Cameron. "It's Dr. Sullivan," the nurse said.

"Cameron, are you sitting down?" Track asked.

"I already know," Cameron replied.

"You know Billy died?"

Cameron nodded, as if the phone could convey it.

"I'm sorry I didn't tell you personally. I've been talking to the family." Track paused. "Maybe I shouldn't have gotten you into this. But it was his only chance."

Cameron touched his eye, and said nothing.

"Dr. Ormsby will have to write the death certificate. We talked about it. He died of liver failure, after one transplant, and a recent operation."

"Yes."

"So you've thought about this, Cameron?"

"No. Deep down I guess I never believed Billy would die. The doctor knew chances were slim. The rest of me couldn't accept that."

"Ormsby listed you as 'advisor' in the operative report. He doesn't have to include your name as assistant surgeon. He wants you out of the death certificate."

"No. Don't do that. Leave it in."

"I told him you'd say that. He'd already figured that himself."

"Let's do it straight."

"You know, Cameron, Ormsby's name and mine would be sufficient for the implant surgery. We could do that. Since I do similar research, no one would question it."

"You considered it before?" Cameron asked rhetorically.

"Not really. Like you, I couldn't see Billy dead. But now, we don't need to drag you through the rest. You're already compromised enough with Q.M."

"That's another reason to do it straight. You've both got more to lose. They'll want a scapegoat, and I fit that best."

"Look, Cameron, it wasn't your fault. I can't let you do that."

"Tell Ormsby that's the way I want it."

"I know you're on call tonight, Cameron. We'll talk more tomorrow. We can't let you take the fall."

Before midnight had brought another day, they had cared for several more patients: Kidney infections and stones, three with pneumonias, one patient with asthma, one stroke, two overdoses, two patients with chest pains that could be anything from blood clots to heart attacks, two with congestive heart failure, and two with infectious diseases of cause yet unknown. It was an average night, of average patients, with average maladies, which meant none of it was *"average"* at all. Life, death, and everything in between came out from the streets of the city by night, and they waited for it here. It happened whether they were here or not, and would continue to happen. At times they were able to change it. Then the night's dragons backed off into corners, biding another time. Until they met again. Here, where battles raged for life, death, and everything in between.

Before dawn, Mrs. Edna Dwyer had come back to them. Outpatient radiation therapy had helped initially, but now she'd relapsed, along with weakness of the entire right side of her body, and both corners of her mouth. Whatever food or water she'd place in her mouth with her left hand had less than an even chance of staying there. She couldn't quite close the corners of her mouth, streaks of saliva pooling crusted white with dehydration.

Cameron finished his exam, and was about to start an IV. "We'll talk to Radiation Therapy and Oncology again, Mrs. Dwyer," he began.

She shook her head with all the emphasis her life could muster, like a limp doll bouncing down a staircase.

"Wo...woo... wooon't be...ne...necess..." she tried the word again, but her tongue glued to her mouth. "No," she finally said. Her left hand pushed his IV needle away.

She'd returned to die.

"You're very dry, Mrs. Dwyer. You sure you don't want the IV fluids?"

She held her arm up, pocked with scars from previous IVs for fluids and medications, then let it fall, weightless and silent. "Woo... wooon't be...long," she said by way of apology, as Cameron was leaving. If a smile's remnant touched her lips, Cameron couldn't tell.

Joel Saxton finished Mrs. Dwyer's work-up before morning rounds, and woke Cameron from his chair.

Cameron heard a question and lifted his head. A crease ran across his brow where he'd slept on his elbow. Joel repeated the question. "Mrs. Dwyer is pretty set on not having more tests or treatments. She can't feed or care for herself, or give herself pain meds. She wants to be here for that."

"I know. We can do that."

Morning rounds began after coffee. Cameron remained a day, a day's night, and a day. He went through it automatically. Automatically too, in the evening when call was done, he gathered a few of his things from his desk, and put them in his pocket.

Joel looked at him but didn't question it. He sat down, placed his hand over his head. "How long before she dies?"

"I don't know, Joel. I can't tell you that." Cameron knew he was talking about Mrs. Dwyer.

Joel closed the chart he'd been studying. "So what does Medicine tell us now, for times like this?"

"It tells us...that sorrow sometimes brings us together. Maybe that's why we care for each other like we do. Maybe, without it, we wouldn't be as human..." Cameron looked away. "What makes us human, Joel? If it was speech that first moved us, was it for joy at a baby's birth, or grief when found a stillborn? You tell me."

Joel put away the chart. "It seems we have many questions we can't answer tonight. You know," he paused, "I wonder how it got this way? Utilization Review has already denied her stay because Medicare and

Medicaid won't cover what they call 'terminal care,' unless it's tied to needles, IV's, and medications."

"She wants to rest. I think we should let her."

"What do we do when they deny her stay?"

"Let the bureaucrats that want to kick her out sign the papers. We won't."

They sat in the lab room, in crumpled whites, disheveled and tired. Joel knew now that he'd been trying to follow in this man's footsteps, to become a doctor like he was a doctor. In the past, he didn't know how. Now Joel felt he understood.

Lucy came into the room, setting her charts down. "Done for today?"

Cameron nodded. "I've set the guard and checked out with the on-call team."

"About Mrs. Dwyer..." Joel began.

Cameron grabbed his shoulder. "You'll take care of her Joel. I know you can." Cameron had already made his decision, even before Mrs. Dwyer's return. He looked at them: "We've had good times and hard times together. From the hard ones we've learned; and the good ones have been their own reward. On call, you've received what the city's night has thrown at you, and learned to listen, examine, evaluate, and care for patients. I can't ask more of you. We've all tried to become above average medically, and if we are, that's good. And if we're really the average, maybe that's even better." Cameron paused, and looked as if he wanted to say more. "Call night and rounds are over, Doctors," was all.

"I wonder what he meant by all that?" Lucy commented. "Maybe he's tired."

"Sounds almost like a farewell. No," Joel shook his head, "rounds in the morning; Cameron will be here."

. . . . .

But Cameron wouldn't be coming back. It wasn't so much that the dragons had won, but that he'd no longer be able to fight them. He went across the parking lot to the lab, to set the rest of his things in order. Much of his work had already been transferred to the simian lab, and what remained, besides the canines, was only a skeletal shadow of the past. Some of the canines howled, as if they knew one of their pack was leaving.

Cameron took out a duffel bag, and cleared his desk. Wildwolf would have been lying next to his side by now. Cameron looked at the empty foot-rug. In the dimmed lights of the lab, Cameron could still see Wildwolf bringing back the leash between his teeth for a run. Cameron took down Wildwolf's collar and leash from its peg on the wall, turned them for a moment in his hands, then placed them within the duffel. The rest was done. He gazed at Wildwolf's empty cage, then closed the bag. At the door, before turning down the lights, he reflexly bent down to shake Wildwolf's paw. It was an imaginary paw. The darkness didn't change that.

In the bright lights of the hall stood a man in a gray suit. Not someone he'd seen before. But somehow Cameron felt it was not someone unknown.

"Why didn't you come in?" Cameron asked.

The man shook his head. "It wasn't the right time. It's your farewell."

There was silence.

"Aren't you going to ask me who I am?"

"I know who you are," Cameron said.

"It's strange how sometimes I get a feeling about the person I'm trying to...track down." The man wasn't satisfied with his choice of words, but let them stand. "What about you? How did you know who I was?"

Cameron shrugged. "Different people cast different shadows. I've felt yours for some time."

"I'm Jacob Werner, assigned to your case."

Cameron remained silent. The silence of a jungle beast deciding whether to allow the intruder to pass, or pay.

"You are John Cameron, M.D., brilliant researcher, and maybe even better doctor."

"Why'd you come after me, then?"

"It was my job. I was assigned. You were a challenge."

The wild beast fought to restrain its leap. "That's it?" You're telling me you were 'doing your job'? That you just 'followed orders'?"

"I didn't come to tell you that. I came to say I didn't kill your dog. I didn't kill Wildwolf. And to say I'm sorry."

Cameron stilled his leap. "I don't know why, but I believe you." It was Jake's turn to be silent.

"I believe you; but I can't forgive you."

"I didn't come for that either." Jake turned before leaving, "I'm sorry the boy died."

"You also know about that?"

"I'm not just a bureaucrat," Jake smiled drily.

"I'm a bureaucrat that's also good at his job. Most of the time."

Cameron returned a wry smile. "Then you're almost a professional."

"I know what I am," Jake's smile was sad. "I have no illusions about that. Anyway, there won't be anything in my report about Billy."

"Why not?"

"You did your best. Who knows? It might have worked."

. . . . .

Cameron returned to pack a few things from his room. He'd already talked to Max, who stood by his decision, though he didn't agree with it. For Track, who would have tried to dissuade him, he left a note. He would miss them all: Friend, coach, and now sister. He still had to face Tammy.

Disbelief came over her eyes like a dust-storm. "You're going to run, just like that?"

Cameron tried to keep it light. "What'd you expect from a track runner?"

"To finish the race."

That's what Track would have said, Cameron thought. He sat down, his suitcase packed. "I have, Tammy. I lost."

"Maybe you have, or maybe you just think you have." She took his hands between hers: "You believed in me, Cameron. That made all the difference in the world for me. And you became the brother I never had. Now I believe in you. I don't want to let you go like this. Besides," she placed her arms around him and hugged him, like a dove's wings hug the air, "I'm going to miss you so much..!"

"I'll miss you too, sis."

"I always thought, you know, we'd have you over for evening dinners ..." with the realization that he was actually leaving, a sob choked within her throat. "Or if you're already tired of my cooking, maybe we'd just watch TV, and have popcorn. We could barbecue on holidays, or go camping, or have picnics in the park after you and Max ran." She placed her head on Cameron's shoulder, like an infant waiting for a bad dream to pass. "Maybe we could run with you; or we could chat on evenings in front of a fireplace, or watch a red sunset."

His sleeve was wet where her head had been. "We can do all those things, sis. Just not right away. Max will always know where I'll be."

"What about me?"

"You'll know too, sis. Max will be by later tonight for you. You should be safe now, sis. Take care of yourself, for me." He kissed her on the forehead. "We will do all those things, you'll see."

Cameron wondered when that would be—another dream of returning on a snowy Christmas.

. . . . .

The pathologist pushed open the door with his foot, gloves and instruments still in hand. "Hey, Joe, come here for a minute."

The other pathologist took his eyes off the microscope, where he'd been studying a breast lump's "frozen section."

"What's up?"

"The Clement case—the boy with the liver transplant. Do me a favor and have a look."

Joe Breneton, Chief Pathologist, donned his gloves and a gown. He entered a room shiny from ceiling lights to steel prosecting table, to cream-tiled floor. A glass cabinet held a variety of specimen jars for preservation and further study—for resolution by the naked eye, down to an electron microscope magnifying one million times if need be, to the crystal details of a molecule, where a spider's single web-strand would look the size a movie theater.

"Hmm... not a bad transplant, that. The central part looks really good. What did he die of?"

"That's just it: They thought the Clement boy died of liver failure, due to organ rejection."

Breneton peered over his glasses. "Sure doesn't look like any rejection to me. The central part looks like healthy liver, though the edges are more ragged. So what'd he die of, Ted?"

Ted Thurston pointed to a jar with a small gelatinous glob: "Blood clot in the inferior vena cava." It rested like a thimble-full of black currant jello, only a little darker than the liver.

"Tragic…" Joe Breneton took off his glasses, trying to clean them, as if that would erase what had happened. "…So he died of a not unusual postoperative complication for this surgery," he said in a soft voice, "and run down metabolic status…such a small thing, bringing down a small boy…"

Ted shook his head. "That's not all. The boy had a second operation, weeks after the first—some kind of fancy new implant: That's what you see in the center. Clean. Functional. The edges are what's left of the failing old transplant. The boy almost made it…"

"I'd say that's a fancy implant indeed," Joe seemed to force a faint smile. "Better save some of these path slides."

· · · · ·

Days later and scores of miles away, Cameron still wasn't used to not having to make morning rounds; and every third night he still woke, feet in his shoes, dreaming he'd overslept a patient admission. Years of university classrooms, hospital corridors, brightly lit libraries, or dimly shadowed old reading lounges imbued with a curious mix of aftershave and antiseptic had been like a second womb, a stone mother with arms of patient-filled wards around him. Leaving suddenly had been like a premature birth, from barely ordered chaos—into unusual stillness. No bright lights to see through X-ray film, or the mind's bolt of lightning to fit an unusual diagnosis. Without the regular wailing of sirens, even the outside streets seemed silent.

Cameron had given himself a week before deciding where he'd go, or what he'd do next. In the meantime, his washed socks dried over a motel's warm TV. Following an antidepressant med commercial showing twirling, dancing figures that did everything but win the lottery, the local news switched to the steps of the State Hospital.

Cameron debated whether to switch it off, or leave it on to dry his socks, until he recognized a face. He turned the volume and sat down. A reporter in an electric-blue suit, loose neck bow and high-collared white blouse held the microphone in front, reading:

> "...According to Medicaid and Medicare rules and regulations, it seems only those hospitalizations are approved which provide intravenous medications, or similar intensive therapy. Patients who decline such therapy, or are hospitalized for basic care of a terminal illness, are refused such coverage." The reporter shifted her microphone: "From a local hospital, we have here with us Dr. Joel Saxton and his patient, Mrs. Edna Dwyer. Dr. Saxton, I understand this is a more common problem than we realize?"

Above the microphone held for him by manicured hands, Joel's face wore stubble dark as the microphone pores; it had been an evening after call, and his eyes sat nearly as deep as Mrs. Dwyer's. He blinked at the lights: "More than a common problem—a common shame." Without his surfer's tan, carefully brushed hair and trimmed mustache, Dr. Joel Saxton looked out of his usual photogenic place. He stood over the wheelchair and adjusted Mrs. Dwyer's blanket around her. The two made an unusual pair before the hospital steps: Joel still in wrinkled whites, Mrs. Dwyer lost within a gray robe atop hospital-issue pajamas. The robe wrapped around her like a swaddling blanket holding an infant. The microphone lowered to Mrs. Dwyer. Her gaunt face was as shadowed as the falling evening. She glanced slowly around her, neck twitching from effort, at the reporter, at Joel, at the police standing by. Then she faced straight ahead.

...Strange how the year had gone, Cameron pondered: Intern Lucy Carlton had resurrected an innovative charting system for patient care from a Resident who had committed suicide; Max McDaniel had lost a chip off his shoulder, and freed his girlfriend from a mob's grip; the girl, Tammy, had become Cameron's sister; Cameron himself had turned up somewhere in a motel, just a few months short of finishing his last

Residency year. And from playboy-accountant to dedicated doctor, Joel Saxton now stood behind Mrs. Dwyer's wheelchair...

Mrs. Dwyer had made one more request of Dr. Saxton: For once she would be doing on her own terms and volition. Her head held steady. Her face, though twisted, showed her final dignity and caught her words, light as autumn's falling leaves:

"...Treat people, not rules."

Cameron raised his fist in the air.

- SOME ENDINGS...
ARE NEW BEGINNINGS

EPILOGUE

Most elements of this story are true to life, including the rationale and possibilities for the envisioned research.

Equally, and unfortunately, true to life are the described impediments to the true care for patients (instead of "services" rendered by "providers").

These obstacles were catalyzed over the last two decades by control over how doctors practice medicine, via corporate-chain and hospital-owned medical practices, and unprecedented strangulation by the medico-industrial complex—comprised of government/ pharma/ insurance/ hospital-merger megaliths.

Conflicts of interest in economics vs. care for the patient abound within this "middleman" riddled medico-industrial complex and its agents, to the detriment of patient care.

Is reversal of this trend possible?

Perhaps, but only with exposure of the truths behind this medico-industrial complex, and through vigilance and willingness of the patient/ public to demand foundational change.

ACKNOWLEDGEMENTS

I remain deeply indebted to my mentors and teachers: Professor Santisteban (undergrad Biochemistry); Dr. Schwartz (Anatomy); Dr. Kirby (Infectious Disease); Dr. Ormsby (clinical Internal Medicine); and so many others at the University of Washington School of Medicine.

They were truly beacons of learning and hope for students, future doctors, and patients. Indeed, if ever we stand high, we do so "on the shoulders of giants"!

I am grateful also for a time when Medicine was taught without political, economic, or faux social agendas masquerading as Medicine.

----More in sequel: "ONCE UPON A TIME THERE WERE DOCTORS"----

Greatest gratitude goes out to my father, J. Mikelionis MD, for inspiration, and his dedication to Medicine.

Additional thanks to Charmaine Hopkins and Tanisha Johnson for their patient help in final manuscript preparation. And Yenny Villegas-Brea for cover graphics.

DEAR READER

Reader reviews really are the author's bread and butter! So, if you enjoyed your read, please leave a review on Amazon and/or Goodreads. If you don't feel like writing much, you can still show your appreciation by leaving a few stars—The more, the better!

For Amazon: Go to the order page, AMAZON.COM/ORDERS
- Click "write product review" next to the book.
- Write review/stars
- Submit

For Goodreads: Go to goodreads.com.
- Search by author, Book title
- Click on star rating under the book cover
- Add review if you wish

You may also reach me at: https://www.bluefirerjmikelionis.com/

THANK YOU, FRIENDS!

R.J Mikelionis M.D

www.ingramcontent.com/pod-product-compliance
Lightning Source LLC
LaVergne TN
LVHW091613070526
838199LV00044B/785